CURSE OF THE NICE GUY

THE EDUCATION OF CLARK WESTFIELD, BOOK TWO

A NOVEL

RANDALL BLAIR

This is a work of fiction. Names, characters, organizations, places, events, and incidents are either products of the author's imagination or are used fictitiously.

ISBN 978-0-9976291-2-5 EBook
ISBN 978-0-9976291-3-2 Paperback

Cover Design by Villa Design

For Mom

CHAPTER 1

London, England * September 1966

Clark Westfield heard the sounds of the demonstration before he saw it. As he approached Big Ben and the Palace at Westminster, he saw a large throng of protestors, seemingly all college students, who packed Parliament Square, the large park across the street from the palace. Many of them carried signs protesting the Vietnam War, while others chanted anti-war and peace-now slogans.

As he entered the crowd, Clark remembered seeing the news on the BBC that Robert McNamara, the U.S. Secretary of Defense, was in town to address the British Parliament on the Vietnam situation. The Brits remained understandably reluctant to get involved in the quagmire of Southeast Asia because they had seen the negative impact on France from its humiliating failure there in the 1950s. No powerful country wanted to admit defeat by a bunch of peasants. And of course the English had their own colonial past to haunt them.

As he moved among the students at the rear of the crowd, Clark blended in easily because he was the same age, twenty, and wore similar clothing. At six feet tall he was a little taller than many of them, but his brown hair was cut moderately long in a fashionable student-style, and his bright hazel eyes were hidden behind a pair of trendy sunglasses that he had purchased the day before on Carnaby Street.

Clark began to take photos took with his Nikon SLR camera. He got some smiles and even a few silly poses, like they were at a party. It reminded him of a pep rally before a college football game at home. But as he got toward the front of the crowd, it became evident that those students were energized in a totally different way. Instead of smiles there were glares of suspicion, a quick hiding of faces, and even a few hands thrust aggressively towards his lens. He thought that for people who advocated peace, they sure acted aggressively. He remembered going to a peace rally in Harvard Square the previous spring, but unlike this, it had been fueled much more by flower-power than by anger.

British policemen, bobbies, stood at attention along the entire street and kept the students confined to the square and safely away from the Parliament building. The bobbies didn't carry guns, as was the British tradition. A BBC Television news crew had encamped in the street between the crowd and the Parliament buildings, but they weren't filming anything at the moment. It seemed all very British in its organization and its controlled energy.

Then without warning, a series of sirens and police whistles signaled an escalation to the confrontation. Five or six paddy wagons arrived on the scene, and the police began to try to aggressively disperse the demonstrators, which caused a wave of anger and fear to swept through the crowd. Many of the students in the rear began to leave, but most of the ones at the front stood fast and even pushed back. The BBC news crew jumped into action.

Clark had started to move away when he noticed one small student, apparently one of the leaders, standing face-to-face with a bobbie, yelling in his face, "You imperialist bloody berk, supporting this illegal and immoral war makes you no better than the bloody blighters who supported the Nazis."

That evidently proved too much for the bobbie, who looked old enough to have fought in the war against the Nazis. He grabbed the student by the arms and then around the chest. She reacted strongly to having her breasts molested and struggled to pull away.

Clark watched, immensely impressed that it was a girl and by how fearless she was. He was captivated by her vivid blue eyes. Her black beret came off during the tussle, and her raven-black hair fell down to her shoulders. She was angry, emotional, and very attractive in an off-beat, revolutionary, street-fighter kind of way.

The bobbie started to drag her off toward a waiting paddy wagon. Down the front line of protestors, other officers carted other protest leaders away.

Clark hesitated a moment but not long enough to fully consider the possible consequences. He jumped through the line of protestors, held his camera up to his face, and raced toward the paddy wagons. He got right up in the face of the bobbie who held the girl and snapped some photos of him. The bobbie stopped, shocked that anyone would be so brazenly stupid when it was well known that the police hated to have their pictures taken. Impulsively, he let go of the girl and reached for Clark. But Clark easily dodged him and sprinted away. The policeman gave chase, leaving the girl alone. She couldn't move for a second as she tried to comprehend what had just happened. It was so unexpected, so crazy. She shook her head in disbelief and then quickly merged into the crowd.

Clark dodged and weaved around clumps of students, then dashed down Whitehall, leaving the out-of-shape, middle-aged, policeman out of breath and far behind. He laughed out loud with exhilaration and the shock of having done something so spontaneous, so out-of-character for him.

Without their leaders to motivate them and no longer having fun, the rest of the crowd soon dissipated. The girl moved carefully in the middle of one glom of students who were headed toward St. James Park, where it would be easy to get lost if any police pursued them. She racked her memory for any sense of recognition of that man who had rescued her. He looked like a student, but she was sure that she had never seen him before.

Clark looked around, hoping to find the girl. He saw different groups of demonstrators headed in all directions, and he followed one large group further down Whitehall toward Trafalgar Square. He didn't see her, but he convinced himself that she was okay. He then headed for the underground station, and he had almost reached it when he saw her run across the street, talking animatedly with a couple of other students.

She noticed him, and after saying good-by to the others, she went to meet him. "That was a very barmy thing to do, but ta you saved my arse for sure."

"You're welcome. That was intense. And fun." The laughter in his voice was fueled by his nervous excitement.

A dark frown obliterated her smile as she now looked critically at him. "Oh bollocks, you're American?"

He nodded slowly, unsure about her new, suddenly negative, tone of voice.

"And you think it's a bloody joke? Well, let me tell you it's not and someday you'll see why, when you're stuck in some bloody, muddy, foxhole getting shot."

Her words stung and hit home. "Sorry, I have this habit of trying to make fun of a stressful situation. It's a weird defense mechanism. If I'm in trouble, I laugh."

"You're not laughing now."

"Am I in trouble?"

She didn't know how to answer that - was he referring to the police or to her? She forced a small smile back on her face. "Well anyway, thanks again," she said as she turned to leave.

"Hey, can I buy you a cup of coffee or tea or something?"

"I've got to make arrangements for my mates who got nicked, get them out of jail. Maybe I'll see you around." She continued down the street quite sure that he was a random tourist and she would never see him again. Then she stopped and turned back toward him just in time to see him disappear down the stairs into the underground station.

The image of the girl stayed with Clark as he rode the underground to his stop at Hampstead High Street and then walked four blocks to his flat on Willow Road. She was very pretty in a tomboy kind of way; she wasn't masculine, but she didn't try to be feminine. It wasn't the look or type that he was normally attracted to, but maybe because of her energy and the intelligence behind her bright eyes, he found her completely fascinating. He wondered if he would ever see her again. Not likely, he feared, London was a big city with many colleges, thousands of students.

The flat in Hampstead was the top floor of a duplex building and had a good sized living/dining room with a nice kitchen. There was a master bedroom with a bath and a smaller bedroom and a hall bath. But the best thing about it was the music system and an incredible collection of record albums. The flat belonged to Clark's half-sister Rita, her husband Keith, and Melody, their three-year-old daughter. Rita worked for EMI Record Studio as a music producer, and had hundreds of albums of all different genres of music, many from artists that Clark had never heard of.

A year ago, EMI had asked Rita to go to Hollywood for a few years to help develop their connections with the film industry. Since it was supposed to be a temporary move, they had decided not to sell the flat that her father, also Clark's father, had helped them buy. All that was before anyone knew about Clark's plan to study in London for his junior year of college.

In less than a week Clark had absorbed much of the strangeness and the sameness of London. It remained foreign, but it had also become familiar. He already felt oddly at home, certainly as much as he had ever felt in any of the many cities in the United States that he and his family had temporarily called home. He felt a slight twinge of nervous anticipation for having to fit into yet another new school. But he knew he could do it because he had done it every school year, kindergarten to college. The only exception being the past year, which had been his second one at Dartmouth College.

It had turned out to be the perfect situation for Clark, and he had already begun to feel more like a resident than a visitor. And now he had had his first real contact with the locals; and it had been with a very interesting girl.

When Clark woke the next morning, Saturday, he felt restless and knew he needed to do something, but he had had enough sightseeing. In his first week in London he had already seen the Tower of London, St. Paul's Cathedral, Buckingham Palace, Piccadilly Circus, the British Museum, Trafalgar Square, Big Ben, and Carnaby Street, the heart of swinging London. Even though he was going to be living there the entire school year, he had wanted to see it all right away. And it had helped immensely that the weather had been unusually nice for London.

Clark decided to try the gym and the track at the University of London. He had briefly checked out the athletic facilities earlier in the week when he had registered for classes and paid the athletic fee. So he threw some gym clothes in his green gym bag and headed downtown.

The facility was open, even though school didn't officially start until Monday, and Clark was happy that he was the only one there. He didn't want to be seen stumbling around as he figured out where things were and how they worked. While most gyms and locker rooms were basically the same everywhere, there were enough differences in England, hot water faucets on the right for example, to potentially cause the foreign guy to look like a pathetic loser.

After several false turns and a few locked doors, he finally found his way outside to a track that circled around a soccer field. He jogged around the 400-meter track probably a half-dozen times before he realized that he was no longer alone. The tone and the energy of the male voices behind him indicated a group of three or four friends with a variety of accents. Three men soon ran past him, jostling each other, bantering and competing in that casual but intense manner common to athletes. They didn't acknowledge Clark, which was fine with him, and proceeded to run past him. Clark continued his steady pace and eventually passed them when they veered off the track and onto the soccer field.

Now warmed up, Clark picked up his pace. He loved to run, and he knew that he was pretty fast. During his senior year of high school, he had convinced his baseball coach to let him run with the track team on the days when he didn't have baseball practice. He had quickly proved to be the fastest boy in school in the 440-yard race and second fastest at 220 yards, and it had given the track coach heartburn that the track meet schedule conflicted with the baseball game schedule. But at the end of the spring sports season, the baseball team had finished early because it failed to qualify for the state tournament. That had given Clark the opportunity to run with the track team in the Penn Relays, which served as the state high school championships. He had placed second in the 440-yard event and fourth in the 220. That fall, when he got to college, he had wanted to run with the college indoor track team during the winter. But the baseball coach had forbidden it, demanding total and exclusive attention to baseball for the entire year. Clark had been angry because he loved variety and change, and that had been the first step in his eventual disengagement from the college baseball team during his sophomore year.

As Clark began another fast lap, one of the other men ran up beside him and seemed to be trying to pass him. His competitive instinct kicked in, and Clark sped up to stay ahead. He got to a straightaway and kicked it into high gear, a full out sprint, and left the other runner far behind. Superiority sufficiently proven, he slowed down around the curve.

"Hey mate," the runner said between deep breaths, "you're bloody quick. Are you by chance a rugger?"

Clark slowed down to a jog to match the other's pace. "Hey. Sorry, I don't know what that means."

"Oh, a Yank," the runner responded, through a broad smile. "A rugger is a rugby player. We all play on the university team." He gestured to the others who stood on the field and watched this exchange.

Clark had little idea what that sport entailed, except that it seemed vaguely more like what he knew as football, not soccer.

Before he could respond, one of the men yelled from across the field. "Arthur! It's bang on noon, we got to chip, union blokes here in thirty."

"See ya Yank," Arthur said, as he hurried off to join his friends, who were already off the field and headed for the athletic building.

CHAPTER 2

That evening, energized by his workout and encouraged by his second positive encounter with a local, Clark decided to go out to a dance club. Rita and Keith had taken him and Sarah, his twin sister, to a club a couple of years before when they had visited London with their parents. His parents had eagerly let the kids go off while they babysat their new granddaughter. The club was in the Soho district near Piccadilly Circus, and he felt more comfortable going to a place he knew. Clark did like to try new things, but he normally preferred what was familiar.

Club Clarisse had opened in 1959 and was one of the first dance clubs in London that appealed to young men and women who loved rock-n-roll music. It had survived and thrived while many others had failed because the owner had been unusually diligent about maintaining a clientele that didn't tend to what he called, "rowdiness."

Clark was one of the few single guys in line, and he had to wait for almost an hour. He thought it was unfair that any single woman got to cut the line and go right in, but then realized that he might benefit once he was inside. As he entered, Clark thought that the club appeared much smaller than he remembered it. Maybe it was because of the size of the crowd or that he felt a little nervous being there on his own. Couples or groups of couples occupied all the tables around the large dance floor. The dance floor was crowded, and the music very loud, played by a DJ with unnatural blond hair, hanging down past his shoulders and streaked with purple. Cigarette smoke hung thick in the close, hot, air. It was an assault on his senses, and he might have left if he hadn't invested so much time waiting to get in.

Clark worked his way to the large bar that stretched along the length of the rear wall. There were a couple of empty bar stools, and he took one at the end that afforded him a good observation point for the entire club. He waited for what seemed like a long time, and neither of the bartenders paid any attention to him. Being invisible was an established trait for Clark and often served him well, but not at times like this when he really wanted a beer. Finally, one of the bartenders headed his way, but then he stopped just short of Clark and took an order from a young woman who had just sat down on the stool next to him. After the bartender took her order, he turned away and didn't respond to Clark's urgent call.

"Sorry, he pays more attention to the women, and he knows me," the woman offered. "Are you an American?"

Her pretty eyes, an unusual light brown with bright flakes of blue and gray, immediately grabbed Clark's attention. Eyes were always the first thing he noticed about someone, particularly a woman. He knew that most of his male friends went immediately to the breasts, but he went first to the eyes, then the breasts. This woman seemed to appreciate Clark's order of priority. And she did have very nice breasts, which were on display beneath a tight, low-cut halter-top. She also had great long legs that were minimally covered by a red leather mini-skirt. He guessed that she was about his age, maybe a little older.

Clark smiled. "Guilty as charged."

He watched her as she quickly caught the bartender's eye and motioned him over. "My American friend here would like a..." She turned to Clark with the unspoken question.

"A pint of bitter, thanks."

The bartender gave him an odd sort of smile and then went back down the bar to the beer taps.

Clark and the woman sat in an awkward silence while they waited. He tried to place her accent. Certainly not British or Irish, it sounded a little like that of the French exchange student who had lived with the family next door to him during his senior year of high school. But this woman's coloring was more Italian, Mediterranean.

When the bartender came back with their drinks, Clark turned to face her. "Cheers," he said, and was rewarded by a great smile.

"Cheers. Are you here on holiday?"

"Yes," Clark replied without thinking.

"Bernadette." She offered her hand.

"Clark," he responded, and liked her strong, self-assured grip.

They chatted about the things he had seen, and she was surprised that he had done so much. She told him that she had moved to London from Corsica over a year ago and hadn't made it to any of the tourist sights. She did know the nightlife, however, and she told him about some of the other clubs she liked in Soho and also a fancy one in Knightsbridge that she went to sometimes.

Bernadette was very friendly but not pushy, and that was the perfect combination for Clark. It meant that he didn't have to work hard to overcome his natural shyness or his fear of rejection. And she didn't smoke. He had never done it, and he really didn't see it as an attractive habit, especially for a woman. But so many did it, particularly at a bar or club.

"What do you do?" he asked, certainly a safe question.

"Oh, I'm a student mostly, at Kings College."

Oh shit, he swore to himself. He had registered for a creative writing course at Kings College, which was part of the University of London. He quickly tried to analyze the odds that they would run into each other there. It was a big school. He considered coming clean on his earlier misrepresentation, but he didn't get the chance.

"Let's dance," she said, as she slid off the bar stool and took his hand.

He followed her to the dance floor and stared at her body - five feet seven or eight, and amazing curves. She moved gracefully, but with a purposeful stride, through the crowd. Her hair was medium-length, a wavy dark brown with subtle blond highlights that picked up the pulsing lights on the dance floor.

Bernadette loved to dance, and her whole body moved in perfect harmony to the music - strong, passionate, and with none of the wild, off-beat gyrations of many of the other women. She drew admiring glances from all the men in the club. Clark also liked to dance because it allowed him to be with a woman and not have to worry about coming up with too many topics of conversation.

It was hot in the club, and by the time a slow song began, Bernadette's body glistened with perspiration, and Clark felt uncomfortable in his sweaty shirt. He didn't mind, however, when she wrapped her arms around his waist and pulled him close. He put his arms around her shoulders and felt the firm tension of her shoulder muscles. He enjoyed the pressure of her breasts as they pressed into his chest, and then the gentle sway of her hips as she moved against his body. It all felt really good. So good that he felt himself getting aroused. He experienced a moment of panic, not sure if she would notice his stiffening penis as she continued to move her hips against him. But she laid her head on his shoulder and emitted a soft sound that vibrated through her body like the gentle purr of a cat. They moved like that for a series of slow songs and then reluctantly pulled apart when a fast song started.

They found their way back to the bar and ordered more drinks. He was more than happy to keep buying her drinks.

One, it was the gentlemanly thing to do, and two, it kept her with him. And now it seemed as if some parts of their bodies, a hand or leg or hip, were always in casual contact. They followed that pattern of dancing and drinking for several hours. The dancing countered most of the effects of the alcohol.

Then after a set of slow songs, she paused and didn't immediately head for the bar. "What do you think about getting some air?" she asked, her eyes smiling at him, a little shy and a little seductive. And without waiting for an answer, she pulled Clark from the dance floor and out of the club. Even at one o'clock in the morning, there were probably twenty people in the line waiting to get into the club. The line had been moving very slowly, and several people mockingly cheered as Clark and Bernadette exited.

"Where's your hotel?" she casually asked, as they walked arm-in-arm toward Piccadilly Circus.

Was this the time for him to come clean, tell her the truth? "Well, actually I'm staying with my half-sister and her family in Hampstead."

"Are they going to be worried? It's pretty late."

"Oh, no. They're okay. I've got a key. They go to bed early. They have a three-year-old. A daughter." He stopped because he was sure that he was rambling on like some retard.

"We could go to my place," she offered, with a very sweet sexy smile and a twinkle in her bright eyes.

Clark was often obtuse to a woman's silent messages but not to this one. He read this one loud and clear. The look on his face must have clearly indicated eager acceptance because she took his face in her hands and gave him a long, sensual kiss.

"The tube is closed, so we can either wait for a bus or take a taxi."

"Oh, let's get a taxi," he responded. He didn't want the moment or the momentum to change by waiting for and then sitting on some smelly bus.

In the taxi, she gave the driver an address on Earls Court Square. Clark thought he remembered that Rita had lived in the Earls Court area when she was growing up. But all thoughts of that quickly evaporated as Bernadette kissed him again. This time she also gently rubbed his leg. Her hand got close to but not all the way to his crotch, which was now full with his erection. He said a silent prayer that she wouldn't touch it. He knew that it wouldn't take much for him to lose control and embarrass himself. That had happened a couple of times with different women and had contributed to his current sexual status. He sensed that this might finally be his night, and he was desperate to not ruin it.

The taxi pulled up to a four-story apartment building, and after Clark paid the cabbie, Bernadette opened the door and led him inside and up two flights of stairs. Her flat was smaller and much older than Rita's, but it was warmly and very femininely furnished. It had a combined living and dining area with a small kitchen off of it. Then, down a short hall, was a bathroom and two bedrooms. It didn't occur to Clark to wonder who used the other bedroom because he was completely fixated on Bernadette as she led him into her bedroom.

She pushed the door partially closed behind them, and they stood there for a moment. Then she stepped close to him and began to unbutton his shirt. As she got it almost open, she paused a moment and then ran her fingers through his dark brown, chest hair.

"Oh, It's so thick and soft."

Over the past few years, Clark had grown to be mostly confident about his hair, which wasn't just on his chest, but covered almost every inch of his body. It had been a major source of angst and embarrassment growing up. But that had changed during his junior year of high school in Denver thanks to Julie Wells, his first girlfriend, who had been okay with it. But he was sure that his hair had been a primary reason why things had never progressed with Molly Connors when he was a senior in Sewickley, Pennsylvania. Molly had never said anything specifically, but she had also never really touched it.

"I hope it doesn't bother you."

"Not at all. Is it, you know, like this everywhere?" Without waiting for an answer, she unbuckled his belt, undid the button and zipper on his pants and pulled them down along with his underwear. His erection jumped out and stiffened further as she touched it. "This little Yank has wanted to come out and play all evening." She laughed, as she knelt down in front of him and put him into her mouth. She began to suck, teased him with her tongue, and then sucked harder as he very quickly lost control. Clark struggled to stay upright as he exploded, and his release washed every bit of strength from his body. She must have felt it, because she guided him over to sit down on her bed and then sat next to him.

"I'm so sorry," he moaned, still feeling the impact of his orgasm. "I didn't want that to happen so fast, but it just felt so, so wonderful."

She smiled at his silly grin and again rubbed her hands through the hair on his chest. "Don't worry silly, that's part of my master plan. You come quickly, and then we begin to have some real fun, slowly. I'll get you up again in no time, you'll see." She proceeded to alternate between rubbing his body and removing her clothes. He had been pretty sure that she wasn't wearing a bra, and that was quickly confirmed as her top came off and exposed her glistening breasts. He appreciated breasts, and these were spectacular. Her short skirt came off to reveal the smallest of bikini panties. When those came off he felt a sensation in his penis but not much growth yet.

She pulled it gently, stretching it a little. "Men's penises are so interesting," she remarked, with a grin, a tease. "Some men have these big things that always hang there like they're showing off. And then when aroused, they're still the same size.

What you saw in advance is all you're going to get. No surprises." She massaged him gently and smiled as a groan of pleasure escaped from Clark. "But then others seem to wait all compact like this, almost like they're shy or don't want to brag. And then when it's time, wow, you never know what you're going to get. They grow and grow. I like to think it's all about how much they want you." She paused and looked at him. "You probably think I'm completely bonkers," she teased.

He thought she was the most beautiful and interesting and sexy thing he had ever seen or dreamed of, but his orgasm had drained his brain of any ability to speak. He did manage, however, to give her a very warm smile and that seemed to be enough. Then he gained some control of himself and reached for her breasts. He had some experience with breasts and proceeded to try to give her his best effort. He kissed and sucked and bit on her firm nipples and soon heard her sighs of pleasure and felt her body respond. Her hands continued to gently massaged his penis, and it wasn't very long before it began to respond with new life.

She started to pull him on top of her, and neither of them heard the door to the flat open and close.

"Bernie, are you home?" A female voice called from the living room. "Where did you go tonight?"

Clark immediately felt his body stiffen and his penis soften.

Before they could react, the door to Bernadette's room swung open and in stepped a woman who looked very much like Bernadette - same features, hairstyle and eyes. The biggest difference was that she was older, with a clear maturity in her face. He expression immediately turned hard and then angry when she saw Clark. "Bernadette! I told you that you can't bring them to our flat. You have to keep work separate, you know that."

Clark struggled to process what he heard as he watched Bernadette's sister examine him with a cold, professional stare.

Bernadette faced her sister, not the least bit uncomfortable with her nakedness or the situation. "Mags, this is Clark, and he's not work. I like him."

Mags' face seemed to soften just slightly. "Oh Bernie we've talked about that." She continued to examine Clark. "And I don't see a condom anywhere. I won't go through that again, and you know mother would have a bloody cow. We didn't come here, sacrifice so much, for you to get careless."

Bernadette reached over Clark to her bedside table and opened a small drawer, pulling out a condom. "Here, we were just getting to that point. I know what I'm doing."

"Well, all I can say is that this won't pay the rent or your tuition." Mags paused, considered. "Does he have any money?" She looked skeptically at Clark.

"I'm not going to charge him. I brought him here because I like him, and he likes me." Bernadette gave Clark a smile that expressed the hope that if he had liked her before, he still did now.

Clark had never encountered a prostitute before, but he knew with some certainty that Mags was one, and he now felt an almost equal certainty that Bernadette was one also. He wondered what he had missed, whether he was a complete idiot. The really strange thing was that he felt oddly comfortable being naked in front of these two pretty women. In fact, as he looked at them, he started to respond again.

Mags noticed it, and she smiled. "Well maybe he'd like to do you for free and pay for me and we'll split it. I had a slow night, and it's been a while since I did a threesome. And oh, that hair looks so nice."

Clark had never thought about it before, but he now felt certain that he didn't want to lose his virginity as part of a monetary transaction. And besides, he was almost out of money after the club and the taxi. He wasn't even sure if he had enough for a taxi home. And he had no idea how much Mags would want, but she looked expensive. He shriveled up again and started to look for his clothes. "I'm sorry, but really I better go. I didn't, I didn't realize what was going on." He stumbled with the words as he avoided looking at Bernadette.

She got his meaning and gave him a weak smile as she picked up his pants and handed them to him. As she did, she whispered in his ear, "I'm sorry, I really do like you, and I wasn't, you know, doing it for..." She finished by nodding her head toward her sister, who enjoyed the awkwardness of the two frustrated would-be lovers. Bernadette turned, grabbed her sister by the arm and led her out of the room and into the other bedroom, leaving Clark alone to get dressed.

As Clark got to the front door, he paused, not sure what to do. He considered for a moment that he was probably a complete fool to leave this. "Bye, cheers," he called, then quickly opened the door and left. Half-way down the stairs he had to pause, his knees weak, and no idea of how he was going to get home.

He found a five pound note in his pocket which he figured would be enough for a taxi, but he had to find one first. He was fairly sure that Earls Court was in southwest London and he had to get to Hampstead in the north. But there weren't any taxis in Bernadette's neighborhood, and he didn't know where he would find a major street that might have some at two thirty in the morning. Struggling to remember how the taxi had gotten to Bernadette's building, he started walking and about fifteen minutes later stumbled onto Cromwell Street and found a taxi. Once home, he had a very difficult time falling asleep. He was beyond exhausted, but sexy images of Bernadette kept merging with images of old girlfriends and past sexual frustrations. Julie Wells was of course his biggest regret - that he had stopped what would have been the first sex for both of them. He had been hung-up on the certainty that he would soon be moving, and then the irony had been that she had moved before he did. And he remembered seeing the movie *Irma La Douce* and how Jack Lemmon was overcome by insane jealousy when Irma, the prostitute he loved, was with other men. Clark had felt bad for Nestor and knew that he could never handle a situation like that. But he had never imagined that he would ever meet a prostitute, and certainly not one as nice as Bernadette.

CHAPTER 3

It was early afternoon on Sunday when Clark finally got up and went to the gym to work out his sexual frustration in the weight room and on the track. Even while he struggled with 150 pounds on the bench press, he couldn't completely repress images of Bernadette, which brought some unwelcome reaction in his groin. He tried to force his mind to concentrate on baseball and whether or not the Baltimore Orioles were going to upset the Los Angeles Dodgers and win the upcoming World Series. The Dodgers were trying to repeat, but the Orioles were really good and were motivated to win their first series ever.

"Hey Yank."

It startled him because he hadn't heard Arthur enter the weight room. Fortunately, he didn't have the weights up over his chest because he might have lost control of them. He sat up to respond. "Hi." Nothing more came to his conversationally challenged brain.

"Do you want to spot for each other?" Arthur asked.

"Sure," Clark responded, as he got up and added another fifty pounds to the bar.

Arthur stood behind the bench ready to help if Clark couldn't get the bar back on the rack, which happened after only three reps.

"I've already done several sets," Clark offered, to explain what he feared was a feeble demonstration of strength.

"No worries." Arthur smiled while he added another fifty pounds to the bar.

Male testosterone dominated the gym, but neither of them got into an overly competitive mindset. Clark watched, impressed, as Arthur did ten quick reps and easily placed the bar on the rack. After Arthur did two more sets on the bench, they both moved to squats. Arthur's legs were noticeably thicker and stronger than Clark's. There wasn't much talking, and both men seemed to be comfortable with that. They did establish that Arthur came from Wales and was in his third and final year at the London School of Economics (LSE), which was also part of the University of London. He seemed pleased to learn that Clark was enrolled in several courses at LSE.

"I'm going out to run," Clark announced after some bicep curls, on which he had almost managed to keep up with Arthur. He was eager to demonstrate that, while not as strong as Arthur, he was faster.

"Before you go, since you're a student here, I wonder if you have a mind to play with us? You've got speed and good strength. I think you'd be a bloody natural on the pitch. We need a winger."

"What's a winger?"

"Oh, he's a back on the edge of the line and needs speed to score but has to tackle as well, we all do. I'm a forward on the edge of the scrum - more strength than speed."

Clark felt tempted to say yes, but hesitated. "I don't know. I've never played it. I didn't play football at home. Our football, not yours."

"Well, I'm sure that you could pick it up fast, and it's a good gang of lads, and after the matches we have some rip-snorter parties with plenty of birds." Arthur could sense that Clark was on the fence. "We have our first practice tomorrow afternoon, come out and see if you like it."

Clark didn't have a class on Monday afternoon, and he knew that birds referred to girls, and he did want to meet them. And there would be no expectations as to his skill level. So, it could be a win-win situation. "Yeah, that's cool, I'll think about it." He hoped he succeeded at being safely noncommittal but not rude. It just wasn't his personality to be, or appear to be, overly eager about something like that. But it did sound like fun.

Clark's first course, Modern Imperialism with Professor Joseph Merkel, began at ten o'clock Monday morning at the London School of Economics. Clark tried to give himself enough time to get to the school by nine o'clock, but he hadn't been on the underground trains and the buses during the morning rush hour, and it took a lot longer than he had anticipated. He ran from the bus stop to the school and then it took him some time to find the classroom.

Professor Merkel reacted with a cold glare as Clark stood just inside the door and tried to catch his breath. It was a seminar course, and fifteen or so students sat around a large table. The Professor stood at the head of the table near the door. Clark fought a surge of panic as he looked for an empty seat. There was only one, and it was in the far corner of the room. The table and chairs almost filled the small room and left very little space to maneuver. As he carefully worked his way around the students, stepping over their bags on the floor, he tried to ignore the grunts of frustration, and what he was sure were stares of total ridicule. He was very careful to not look directly at anyone.

"Well, by process of elimination of the students who were on time to class, this must be Mr. Westfield, our transfer from America," Professor Merkel mocked and put a very negative inflection on the last word.

"Sorry sir," Clark offered weakly. "I'm not used to the trains and busses yet."

"Did I ask for an explanation Mr. Westfield?"

"Uh, no sir."

"All right, now that Mr. Westfield has graced us with his presence, we can continue. As I was saying, the premise of this course is that imperialism is alive and well today with a modern manifestation and new centers of power in Moscow, Peking or Beijing, and Washington. The reading for the course will come from my new book, that I see most of you have, and obviously Mr. Westfield has not yet found the bookseller. I trust that you have all read the first two chapters for today. The other reading for the course will be my expectation that you peruse the *London Times* and the *Herald Tribune* on a daily basis." Professor Merkel paused to let that sink in. "We will begin this morning with a review of the history of imperialism beginning with the Romans in 600 AD, and we will quickly work our way to the obscene abuse of power being used by Mr. Westfield's country in Vietnam."

As the Professor droned on, Clark realized that he knew most of the history in general terms but not all the specific dates that seemed very important to the professor. He then allowed himself the opportunity to glance around the room at the other students. Almost the first person he saw was Protest Girl who stared at him with a curious sly smirk on her face. Clark tried to keep his reaction modest, which belied the enormity of his relief at seeing a friendly face and his happiness that it was her face.

Protest Girl turned her attention back to the professor and seemed to eagerly soak up every word he uttered. Words that Clark had already decided were pedantic and boring. Clark's focus on Protest Girl was then distracted by the girl seated next to her. She was the most beautiful, most exotic girl, woman, that Clark had ever seen, and she happened to be staring right at him. Exotic Girl then smiled at him. Clark wasn't sure if he managed to smile back, but he felt a warm blush spread up from his neck to his ears. Exotic Girl's long black hair was pulled back in a ponytail, and her finely chiseled facial features were exquisite. Her eyes were dark pools of passion, and Clark felt himself falling into them.

"Mr. Westfield!" The Professor's voice elevated enough to break Clark from his fixation on Exotic Girl. He turned to face the Professor, who stared at him with a malevolent intensity.

"Sir?"

"Ah, Mr. Westfield has returned to the land of the living. Can you tell us what we should have learned from the experience of the Romans after their failed campaign in France in seven fifty AD?"

Clark hadn't been listening, but he did have a good grasp of ancient history from having taken it two years in a row, thanks to attending three different junior high schools. He frantically tried to remember the Roman invasion of France that had ended so badly. He tried not to look directly at Professor Merkel, who was enjoying Clark's discomfort far too much. Nor could he look over toward the two women.

Professor Merkel evidently thought that his victory was complete and was preparing to push the knife further in, but stopped when Clark spoke.

"Well, I would say that the primary lesson would be that supply lines are critical in any campaign or occupation so far from home. The Romans got greedy and stretched themselves too far, especially when they invaded Britain around the same time. That began an inevitable-"

The professor cut Clark off. "Okay, fine, Mr. Westfield, now let's move on."

The remainder of the two-hour class dragged on for everyone except Clark, who felt emboldened by his answer. He noticed that no student ever asked a question, despite seeing what he was sure were perplexed expressions on many of their faces. And the professor did occasionally zap out a question to a student, and it was clear that this was always to someone whose attention had seemed to wane. Clark thought that none of them recovered as well as he had.

At first he tried to ignore it, but he was soon mesmerized by the little glances that kept coming at him from Exotic Girl. And he was also fascinated by Protest Girl and her ability to concentrate. Those pleasant distractions helped him pass the time. When the class was finally over, Professor Merkel abruptly left the room, leaving no opportunity for any student to make contact with him.

As Clark left the room, he noticed that both women stood a little way down the hall, chatting. He wondered if they had waited for him. It turned out that they had, and they motioned at him to join them.

"Bugger all, why didn't you tell me you were a student? I thought you were a bloody tourist," Protest Girl immediately challenged him.

"I never had a chance because you wouldn't have coffee with me. Oh, did you get everyone out of jail?"

She nodded, "Yeah, of course."

"That was so great that you shoved it back at Professor Merkel. He's such an ass, and he really hates Americans," gushed Exotic Girl.

"This is Cynna Moustakas, she's from Greece." Protest Girl motioned to Exotic Girl, who responded with her exotic smile that had captivated Clark for the past two hours. He didn't know whether to shake hands with her or not, so he just stood awkwardly and tried to smile naturally. "And my name is Gwen Thomas," Protest Girl continued, as her vivid blue eyes came to life and focused completely on him. She aggressively thrust out her hand and waited a second while he recovered enough to shake it. She had a very firm grip, and he thought she might be trying to prove how strong she was.

Clark recovered quickly enough to reply, "I'm Clark. Nice to meet you Gwen and Cynna."

"We were just going to the pub for nosh and a pint, want to join us?" Gwen asked.

"Sure that's cool." Clark tried to be casual but he couldn't think of anything he'd rather do. As he followed them, he was struck by the dramatic physical differences between the two women. Gwen looked smaller than he remembered from the protest. Maybe it had been the nervous energy that had poured out of her that day, like a boxer bouncing on her toes, ready to fight. Her figure was what he thought was called petite - slender with narrow hips and only a hint of breasts. All of it hidden under her loose-fitting pants and baggy shirt.

Cynna was a dramatic contrast in every way. She was maybe five feet eight inches, a good four or five inches taller than Gwen; with a voluptuous figure, one that a sculpture would love to have as a model. And she was dressed as provocatively as would be appropriate for a college classroom - a revealing top and short mini-skirt, not unlike many of the women he'd seen at the dance club.

Clark instinctively categorized Cynna as a lover and Gwen as a friend.

The Three Tuns Pub was the student pub at LSE, and on the first day of the fall term it was crowded with students catching up with friends who they hadn't seen during the almost four-month summer break. Austere and functional were Clark's first impressions of the pub. A few old photographs hung on the walls in a haphazard fashion, as if put there by different people at different times with no thoughts of coordination - not very British. Half of the long bar that ran the length of the room was devoted to multiple beer taps, with no other alcohol on display. The other half of the bar held large plates with sandwiches that sat unwrapped and didn't look very appetizing.

The plain surroundings didn't stop the crowd from having a good time. Some women friends of Gwen called to them to join their group, which was seated around three tables jammed together. Most of the women greeted Gwen warmly and treated Cynna more casually, carefully.

Clark thought he might try to sit next to Cynna, but suddenly Arthur appeared and pulled him toward a group of men, which included the others he had seen on the track. A pint of beer magically materialized in front of him.

"So I see you've met my knobhead brother," Gwen said, as she appeared at the guys' table and playfully punched Arthur on the arm.

"This is the Yank I told you about," Arthur said as he smiled at his sister. "I hope he's going to come out for the team."

Gwen smiled as she rolled her eyes and went back to her table.

"Looks like Arthur has a new recruit," Cynna remarked to Gwen.

"I wouldn't bet on it. He seems, I don't know… too intelligent for those prats."

Arthur and the other men on the team talked a little about the courses they were taking, but the majority of the conversation was about rugby. They had seven games scheduled for the fall term, and the highlight was a trip to Amsterdam and Paris in late November.

As the group ate and drank, Clark was surprised that most of them smoked. He had known athletes in high school who had smoked, but almost no one on his college team had. Clark listened and nodded occasionally without commenting, but mostly he surreptitiously watched Cynna. She seemed to hover on the edge of the women's conversation, much as he did with the men. She took small bites of what looked like a plain cheese sandwich on thin white bread and sipped lemonade in a pint glass. Several times she glanced over in his direction, and he quickly looked down or away. There was still an empty seat next to her, but he couldn't get up the nerve to move and talk to her. She seemed aloof, and she was beautiful - too beautiful for him to feel comfortable. He was in a great spot to watch her, and that was perfect. It made him happy to see that she didn't smoke even though most of the other women did, including Gwen.

Gwen filled her friends in on her narrow escape the week before. They all looked over at Clark when she described her rescue. A few of them had been there, but mostly in the rear. Over the summer break they had all scattered to the far corners of the British Isles, and none of them had had the opportunity or the inclination for any serious political activity. That was fine for them, but not for Gwen, who described how she had gone stir-crazy being home in Cardiff, working as an intern in her father's bank. Her real passion was political activism, and she joked that, "The last political protest in Wales was the Magna Carta, seven hundred and fifty some years ago."

As she talked and interacted with her friends, Gwen stole a few glances at Clark. She noticed him looking over at Cynna. She laughed to herself that he was daft as a bush; Cynna was way out of his league. She tried to pull Cynna into her conversations, but the Greek woman didn't have much interest in politics. She was an economics major.

Clark had consumed his first pint quickly, but then he carefully nursed his second one while most of the others got slightly pissed.

"You could dash home and get your kit and meet us at the pitch. We start at half three," Arthur implored Clark.

Clark felt comfortable enough with them that he decided to do that. He thought he saw an expression of surprise on Gwen's face as he passed her on his way out.

Clark was glad for the excuse to leave the pub. He was sure that Gwen had noticed him staring at Cynna, but he wasn't going to let that bother him. Senior year in high school, his girlfriend Molly had a best friend, Lindy, who had been just like that. Lindy and Clark had clashed constantly, and he knew that she had been a big reason that Molly never did it with him. It seemed like Lindy had some sort of weird radar. Whenever he thought he had made a breakthrough with Molly and might get beyond second base, Lindy appeared. She would magically materialize out of thin air. Sometimes she had been there physically. Sometimes she'd been on the telephone. Other times Molly would suddenly remember that she had to do something that involved Lindy. He could laugh now, but what an annoying girl she had been.

A protest by the transit workers' union for higher wages caused the trains and busses to run irregularly and slowly. By the time Clark reached Hampstead and got his gym stuff, he knew he was running late. He almost stayed home. Being late would make him the center of attention and that was not where he liked to be. But he thought he had seen Cynna smile at Arthur's mention of rugby, so she might like it, and that was sufficient motivation for him to jog out to the field and join the practice.

Arthur welcomed him and immediately turned him over to Charles, who inserted him into the drills with the players called the backs. The first drill involved sprinting for a short distance, five to ten yards, then spinning around a player who tried to tag him and then a sprint to another player, spin, and so on. Then the runner took the spot at the end of the chain and the player at the front began to sprint and spin. The sprinting part was easy for Clark, but the spinning proved disorienting. He stumbled several times on each of his turns through the group, and he fell down once. He anticipated some snickers or laughs from the others, but none came - probably because most of them has also tripped or fallen. Clark's experience with sports teams was not that extensive, but he immediately sensed that the concept of sportsmanship in England was maybe different than in America.

They then drilled on passing the rugby ball, which looked like a pregnant American football - bigger and fatter. His father had given him an NFL football for Christmas a few years before, but he hadn't used it much and certainly couldn't throw it very well. That didn't matter now because the rugby ball wasn't thrown anything like a football in America. It wasn't thrown with an overhead motion, and it was never thrown forward. It was tossed underhand, pitched they called it, sideways and backward to a player who ran next to, but just behind, the player with the ball.

From the side of the field, Clark watched a short practice game along with the four other men who were new and trying out for the team. Sean, a player with a broken foot, stood next to them and tried to explain the rules. The most interesting part of the game for Clark was what they called the scrum. At seemingly random times, eight of the men, called the forwards, would bundle together in a formation of three rows that resembled an American football huddle. Then, bent over at the waist and holding on to each other, they would butt up against a similar formation of the other team's forwards. One of the backs would toss the ball on the ground between the two groups. They would then use the strength in their legs to try to push ahead against the other team and hook the ball with their feet to propel it back to one of the backs who waited for it to emerge from the rear of the scrum. Then the ball could be advanced by the backs.

When Sean began to explain rucks and mauls, Clark felt overwhelmed and begged the guy to stop. He was glad to see that at least two of the others looked as confused as he felt.

After practice, Clark walked into the locker room and faced an old anxiety. It happened every time with a new team, a new group that had never seen his hairy body. Here he was a stranger in a strange land. Plus, he knew from his brother-in-law Keith that body hair was not a common characteristic of British men.

As Clark undressed and headed for the shower room, he noticed the reactions - they always happened. But these were different. He felt only positive energy. There were none of the caustic negative jokes that he had heard since seventh grade, when he had begun to shave. Sure, someone whispered about, "Grizzly bears in America", and someone said, "What a beast", which had been his nickname on the baseball team, senior year of high school. But tone was important, and this tone was positive and even admiring, in a manly way. Clark didn't realize that he had been slouching until he felt himself stand up taller in the shower and let the hot water run down his back.

He was putting on his shirt, when one of the forwards, Martin, called out, laughing, "Blimey Yank, I got to keep you away from Emily, my bird. She's totally bonkers over men's body hair. She'll be wanting to shag you on the spot."

"Martin's bird will shag just about anything, so stay away from her," Arthur loudly cautioned Clark, but he barely got it out because he laughed so hard. "Some of us are back for a pint. Care to join?"

Clark was tired but felt very good about the day. He didn't want to push his luck, so he declined and headed home. He had a lot of experience being in new situations with new people, and he had learned that it was far better to take it slowly, one step at a time. And this had been a very good first step.

CHAPTER 4

Clark ate his breakfast the next morning and sang along as the Beatles sang *Got to Get You Into my Life* from the *Revolver* album. "I was alone, I took a ride, I didn't know what I would find there..." He liked to sing but only sang when alone because he knew he didn't have a good singing voice, not like his sister who was majoring in musical theater at NYU.

He looked over the mimeographed course information sheet from Professor Merkel. There were readings listed for each week, most of them from the professor's textbook. It looked like fifty or more pages a week, which wasn't too bad. What struck him as strange was that there were no papers or exams listed on the schedule. So he wondered whether he had missed something. Maybe this was a question that would provide him a good reason to approach Cynna. He hoped that she might be in his next course, which met at two o'clock that afternoon.

Cynna wasn't in the course, Political Realities of the Middle East, but Gwen was. She talked to another student, a thin male with black curly hair, who sat next to her. It appeared to be a very intense conversation. Clark had a momentary impulse to sit near her, but when she looked up at him there was just the smallest hint of recognition, almost no warmth, and a barely perceptible nod of her head. So Clark took a seat across the table and glanced at the course information sheet that he had taken from a stack at the head of the table. There were readings, but no papers or exams were listed for this course either. He knew that he must be missing something, something that had the potential to make him look stupid if he asked a question.

Professor Isaac Cohen entered and immediately started to lecture. He offered no greeting, welcome, or any other pleasantry. He didn't bother with his attendance list. "The political reality of the Middle East, as you will learn in this class and from my new book, is that the creation of the state of Israel in 1946 by the British Government, with the blessing of the other allied powers, was the biggest mistake of the twentieth century. Bigger than the League of Nations. Bigger than the appeasement of Hitler. Bigger than the atomic bombs on Japan. And much bigger than the so-called Cold War."

Clark felt tension flood the room like a damn had burst. Gwen and the curly-haired student next to her gasped and stared, seemingly shocked and horrified. Their reaction was echoed by many of the other students. But not all of them. Several students, who seemed to be from the Middle East or possibly Africa, appeared to try to hide their smiles. Their reactions were careful and quiet, but they were clearly in some agreement with the professor.

With a little smirk, as if he had anticipated the reactions, Cohen continued. "Now I know some of you, probably most of you, think this is heresy, sacrilege. But I'm a Jew, and I'm not a traitor to my faith because I believe that this folly will eventually lead to a greater threat to our people than the Holocaust."

Clark braced himself for the uproar that he would have expected from a class at home, but there was only dead silence. Had a pin hit the floor at that moment, the sound would have reverberated around the room like a cannon blast. Damn these people are polite, Clark thought. But then he wondered if they were somehow intimidated. Or maybe many of them, like

Gwen and Curly Hair next to her, were just too shocked to speak.

"That's enough for today. I want that to sink in while you do the reading for next week," the professor announced, and then abruptly left the room. It was less than five minutes into the scheduled two-hour class.

Clark watched the students who had seemed to agree with the professor quickly leave the room, like they were being sucked out in his wake. The others, the dissenters, the disbelievers, including Gwen and Curly Hair, all began to speak at once, intensely but quietly. Clark got up to go. As he reached the door, Gwen grabbed his arm.

"So Yank, what do you think about that plonker?"

He knew he had to be careful. She had asked a question, but her facial expression and body language clearly indicated that she wanted to hear the correct answer. "Pretty incendiary. Could be an interesting course or maybe he's trying to get people to drop it. It's crowded in here."

Gwen considered that and seemed to relax a little bit. She then remembered Curly Hair who now stood next to her. "Clark, this is Nigel. Nigel, Clark."

Clark nodded at Curly Hair aka Nigel, who paid attention only to Gwen.

Nigel was red-faced with simmering rage. "I'm going to file a complaint against that arse-hole. I'm sure they thought a Professor Cohen would be a good Jew when they hired him. Did you know that we only had two Jews on the faculty before? Middle East expert, what a load of bloody rubbish." Nigel stormed away without ever acknowledging Clark or saying good-bye to Gwen.

She forced a smile. "He gets pretty intense, especially over Israel, and that was a bloody shock." Clark nodded as she continued. "His father is a nob with some pull on the Board of Regents, so maybe that will be our first and last class with fucking mingebag I'm-a-Jew Cohen." Then she quickly changed gears. "How was your knock-about yesterday? I don't imagine those prats took it easy on you."

It struck him that her moods certainly changed very quickly, and he was intrigued by her colorful language. He also liked her smile - friendly and accepting. It merged with her blue eyes, and for a moment she looked quite pretty. Then her smile disappeared like a lost treasure, and with a quick wave of her hand, she scooted off down the hallway, not waiting for him to answer what he thought had been a question.

Clark was glad the class had let out early because it gave him an opportunity to find the shop that Arthur had recommended and buy a pair of rugby boots and a mouth guard for practice that afternoon.

When he arrived at the field, Clark felt comfortable because it seemed like everyone on the team had accepted him despite his inexperience. In fact, it seemed that they were going out of their way to welcome him and to try to get him excited about their game. And it was a perfect game for Clark because it didn't require special skills as did baseball, which had taken him many years to learn. In rugby, it seemed as if his natural speed was almost all he needed. The only thing that he had never done before was to tackle someone.

The day before he had watched and cringed at the violent collisions between tacklers and ball carriers - and without the benefit of padding of any kind or helmets on their heads. He had almost decided to call it quits, assuming that he would never learn to or like to do that. As he had continued to watch the game, however, he realized that it didn't seem nearly as violent as the tackles he had seen in high school and college football games. And then he had noticed that no one ever hit anyone except the ball carrier. There wasn't the indiscriminate hitting that happened to everyone in American football.

They were about to start a tackling drill, and Clark was nervous. He wasn't particularly fond of pain and certainly didn't have a death wish. Arthur took the forwards and Charles took the backs, which included Clark.

"All right you lot, our tackling last season was pathetic, little bloody Sloane Rangers could have done better." Charles tried to keep a straight face, but no one seemed to be buying it. He looked directly at Clark. "No padding means you have to use your hands more than your shoulders. Grab them, slow them up, drag them down."

The backs then lined up in two groups and stood ten meters from each other. When Charles shouted, "go," the player with the ball ran toward a player in the other group, who had to tackle him. The ball carrier could spin and dodge to avoid the tackler, but he could only move within a set parameter. It was immediately clear to Clark that almost no one relished tackling, and that it was fairly easy for the ball carrier to elude the tackler.

On his first try as a tackler, Clark wasn't very aggressive and completely missed the ball carrier. And when his first turn came to be the ball carrier, he successfully avoided the tackler. That happened for most of the backs, so Charles narrowed the corridor for the ball carrier. On his next try, Clark managed to grab the ball carrier and hang on until he dragged him to the ground. As he got up, he realized that it had felt pretty good. That lasted until he carried the ball, and Charles hit him hard and knocked him off his feet. Shit that hurts! he yelled at himself. The hurt, however, motivated him to get retribution when Charles was the ball carrier.

"Smashing tackle Clark," Charles said, as he got up off the ground.

Clark felt good despite the sensation that his left arm was probably going to fall out of its shoulder socket.

Clark's shoulder was still sore the next morning as he made his way to Kings College and his first class in creative writing. But the pain didn't dampen his excitement. This was a course that he never would have had the opportunity to take at his college. Plus, he had never had a woman professor and didn't know what to expect. What he certainly hadn't anticipated was that the first person he saw in the class was Bernadette.

Clark had often thought of that night, how exciting she had been, and how he had reacted. He had fought an impulse, several times, to go find her. He remembered where she lived, but he hadn't done it, partly from embarrassment, but mostly because he didn't think he could resist her again if she offered.

A torrent of panic raced up his spine as he quickly looked around the room for an empty chair away from her. He spied one and hurried to it. He didn't look at her and hoped she hadn't seen him.

She had seen him, and a wicked little smile crossed her face as she started to get up to move next to him. The sudden and dramatic entrance of Professor Hammerly caused Bernadette to sit back down and the room to go dead quiet.

Maya Hammerly had a well-deserved reputation around Kings College. Her novels and short stories had earned her an international reputation as an avant-garde writer with two dominant themes: blacks in Scotland and feminism. Her black Scottish female protagonists were tough and often aggressively bisexual. They took no prisoners, and Professor Hammerly did the same in her classroom.

She took the two books that her department chair required her to use and slammed them down on the desk, causing one to topple heavily to the floor. "These are pure rubbish, and we won't be needing them in this class." She paused to gauge the reactions of the students. She fully expected to lose a third of them, mostly the men, by the time the morning was over.

Clark was immediately both impressed and intimidated by this woman with her very short kinky hair, mocha skin, and large, thick eyeglasses. He ventured a glance across the room at Bernadette and saw a cautious smile on her face, as she stared at the professor.

"We're going to write in this class, and I expect to get stuff from your gut, from your soul. I don't want to get what you think I will like. Nothing is off the table, off limits. If you want to describe the best fuck you ever had, that's fine. Or if it was rape or incest, let's hear about it with all the gory details. We are going to learn to be brutally honest with ourselves, just as writers must be." The professor paused again and could now clearly identify several students, all men, who would soon leave. It was then that she noticed Clark, who continued to stare at Bernadette. She followed the direction of his gaze and decided to have a little fun. "So you there with the sexy hairy arms, I want you to tell us what you think of as you look at this woman here." She pointed at Bernadette. "Describe her as we meet her in your story."

Clark looked at the professor to confirm that she had indeed called on him. He felt oddly confident and empowered because no one knew him. That was a situation he knew well. Bernadette. Several images flashed through his mind: her body moving to the music, her naked body under him. Without looking at her, he began, "Pulsing moving rhythmic feet. Brilliant smile lights up the street. Layers hidden none to see. Embarrassed boy who can only flee. See naked breast and imagine the rest." He stopped and felt a hot blush rush across his face. He didn't dare look around at the other students, who sat there very quiet, surprised.

Maya smiled, and her face relaxed. Well, interesting, not complete rubbish, she thought. From his accent, she assumed that Clark must be the American who had wormed his way into her class without any of the prerequisites.

Bernadette was not easily surprised by people, especially men, but she sat there unable to react. He had created a poem to her in front of a class of strangers. She hadn't felt this unsure of herself since she was sixteen and had had to tell her mother that she was pregnant.

For Clark, the rest of the class passed like an out-of-focus silent film. He was vaguely aware of the story ideas that some of the other students pitched. He didn't pay much attention to the professor's reactions except to form an impression that she wasn't pleased with very many of them. He found that he couldn't look at Bernadette without seeing her stare at him. After he responded with a couple of weak smiles, he stopped looking. He was preoccupied with what he should do after class - should he talk to her or not. He decided that if she hung around, then he would talk.

As the class ended, he stalled and watched Bernadette leave and thought that maybe it meant she didn't want to talk. But when he came into the hall and saw her leaning against the wall, he knew that wasn't the case. He smiled sheepishly as she approached her. "Hi," he offered, as he leaned on the wall next to her.

"Clark. So I guess your tourist visa got extended." She tried to keep it light. She wasn't mad, she wanted to tease him.

"Yeah, sorry about that. I wasn't really thinking clearly. Maybe I can blame it on jetlag, I had just arrived a few days earlier."

"Pretty big coincidence, same college, same class."

"Yeah. I'm doing this class and three at the London School of Economics."

"Oh, I detest economists. They're a step below lawyers on the circles of hell. We have one who is currently running and destroying my country."

He laughed nervously. "Yeah, but I'm there for the political science part of the school." He tried to decipher his feelings. All he knew for sure was that he wanted to continue to talk to her. "Would you like to grab some lunch?"

They went to a small but brightly lit pub near the college. After a few awkward moments, they settled into a comfortable exchange of their opinions of Professor Hammerly and then stories about other interesting professors. She was much better at innocent small talk than he was. But there was a strong and very strange undercurrent of familiarity between them because they had, after all, seen each other naked and more.

Clark was eager to keep it light and friendly. He enjoyed her company, and as a friend he could possibly accept her choice of how to live her life.

"I really did have fun the other night, and I'm sorry about Mags, she can come on jolly strong."

He was glad that she had brought it up and out into the open. "That's okay, yeah I did also." He felt awkward but not uncomfortable, and he sensed that she felt something similar.

"So, friends?" she asked, as she held out her hand, official but fun.

"Friends," he confirmed. But as he shook her hand, he wondered if that were really possible with such a beautiful, sexy woman.

After lunch they parted with a European-style semi-hug and kisses on the cheeks.

Clark had a couple of hours to kill before rugby practice, so he hopped on a bus to LSE and the library. He thought he would try to find anything written by or about Professor Cohen to see how he had developed his seemingly radical and unpopular views.

Clark wandered around the crazy rabbit warren of buildings that had become the London School of Economics as it had grown during the 1900s. Some buildings had connecting halls or doors, but not all of them. A few of the buildings were of recent construction but most were pre-war, World Wars I and II. And some were much older, early 1800s, and the library was in one of those. Like a room in an old castle or cathedral, the main room of the library had tall ceilings with stone pillars and arches. Stained glass windows depicted scenes of monks reading and writing books. Clark liked it immediately and imagined that this was probably what the library would be like at Cambridge or Oxford.

There were students sitting at almost all of the large wooden tables in the main room. Clark found an empty one in the back next to a large, clear, leaded-glass window that looked out onto Houghton Street. He left his bag on a chair and ambled down the aisles of wooden shelving, trying to figure out the cataloguing system, but it wasn't what he was used to. He finally went to the front desk to ask for help. After he retrieved a couple of books, he returned to his table and found Gwen and Cynna sitting there, talking quietly. He suppressed a nervous urge to grab his bag and leave. But he decided to stay, partly because he had been there first, and mostly because he hoped he'd get a chance to talk to Cynna. Both women looked at him and gave him a smile as he sat down. Gwen's smile was accepting but not eager, while Cynna's was circumspect, curious.

Clark tried to concentrate on his research, but his attention was constantly pulled away by his interest in what the two women talked about. It seemed that a friend of Gwen's had been working at a school for gypsy children in the Macedonian district of Greece, where Cynna was from. Gwen's friend was missing, and she feared he had been abducted by one of the anti-gypsy groups in that area. She wanted Cynna to ask her father to check into it. But it was clear to Clark, if not to Gwen, that Cynna wasn't that eager to get involved.

Clark almost missed an old newspaper article stuck in one of Professor Cohen's books. It was from the *London Times* in July, 1948, and told of how Isaac Cohen had been tossed out of Israel after he had tried to create a political movement that would include Arabs in the governing body for the new country. This had been considered political heresy among the Jews, who had fled persecution in Europe and had fought the Arabs for every inch of territory. Cohen, once a diehard Zionist, had been vilified because he had suggested that there were similarities between the displacement of Jews from their homes in Europe and the displacement of Arabs from their homes in what was now Israel. As he finished the article, it seemed to Clark that there had been no place for compromise in the Israeli nationalization process. Clark looked up to share this with Gwen and found that both women were gone.

Clark had almost reached the athletic building at the university when the sky opened up, and he got soaked by the first heavy rain since he had been in London. He wondered if there would be a practice.

"We love the mud," Charles shouted as they ran out to the field.

Later, Arthur and Charles finally ended practice when the conditions became more treacherous than fun. After very long and welcome hot showers, they all headed to The Herald Times, the student pub at the University of London. While not as small nor as austere as the Three Tuns pub at LSE, The Herald Times certainly wouldn't make anyone's pub-tour list. It was in one of the university's newer buildings and had a main public room with a full bar to complement the obligatory beer taps. There was also a snack bar with a grill manned by a work-study student and a short-order cook. Another large room had a couple of billiard tables, pinball machines, and several clusters of comfortable couches and chairs.

Clark examined framed photos on the wall of university sports teams and students engaged in other activities. He found several of the rugby team and could pick out Arthur, Charles and a couple of the other players he knew.

"That was my first year," Charles said, as he came up next to Clark. "We won the Queen's Cup that year. Just missed last year, but I think we've got a chance this year."

"I'm curious," Clark asked, as they walked to the bar. "Don't get me wrong, you and Arthur do a great job, but why doesn't the team have a coach?"

"Bloody budget cuts. Priorities. The regents decided that a new science building was more important than athletics. Bloody wankers." Charles finished with a wry smile.

Clark nodded sympathetically as he remembered seeing the large construction project and sign for the new science building.

"They wanted to demote us to a club, but we got them to keep us officially a varsity team that we coach ourselves," Charles continued. "Problem is there's no queue of new players, and we're really glad that you've signed on." He then bought Clark a beer, and they mockingly toasted to the value of academics over sports.

After a few beers, Clark knew he should go home. He had another class the next day. But as the group thinned out, he found himself alone with Arthur, who seemed to want to talk. Clark felt comfortable around him, and it helped that Arthur's main topic of conversation was Cynna.

"She spent the summer in Cardiff with Gwen and me. Our fathers know each other through the Rothschild Bank. The girls both worked at the bank. It was a right corker despite Cynna's bloody minder."

Clark was about to ask what a minder was when Arthur pushed on. "So what do you think of her?" Arthur asked.

"She seems nice, a bit exotic," Clark ventured carefully.

"Exotic?" Arthur snorted his beer. "Gwen?"

Clark realized his mistake. "Oh, Gwen, sure, yeah she's also in my Political Realities course. Now that prof is really intense, and controversial."

"Oh, I heard. Cohen. Gwen said he's an arrogant toe-rag. But you should give Gwen a chance. Under all that bolshie proxy rhetoric and tough exterior, she's a sweet girl, and she really appreciated what you did for her last week. If she keeps getting nicked at those things, our old man is gonna make her come home for good."

Arthur had to go settle an argument between two others on the team, and Clark realized that he had had more than enough to drink, so he headed for the bus stop. It took him over an hour to get home because of the night schedule. Twice he had to switch busses. And at one stop he was accosted by an unpleasant drunk with a very thick Jamaican accent. Clark was about to flee when the bus pulled up, and the man disappeared back into the shadows.

Clark finally got up about noon the next day, Thursday, with a lingering hangover and the smell of cigarette smoke in his hair. He showered and managed to get to LSE by two o'clock, just in time for his last class of the week - Philosophy of International Law. From its catalogue description this had been the course that had most interested Clark, other than creative writing. If a career as a writer didn't materialize, he thought that international law might be a possibility, despite his inability to speak any other languages.

Clark was immediately rewarded by the sight of Cynna, who sat in the last row with an empty chair next to her. He made an uncharacteristically bold move and sat next to her. It paid off with her quick smile and bright, "Hello." She seemed happy to see a familiar face.

Professor Jason Doctor made a quiet entrance, stood at the head of the room and waited a moment for the students to acknowledge him and settle down. In a very quiet voice, he introduced himself as foremost a philosopher and secondarily a lawyer.

The room was warm, the professor's voice a quiet monotone, and Clark had a hard time staying awake. He was afraid that the rumbling noise from his empty stomach was loud enough to raise the ire of yet another professor. But the only one who seemed to hear it was Cynna, who smiled and wrote 'hungry?' on her note pad. 'Yes' he replied on his notebook, adding a smiling face, which he regretted as soon as he drew it. He knew that she would think he was a real loser. Cautiously, he looked over at her and was rewarded with her best smile yet.

Cynna had met only one other American in her life, and he had been a lecherous jerk. So she was pleasantly surprised by this seemingly sweet, innocent boy who was silly enough to draw a smiling face. She realized that Mrs. Rovsek would probably not see him as a threat.

As class ended, Clark mustered up his courage and turned to Cynna. "Would you like to get something to eat or drink?"

She smiled as she shook her head. "Maybe some other time," she offered, and Clark hoped that she was serious and not just being polite.

Clark liked the rain. He had been the only one in his family who had enjoyed Seattle when they had lived there when he was in the seventh grade. Today he loved the heavy rain because practice was canceled and he could go home and collapse. He had felt conflicted about whether or not to suck it up and go. Now his conscience was clear as he grabbed a sandwich at a kiosk outside the underground station and headed for the train.

When Clark woke Friday, it was late morning and he felt good, not just physically, but also because it had been an interesting and overall very positive first week of school, first few weeks of living in London.

All his life, moving every summer to a new city, he had dealt with change and new surroundings, and often he had hated it. But this was different; this time he had purposefully caused it. It had started midway through the previous school year, his sophomore year at college. At the beginning of that school year he had felt comfortable being in the same school for a second year - the first time that had ever happened for him. The same surroundings, the same people, the same dorm room, the same routine, had all made him feel good at first. But then things had slowly changed. By the middle of February, he had realized that he was bored. Moving and change were an ingrained part of who he was. Almost like an addiction, he needed a change. Dartmouth's isolation from the rest of the world certainly hadn't helped. Nor had the fact that it was all men, and the closest college with women was an hour away. Boston, the nearest big city, was over four hours by car.

When he had heard the news that Rita was moving to Los Angeles for a few years, leaving her flat empty, an idea had taken shape. He had always wanted to travel around Europe, to live there, so why not go to school there. The fact that Dartmouth didn't have a formal program for students to study abroad hadn't been an unsurmountable obstacle. The University of London accepted hundreds of international students from all over the world and had promptly responded with an application packet. He had waited until he had been accepted before he had broached the idea with his parents.

At Dartmouth, he'd had the nearby safety net of his family, particularly his mother who had held their family together while his father constantly traveled for work. In London, he hadn't been too homesick, but he had occasionally felt exposed. That safety net was now thousands of miles away. Rita's flat had quickly become an oasis, and now it really felt like home.

Clark spent the early afternoon reading and working on his story ideas for creative writing class. He had several ideas but wasn't excited about any one of them. He really wanted this first one to make a good impression on the professor. And he also wanted to impress Bernadette. Most of his writing in the past had been about or for a girl in his life or one he wanted to be in his life. Margaret, Julie, Molly, Rebecca - all had inspired angst-ridden poetry and short stories. He knew that the way he had met Bernadette would make a great story, but he obviously couldn't use that for the class. Frustrated, he finally abandoned the effort and made his way into town for rugby practice.

Practice was light because they had a match the next day against the team from Cambridge University, which they had barely beaten last spring in the national tournament. Even though they called this a friendly, meaning it didn't count as an official game, Arthur and Charles were clearly nervous as they repeated bits of strategy and went over the rules, many of which still baffled Clark. He was constantly off-sides and had a hard time internalizing what that concept meant. It wasn't in his nature to hold back when he saw an opening, but that was what he was supposed to do, not get ahead of his teammate who had the ball.

They all went easy on the beer after practice. No one was prepared to give it up entirely, and most of them figured that two or three pints wouldn't hurt. Plus, the friendly wasn't scheduled until three o'clock in the afternoon, so there would be plenty of time to sleep it off.

After a week, Clark had gotten familiar with many of the personalities on the team. Charles, the leader of the backs, had been the fastest man on the team until Clark arrived. He didn't seem to mind Clark beating him, as long as it helped them win. Robert, a forward, was even quieter than Clark. Craig, another forward, was easily the strongest on the team but not the brightest. Winston, named after Churchill, was a back, and a very sharp dresser. Heath, a forward from Scotland, was the joker on the team but also either a racist or not very sensitive to the kind of jokes he told. Martin, the biggest man on the team, had the girlfriend who liked hairy men. And Henry, a third-year back, seemed to resent Clark because he was afraid that Clark might supplant him as a starter.

And then there was Arthur. He clearly had strong leadership talents. He also had a reputation as a wild playboy who had supposedly gotten at least two co-eds pregnant in his first two years at the university. But this year the conversations centered on how much he seemed to have changed. No one could recall seeing him with any bird since the start of the term.

Clark left the pub fairly early because he didn't want to miss the last bus that went directly to Hampstead. He waited impatiently at the bus stop, not sure if the bus was late or whether he had missed it. He planned to call his father on Sunday about a car. When he had decided to come to England for the year, Clark and his father had agreed that he would sell his Ford Mustang and buy a car in London so he could explore the country and the rest of Europe. He had waited while he learned his way around and settled in, but it now seemed like the time to do it. He sorely missed the freedom and independence that he had enjoyed with his car. But it was interesting that no one he had met so far seemed to have one. He wondered if it was just an American thing.

CHAPTER 5

The friendly rugby match with Cambridge began promptly at three o'clock Saturday afternoon on the stadium field of the University of London. Clark thought it was a surprisingly modest stadium that at home would compare more to a high school than a college facility. A light rain filled the air, and only a few spectators were dedicated enough to get wet watching a game that didn't count. Gwen had braved the elements but not Cynna.

As the home team, the University of London received the ball in a drop kick from the Cambridge team to start the game. The first forty-minute half went by with only one try, or score of five points, for each team. But Cambridge managed to kick the ball through the uprights of the goalpost for the two extra points, while the London team had a much harder angle and missed their kick. The rain stopped during the first half, and the sun came out, soon making it unusually warm and humid for late September in London.

After a ten-minute break, the second half started, and Charles told Clark to be ready to go in for Henry. "It's the first friendly and everyone plays."

Clark had already learned that rugby was a lot more unstructured than American football, much more like soccer. There was a premium placed on a player's ability to see and anticipate the flow of action on the field and to take advantage of an opportunity when it presented itself. But there were also a lot of rules, and he still felt overwhelmed as he struggled to follow or anticipate all that went on during the game. He tried to push that aside when Charles told him to get in the game at wing. "Good game," he said to Henry, as the other winger came off the field. But he only got a sour look in response.

Clark may have been the fastest man on the London team, but he wasn't the fastest on the field. That was the left wing for Cambridge, who raced by Clark and headed for the goal line. Only a desperation tackle by Charles kept him from scoring. London won the scrum and methodically moved the ball downfield. Clark waited for the ball to get to him, but it never came past the inside center back before there'd be a tackle and another scrum. Then Cambridge won a scrum, and they began to move the ball the other way. This time Clark stayed close to the Cambridge wing, and the ball didn't get out to him again. Control of the ball changed frequently, and Clark became more comfortable with the pace and intensity of the game, compared to what they had done in practice. It was substantially faster and the tackling was harder.

During a set-up for a lineout, which occurred whenever the ball went out of bounds, Clark took a moment to look at the spectators and saw that Cynna had joined Gwen. Her bright yellow tank top and white, very short mini-skirt were quite a contrast to Gwen and her nondescript pants and shirt.

The ball was thrown down the middle of the lineup and no one grabbed control of it before it came to Clark. It took him a moment to realize what had happened, and then on instinct, he sprinted toward the goal. He was amazed that he made it so easily. But when he looked back, he saw that everyone stood and watched him. He heard the whistle blown by the official, who signaled for an offside.

Clark felt pretty silly as he jogged back with the ball and tossed it to the official. Arthur came up to him. "Nice try Yank." He grinned and playfully slapped him on the back.

Clark carefully avoided looking at the spectators. He quickly calmed down because no one seemed to care and the action started again.

As the game got close to the end, the pace increased because the score was tied. Each team had had another try, and the University of London team had kicked their extra points, and Cambridge had missed. Clark by now had a much better sense for what constituted an offside and how to avoid it. Sometimes it meant slowing up or a quick pass back to a teammate who was not offside.

The Cambridge inside center back suddenly broke free and headed for the London goal. Clark thought he might be offside but didn't hear a whistle. He was not the closest player, but he took off and sprinted to tackle the Cambridge player a few meters from the goal line. Even during the tussle of the resulting scrum, Charles was able to shout, "Great tackle Clark."

Clark was so pumped up with adrenalin that a short time later, with under a minute left in the game, he grabbed the ball from the ground where it had been dropped by a Cambridge back and sprinted forward. The whistle blew, and Clark was angry. He knew he hadn't been offside. He hadn't been, but he had still committed a penalty, and the Cambridge team got a penalty kick close to the London goal posts. They made it and won the game 15 to 12. Clark felt terrible, his mistake had caused them to lose.

Charles found him after the teams had lined up and shaken hands with each other. "Don't fret on it mate. You played well, and there are a lot of bloody rules. You'll get it soon. That's what friendlies are for."

"Thanks. I felt really stupid a couple of times, but it was a lot of fun."

The mood in the locker room didn't reflect the fact that they had lost the game. Laughter, teasing, and a general good humor prevailed. Some players sang what Clark would learn were traditional rugby songs, which were sung whether the team won or lost. Clark received his share of teasing, but so did others. There had been plenty of mistakes to go around. It was the most positive locker room that he had ever experienced after losing a game, and he was really pumped-up as they all headed for the Herald Times and the after-game party.

Clark still had a lot to learn about rugby, but one thing immediately became very clear. This was a sport that put a lot of importance on attitude and a good party. Customarily both teams got together and got drunk after every match. In fact, it seemed to Clark like the party was more important to some of the players than the match itself. And he wasn't wrong about that.

They were in a private party room at the pub that Clark hadn't seen before. A large space, it had tables, chairs and its own tap system. The floor was linoleum, which didn't absorb any of the beer spilled during the evening. Clark felt a sense of Déjà vu. It seemed so much like the party rooms in the basements of the fraternities at Dartmouth. The biggest difference was that there were a lot more women in the pub.

When the players arrived, there were dozens of pint glasses pre-filled so they didn't have to wait for a beer. Clark grabbed a glass and downed it quickly. He wondered where all the women had come from. They certainly hadn't all been at the game, although more had shown up in the second half after the rain stopped. He assumed that the Cambridge team must have brought their birds with them.

He noticed that Gwen stood with several of the players and talked and joked like one of the guys. He looked for Cynna but didn't see her, and he felt a pang of disappointment. It seemed like most of the other women were paired up with a player, so he wandered around and tried not to look like a loser without a date.

A group of players from both teams, led by Winston, began to sing a rugby song about virile men and willing women. A few of the women joined in but most of them just stood by and tried to look nonchalant. One song led to another with much the same theme, but more risqué. By now Clark was loose enough to join in, even though he didn't know the words.

"There he is. Grizzly, come meet my Emily," Martin yelled across the room, causing a lot of heads to turn.

Buoyed by, but also a little embarrassed by the attention, Clark moved over to where Martin stood with Sean and two very pretty girls. Martin had his arm around his girl who looked like a midget beside him. About the same size as Gwen, she was dressed like a woman who desperately wanted men to notice her assets, the most prominent of which were breasts that seemed far too big for the rest of her. Maybe it was the skimpy top or the way she stood with her chest thrust forward. She smiled when she saw that Clark had noticed. Without a word, she stepped up to him, unbuttoned two of his shirt buttons, and began to rub her fingers through his chest hair.

"Oh, you were right Martin, it is smashing," she purred, as Clark's face started to turn red. "Is it everywhere?" She looked down toward his crotch. He held his breath, unsure whether she was going to reach down and grab him.

"Oh Clark, there you are, I've been looking for you."

He swiveled his head to see Gwen standing beside him. She grabbed his arm and gently pulled him away from Emily, who wasn't at all happy to have her fun ruined.

"Gwen, I didn't see you there among the other boys," Emily sneered with a fake smile.

"Emily, always nice to see so much of you," Gwen replied, pointedly looking directly at Emily's breasts. "Clark there's someone I want you to meet," she continued, as she pulled him further away.

Clark slowly got his wits together as they crossed the room. "Uh thanks for that, I was ..."

Gwen laughed. "No problem, Grizzly. Emily's got a rep as big as her knockers. She's an outrageous tease, but you were safe, she won't shag anyone but Martin." She still held his arm but quickly let go as they reached Cynna.

Cynna seemed preoccupied, nervously scanning the room, and she barely acknowledged Gwen and Clark. Clark's attention was drawn to a flash of movement and sparkle in Cynna's right hand. She held what reminded him of a Catholic rosary, made with silver beads. She moved the beads quietly and methodically with her fingers. It was a practiced, automatic movement, and Clark wondered if she was praying.

Clark then shifted his attention to the odd woman who stood next to Cynna. She looked to be on the far side of middle-age, a formidable person with what appeared to be a permanent scowl. Her conservative drab attire didn't make a big impression on him, but her shoes did. There were black and heavy, almost boots that covered her ankles and looked like they were designed to kick the shit out of someone.

"Mrs. Rovsek, I'm with her if you want to leave," Gwen offered.

"Her act strange late. Rovsek is worry," the woman responded, as if Cynna wasn't standing right next to her. She had a thick accent that Clark didn't recognize but thought it was from Russia or Poland or somewhere like that.

"Don't worry, we're all just friends here. We won't stay out too late."

Mrs. Rovsek considered for a moment and then, seemingly convinced, turned and left.

Cynna watched her leave and immediately relaxed. She smiled at Gwen and then at Clark. "Thank you. I'm getting a drink. Do you want one?"

Gwen shook her head as she held up her half-full beer glass for examination. Cynna headed to the bar before Clark could respond.

"Who was that?" Clark asked.

"Oh, that's Helga Rovsek, Cynna's chaperone, hired by her bloody father to keep her safe."

"Safe from what?"

"He's a big nob in Greece and very conservative, supposedly an Onassis buddy, thinks the West is too decadent, the women too loose - we're all trollops and floozies, bad influences. Balls off for her."

Clark tried to process all that as Gwen drifted away to join a group that was discussing the recent arrest of Buster Edwards, a suspect in the Great Train Robbery. Their conversation led to loud criticisms of Scotland Yard and its general ineptitude. Gwen had a lot of direct experience with that.

Clark wandered around, lingering on the fringes of several groups and their conversations. No one excluded him, but few went out of their way to include him. It was nothing personal. Everyone on the team was by now drunk and with their girlfriends or dates. He looked for Arthur or Cynna but didn't see either one in the room.

Clark knew he had to go easy on the beer or he wouldn't last much longer. Singing helped, and he knew dancing would be better. But no one danced, despite the popular tunes that played on the jukebox. He noticed Cynna enter the room and urgently whisper something into Gwen's ear that clearly upset her. Gwen strode toward the door, where a thin, young black man had appeared and stood hesitantly as if an invisible force field prevented him from entering the room. The man had interesting features, a combination of African and European, a skin color that was dark but not black. He appeared to Clark to be older, maybe late twenties or even early thirties.

"That's Ezekiel," Cynna offered, as she came over and stood next to Clark.

"Who's Ezekiel?"

"This bloke who has been pursuing her for almost a year. He's a musician, a drummer, from east Africa somewhere. Kenya, I think."

They watched what appeared to be an intense conversation between Gwen and Ezekiel. He put his hand on her arm and seemed to try to pull her out of the room, but she stood fast, her body levered against the doorframe.

"Should we go help her?" Clark asked Cynna.

"Oh, our Gwen can take care of herself. She's stronger than she looks."

"What the hell is that bugger doing here?" asked Arthur, as he joined them. His protective brotherly instincts kicked in, heightened by the beers. "I'm gonna get rid of him."

Cynna reached across Clark and grabbed Arthur's arm before he could move. "She'll be pissed, you know that. They had a date last night, but he never showed. I'd love to hear his lame excuse this time."

"Bloody… bastard," Arthur fumed.

Clark noted a slight pause between his words and wondered if Arthur had edited out a racial reference. There were no blacks or other non-white races on the rugby team, which had struck him as strange. He wondered if they would be called African English like African American? He thought it best not to ask, at least not at that moment.

Gwen and Ezekiel's argument had reached an intense stare-down stage, and then he suddenly turned and left. She paused a moment, gathered herself, and joined the group.

"Don't say a fucking word!" she preempted Arthur, who was obviously about to speak.

"Well, he's-"

"Stop!" Gwen abruptly cut him off and pulled Cynna away.

Arthur stared after them as they joined some other women. He turned to Clark for support. "Cheeky bastard has been causing her grief for too long. I just can't understand why she puts up with him and his shite."

Clark nodded. It had been his experience that some women did seem to be attracted to guys who were wrong for them. There had been a nice girl, Marnie, in high school who dated a teammate of his on the baseball team who was a real jerk. No one liked Cliff except for Marnie. When she finally decided to dump him, he got so angry and threatening that her parents had to go to court to get a restraining order to keep him away from her. But Clark also knew that the perceived wrongness in a relationship could be based on interpretations or prejudices.

"What does he do? Is he abusive?" Clark asked tentatively.

"What? Oh, no, not that, but he's constantly breaking dates, leaving her stranded while he's off with some grotty band or other. And I think he's been trying to get her to do drugs and …" Arthur couldn't finish his sentence because the thought of his sister having sex with Ezekiel was just too appalling.

Clark didn't have a response, but fortunately Cynna came back and joined them before things got too awkward. She tried to change the subject and asked Arthur if he was pleased with how the game went. Despite the loss, this proved to be a much better topic for Arthur, and he relaxed as he described the progress he had seen with the team.

Clark got a strong sense that Cynna only pretended to be interested. He didn't know why, but he began to feel a little like an interloper with them, so he casually moved away and headed for the bar. He needed another beer after all that tension.

After a while the crowd thinned out. Most of the Cambridge players and their birds had left. Clark sat alone at a small table. Tired and talked-out, he was perfectly happy to just observe as the party wound down. He saw Gwen across the room and gave her a careful smile, but it surprised him when she came over and sat next to him.

"Sorry that my bloody brother was bending your ear so much," she started tentatively. "He goes mad as a bag of fucking ferrets when Ezekiel's around."

Clark wanted to respond that that was putting it mildly, but instead he said, "it's okay."

"He's not really a rotter, Ezekiel I mean, but he does rub some people the wrong way. And I think Cynna and my brother are maybe both a little racist."

Clark looked and listened but didn't react, which turned out to be perfect for Gwen.

"Arthur thinks that Ezekiel is trying to get me high and into my knickers, which he is, but I'm a big girl. He thinks he always has to be the big brother and protect me." She smiled and shrugged her shoulders, although it was hard to see under the loose fitting jacket she wore.

"Ezekiel's a drummer and has been in some bands that made hit records, but he never seems to stick with them very long. I think it's probably his fault, even though he always has an excuse. He's wired pretty tight and pisses off a lot of people."

Clark wanted to ask her why she was interested in him, but didn't. He waited.

"I just find him interesting. I love music but have no bloody talent or desire to do anything but listen. And maybe I get a little thrill from the fringe by being with Ezekiel. Oh, bloody hell! I just realized, I'm a fucking groupie!"

He could tell that she didn't really want to believe that, so he replied as firmly as he could, "No, not at all."

Clearly the right response, she smiled warmly at him. "You're a good listener Clark. Thanks for letting me waffle on."

Clark woke up late Sunday morning exhausted and hung-over, again.

London Transit bus drivers had gone on another impromptu strike for the weekend, and Clark had walked home after the party, a little over two miles, through some rather dodgy neighborhoods. He had money for a taxi, but the weather was good, and he had just felt like walking.

He'd had a series of dreams, or rather fleeting images more than dreams, which left him restless and frustrated. The images, some sharp but mostly fuzzy, were primarily of women from his past. Julie Wells crying as she left for Arizona with her father. Molly Connors at high school graduation, breaking up with him. Rebecca Watson from Green Mountain Junior College, who morphed into her staff sergeant father. And Lucy Giordano from Sewickley, breathless with excitement over a piece of her artwork. But Cynna and Bernadette and even Gwen had also found their way in. Nothing really happened, no substance to anything, and that was a big part of his frustration - he couldn't even get laid in his dreams.

Clark made some instant Nescafe coffee and ate a roll that was just shy of being stale. The thought of cooking anything made his stomach flutter a warning. His cooking skills were just above the staying-alive level, and he was grateful that his mother had insisted on some rudimentary lessons before he left for England. Maybe a late lunch, he thought, as he sat down and stared at the textbooks that waited to be read.

More than a little overwhelmed by the number of pages that had been assigned, he kept telling himself that it wouldn't be too bad if there really were no papers or tests. But he still had to come up with an idea and a pitch for a short story for creative writing class. Pondering all the work pushed him into a catatonic state, which he tried to break out of by putting on some music - the *Do You Believe in Magic* album by the Lovin' Spoonful - and writing some poetry. As Clark wrote, he heard a melody in his head and realized that what he was writing a rugby song. Either that or he had a country music song in his head, and he simply refused to accept that - he hated country music.

Early afternoon, he finally showered and realized that he didn't have any clean clothes, particularly underwear. So he gathered up his dirty clothes from the floor of the closet, put them in Rita's laundry bag, and headed for a laundromat that he had seen just off Hampstead High Street.

The Wash-A-Matic laundromat consisted of one large hot and crowded room with a dozen washers and five large dryers. It was presided over by an old Sikh man in a turban, who sat by the door and carefully scrutinized everyone who walked in. He gave Clark a particularly hard stare because he was the only other male in the place. Most residents of Hampstead were elderly or middle-aged couples and only a few younger couples with children. It was much too expensive for single young men. Hampstead was isolated from the loud and hectic pace of central London, and the residents wanted to keep it that way. The Sikh didn't live there, but he was very protective of his clientele.

Clark found an open washer and started to dump his clothes in. As he finished, he got the sense that the person next to him was staring. So he paused and turned to see a pretty young woman, probably in her early thirties, holding an infant in her arms.

She looked at him with a bemused smile. "You need to sort those things love. The colors will all run together and ruin them."

It took Clark a second to register what she said and to recall a similar admonishment from his mother in one of her housekeeping lessons. "Oh, yeah, right, thanks." He smiled as he began to pull everything out of the washer.

"Canadian?"

"No, American," he responded, as he noticed that she was cute in her baggy t-shirt with the big tongue logo of the Rolling Stones. He sorted his clothes on the floor, all the while stealing glances at the woman. Her wash had just finished, and she pulled her clothes out of the machine and into a wicker basket, all without taking the baby from her hip. When her basket was full she placed the baby on top of the clothes and carried it over to one of the dryers at the rear of the room. He noticed her very firm butt that moved nicely under her loose-fitting shorts. She was definitely dressed for comfort and not style.

There was no one else waiting for a washing machine, so he used his and hers to wash his two piles of clothes at the same time. While he waited, he tried to read the book for his Modern Imperialism class, but it was too boring and the young woman was too interesting. She read a *Life* magazine, and he was pretty sure that she more than once looked over at him also. Then it happened that they glanced at the same time, and caught, they smiled at each other.

Clark was pleasantly surprised when his washing machines both finished and she was still there drying her clothes. There was an empty dryer next to her, and he tried to remember his mother's instructions on drying as he walked over. Almost sure that he was right, he put all of the clothes in the one dryer and set it on a low temperature. Before he pushed the button to start it, he looked over at her, and she nodded approval.

"New to the neighborhood?"

"Yes, just a few weeks."

"Are you here with family?" she asked, and instinctively looked at her baby who slept quietly in the laundry basket on top of a pile of clean, warm towels.

"Oh no, I'm alone. I'm going to the University of London for the year."

"Well, that's blooming unusual around here. We got mostly diamond geezers and pensioners. The night action on

High Street is so bloomin' tame. I lived right in London center, near Carnaby Street, before I got married and, you know, up the duff." She pointed at the baby and shrugged her shoulders. "Oh, my name's Tildi, for Matilda."

"Hi, I'm Clark." He didn't know whether to shake her hand or not, so he settled for a little awkward wave of his hand.

She asked him what he was studying and seemed most interested in the creative writing course, telling him that anything that involved romance novels and travel excited her. Her dryer had stopped, but she didn't make a move to leave until he was done and packing up. Her baby was now awake, and Tildi had to hold her while she tried to pick up the basket.

Clark noticed and moved to help. "Here, let me help you with that."

"Oh no, I'm fine, you don't need to."

"You saved me from a washing disaster. It's the least I can do." He tried to make light of it.

"Well, Stan, that's my husband, often helps me, but he's in India for a month on business." She let go of the basket and held the baby more securely in her arms. "We're just down Hampstead High to Perrins Lane."

As they walked, she maintained a steady chatter about her previous life as a hand and foot model for Harrods and other stores, and the nightlife she used to enjoy. She kept assuring him that she really loved her new life, but her face really lit up when she described how the photographers would lavish gifts on her so she would model for them. "And not just hands and feet. Some liked the rest of me as well," she added, with a sexy little smile.

They arrived at her house, a large single family Tudor. She unlocked the front door and ushered him inside. "Let me get you something to drink."

"Oh no, that's okay."

"Don't be daft, we're neighbors being neighborly."

She put the baby on a blanket that had been spread out on top of the rug on the floor of the living room and went into the kitchen. He heard the sound of a cork coming out of a bottle, and a moment later she returned with two glasses of red wine. He remembered that he still hadn't eaten.

"Oh ta very much but I can't-"

"Relax," she cut him off. "I'll show you some of my stuff." She pulled a scrapbook from the bookshelf and opened it to photos of her hands, wearing various rings, bracelets, gloves and watches. He knew they were her hands because she now had one of them resting on his leg, midway between his knee and his crotch. Then there were shots of her feet slipping into boots and slippers and socks. Her feet, now bare, found his legs and rubbed against them. He was glad he held the photo book on his lap because it covered his steadily rising erection.

The next photos were of her naked, and he stared at them, afraid to look at her. She took control, grabbed his head, turned him toward her and kissed him. He didn't respond at first, and she pulled back. "What's wrong, don't you like me?"

"Sure, yes I do, but you're married and there's…" He pointed toward the baby who kicked her feet at the light fixture on the ceiling.

"Don't be daft. He's away, and she's only five months old, and I'm bloomin' randy."

She tried another kiss. This time he responded, and she got her tongue involved. They kissed for a while and then took a break for a sip of wine. Then she lifted her t-shirt over her head and revealed her very nice breasts, which were firm and full for feeding. He was about to move to them when she reached down and picked up her baby, which she placed on her chest so the baby could suck on her nipple. Clark had never seen anything so sexy. He really envied that baby.

"This doesn't turn you off?"

"No, no on the contrary I think it's incredibly sexy. I want to be her."

Tildi laughed and put her hand down to feel for his belt and then zipper. With one hand she expertly managed to open him up and reached in to grab his very erect penis. "Stan gets turned off by this. Do you know how frustrating that is? I've never felt more like a woman, and he can't get it up. And I'm stuck here all day, alone, because I gave up my job, everything, to get married." She switched the baby to her other nipple and continued to stroke him. She seemed to have a sense for him and pulled back just before he lost control.

He realized that she really knew what she was doing and that maybe a mature woman like her was just the thing he needed to lose his virginity. He could probably deal with the married thing. And maybe it was even a plus - no issues with commitment.

He reached over and put his hand on her leg and moved it up under her shorts. They were loose enough that he easily reached her panties, and they felt moist to his touch. Her body reacted, and she almost dropped the baby. He moved his fingers over her panties, and she moaned as she enjoyed his gentle massage. As he started to explore more with his fingers, she pulled the baby off her breast, held her up on her shoulder and began to burp her.

"Clark, this is going to be grand, but let's get the silly business stuff out of the way first, shall we. I think twenty quid is fair, don't you? We've got all day and night if you want."

For a moment he didn't comprehend what she meant. This was a married woman with a baby. Then he moaned. Jesus, he thought, what is it with prostitutes and me? Was there some sign on my forehead - desperate virgin you can screw with. He pulled his hand back. He stood and was pulling up his zipper before she spoke.

"What the fuck Clark, I thought we had an understanding here. I can tell you want to have it off with me, and I want you love."

Clark looked down at her, then the baby. and headed for the door.

"Fine, go, but you know where I live, and you can come back any time 'cause Stan's almost always gone."

He stopped at the door and looked back at her, trying to concentrate on her face, not her breasts. "Why? Why do it when you've got all of this?"

"Well silly, I'm bored. And I need some spending money because my cheap husband never gives me enough. I learned a long time ago to never give it away for free. Jewelry, money, marriage, whatever men will pay." She touched herself seductively.

He had to flee before he changed his mind, but in his haste, he forgot his bag of laundry. When he came back ten minutes later, he found it on the front steps with one of Tildi's nude pictures attached to it with a big pink diaper safety pin.

Back at the flat, he sat down and began to write a synopsis for a story that involved a naive boy and a bored housewife-prostitute with a baby. It poured out easily in prose with some poetry mixed in. He didn't know if Professor Hammerly would be cool with that, but it felt right.

CHAPTER 6

Clark entered Professor Merkel's seminar room on Monday morning feeling rested and prepared. He had finally eaten the night before, and the encounter with Tildi had energized him sufficiently to complete a good first draft of the synopsis for his short story and finish the reading for this course.

Gwen and Cynna were already there, and Cynna motioned to an empty seat next to her that she saved for him. Clark tried to think of a good conversation opener, but then Professor Merkel entered, and the room immediately went dead quiet.

Merkel looked around the room with his dour expression. Clark noticed that Merkel paused ever so slightly on him, but told himself to not be so paranoid.

Without any pleasantries, Merkel launched immediately into his lecture, which he knew was exactly 45 minutes long. The class may have been scheduled for two hours, but he felt no obligation to spend all of that time with these students, whom he considered to be mostly imbeciles.

This lecture presented one of his pet theories, that imperialism in the Middle Ages was a reflection of the rulers, mostly inbred twits and tossers, who used aggression and conquest to prove their manhood. And many were demented enough to believe that a god had chosen them to rule and conquer. Merkel had just finished what he believed to be a logical extension of this thesis to describe the Crusades, when he felt a disturbance pulsate through in the room. He looked over to see Clark with his hand in the air and everyone else staring at him.

Gwen tried to reach around Cynna to get Clark to pull his hand down, but it was too late.

"Mr. Westword, you don't need a hall pass to use the loo."

None of the students laughed because they knew it wasn't meant to be funny.

"Oh, no sir, I had a question."

"Really? A question, how American. But by all means, what is your question that is so important as to interrupt my lecture?"

Clark could tell that the professor was upset, so he paused, confused. But he had started this, so he pushed ahead. "My question is that after reading your chapter on the Crusades, I was not convinced that they weren't really more defensive than offensive. The kings and the popes didn't seem interested in conquering and ruling that area, or those people, as much as stopping what they saw as a threat to their religion. I, I thought that maybe I missed something." He tried to end on a non-confrontational note, but it didn't work.

"Well, I would say that there are many things that you have missed, including years of research." Merkel paused. He wanted to put an end to this question nonsense. He could do it quietly as a learning moment, or he could go for the drama. He went for the drama - slammed his notebook closed and abruptly left the room.

The stunned silence lasted almost a minute, until the students determined that Merkel wasn't coming back. They would have cheered, but they were British. Instead, they all rushed from the room. Cynna left with the other students, but Gwen held back to talk to Clark.

"We don't really do that here," she offered, as she tried unsuccessfully to hold back her smile, brought on by his look of utter confusion. "It's a thing with us. Teachers and professors are considered infallible."

"You don't ask them any questions?"

"Not to most of them. Especially the older wankers like Merkel or Cohen. We've grown up with that so we're used to it, but I don't really like it personally. I think it makes us intellectually lazy." She had read the same chapter and just accepted it as true.

"Wow, that really, sucks."

She laughed and nodded in agreement. Her eyes appeared to be teasing him as she said goodbye and headed off to the library to read that chapter again.

Clark appreciated Gwen's support, but he despaired that he certainly wasn't making any friends among his professors. Not that they seemed the slightest bit inclined to be friendly.

It was a nice fall day in London, and Clark took the opportunity to walk on the Victoria Embankment along the Thames River toward Westminster. He watched the boat traffic, which was all industrial, a fascinating array of different styles of boats and barges. He didn't see anything that resembled a pleasure craft. When his family had moved to Seattle, his father had bought an 18-foot speedboat, which they took with them when they moved to Los Angeles. Clark really loved being on the water - the ancient highway to explore the world, to find adventure.

Eventually he got hungry and stopped at a fish-and-chips shop. He brought the bag of greasy food to a bench to sit and eat, but aggressive pigeons forced him to keep moving. He didn't remember the pigeons in New York being so unafraid of humans. But he had only been fourteen when they lived there, and his perceptions may have been off.

Later he went to rugby practice. Arthur and Charles worked their groups hard to bolster what had gone right in the friendly and correct what had gone wrong. But they didn't project any sense of frustration because they both felt that more had gone right than had gone wrong.

The next afternoon, Clark didn't look forward to the Political Realities class, but he was prepared. He had done the assigned reading, and he had the article on Professor Cohen.

Before class, he ventured into the LSE pub to get a sandwich and hopefully see Cynna, but she wasn't there. He did see Nigel, who sat with some other men at a table across the room. He didn't look very happy. Then Clark heard Gwen's voice, and upon closer examination, saw her there with Nigel and the others. She wore a brown fedora hat along with her normal unfeminine attire. He smiled at what an odd bird she was.

When Clark entered the classroom, there wasn't an open seat next to Gwen, but there was one next to Nigel. Clark opted to take another seat, across the table from them. He observed that, similar to Merkel's class, there were noticeably fewer students present than had been there at the first class meeting. There seemed to be some point-of-pride for these professors to scare students from their courses. Even Professor Hammerly seemed to do the same; but not Professor Doctor.

At exactly the top of the hour, Professor Cohen marched in and dumped his heavy briefcase on the table, sending shock waves through the wood, causing a female student to jump, startled out of her daydream. A little smirk crossed Cohen's face as he looked out over the room. "So I assume that if you've come back you don't think I'm completely off my rocker with my premise. Or you haven't figured out a good alternative for two o'clock Tuesday afternoon."

Nigel's face started to turn red. Gwen put her hand on his arm and squeezed it until he finally took a breath. Clark, struck by how angry and intense Nigel seemed to be, wondered why he hadn't just dropped the course.

Professor Cohen proceeded to lecture about the condition of Palestine under British rule before and during the Second World War. He briefly recounted the toll of the Holocaust on Jews in Europe and their desire to find a homeland. He admitted that Palestine seemed like a logical place, but the problem was that it was already populated. "There was some vacant land, but it was not very hospitable for settlement. Its lack of perceived value is what encouraged the western powers to concede it to them. And it assuaged the increasing moral pressure on the Allied leaders that came from the survivors of the Holocaust." Cohen offered that there might have been far better places if the Allied leaders had taken the time to think it through. But they didn't because everyone wanted to forget the war as soon as possible and enjoy the peace. "The Jewish leaders saw an opportunity, and they took it, ignoring the potential problems."

Finally, Nigel had enough and blurted out, "But it's our homeland, the land of Moses, Abraham, David."

"Also the homeland for two other major religions, and the birthplace for almost a million Palestinians who lived there," Cohen rebutted. "The native-born Jewish population was less than ten thousand at that time. Not exactly a moral imperative, wouldn't you agree?"

Nigel couldn't agree or disagree because he was too angry to speak. His frustration was exacerbated because his father had refused to intercede with the Board of Regents. Nigel had instead gotten a familiar lecture from his father about fighting his own battles and being a man. He was going to be a man and not drop this course, but he wasn't going to stay quiet like a good English schoolboy.

"They were the ones who started it."

"Well, mister..." Cohen paused, waiting for Nigel to respond.

"Barrington, Nigel."

"Well, Mr. Barrington Nigel, if someone invaded your home and wanted to force you to move what would you do?" He didn't wait for an answer. "Most people would fight. So our people, ravaged by war, having suffered the most horrific conditions imaginable, proceeded to force themselves on another people, to effectively put them into camps. Can you come up with a justification for that?"

Nigel sat catatonic with anger and hate. Gwen looked back and forth between the Professor and her friend. The air in the room was thick with tension, ready to explode, needing only a spark.

"But professor, didn't you initially participate in the negotiations that legitimized that situation and actually argue vehemently for a partition after the British had conceded their authority?" As he spoke, Clark removed the *London Times* article from his notebook and laid it on the table in front of him.

Professor Cohen stared at the article like it was a cobra let loose in the room. "That, that thing," he stammered, "is not accurate. Where did you get that?" He made a quick move to reach across the table to grab the article, but Clark pulled it back. Incensed, Cohen picked up his briefcase and stormed out of the room.

Absolute silence hung over the room as the students drifted out. Some stole a glance at Clark, but no one said anything. As he packed up to leave, it dawned on Clark that in two days he had caused two professors to storm out of their classrooms. He assumed that that must be some kind of a record, but not one he wanted to have.

"That was bloody brilliant, wasn't it Nigel," Gwen almost shouted. "I'm beginning to like how you Americans do things."

Nigel looked over at Clark, his expression definitely not friendly. "I don't need a bloody Yank to fight my battles!" Then in his rush to get up and leave, he knocked his book on the floor. His anger only increased as he had to bend down and retrieve it. He practically flew out the door.

"Don't worry, he'll get over it. He's got a lot on his mind right now," Gwen offered. She didn't know that Clark had already written him off as an asshole.

Later at rugby practice, Clark noticed that Gwen stood on the sidelines and watched, and then she spent some time talking to Arthur and Charles. He couldn't really focus on her because he was too busy dealing with the vitriol coming from Henry. Charles had said at the beginning of practice that Clark was going to share time with Henry, playing with the starters. The third-year player didn't take it well. And then Henry's resentment caused him to lose focus and make mistakes. That turned his resentment into anger.

Clark didn't have particularly positive feelings for Henry, but in his conflict-adverse way, he also didn't want to ruin the nice vibe of the team or the atmosphere in the locker room. He did believe that he had already become, in some ways, a better player than Henry. So he did what he usually did in such a situation, he didn't do or say anything.

The next morning, Clark was excited to see Bernadette in class. She was, of course, no longer his only prostitute acquaintance. He had to laugh at himself, at those crazy encounters, and yet he was still a virgin.

He played a little game by timing his arrival for just before class was scheduled to begin. If Bernadette saved a seat for him next to her, then he would sit there. Otherwise, he would sit wherever he could.

She had saved him a seat and gave him a big friendly smile when he took it. He noticed that she again dressed fairly conservatively in a loose fitting blouse and bell-bottom pants. Her hair was pulled up in a bun, and it accentuated her fine features. It was a very attractive look without screaming sexy. They only had time for brief pleasantries, starting with cheek kissing, which she of course initiated, before the professor walked in.

Professor Hammerly immediately took control of the dynamic in the room. "Good morning, I'm surprised to see that so many are sticking with me. Beginning now, I want you to call me Maya, and I will presume to address you by your first names. I know that's unorthodox, but we are going to be sharing some intimate stuff, and I want us to be completely open with each other. Every story you write will be read and critiqued by me and by two other students in the class. We will all respond with constructive feedback and suggestions. There's nothing that can't be written in this class. No taboos. All language is acceptable if it fits the context of the story and the characters. If your character constantly says fuck or worse then that's what you write and what we read. I trust that no one has a problem with that. If so, it's still not too late to drop."

Clark wasn't sure how he felt about that. He wasn't someone who swore a lot, but he appreciated it as an interesting character trait. And he had a good model in his twin sister, whose foul mouth would make a sailor proud. As he glanced around the room, he noticed that Bernadette seemed to be the only one who looked totally comfortable.

For the remainder of the class, students took turns giving short pitches of their story synopsis and getting feedback from the professor. Many of them had stories that struck Clark as fairly pedestrian. He noticed that Professor Hammerly, Maya, seemed to react the same way. But even when she was critical, she managed to maintain a positive attitude with her comments. He was impressed with how quickly she could come up with good ideas for improvements to any idea.

As they rounded the room and came toward Clark and Bernadette, he felt a little apprehensive. But he noticed that she seemed extremely nervous. Her hands trembled, shaking the paper she clutched tightly. A fine sheen of perspiration had formed on her upper lip. The way there were proceeding, it would soon be Bernadette's turn, and he would be last. He looked at his watch. It was almost noon and time for the class to end. "Do you want to switch places and go last? We might not get that far," he whispered to her.

Her eyes lit up in appreciation but then firmed with resolve. "Thanks love, but I need to do this and get it over."

After two quick uninspired stories, it was Bernadette's turn. She took a deep breath. Clark had to fight his impulse to take her hand for support.

"Okay then, Gabriel is a DJ at a very fancy and successful night club who has lots of admirers and gets lots of girls and lots of sex." Bernadette started reading in a rush and then took a deep breath. "But one day he wakes up, and he's totally deaf. The doctor tells him that it might be permanent. He tries to hide his affliction so he can keep his job and his lifestyle. That brings him into conflict with the owner of the club and with the one girl who loves him for who he is, not for his famous self."

As Bernadette read, Clark noted a positive reaction from Maya. He had been studying her for the past hour and thought he knew her telltale mannerisms. There was her encouraging smile versus the smirk. Tugging on her left ear seemed to mean that she couldn't can't wait for this to be over. And if a story hooked her, she leaned in slightly toward the student as they finished. Bernadette got both the encouraging smile and the lean.

After she made a few comments to Bernadette, Maya turned to Clark. "Clark, we have five minutes remaining. Please begin." She didn't have to tell him that he had a hard act to follow.

"Lizzie is a housewife, in Hampstead, who has a baby and a husband who travels a lot," Clark began. He could almost hear the whispers - boring. "Lizzie is doing her laundry at the laundromat when she meets Reggie, a college student, also doing his laundry." He almost stopped when he saw Maya tug on her left ear. "They make a connection, and she invites him home with her, where she gives him some wine and propositions him for sex. She figures twenty quid would do it for the afternoon and night, with some time out for taking care of the baby, of course." He noticed that Maya had stopped tugging her ear. "They are in the midst of sex when Lizzie's husband comes home. Reggie flees out the back door with his laundry basket." He sees a very slight lean from Maya, and he confidently goes for the finish. "But he doesn't realize, until he gets home, that the baby had crawled into his basket and fallen asleep under the warm clothes."

Maya grinned, glad that she hadn't misjudged him. "I love the twist. The potential complications can take the story in a number of interesting directions - comedy or tragedy."

The class was over, and the students all paused, surprised that Maya had not raced out ahead of them. A few stayed and asked her questions. Clark and Bernadette walked out together, having agreed to get lunch.

"Yours is such a great idea," he said as they walked. "I can't wait to see how it goes."

"Me too," she laughed. "I've got some thoughts but haven't decided. I got the idea when I was in a club, our club." She smiled at him as she continued. "And I realized how loud it is for the DJ and wouldn't that damage his ears. You should come back you know, I liked dancing with you."

"Oh, I'm sure there are plenty of people to dance with, and aren't you usually working?" He tried to sound very matter-of-fact and not judgmental about her job.

"Well, sometimes, but I'm very picky. It has to be a rich tourist with a nice hotel room. No standup quickies for the Ochera girls."

"So how do you pick them?" he asked, curious as to why she had come on to him.

"It's not too hard. They should be older than you. Oh, but you weren't a mistake, I just liked you, and I really wasn't working that night." She leaned her body over to give him a kiss on his cheek. "And mostly Europeans, although I don't do Germans - they're too aggressive. I do like Japanese men, they're often into some interesting kinky stuff, sort of S and M but not violent. And Americans…"

She paused because they had entered the same pub as before. They got some bar food and found a table.

"You Americans," she reflected as she looked at him. "I love them the most because they're so naïve, even the older ones, married and all, so clueless about sex. I can make them come before they get their pants down if I want to. But where would be the fun in that," she teased. "And I'd feel bad getting paid for that kind of orgasm. I have standards you know, or don't know as the case may be. But don't worry, I can keep your secret."

"What secret?"

"That you're still a virgin."

Instinctively, he glanced around the room to see if anyone was listening. "What makes you say that?" He tried to be indignant, but realized that he wasn't.

"Come on Clark, I'm sure that's why you couldn't or didn't the other night. And I don't blame you. Everyone wants to do it for love the first time, not with a prostitute… even one as nice as me," she exaggerated and laughed at herself. His quiet lack of response confirmed her assumption.

"I've had some bad luck," he finally replied, almost whispering.

"Like what?"

She didn't really think he would answer, not now, and he didn't.

"Where are you off to, rugby practice?" she asked as they finished and left the pub.

"Well, I'm off to Brentford," he announced.

"Mon Dieu, that's half-way to Heathrow. What's in Brentford? Or should I ask who's in Brentford?" she teased him.

He laughed. He felt more and more comfortable around her. And it was so much easier now that his secret was out. There were very few people who knew it.

"I'm looking for a car, and this dealership there has a sale going on. They say that they're the largest dealer in the area."

"Groovy. What kind of car? A Mini Cooper? I love minis."

"An MGB, I think. They also have the Triumphs, and I like the Spitfire too. I'm going to see them and decide." He thought for a moment. "Would you like to go with me and help me decide?"

"Just like that, you're going to buy a frigging car? Blimey mate, Americans always amaze me."

As they rode the Piccadilly line train to Northfield, Clark explained his car situation, and the American obsession with cars and the independence they offered in a country where everything was so spread out, and without much public transportation. The train ran above ground much of the way, and they sat and looked out at the middle class neighborhoods that passed by in a boring monotone of gray, green, and brown.

Finally, Bernadette had to ask. "Okay, I have to know about your story and this other prostitute in your life." She smiled and tried to keep it light and hoped that he didn't detected any hint of jealousy or judgment in her voice.

He had wondered when she would ask him about that. He had tried to anticipate her reaction ever since he started writing the story. The fact that she delayed, and then seemed so cool with it, helped him relax. "Oh you know, just an active imagination."

She stared at him, not buying that at all.

"Okay, it happened Sunday afternoon," he confessed. "All except the husband and the baby in my basket. She carried it in her basket, and that gave me the idea."

"But you didn't…"

"No, no, if I was going to do that, I would want to do it with you." He had thought about this a lot and surprised himself that he could say it so calmly. She simply smiled as she took his hand and squeezed it.

They arrived at the Northfield station and took a taxi to the dealership. They were both too excited to wait for the bus. Walking into the dealership with Bernadette on his arm, Clark felt like king of the world. He noticed the salesmen's heads turn to look at her. She looked stunning, having unbuttoned the top of her blouse and tied up the bottom, exposing her midriff. She had also let her hair down, and it flowed around her shoulders. And while her bell-bottom pants were loose at the ankles, they were alluringly tight around her firm butt.

Clark and Bernadette spent the next hour jumping in and out of sports cars, laughing or being mock serious as they considered different features. He finally decided that he liked the MGB Roadster convertible the best, and she loved the deep blue color. It reminded her of the sea and home.

Bernadette kept looking at the prices on the window stickers. "Bloody hell Clark, a thousand quid. I could buy a mansion at home for that."

Clark did the pound to dollar conversion in his head. At $2,790, the MGB cost just a little more than his 1965 Mustang convertible, which he had sold before leaving for England. That put it within the acceptable price range that he had discussed with his father.

They would have driven off with a car that afternoon except Clark wanted one with the steering wheel on the left side.

"You'll go bonkers driving here. How can you see properly if you're sitting over there? Mags and I don't even think about driving in this country. It's just too bloody difficult driving on the wrong side of the road."

He explained that he intended to ship it home at the end of the school year and also planned to drive it to the continent, where they drove on the right side of the road.

The dealer could do it as a special order, but it was going to take a few weeks, maybe a month, to get it assembled and shipped from the factory. Clark almost changed his mind because he really wanted to drive it home that day with Bernadette. But he had promised his father that he would be sensible, or at least as sensible as he could be when buying a new sports car.

"We'll come back together and get it," he promised her, as they rode back to London on the train.

Cynna didn't appear the next day in the Philosophy of International Law class, and Clark wondered if she had dropped it. He was disappointed, but the engaging lecture by Professor Doctor soon distracted him. And this professor didn't get upset when he asked a question.

After class he had some time before rugby practice so he wandered around the halls of LSE. There were still several buildings that he hadn't been in. In one of the oldest, Clark imagined that Charles Dickens might have once walked there. In fact, the actual Old Curiosity Shoppe of the Dicken's novel was only a block away. He discovered a student lounge that offered a casual place to hang out. Everything about the room was old but comfortable. Small groups of students talked quietly, but not library quiet, and several other students slept on the big padded leather chairs. Clark really liked the place.

On the walls were several bulletin boards covered with flyers and notices, tacked on in neat rows. One board held notices posted by students looking for housing or for roommates. He briefly considered whether he should post for a roommate for the extra bedroom in the flat. But he quickly discarded that thought. Despite the allure of a little extra spending money, he couldn't imagine having to deal with someone all the time, particularly in a place where he now felt so comfortable. And besides it was Melody's room, with her small bed and juvenile furniture.

On another board there were flyers for plays, concerts and other shows in the vibrant theater world of London's West End, where LSE was located. *The Sound of Music*, *The Mousetrap*, *Oliver*, and *Marat/Sade*, were all in theaters within walking distance. When he had anticipated his time in London, Clark had intended to take advantage of his access to London theaters. But so far he had been too busy with classes and rugby. A Royal Shakespeare Company flyer caught his eye. It was for a limited run of a new anti-Vietnam War play titled *US*. The company was performing it at the Aldwych Theater, only a block from LSE. As did most theaters, the Aldwych offered discounted admission for students on Thursday evenings. He decided to go that night after practice.

Clark had passed by the Aldwych Theater on numerous occasions and admired its baroque architecture. The Aldwych was the Royal Shakespeare Company's London home, while its older, traditional home was at Stratford Upon Avon. After he got his car, Clark knew he would have to go there.

The admission price for students was only one pound, an eighty percent discount. He paused in the lobby to examine a poster for the play *Marat/Sade*, also performed by the Royal Shakespeare Company. It was a show that he had wanted to see since the previous spring when the New York production of the play had won the Tony Award for best drama.

He entered the theater and stopped - impressed by the ornate sculptured woodwork, gilded fixtures, and lush velvet curtains and seat covers. Clark had been in theaters and opera houses in many American cities but none had been as impressive as this. And he knew that the Aldwych wasn't considered one of the most opulent of the London theaters.

Clark found his seat in the first row of the student area, which was the last ten rows of the orchestra section. A few other students were scattered about in that area, and the rest of the theater was almost empty.

Clark was unequivocally opposed to the Vietnam war. He regularly watched and read the news and had taken a course in the history of Asia in his first year of college, so he felt he had a solid understanding of the history and politics of the American involvement in Southeast Asia. He knew that the ones who were suffering were the poor people of Vietnam and the hundreds of thousands of young American men who were drafted and shipped off to fight and die. However, unlike many in the anti-war crowd, Clark had lived all over the United States and appreciated the diversity of the land and the people. His anti-war feelings had not turned him anti-American as had happened with so many people.

Clark responded mostly positively to the play even though he thought it contained a lot more rhetoric than facts. The stagecraft was very powerful, including the projection of film and photographs of the war on several large white backdrops. But the violent and vivid imagery, particularly the film of a baby being burned by napalm, shocked him. At that point, several people in the audience left. The images got progressively more violent toward the end of the eighty-five-minute play, and he understood why there hadn't been an intermission. Few people would have returned. The curtain came down, and the audience waited for the actors to appear for their applause. But nothing happened. The small crowd then applauded politely as they slowly got to their feet and filed out.

Clark tried to imagine how Denis Cannan, the play's author, would feel to have his work performed and provoke such a reaction. Clark had written a one-act play during his senior year of high school that had won a competition sponsored by the Pittsburgh Theater Guild. His had been one of three plays selected and performed at the Melon Playhouse. On the evening of the one and only performance, he hadn't been able to sit in the audience with his parents and sister. He had paced the lobby, listening for the audience reactions. His play had been second on the program, and it had gotten more applause than the first. But it had been far less than the last play, which brought down the house.

Someone came up behind him. "Clark?"

Pulled back to the moment, Clark turned around and was surprised to see Nigel.

"An ace of a play wasn't it. Are you a dissenter?"

"Against the war, yeah, sure. I could get drafted next year."

"Would you go?"

"No."

Nigel nodded solemnly. "Well I, I just wanted to thank you for what you did the other day with Cohen and to say that

I'm sorry I acted like a total sod." He finally exhaled and looked relieved. It didn't seem like apologizing was something he did very often.

"No problem man."

"Okay then, see you around." Nigel left to join two guys who waited for him by the exit. One of them gave Nigel a little hug, and Clark's impression of Nigel got a bit more complicated.

CHAPTER 7

When Clark arrived at the University of London stadium field for the friendly against Northampton on Saturday afternoon, Charles told him that he would start the second half at right wing. He was thrilled but apprehensive. He knew it would upset Henry, who continued to be very vocal with his negative comments about Americans taking over everything.

Clark had had a couple of good days and didn't want anything or anyone to ruin it. He had practiced hard all week and looked forward to this final friendly match before the regular season started. Everyone said that the Northampton team was better than Cambridge, so this should be a real test for the team and for Clark. He had begun to feel comfortable with strategy and the rules, even though new rules seemed to come to light every time he played.

One of the things that he continued to have a hard time with was the dropkick. If a player who carried the ball thought he was about to be tackled, he could kick it forward. And kicking the ball through the goalposts, scored three points. For Clark, the decision point about when to kick and when to keep running remained fuzzy. But playing winger meant he would be one of the players likely to be in a situation where he could or should dropkick. The difficulty was that the ball had to be dropped on the ground first. The physical coordination and timing required to kick the odd shaped ball as it bounced off the ground had proved very difficult for Clark to master. It was one thing that Henry could do well that Clark couldn't, so he had resolved to learn. After one disastrous attempt during practice, he bought a rugby ball and found a pitch in Hampstead Heath, not too far from his flat. Over many hours during the past week, time that he probably should have used to read for school, he had worked on the dropkick. He didn't consider it ready for a game yet, but he was getting close.

It was a cold, cloudy day, which heralded the late fall and winter months of dreary London weather. The few spectators at the game bundled up in winter coats on the sidelines. Gwen wore a black Macintosh with a fleece lining. Cynna was nowhere to be seen.

Clark didn't notice a woman on the other side of the field. She stood near the Northampton team and supporters, but she cheered quietly for UL. Bernadette's wide-rimmed rain hat shadowed her face, and she tried not to look directly at Clark.

The friendly began poorly for the University of London squad and then got worse. The Northampton team was very good, and the UL team could not get in sync. It seemed like the players were never in position to make a play or help a teammate. Arthur and Charles became increasingly vocal, and their exhortations to the team went from encouragement to frustration to downright anger.

The only player who seemed to be totally focused on the game was Henry. Clark laughed to himself as he realized it represented a classic case of trying harder when you know someone wants your job. Clark was a team player first and foremost. He had always been that way, even as a baseball pitcher who performed one of the most solitary jobs in sports. He would gladly accept a role as reserve on the sidelines if it would mean a victory for his team. During the break at the half, Clark approached Charles. "Henry is playing really well, and I don't have to go in."

Charles took a moment to process that and reconcile it with the fact that he wanted to win. But they were already behind 25 to 10. "That's noble mate, thanks. But I will get you in. It's a friendly and everyone plays."

A few minutes later, Clark saw Charles speak to Henry, and then Henry glanced over at him. Clark couldn't read the expression on his face except that it seemed to be less negative than what he had been used to getting from the third-year.

By the time Clark got in the game, the score was 30 to 15, and Northampton was also playing their reserves. Clark had become stiff and cold standing on the sidelines, and he had a hard time getting into the flow of things. The first time he had the ball, he was tackled hard and was slow to get up. But the physical contact and pain got his adrenalin pumping, and he played decently the rest of the game. He didn't score, but he made two good tackles that prevented Northampton scores. He found himself in a position at the very end where it might have been appropriate to try a dropkick, but he hesitated too long and got tackled.

The team's mood in the locker room didn't reflect their loss for very long. Soon everyone recovered with loud macho banter and rugby songs. Clark wondered if it would be the same if they lost a real game. And it surprised him to get a complement from Henry on his tackles.

When Clark entered the pub and got a beer, he noticed that Gwen sat alone at a table. She seemed engrossed looking over some papers and what looked like travel brochures. He debated whether to join her or not. Before he could decide, she looked up and saw him, smiled, and waved him over.

"Hi Clark. I'd like your opinion on something."

"Sure. What?"

"Well, you probably know that the team takes a trip to the continent each fall to play a couple of friendlies at different universities, and this year we're going to Amsterdam and Paris."

Clark did know that, and it had been a big factor in his decision to try out for the team.

"I'm the travel person, secretary, some bloody thing, and I have to pick the hotels. I know Paris, but I've never been to Amsterdam and can't decide between these two." She handed him two hotel brochures. "I got them from the auto club travel people, and they said that both would be okay with a student group. Not all hotels are, you know."

"I know," he laughed. When he had traveled with the Dartmouth baseball team, they had stayed in hotels and often left a mess, if not real damage. Their best catcher had been tossed off the team, and his parents had had to pay more than five-hundred dollars for the damage he had caused in a hotel room in Philadelphia.

"Okay, so which do you think?"

He looked them over but didn't see any real difference. "I can't tell. They both look fine."

"Quite, I fancy them both, but you decide. Don't worry, I'll tell everyone it was my choice if it turns out skanky." She laughed.

She was pretty when she laughed, and he thought she should do it more often. Clark made a random decision and chose a hotel based on its location next to a canal. Gwen noted it on her papers.

"Can I ask you what's probably a silly question about school, classes?"

"Sure."

"Okay, so I'm confused because there don't appear to be any tests, exams or even papers in the courses."

"Well, these are courses for second years like me, Cynna, and I guess you. We don't do exams or papers during second year. We have three years at university, and we do exams at the end of the first to allow us to continue and at the end of the third year to graduate."

"So the second year is..." he couldn't find the right word. "How do you get grades?"

"We don't have grades in each course, but each one gives us the information we need to pass the third year exams. It's a cumulative knowledge kind of thing, and the only thing that matters is passing those exams."

Clark had to process that because, if there were no grades, how he would get credit for the year.

"Is that a problem for you?" she asked.

"Oh, I certainly don't mind not having exams or papers, but I do need grades of some sort to prove to my college back home that I should get credit, so I can continue in school and not..."

"Not get drafted?"

He nodded.

"If you did, what would you do?"

He hesitated. He knew, but he wondered whether he should share. "I'd move to Canada. Or here preferably, but there's extradition from England and not from Canada."

"We would hide you." She grinned, but she was very serious. Then her attention turned to the door, where Cynna stood and looked around.

Clark followed her look. Over the past weeks he had spent a lot of time thinking about Cynna. He had been encouraged by the fact that Thursday afternoon she had saved him a seat in the Philosophy of International Law class. They had only exchanged pleasantries, but that was more than enough for him. He had been disappointed when she quickly but politely said goodbye after class and walked away. She had given him a friendly smile, but he desperately wanted more.

Cynna joined them at the table. Clark thought she seemed more reserved and distracted than normal. Her fingers furiously worked her silver beads. Gwen offered to get her a drink and then went off to get it. Cynna turned her attention to Clark.

"Clark, tell me about you. Gwen thinks that you are an interesting person, for an American."

He wasn't sure how to react to the question, or the statement, or the subtext. He decided on the straightforward approach. "Oh, I'm just the normal All-American boy," he said, as he tried to keep it light.

"Are you from New York City?" she asked hopefully. She had always wanted to go to New York.

"No, but I lived there once. Now I live in Pennsylvania. But I've also lived in a lot of other places, Boston, Washington, Atlanta, Chicago, Denver, Dallas, Los Angeles, Seattle." He normally went from east to west when he described the many moves his family had made.

"My goodness, do all Americans do that?"

"No, not really, my family is different. My father's job had us moving pretty much every year."

"What is his job?"

"Well, it used to be the telephone company, but now he's the head of a manufacturing company that makes automobile parts." He knew that wasn't very exciting, so he added, "And he might be running for the senate next year. If he wins, we'd move back to Washington." He couldn't tell if she was impressed or not, so he nervously pushed on. "And you're from Greece. I'd love to go there some day."

"Not Greece," she spat on the word. "I am Macedonian. It is very different. You know Alexander the Great? He was Macedonian, and I'm named for his sister. We once ruled once Greece."

He was surprised at this first hint of excitement that he had seen her display. "Wow, sure, that's cool." He noticed her glance over toward the bar where Gwen had gotten involved in a discussion with Arthur.

"But it is pleasant to talk to you. We should do it more," she added, like she assumed that he would want to.

Of course he did. He wanted to talk and a lot more. He then surprised himself by asking, "Sure, maybe you would like to go to dinner with me next week, Thursday night after Philosophy class?" He knew it hadn't been artfully worded, and he waited while she processed the invitation. What he didn't expect was for her to laugh.

"Oh yes, but you know it would be three of us."

"Three?" He was confused.

"You, me, and Mrs. Rovsek. I can't go on a date without my chaperone. My father's orders."

"Really?" All sorts of questions and comments ran through his mind as he tried to imagine any girl he had ever known who would follow her father's orders like that. It certainly wouldn't happen with his sister and their father. About to make light of it, he remembered that she came from a different culture, and he wanted to establish a relationship with her. He needed to be more sensitive, so he tried to come up with a compromise. She'd given him an opening here, and he was desperate to exploit it.

"Well, sure, three is no problem. I'm sure we'll be able to ignore her." He remembered the impressive Mrs. Rovsek and her shoes and wasn't nearly as confident as he tried to sound.

"A marvelous idea Clark, it's a date." She seemed happy but not ecstatic. She gave his arm a squeeze before she wrote down her address and phone number. Then she got up and joined Gwen, who had moved on from Arthur and was talking with a group of the rugby team girlfriends.

Clark watched Cynna go and brimmed with excitement. He wished he had someone he could tell. Bernadette came to mind, but he quickly dismissed that idea. She was probably working. Then he had to laugh at this odd circle of women in his life: a stoic Greek, a Welsh tomboy, and a Corsican prostitute. He purposefully left out Tildi. Things were outlandish enough without including a married hooker who picked up business with her infant in tow.

The sales manager from the car dealership called Tuesday morning to report that they had found the car Clark wanted at another dealership and that Clark's father had wired the money. Clark forgot class and immediately called Bernadette.

"I'm in shock that you remembered to call me," Bernadette said, as she sat down next to Clark on the train. "Mags bet me a fancy dinner that you wouldn't."

Clark smiled at her. He enjoyed her company, and he also liked the envious looks he got from every male they passed. She looked really good, like a fashion model parading down Carnaby Street to lure tourists into the trendy shops. Her tight mini-skirt was accentuated by a t-shirt printed with a Union Jack that waved over her partially exposed breasts. It was a very sexy woman who held his arm as they walked into the MGB dealership.

Clark had to spend only twenty minutes doing the final paperwork, and soon they drove off in his new dark blue MGB convertible.

It became immediately and frighteningly obvious that Bernadette had been right about the difficulty of driving on the left side of the road with a steering wheel on the left side of the car. Without her help as a spotter, Clark would never have been able to pass a vehicle on the motorway. He tried staying out in the passing lane, but faster drivers roared up behind him, flashed their lights, and demanded to pass. Clark was totally frazzled by the time he got off the motorway and came to his first roundabout. That proved an even greater challenge as he got swept along in the heavy flow of traffic. Clark couldn't remember ever being as nervous, and then embarrassed, and then outright scared. The steering thing was going to get them killed.

Bernadette remained mostly supportive, but she screamed in terror a couple of times, once on the M2 and again on the roundabout. Not a person to normally say, "I told you so," she really wanted to. And she knew that she would be completely justified.

They finally got to Bernadette's neighborhood just as the sun made a brief appearance in the otherwise depressingly gray sky. Clark managed to parallel park after only four attempts, and they stumbled out of the car. They found a small Italian restaurant where they collapsed into a booth, exhausted and ready for a late lunch. After a beer and a glass of wine, they began to relax and tried to put the harrowing drive behind them.

"What do you think of Colin's story? Isn't is lame?" Bernadette asked him.

"I kept waiting for Maya to pounce on him. I know she promised to be open to every story, but she has to have some limits."

"The penis envy thing didn't surprise me, he's a guy after all, but the graphic incest scene was too much."

"I thought she was going to pull her left ear off, it was so red and sore." Clark had previously shared his insights about Maya's quirks.

Their lunch arrived, and they ate in silence, both hungry. Then she smiled at him. "Why are you staring at my breasts?"

"I'm not."

"You know what they look like, or do you need a refresher?" she teased.

"I wasn't staring, but they are right there and very nice."

"Oh, please, all men stare at women's breasts. Big or small it doesn't matter."

"Small men or small breasts?" he tried to tease back.

"You know what I mean." She playfully hit his shoulder. "I'm serious actually. Most men look at them first. Oh hi, I'm Fred, nice breasts you have there. But you didn't, and that's what I immediately fancied about you that night at the club."

They sat quietly for a moment, both still exploring the boundaries of this odd friendship. Then he told her about his pending date with Cynna, and Bernadette ventured into her favorite area, sexual banter, innuendo, and human foibles. She knew that he was very limited in that area but thought that he seemed to like it. "So you think this Cynna might be the one to finally get it done? Do you know if she's experienced? Two virgins going at it the first time can get very messy, trust me."

"Did that happen to you?

"Oh, Christ no. Far from it."

Her tone caused him to back off from that line of questioning. "Well, she has a chaperone who looks like a policewoman from Russia, or Siberia. So my guess would be that she's pretty sheltered."

"A commie chaperone? Jesus Clark, you don't make it easy for yourself do you?"

He shrugged his shoulders and smiled a sheepish smile.

After lunch he dropped her off at her flat. She feared for his safety as he headed off for Hampstead. Clark knew that if he took Cromwell Road, the A4, from Earls Court into downtown and could find Piccadilly Circus then he probably could find the University and then home by following the bus route. He found Piccadilly Circus without too much problem, but almost got smashed by a double-decker bus as he tried to navigate that crazy intersection of five busy streets with no traffic signals.

By the time he reached Hampstead and home, Clark was exhausted and his hands shook from the tension of the drive. Fortunately, Rita's flat had a parking enclosure, and he didn't have to try to park on the crowded street.

Clark wanted to impress Cynna with his new convertible, but it rained all day Thursday. It was October in London, and the forecast called for rain for the next week, maybe more.

Cynna seemed to be impressed, however, even without the top down as they drove from LSE to her flat on Thursday afternoon after class. He had spent hours poring over the *London A to Z Street Guide* to find the best route. He wanted her to think that he really knew his way around. The reality was that he had, in fact, learned a lot because he loved maps. When his family moved to a new city, Clark would immediately pour over a map and soon know his way around like a native. It had helped him gain a sense of belonging and not feel so helplessly out of place. London was by far the most difficult city he had ever encountered. There was no pattern to the streets, and the Thames River curved through it like an inverted horseshoe.

Cynna's flat was in a very attractive three-story building in Knightsbridge, a trendy and expensive area of London. She shared the flat with Gwen and Mrs. Rovsek, the chaperone. They each had their own bedroom. Her father was paying for the entire flat so Cynna got the bedroom with its own bathroom. Gwen and Mrs. Rovsek shared the hall bathroom in an uneasy détente.

Cynna had been quiet on the drive. She seemed to be preoccupied, as she had been earlier in class. Normally that would have been fine with him, but today he felt some compulsion to start a conversation. He had asked her if she was okay, and she had responded, "Yes," with a quiet smile and casually put her hand on his arm.

As they walked to her building, he commented on how nice the neighborhood was. She asked him where he lived and seemed pleased to hear about his flat in Hampstead.

As they entered the flat, Gwen came out of the bathroom wearing only a towel casually wrapped around her body. Her important parts were covered, but that didn't stop her from screaming at them. "Jesus Christ, what the fuck are you doing here Clark?" Her voice trailed off as she raced to her bedroom and slammed the door.

"Sorry Gwen," Cynna called out. "I thought I told you he was coming over. Oh hi Mrs. Rovsek," she continued, as the chaperone, thankfully fully dressed, emerged from her bedroom to see what all the ruckus was about.

Cynna showed Clark into the living room to wait while she changed. He sat stiffly on the couch while Mrs. Rovsek stood guard in the doorway. After a few minutes, she evidently determined that he posed no immediate threat, and she went into the kitchen. Clark relaxed a little and examined the room. It was decorated in an eclectic mixture of conservative but expensive-looking furniture, a large oriental rug, and a few pieces of modern artwork on the walls. There was a framed poster for the Beatles concert in Candlestick Park in August. He remembered seeing one for sale in a store near Piccadilly. Then he got up and moved over to examine a painting that looked like something that Salvador Dali might have painted. It was an original oil but had no signature that he could see.

"It's a very early work of his."

Clark hadn't noticed that Gwen, now dressed in her usual baggy, boyish, clothes, had come into the room. He turned to look at her and must have appeared confused.

"Dali. He was an acquaintance of Cynna's grandfather from somewhere, Spain I guess, when they were young."

She moved around cautiously. "I'm sorry about before. You surprised me. Neither of us bring men here."

"Not Ezekiel?"

"No, not Ezekiel. Even Arthur has only been here once, briefly."

"Where does he live?" Clark thought he knew, but it seemed like a safe question.

"Ezekiel?"

"No, Arthur."

"Oh, Bloomsbury, near the university, with two other blokes on the team, Charles and Owen. It's a bloody skanky pig sty, I warn you." Her mood improved.

"This is a very nice place."

"The best that Cynna's father's money can buy, or lease as the case may be. He needed a place with an extra bedroom for Mrs. Rovsek and Cynna wanted a friend with her, so here I am. Lots of bloody house rules though. No parties, and I thought no men, but maybe that's changed."

"I just drove her home so she could change and go to dinner. With Mrs. Rovsek," he added, with a weak smile. "Are you going out?"

It took her a moment to answer because she was still getting used to the idea of Cynna going on a date. This was the first one that Gwen was aware of. The only times Cynna went out had been when she attended some event on the diplomatic social calendar. She would be escorted by someone from the Greek embassy as a courtesy to her father. Not really considered dates.

"No, some of us need to study," she finally answered, and then quickly added, "Actually I might go to a club later to hear this American singer/guitarist Jimi Hendrix. Do you know him?"

"Yeah, but he's too much for me. They're now calling that hard rock, and it's not my style. I like good old standard, blues-based rock and roll."

"I agree personally, but the Hendrix type of sound is becoming the anthem of our protest movements. The old protest folk songs of Guthrie and Seeger and even Dylan are just too tame."

"Who's too tame?" Cynna asked from the entrance to the living room. She had changed and looked stunning in a purple dress with a plunging neckline that showed off her ample breasts and a tight waistline that accentuated her other splendid curves. Clark immediately felt inadequate in his simple dark blue cotton pants and dress shirt. He wore his dark brown, European-cut, suede jacket that had been a Christmas present from Rita and Keith. But it was showing some wear because he wore it everywhere.

"Oh, just some music stuff," replied Gwen.

"Wow, you look great," stammered Clark.

"Well, have fun you crazy kids." Gwen used a mock-serious, parental voice.

The night had turned cool, and as they walked down the street, Clark noticed Cynna shiver. He debated whether he should or could put his arm around her. But one glance at Mrs. Rovsek, who walked several paces behind them, answered that.

"Are you cold? Take my jacket." He started to take it off.

"Thank you, no I'm fine. This air temperature reminds me of home in our mountains."

"Well, I'm sure the air there is probably a lot cleaner," he joked, referring to the recent smog alert for central London.

She laughed in agreement.

It only took a minute to hail a cab, and when it stopped, Clark opened the door for Cynna. He had good manners, instilled by his mother, and both women noticed.

The New Delhi Restaurant had recently opened and offered a northern Indian cuisine that Cynna wanted to try. The restaurant advertised simple Indian food, but its decor was elaborate Indian Raj, and its prices were princely. Even when it became clear that he didn't have to pay for Mrs. Rovsek, who had disappeared into the woodwork, Clark knew the evening was going to put a real strain on his budget. He searched the menu for the least expensive items.

Taking Bernadette's advice, Clark struggled to keep his eyes focused on Cynna's dark eyes and away from her breasts. She wore her hair pulled up into a fancy bun, and it showed off her long elegant neck. But eventually her breasts were impossible to ignore.

Cynna noticed when he finally looked. She smiled to herself - his restraint was some sort of record - and she relaxed a little. She considered Clark cute in a schoolboy kind of way. Wholesome and seemingly naïve. He appeared to be safe enough that Mrs. Rovsek had already exhibited signs of relaxing her vigilance. She asked Clark about his courses. They had the two courses in common, and he responded with what she thought was as an interesting approach to the philosophical legal and moral dilemma that had been raised by Professor Doctor during their class that afternoon. It surprised her that a question about rugby didn't keep him talking for hours. She knew that it would have for Arthur.

Clark felt good about how the date was going. He knew he wasn't the most interesting conversationalist, but she was surprisingly easy to talk to. And she was gorgeous - anyone would want to be with her.

When their food came, Cynna said she wasn't all that hungry and grew quiet. He noticed that she now had her silver beads in her hand.

"Those are very nice," he said, nodding at the beads. "Is it a rosary?"

"Oh, no," she replied, with a forced smile. "We call them worry beads. It's an old tradition in my part of the world and into the Middle East. They can bring good luck, but mostly help pass the time, or relieve stress. But not religious."

Soon after, having passed on dessert, they left the restaurant. Mrs. Rovsek appeared out of the shadows. She had evidently seen them coming and had already hailed a taxi.

"Clark and I want to go for a short drive in his new car," Cynna told her chaperone, as the taxi pulled up in front of her building.

This came as news to Clark, but he didn't say anything. He watched as Mrs. Rovsek seemed to carefully process the request.

"But it only has two seats," Cynna added.

"Da, that is okay for short time."

It was just after nine as Clark drove around Hyde Park and then passed by the American Embassy on Grosvenor Square. He really liked showing off his new car - an extension of his manhood.

She smiled at him, and her mood seemed to lift before she surprised him by saying, "Clark, I'm really tired, and my stomach is a bit upset. Do you mind taking me home?"

Disappointed, Clark wondered if he had done or said something wrong. He didn't think so. He took her home and walked her to the door of the building. He didn't expect or make a move for a good-night kiss. As he drove home, Clark chalked it all up to an expensive experience and another dead end in his quest to get laid - not that that was likely to happen with the commie chaperone around. But it surprised him that he hadn't felt more of a sexual attraction to Cynna despite how great she looked. And it seemed pretty clear that she hadn't felt anything like that for him either.

It was still early, so when he got back to Hampstead, he found a parking spot near the New Holly pub, which he had wanted to check out. It was included on most of the tours of famous pubs in London. He didn't expect it to have much of a tourist crowd on a Thursday night, but he was wrong. A large group of middle-aged Germans, well into their pub tour and very drunk, packed the place. He was turning to leave when he saw a cute young woman who looked English and seemed sober - the tour guide, he assumed.

Hope springs eternal for a virgin on a quest, so Clark grabbed a pint at the bar and stood where he could watch the tour guide and look for an opening. Unfortunately, he wasn't very good at either spotting or acting upon openings. And the tour guide, frustrated with her drunken clients, had no interest in being picked up by Clark or anyone else - unless it happened to be Paul McCartney.

Later, as he drove home, Clark made a detour down Perrins Lane and checked Tildi's house. There were no lights on, and he realized that that was undoubtedly a good thing.

CHAPTER 8

Clark debated whether or not to drive to the rugby game. It was Saturday, so traffic wouldn't be bad. But there would be the party in the pub after the game, so he would have to stay sober enough to drive home. In the end, the desire to show off his new ride overcame his caution. It was a beautiful sunny day, and he put the top down as he drove down Hampstead High Street toward Camden Town and then Bloomsbury. The warm sun, the new car smell - Clark thought that even Bonnie Prince Charles couldn't have felt better than he did at that moment.

The first official game of the rugby season was against Leeds University. From the sideline, Clark watched as his team jumped to a fifteen to nothing advantage. They could have had a bigger lead, but Henry seemed to have lost the motivation that had driven him in the last friendly. It was so bad that Charles yelled at the third-year and gave Henry until halftime to shape up. When he didn't respond, Charles replaced him with Clark right before the end of the first half.

As Clark went in, he didn't sense any resentment from Henry. In fact, he thought Henry looked relieved. The Leeds players weren't exceptionally fast or athletic, but they were big and tackled very hard. They had a couple of forwards who, based on size and level of aggression, could have started as linebackers for the New York Giants. One of them had leveled Henry at the beginning of the game, and the other had pummeled him right before Charles pulled him out. Clark knew that he should stay away from them, if he could.

Clark played a decent game. He made some good tackles and managed to avoid the bruisers from Leeds, although they tried to flatten him a couple of times. Then, with two minutes to go in the game, he received a pass from Owen, who played next to him at outside center. Clark saw a narrow opening down the side and sprinted toward it. The Leeds winger totally misjudged Clark's speed, and Clark raced untouched across the Leeds goal line. He even had enough time to down the ball right in front of the goal posts for an easy conversion kick. It wasn't a game-winning goal because they were already ahead, but it was impressive nonetheless.

As the teams shook hands after the game, Clark overheard the Leeds captain comment to Charles, "So that's the secret Yank I've heard rumors about."

"Well, I guess he's not a secret anymore," Charles laughed in response.

As Clark had expected, there was a big difference in the locker room and the pub after winning a real game, compared to winning a friendly. Everything louder and bigger. More spectators had been at the match, and now more people were in the pub. For the first time there were plenty of unattached women at the party. Enthusiasm for the game and a few beers soon had the players singing, more like shouting, rugby songs. And even though the lyrics were often very sexist, many of the women joined in.

The Leeds players were heavy drinkers, and they had very attractive girlfriends. Not that the UL players' girlfriends weren't pretty, they were, but the girls from Leeds seemed hotter because of how they dressed, their makeup, and their eager alcoholic consumption. Every Leeds player had at least one very hot bird who hung on him, and several players, including the big guys from the scrum, had two girls.

"I should tell them to go get a bloody room," joked Gwen, who joined Clark as he stared at one Leeds player and his girlfriend, who were engaged in a passionate embrace, their hands groping everywhere, including places normally considered inappropriate for touching in public.

Clark nodded and turned to face Gwen and Cynna, who stood next to her.

Cynna smiled as she said, "That was a very impressive score Clark."

He tried to be modest, but his grin betrayed him.

"Yeah, the look of surprise on that winger's face was the dog's bollocks," Gwen added. "Zoom, you were right by him. Arthur said you were bloody fast, but I hadn't seen it before today."

Gwen wore her typical uniform of baggy clothes. But Cynna also wore loose fitting clothes, which was unusual for her, and she seemed to already be tired. Gwen left them and went to the bar to talk to Arthur, who stood quiet and alone.

Cynna watched her go and then turned back to Clark, giving him a half-hearted smile. "I'm sorry Clark, but I'm really tired and I'm going home. Enjoy the party, you deserve it." Before he could respond, she gave his arm a little squeeze and left. He briefly fought an urge to run after her and offer her a ride home. But he knew that that would likely lead to a frustrating end to the evening. And just then a Leeds female student, who had bright pink streaks in her blond hair and very red lipstick on her full lips, grabbed him. She had obviously had a few beers, and she pulled Clark over to a group of girls who proceeded to fawn all over him. This was Clark's first taste of a celebrity treatment given rugby and soccer stars, even the minor ones. He soon forgot all about Cynna.

By the time the party ended, Clark had the names and phone numbers of two very hot first-year birds. He doubted that they would remember him in the morning, and he couldn't accurately connect faces with either of the names. The night had been good for his ego, but he hadn't been interested in any of those girls for his first sexual partner. Even with Cynna no longer a viable option, he remained optimistic for someone better. On a silly impulse, he tacked the names and numbers on a bulletin board outside the Student Union.

Clark got very few phone calls, so he was surprised when the telephone in the flat rang late Sunday morning.

"Hi Clark, its Bernie, and I wonder if you'd like to come over for supper this evening. Full disclosure, it's not a free meal because I need your help with my story. I'm stuck, and you have such good ideas. Oh, yes, and Mags would like a ride in your car." Bernadette finally had to take a breath, and Clark readily agreed to the invitation.

After he hung up, he wondered if Bernadette's invitation qualified as sort of a date. But he quickly squelched that idea. They were becoming good friends, and he liked that.

He arrived at Bernadette's flat promptly at six o'clock. The rain had stopped, but it was dark and a heavy cloud cover hung oppressively low, almost a fog.

Bernadette and Mags both responded to the doorbell, and Mags immediately hopped into the car for her ride. Clark had to laugh at her enthusiasm. He couldn't imagine that she had never ridden in a sports car before. He put the top down for the full effect and hoped that the rain would hold off.

"Oh, Bernie was right, this is fun," Mags yelled, as they drove down Cromwell Road and past the Royal Albert Hall. She only flinched and squealed once, when he started going the wrong way at a roundabout.

Clark didn't know how far to go or how long to be away. He continued east on Cromwell Road and turned south toward the river on Queens Gate.

"I need to talk to you Clark," Mags said, suddenly very serious.

He wondered if he should pull over and stop, but he didn't.

"You know what we do, and you might think you know Bernie, but trust me you don't."

Clark wisely kept quiet and let her talk.

"She's the first in our family to go to college, and we all support her, but we're also afraid for her. Our profession is normally a very solitary one. We can't afford to make friends because eventually they start to judge us or try to change us. And relationships are out of the question. I've never seen it work for one of us to have a male friend and not have it end in heartache or tragedy. And despite what Bernie says, I seriously doubt that you will be any different."

Clark concentrated on turning west onto Old Brompton Road and toward the flat in Earls Court. He gathered his thoughts. "I really like Bernie as a friend, and I would never do anything to hurt her."

"Nice sentiment, but very hard to maintain. Listen Clark, Bernie's often too sensitive for her own good, especially for someone in our profession. I don't know if this college thing will work out for her or not, but she says she needs a friend and that you're it. My job is to protect her, and I don't want to see her get hurt, by you or anyone else."

"I understand. But I still want to be her friend."

"But can you keep it that way? I understand that you're still a virgin. I know she likes you and would fuck you any time you want."

"No, just friends, I, I couldn't handle…" He didn't know what he should call it.

"Her professional life?"

He nodded.

"Well, that's good that you can admit it. Sensible. Too many men equate fucking with love and then try to save us."

Clark parked in front of the flat and hesitated before getting out. He wondered if he should go home. His confused expression made her laugh. "Oh, come on in, I just wanted to make sure that we had an understanding. Bernie's waiting for you to help her with that story of hers."

The rest of the evening turned out to be great fun. Mags was an outstanding cook and an unfailing cheerleader for Bernadette and her schoolwork. Clark worked with Bernadette on her tenses - she had a tendency to switch back and forth between present and past. She also needed help with a story point - how in a realistic way to connect the deaf DJ with the girl.

During dinner, Clark found that he felt comfortable with and could more easily engage in their banter about men and sex and their profession. The hardest thing was to keep his mind from wandering to thoughts of sex as these two great looking women communicated with their hands. Mostly they waved them around for emphasis, but they frequently put them on Clark. And they were wearing very sexy clothes. He began to worry that the whole friendship thing was going to implode because he couldn't stop his erection. He tried to hide it, but Bernadette noticed and pointed at it.

"Look, little Yank has joined us."

"I'm so sorry, I should go."

"Why?" they both asked.

"Well, I guess maybe I can't maintain this friends-only status after all."

The both laughed. "Clark, it's normal," Mags replied. "Just because we're all friends doesn't mean that you can't get a stiffie, as you Americans call it. And we have been pretty raunchy. Blimey, we'd be worried about you if you didn't respond." She paused as a big smile crossed her face. "And the best part is that you're with two friends who know what to do about it." She knelt down in front of him and unzipped his pants. She had his stiff penis in her mouth before he could react.

He looked at Bernadette, confusion in his eyes, pleasure on his face.

She smiled. "Just relax and enjoy it, Mags is world-famous for her blowjobs."

He didn't really have any choice because Mags indeed knew exactly what to do with her mouth and tongue to get him to the edge but not over. Minute after minute of exquisite pleasure flowed through him. He closed his eyes and images of different girls from his past and present played behind his eyelids. Finally, when he thought he would go crazy, he opened his eyes, saw they two of them, and exploded. He felt like he would pass out. Mags gently put his penis back in his pants and zipped him up before as she left for the bathroom.

Bernadette moved her chair next to his, ready to stabilize him if he began to topple over. She'd seen it happen after one of Mags' blowjobs. It made her a little jealous actually. "So, how does that compare to mine?"

"Oh my god, no comparison." He then paused as he came to his senses. "I really loved yours."

She knew what the honest answer should be, but she really appreciated his attempt to make her happy. Impulsively, she gave him a quick kiss on his cheek.

By the time Mags returned, Clark could function again, and they resumed work on Bernadette's story as if nothing had happened. When Bernadette was finally happy with their progress, Clark got ready to leave.

Mags put her hand on Clark's arm. "I hope you appreciate good friends and the occasional benefits they can provide, but this is just between us. Understand?"

As he drove home, Clark marveled at his situation, his good fortune. He wrestled with the question that if he could accept a blowjob from a friendly prostitute then why not real sex. He couldn't articulate it, but he knew it was different and not what he wanted. He felt it had something to do with love, but he had begun to realize that love was much more of an elusive and complicated concept than he had ever imagined.

When Clark arrived the next morning at his Modern Imperialism class Cynna gave him a nice smile and motioned for him to sit next to her. Gwen casually acknowledged him with a slight nod of her head.

After class, as Clark started to leave, Cynna grabbed his arm and pulled him close to her. "Clark, I had such a great time the other night. I hope you did too. I'd love to do it again this week, if you'd like to."

Even though he couldn't reconcile her enthusiasm with his memory of their date, he readily agreed and then asked her to have lunch. Maybe then he could figure out what was going on.

"Oh, I'd love to, but my stomach is still acting up, and I'm going home to rest. I'll see you in class on Thursday."

He watched her as she walked down the hall. Suddenly she turned and dashed into the women's bathroom.

The next few days flew by in a swirl of classes and rugby practice. He felt disappointed when Bernadette wasn't in class on Wednesday. He thought about calling her because he wanted to tell her about the strange turn of events with Cynna. She had, after all, advised him that Greek women were quirky and for him to be patient. He had gotten the sense that Bernadette and her sister didn't think very highly of Greek women.

He arrived at Cynna's and Gwen's flat right on time Thursday evening. Cynna appeared, dressed much more casually than she had been for their first date. But she still looked great. Mrs. Rovsek seemed to wear the same clothes all the time. He equated that with a civilian uniform, and it occurred to him that Gwen did much the same thing. He looked around for Gwen, but she didn't appear to be home.

Cynna noticed. "Gwen's leading a student rally to raise money for the victims of Hurricane Inez, you know, the one that hit Hispaniola a few days ago."

"Oh yeah, I wonder if Arthur's there too," Clark replied, as much from an effort to make conversation as from actual curiosity.

"Arthur? Blimey no, he wouldn't be caught anywhere near such a woman's thing. He's probably getting drunk with his mates." The tone of her voice was slightly judgmental but not hostile. Then she asked, somewhat cautiously, "Why do you ask?"

"Oh, no real reason, I just can't figure him out, that's all. He's friendly at rugby but... Anyway, no big deal."

They both seemed happy to drop the conversation and leave for dinner. They went to a Greek restaurant where the maître d' knew Cynna and gave them a nice table at the front window. He knew that it would be good advertising to have such a beautiful young woman sit on display.

Clark felt a different energy flowing from Cynna. Her eyes glimmered, and she seemed glad to be there with him. She had taken his arm as they walked from the taxi into the restaurant. And as they talked about school, she occasionally reached across the table and squeezed his hand. It wasn't the kind of behavior to get him aroused, but it was enough to make him much more hopeful about a potential future.

The evening took a turn, however, when their food arrived. After the first bite, Cynna looked like she was going to vomit. She jumped up from the table and rushed to the bathroom, where she stayed for a long time. Clark didn't see it when Mrs. Rovsek went to investigate. When Cynna returned to the table, she looked pale and asked that he take her home.

The fresh air seemed to make her feel better, and they kept the windows of the taxi rolled down. When they arrived at her flat, Cynna asked if he could give her a ride in his car with the top down. As Clark prepared the car, Mrs. Rovsek assessed the situation and then went inside to go to bed.

Clark opened the car door for Cynna, and as he walked around to the driver's side to get in, he noticed that she was fumbling with her arms under her blouse. As he sat down and turned to her, she pulled her bra out from under her shirt and breathed a big sigh of relief.

"Oh God, that was killing me."

He knew it had something to do with her breasts, but he didn't feel comfortable enough with her to ask. She wasn't Bernadette after all. She unbuttoned the top of her blouse. Her breasts weren't uncovered, but they were exposed more than they had been before. He quickly looked away when she looked over at him, and he didn't notice her little smile.

Clark didn't have any big expectations for the drive. She seemed to enjoy the fresh air, and a couple of times she put her hand on his arm. But as they drove toward the river, she told him that she was tired and needed to go home. They exchanged kisses on the cheek at the front door and a brief hug. He enjoyed the feeling of her firm body pressed briefly against his, and he felt a stab of desire to do more.

CHAPTER 9

As Clark got on the old school bus with the rugby team, Charles approached him and told him that he would be starting at right wing. Clark wanted to ask about Henry, but the bitter expression on Charles' face warned him off. Later, he learned that Henry had given Charles an ultimatum that either he started or he would quit. Charles had called Henry on what he was sure was a bluff and found out that Henry was indeed serious. Charles was upset because even though Henry wasn't as good as Clark, they still needed him as a reserve.

The game that Saturday was at Oxford, and Clark had been looking forward to seeing that campus. He brought his camera, hopeful that he could find time to take some pictures. But cold rain and a dense fog hung over everything, obscuring the landscape in a dull British gray - a thoroughly miserable day. It never stopped raining except to drizzle, but rain wouldn't stop a rugby match.

The pitch quickly became a slippery quagmire. For a while the players enjoyed sliding in the mud, but soon they were soaked, cold, and caked in muck from head to toe. Both teams struggled to generate any kind of a scoring effort. The conditions almost completely negated any advantage that UL had in speed. At the half, the game was tied three to three on penalty kicks for each side. During the halftime break, the players jogged around, trying to keep from getting stiff in the cold - a futile effort as the temperature continued to drop.

Midway through the second half, Oxford managed a try but missed the conversion points. UL almost scored right before the game ended but had to settle for a narrow loss. Clark hadn't distinguished himself, but he hadn't embarrassed himself either.

The players lingered in the hot showers until they could feel the warmth soak in and drive the chill from their bones.

Clark was disappointed with the score, but not with the pub, which looked just as he had imagined a pub at Oxford would. Old carved woodwork surrounded stained glass windows that depicted scenes of people in a market, working in a field, making wine, and drinking in a pub - a veritable shrine to the Greek god Dionysus.

"Impressive isn't it," Gwen remarked. He had seen her briefly during the game, huddled up in a rain slicker. He looked around for Cynna.

"Cynna didn't come. She was living in the loo most of the morning."

Clark nodded, and a half-formed thought nicked away in the back of his brain but couldn't quite grab his attention. "Did you manage to stay warm?" he asked her. He noticed that she wore a blouse and pants that were much more feminine that her normal attire. It looked more like something that Cynna would wear.

She saw his glance at her outfit. She knew that men responded more to Cynna's style of clothes than they did to hers, and it felt good to be noticed. She wondered why she felt so conflicted around this man. Clearly he made Cynna happy because the dark cloud that had hung over her roommate ever since they had returned to London after their summer in Wales had now lifted. The problem for Gwen was that Clark just didn't seem like the type of guy that Cynna would be attracted to. He seemed innocent and strangely naïve. But she had decided to make more of an effort to be friends with him in order to be a supportive friend to Cynna.

The crowd in the pub seemed unusually subdued for a rugby group. Maybe it was the rain or the disappointing game or just the refined atmosphere of the pub - so different from the typical bawdy beer hall. Even the Oxford rugby songs were more literate than what Clark had heard on other occasions.

After a while, Clark noticed that Gwen wasn't making a move to hurry away as she normally did, and he asked if she wanted to find a table and sit down. He was surprised when she agreed and actually seemed pleased. He sensed a change in her, but he figured he was probably mistaken. It certainly wouldn't be the first time that he had been wrong about a girl and her moods. Nevertheless, he felt a little less awkward then he normally did when he was around her.

She commented, "You probably won't see us much anymore in Merkel's class or Cohen's."

"Yeah, they're pretty useless. All they do is lecture from their books. And discourage questions," he added with a smile. "But my Philosophy of International Law course is different. That prof is fairly cool." Clark didn't mention his creative writing course.

"Well, that's true, but it's also tradition for second years to skive classes on a regular basis. For me it means more time to participate in my, you know, outside stuff. For many second-years it means more parties, more drugs, and more unwanted pregnancies." She finished the last comment with a nervous laugh.

Although still early, they were both tired. The team bus wasn't scheduled to leave for another two hours. She had come on the train, and they decided to take one back together.

The rain had stopped, and an almost-full moon bathed the campus in a blue-white light that sparkled off the wet surfaces - a very beautiful and romantic setting that wasn't lost on either of them. As they crossed the ancient stone bridge over the Castle Mill Stream, which separated the campus from the town, they paused to admire the view. Clark took a photo of Gwen with the campus buildings behind her. As the moonlight washed across her face, he was struck by how serene and attractive she looked.

On the train they sat quietly on benches facing each other, and Clark asked her about her protest activities, and she spent most of the trip describing current issues in Rhodesia, South Africa, and Vietnam. She offered to let him know when the next rally against Vietnam happened, and he tried to muster an enthusiastic response. It wasn't that he was unconcerned, he just didn't feel comfortable with a public display of his feelings.

The train was a local, but there weren't many passengers, so it took only fifty-five minutes to reach King's Cross Station. As they walked to the taxi stand outside the station, Gwen noticed a pair of women lurking in the entrance to the station. They were terribly under-dressed for the cold night. "Oh, the poor things," she lamented.

Clark turned to follow her gaze and realized that they were prostitutes.

"They're everywhere in London, mostly foreigners - abused and uneducated. It's terrible how they're forced to live."

Clark responded, "Yeah, that's awful." These women were vastly different from the prostitutes he knew, but he certainly wasn't going to bring that up with Gwen. At the taxi stand, he offered to ride with her to her flat to make sure she got home safely. She wouldn't hear of it, but she did appreciate his gesture.

Clark spent most of the day on Sunday in bed resting and trying to get in front of the head cold he felt coming on. It didn't get worse but it didn't get better quickly, so he laid low Monday and Tuesday, skipping classes just like Gwen and the other second-years. He kept sampling albums in Rita's collection from singers and groups that he hadn't heard of like Francoise Hardy, the Monks, and the Fugs.

He used what energy he had to work on his story for creative writing. He felt okay about it, but he knew that Bernadette's was better. And Clark wanted to impress her. He had the inciting incident for the story, and he had fleshed out the middle, but the ending was giving him trouble. Should I go for a comedy or a tragedy? he asked himself, leaning one way or the other depending on his mood. Today, influenced by the pressure in his sinuses and the jazz of Eric Dolphy and Ornette Coleman, he swung toward tragedy. But he found that his heart wasn't really in it. Deep down, he believed tragedy represented a waste of human potential and generally should be avoided. Of course he knew that most of the classics of literature were tragedies, but he had never felt it necessary for both Romeo and Juliet to die, or that Hamlet shouldn't be able to get revenge without dying. Sure, he thought, tragic deaths did tie things up in a nice neat package. But with a little more imagination, couldn't it be different? But then he would ask himself - who am I to argue with the success of Shakespeare?

He did drag his butt to practice on Tuesday afternoon. And on Wednesday morning he pushed himself to Creative Writing, only to be disappointed that Bernadette wasn't there for the second week in a row. He debated again whether or not to call her, but in the end he didn't.

Feeling fine as he entered the classroom for the legal philosophy class on Thursday, Clark was rewarded with a warm welcoming smile from Cynna. She declared that she was having a marvelous day. That seemed to last for most of the two-hour class. Then ten minutes before the end, she leapt up from her chair and rushed out of the room.

After class, Clark waited in the hallway near the women's bathroom, and when Cynna finally emerged she looked pale and tired. Her fingers worked furiously with her worry beads.

"Can I do anything for you?"

"Thank you Clark, but I just need to get home and take a nap to be ready for our date." She smiled at him and a little color returned to her cheeks.

"We don't have to go out if you're not feeling well," he offered.

"Oh don't be daft. I'm fine really. I've always had a nervous stomach. I'm not really sick."

When he walked up to Cynna and Gwen's flat that evening, Clark wondered what he would find. Suddenly Clark's memory flashed back to images from three years earlier, in Denver, Colorado. His half-sister Rita rushed to the bathroom sick to her stomach; she complained of her breasts being sore; and then she stood naked in the hallway with her baby bump clearly showing. No, Cynna can't be pregnant, he thought. It was impossible with Mrs. Rovsek always around. He immediately dismissed the idea, knowing that he knew far too little about women, their bodies, and their health, to make such a crazy assumption.

The first thing he noticed when Cynna answered the door was that her eyes seemed a little puffy. The second thing was that she didn't appear to be wearing a bra under her colorful, loose-fitting, blouse. He also thought that her breasts looked bigger. He didn't really know if it worked that way by just not wearing a bra, but he liked what he saw. He may have looked a little too hard and long.

Cynna, with a little conspiratorial smile, said, "Let's hope that Mrs. Rovsek doesn't notice. Proper young women always wear bras."

Clark smiled in a way that he hoped communicated, "Ha, ha, I'm in on that joke."

Ironically, it was Mrs. Rovsek who felt sick. She hesitated, knowing her responsibility but not wanting to ruin Cynna's evening. Convinced that this boy posed no threat, she made Cynna promise to be good and let them go out alone.

They went to a little fish-n-chips place near Trafalgar Square. It was popular with tourists, particularly those from America, and because of that it offered tomato ketchup, which would never be found in a traditional English fish-n-chips shop. Cynna had a strong craving for ketchup and knew this place offered it. "Yesterday, I spent two bloody hours shopping for tomato ketchup. There isn't a store anywhere in England that carries it."

After ordering, they ate in the MGB because the shop was too small, and the heat and smell from the deep fryers too intense for both of them. Their conversation started with small talk and soon dwindled. Cynna didn't seem interested or motivated to do much else besides eat, and an awkward tension developed between them. Clark's fragile sense of confidence started to unravel, and he began to think of ways to end the date.

Cynna then inexplicably perked up, put her hand on his, squeezed it firmly, and smiled. "Would you like to kiss me?"

It took him a moment to rally a response. "Yes." Succinct, it was the best he could do, but she acknowledged it with another smile. She leaned in toward him, and he leaned toward her. The kiss that resulted in the middle was nice but tentative. The second kiss proved more energetic, but brought their bodies hard against the gearshift, the handbrake, and the console that divided the two bucket seats. He tried to shift around and in the process bumped her left breast, which caused her to wince.

"Just a little sore. You know, that time of month."

Clark nodded knowingly, despite his dearth of knowledge about female biology.

Back at Cynna's flat, after she confirmed that Mrs. Rovsek was asleep and Gwen wasn't home, they sat on the couch and resumed kissing. Their tongues got involved, hers first. He noticed a subtle cinnamon taste and appreciated it that she didn't smoke.

Clark considered himself a pretty good kisser, and he tried to do his best with Cynna, and she responded. Then be began to wonder what to do next. He would normally try to kiss her breasts, but she had already said that they were sore. He turned his body so it more directly faced her and tried to gently pull her body to his without putting too much pressure on her breasts. This awkward position proved to be unbalanced, and their bodied toppled over on the couch, hers on top of his.

She quickly bounded back up and put a hand on his chest. "We can't, she has radar for this."

"Who? For what?" He assumed that she meant Mrs. Rovsek and not Gwen. But he couldn't imagine that kissing and hugging would be considered dangerous.

"To keep my passionate nature from getting me in trouble, silly. To make sure that I stay pure for my wedding."

At first Clark thought he had misheard her. For one thing, his experience so far with Cynna would never have led him to label her as passionate. And second - what wedding? Hesitantly he asked, "Are you engaged or something?".

"No, not yet. But as the eldest daughter, I am expected to marry a man from a prominent family in Greece and bring honor to our family."

Clark momentarily doubted her sincerity because she said it too perfunctorily and it seemed so old fashioned. So he tried to keep it light. "And you're okay with that? Do you get to select this prominent man?"

She shook her head and couldn't conceal the sadness that appeared in her eyes. He sensed that she thought of something or someone as tears began to form and then slipped gently down her cheeks. Confused but concerned, he leaned in and tenderly kissed her tears. He then did see a flicker of passion in her eyes, but it quickly died as she struggled to compose herself.

"My father is a very strong and powerful man. It is an honor to please him." She paused. "But now I am tired. Next week?"

Clark agreed, but as he drove home, he wondered what might be the future, if any, of this relationship. Sure the kissing had been very nice, but she had made it clear that nothing else would ever happen. Not unless he somehow became a prominent Greek. Did she consider him simply a diversion from boredom? That was hard to believe - mostly because there were scores of more interesting men out there. She could easily get a date, and plenty of diversion, with any of them. To Clark all women were complicated, but Cynna was in a class all by herself. He tried to recall the feeling of her lips and the sensation of her kisses, but it kept slipping away, more like a dream than reality.

Clark spent the next morning visiting three different art schools in London. He had hundreds of photos that he wanted to develop and print in a darkroom, but he didn't have access to one. The previous two years he had had a convenient freelance arrangement with *The Daily D*, the student newspaper, where he had provided photos to the paper in exchange for some film and access to their darkroom.

Only one of the schools he visited had a darkroom, but it was restricted to use by their students, no exceptions. Already frustrated, he became really unhappy when the weather deteriorated quickly, and he got caught in a cold rain. He had barely kept a cold at bay all week, and as he walked home, his body told him that simple rest wasn't going to save him this time. He stopped in a chemist shop and got some cold medicine, then at the grocer for juice, tea bags and honey.

His body hadn't lied, and even after a long night in bed, he felt terrible the next day. He tried to get up, but he felt light-headed and weak. Reluctantly, he called Charles and told him that he would miss the game that afternoon.

Over the next four days he took care of himself, modeled on how his mother would have done it. It also made him to feel a little homesick. He wasn't bothered by missing classes again on Monday and Tuesday, but he was determined to make it to Creative Writing on Wednesday. He hadn't seen Bernadette in weeks, and he had a lot to tell her.

The only interruption to his quiet seclusion was a phone call from Gwen to ask how he felt and report that the team had barely managed to beat Cambridge on their pitch. He really regretted not getting to see Cambridge, but as Gwen pointed out, he could drive there whenever he wanted. He later thought that he had heard her say, "We could drive there." But his head had been stuffy, and he figured that he was probably wrong about that.

Cynna called him Tuesday night to see how he was and to confirm their date on Thursday. He thought that she had initially sounded concerned and then relieved when he assured her that he was okay and that their date was on.

Bernadette looked wonderful for someone so obviously nervous. She gave him an enigmatic Mona Lisa-type smile when Clark gave her a quick friend-hug before class started Wednesday morning. He felt really happy to see her, and his cold was mostly gone.

Bernadette had to read part of her story to the class. "I don't know if I can do this Clark," she fretted.

He assured her that she would do great and then watched as she nervously fiddled with her pencil while Professor Maya lectured on flashbacks, which she detested as a narrative device. Maya then called on Bernadette to read first because she had been absent for her scheduled time the last two weeks. Bernadette's dark complexion turned pale. She asked if she could read from her seat, and Maya must have sensed Bernadette's nervousness because she agreed, even though she had encouraged others to stand in front of the room to read. Bernadette's voice started off so shaky and weak that Clark had a hard time hearing her, and he sat right next to her. Maya asked her to stop and start again, louder, so that she and the class could hear. Before she began again, Bernadette turned to Clark, gave him a smile and a raised what-the-hell eyebrow, took a deep breath, and found strength for her voice.

Clark watched Bernadette and then looked over at Maya as the story got to the first beat, the one he had helped Bernadette with weeks ago at her flat. The expression on the professor's face as she leaned forward indicated that it clearly worked, and Clark relaxed. He didn't know if Bernadette had also seen Maya's reaction, but her voice and her overall presentation did get stronger. And she finished with a flourish.

"I was so bloody nervous," Bernadette said, almost shouted, as they walked to the pub for lunch. "I couldn't have done it if you weren't there."

He assured her that she could have and reminded her of the very positive things that Maya had said to her. He really wanted to know where she'd been the past two weeks. But she spoke first and asked him about how things were going in his life, particularly with rugby and Cynna. She added a sly wink to her grin as she said Cynna's name.

"It's confusing for sure. Just when I think it's never going anywhere, a waste of time, she asks me to kiss her."

"She had to ask you to kiss her?" Bernadette tried unsuccessfully to keep the shock and disbelief from her voice. But then she remembered that she had been the one to initiate things the night they had met.

When she responded that way, he felt foolish and a little embarrassed. But before he got too upset, he realized that it was indeed odd, and that it said a lot about his conflicted feelings for Cynna. "Yeah, I know, I'll never get laid that way."

"That's for bloody sure," she laughed, and her laughter broke any lingering tension. "So did this kissing go well? As I remember you do know how to kiss."

"It was pretty good, I guess, but…" he paused, not sure he could describe his feelings.

"Well, Mags and I warned you about Greek women. They have many layers, like an onion, and all of them can be devastating to men - far beyond just making you cry. Remember, one Greek woman, Helen, started a big war all by herself."

He nodded, wanting to change the topic. "So where have you been? I hope you weren't just avoiding class so you didn't have to read."

"Oh no, I dreaded it, but not that much. Mags and I had to go home to Corsica for a while to see our mother. She's been sick and wants us to come home and help run the family business."

Clark feared he knew the answer but had to ask, "What's the family business?" He hoped that it was an olive grove or a tea shop.

"The largest, and certainly the best brothel on the island," she answered proudly.

Just as he feared, and he struggled to keep his facial expression positive or at least neutral. "So your mother is also a…"

"A prostitute? Yes, Clark, we're a long line of women who pleasure men for money. My mother, grandmother, great-grandmother, and so on. My great, great grandmother fucked Napoleon before he went all Napoleon-like. Grandmother did Mussolini during the war - but we stayed neutral. And mother has been with Fellini many times. He even offered her a role in one of his films."

"So are you going to do it, move back home?" He knew that he hadn't been able to keep the disappointment from his voice.

She noticed and rewarded him with a quick kiss on his cheek. "No, at least not for a while. We like it here, and everyone wants me to finish school. I'm the very first in my family to go to college," she added proudly. "And the trip actually helped my story. Mother happens to have a client who is a deaf musician. He told me about feeling the beat of music like the pulse of his heart."

"Oh yeah, I really liked that metaphor. You're such a good writer, and it would seem such a waste to give it up for, you know…"

"Well, there are a lot of good stories in our world. I could do a novel, Confessions of a Teenage Prostitute. And I have my expensive standards to maintain. I refuse to be a starving artist huddled cold and hungry in a dirty attic."

Clark agreed on the cold and starving points, but he did have a romantic fantasy to lead the international life of a writer, or maybe a photographer.

Before he left for practice, Clark accepted her invitation for dinner on Sunday. "Mags has this new dish that she wants to try out."

The next day, Clark assumed correctly that Cynna would not be in the Philosophy of International Law class. He had come anyway because he enjoyed the subject and appreciated Professor Doctor's attempts to relate the material to current events. They were deep into a discussion about morality and the prerogative of rulers to make decisions that were contrary to the interests of a majority of citizens but were said to be justifiable on the basis of divine right. It fascinated Clark the way that legal systems evolved over time and served as a reflection of the various interests that dominated different societies. England was of course a fascinating example of a society undergoing great change and growth as a democracy. Yet the country, the citizens, were still hung-up on a traditional royal monarchy.

After class he called Cynna to confirm their date, but despite her affirmative words, he couldn't decipher whether she was really pleased. Bernadette had told him the day before that while he wasn't very experienced with women, he had pretty good instincts for people, and he should listen to those. Not sure he believed the second part, the first observation rang painfully true.

When Cynna opened the door to the flat for him, she looked more like she planned to go to bed than out on a date. He had never seen her dressed so casually - a loose white t-shirt, baggy gray cotton pants, and bare feet. And clearly she wasn't wearing bra, as evidenced by her nipples that poked up under fabric of the t-shirt. It created a very sexy look, and Clark felt a rush of anticipation that maybe he was once again wrong about a woman. His excitement grew when she told him that both Gwen and Mrs. Rovsek were out for the evening.

She had begged him to stop for take-away at the fish-n-chips shop at Trafalgar Square. As he presented her with the take-out bag, there was an undercurrent of desperation in her voice as she asked about the ketchup. He dramatically handed her the separate container full of ketchup. "Oh, thank you

Clark, you're a life saver," she gushed, as she grabbed the bag and the ketchup container and rushed to the kitchen.

They ate at a small table in the kitchen, and he marveled at the amount of ketchup she put on everything. As an American he liked ketchup, but her behavior struck him as definitely weird. He told her about the legal philosophy class, and she listened but didn't seem very interested.

After they ate, they went into the living room, and Cynna picked a few albums from an impressive and slightly eclectic record collection that included Beatles, Rolling Stones, The Who, the Mammas and Pappas, Peter and Gordon, The Monkeys, and Bob Dylan. She put one on the turntable of a very expensive stereo system, and Clark was surprised to hear John Mayall and Eric Clapton sing the song *All Your Love* from the recent *Blues Breakers with Eric Clapton* album. It wasn't what he would have expected her to like. But he realized that he didn't really know much about her likes and dislikes - except for ketchup.

They sat on the couch. She sat cross-legged and faced him, which didn't leave a real opening for any kissing. He asked her about the music, and she admitted that the record collection was Gwen's. Her contribution had been the stereo system. The conversation lagged, and his uncertainty grew, until he thought he might as well leave. Maybe sensing this, Cynna suddenly moved over to sit on his lap. Her legs straddling his, she kissed him. Surprised and confused, he nevertheless eagerly reciprocated. After a little while, her kisses and the pressure of her crotch pushing up against his began to get him aroused. He thought he knew what to do next, so he gently moved his hand under her t-shirt to her breast.

She flinched in pain. "Still sore, the period thing. Sorry." She then seemed to feel his erection growing under her because she pulled her body back along his legs. She looked down at his crotch.

He held his breath and wondered what she would she do or say. He never found out because at that moment the front door opened, and Gwen came in. She stood still in the hall for a moment, processing what she saw in the living room. It wasn't a complete surprise because she had assumed that they were having sex. She just hadn't expected to come face-to-face with it in their living room.

Cynna quickly moved off Clark and sat with her legs pulled up underneath her.

Clark felt exposed and crossed his arms across his lap.

Gwen tentatively entered the living room and smiled, trying to appear as if this were an everyday occurrence. "Sorry, I thought you were going out."

"What happened to your date?" Cynna replied.

"Oh, it wasn't a date. My anti-Vietnam gang had a party with some big muckety-muck student leader from Columbia University in New York. He was bloody intense with his willy-waving," she added with a forced smile. "But then I found out that Arthur had hurt his back in practice, and he needed a warming pad. I just came from his place."

"Is he okay?" Cynna asked.

"He's out of commission for at least a day or two, and he might not be able to play Saturday. It happened to him this summer, remember? He's such a baby."

Cynna didn't respond except to quietly get off the couch and go to her bedroom. Clark and Gwen stared at each other. Neither had any idea what to do. After several very awkward minutes, it became obvious that Cynna wasn't coming back.

Clark said good-bye and left.

Gwen shook her head, very confused as to what had just happened.

Clark sat in his car for a while before he drove off. He thought he should be upset that Gwen had interrupted things, but he didn't really think that anything would have happened.

He couldn't shake the feeling that Cynna was toying with him for some reason and that ultimately everything would prove to be a big tease - he still wasn't a prominent Greek.

CHAPTER 10

The next day, while riding the subway train and bus to school, Clark overheard people talking about a place called Aberfan and some tragedy that had happened there. It wasn't until he got to school that he found out that Aberfan was a small mining village in South Wales, and that the day before a mountain of rock and sludge had engulfed the village, burying men, women and children. It wasn't clear to him what could cause something like that, short of an earthquake. The tragedy devastated everyone, especially those from Wales like Gwen and Arthur. He didn't see them because they had already left for home to help in the rescue effort. Ironically, the rugby team that they were scheduled to play the next day was from the University of Cardiff, and they had canceled the match.

Clark wandered over to the student union at LSE, and the first person he saw was Nigel, loaded down with a large leather camera bag and a suitcase.

"I'm joining Gwen in Wales and taking some snaps for the news," he offered to Clark without being asked. "You should come help. It's just unbelievable how negligent that bloody mining board is."

Clark didn't have to come up with an answer or an excuse because Nigel immediately raced off to catch his train.

On Sunday, Clark drove to Bernadette's flat in Earls Court. The evening started off fairly quiet given the news of the past days, but it picked up considerably when Mags presented her new dinner creation - eggplant parmesan. Clark had never eaten eggplant and was surprised to find that despite its unique texture, he liked it. A few Peroni beers, imported from Italy, helped.

The women gave Clark a quick history lesson about Corsica and then waxed on about how beautiful it was, the great weather and nice people. It was obvious to Clark that Mags felt homesick, but Bernadette not as much.

"One thing I don't understand," Clark said to them. "Your island is mostly Italian, also a lot of French, but your English is wonderful, and it's more American than British."

"Roberta," both women responded immediately, and then laughed. Mags continued, "Roberta was an American nurse during the war. After Corsica was liberated, it became a big air base for the Americans. Roberta was stationed there, and she fell in love with a Corsican, who it turned out, had unfortunately been a collaborator with the fascists. He was arrested after the war and became one of several who were eventually hanged."

Bernadette picked up the story. "She said that she debated between suicide, going into a convent, or a brothel, and she chose us."

"But…" Mags prompted, and Bernadette continued. "But she was a terrible whore. She fell in love with all her clients, so our mother convinced her to use her medical skills to be our nurse and our nanny. She taught us all English, and she became fluent in Italian and French."

"And no one ever gets a disease from the Ochera women," Mags boasted.

It was an unusually warm evening for late October, and Mags suggested that Clark take Bernadette for a drive while she cleaned up and went to bed. Bernadette wanted to help clean up, but Mags insisted. As they drove away from Earls Court, Clark asked her if there was somewhere she wanted to go.

"Well, I'd love to see where you live, if that's okay. Unless you have women tied up in the closet for sex slaves or other kinky stuff," she teased, barely able to hold back her laughter.

Clark grinned and tried to remember what condition the flat was in. He certainly hadn't anticipated having a guest. "No sex slaves, but a lot of dirty clothes and dishes."

"Ah, the typical male abode. I can't wait." She kept up a steady commentary on what she saw as he drove through Hyde Park and then north toward Hampstead. He took a slight detour through the Heath and then up Hampstead High Street, which for a Sunday evening seemed unusually busy with a mix of natives and tourists.

Pleased to learn that she was his first visitor to the flat, she forgave him for the man-sized mess. "Well, it's certainly lived-in." She laughed as he swept books and dirty clothes from the couch so they could sit.

He wanted to offer her something to drink, but he didn't have anything. He kicked himself for not being stocked for company with beer and wine. Recently, one evening after practice, he had gone to the flat shared by Arthur and Charles and had been impressed that they had an extra refrigerator just for beer and wine. That evening had been fun, but he had felt weird vibes coming from Arthur for quite a few weeks. And it seemed like they had been getting stronger. Several men on the team mentioned that Arthur had changed, so he tried to not take it personally.

"So any progress beyond kissing with the Greek?" Bernadette teased him as they sat on the couch and listened to Otis Redding's album *Otis Blue*.

He shook his head. "I made a move on a breast, but she was still sore from her period."

"Really? Didn't she say that the week before also?"

"Yeah. Isn't that normal?"

"Maybe for Greek women, but not for any others." She noticed his confusion and concern, so she backed off the topic and slid closer to him. "So maybe you're not doing the kissing correctly. Why don't you show me your technique?" She leaned toward him and kissed him. It only took a moment before he eagerly responded. Friends or whatever, she was really good-looking, and he had become almost blasé about her profession.

"Okay, your technique is quite satisfactory," she reported, as she came up for air.

He paused and wondered if this was a test. He leaned toward her, and she answered his question as she quickly met his lips with hers.

She noticed that his little Yank had started to come to attention, but she didn't make a move toward it. As far as she was concerned, kissing was still within the bounds, the very loosely defined bounds, of friendship. She'd probably even include a blowjob in that category, but she knew that she didn't want to go that far. Not for her own sake, but because he seemed so confused over his feelings for the various women in his life. She wondered where she fit in, but she knew that Mags was right that he would never be able to reconcile romantic feelings for her with her profession.

He moved his hand and cupped her breast, then waited to see if she objected. When she didn't, he carefully unbuttoned a couple of buttons on her shirt and tentatively kissed her bare breasts.

She remembered that he had done really nicely with her breasts that first night, and she relaxed and enjoyed it for a few minutes. Still friends, she thought to herself, but she knew that she had to stop because of what should logically happen next. Reluctantly, she pulled him off and looked him in the eyes. "I think we should stop now, before we can't."

He knew she was right, but that didn't make it easy. It helped immensely that there wasn't any awkwardness between them.

As October rushed to an end, the weather shifted from unseasonably warm to more typically cold and wet. Clark had heard about the miserable weather in London from Rita, and it arrived like an unwelcome guest. In the gray light and bitter wet wind, everything lost its color and seemingly its very life. People on the street, never that cheerful to each other in the best weather, became downright hostile as they thrust their umbrellas around like medieval shields. Clark had learned to hate umbrellas when they lived in Seattle. But people in Seattle had never used them as aggressively as did Londoners as they rushed down the crowded sidewalks.

As much as the color and the life seemed to be sucked out of everyone and everything outdoors, Clark was surprised by the increased warmth and vitality that people exhibited when they were inside the pubs. Everyone seemed more friendly and energetic in a place of refuge from the depressing elements. Clark wondered if that explained the high rate of alcoholism in the country.

Most of the people in the traditional pubs, however, were middle-age. To find people his own age, Clark had to go to the college pubs or get invited to the small gatherings, parties, that happened nightly in hundreds, maybe thousands, of flats across the city. And a significant element of student life was the availability of a variety of stimulants. There was alcohol, mostly beer and wine, a cigarette in every mouth, a lot of marijuana, a little LSD, and occasionally cocaine. Clark had smoked marijuana a couple of times and enjoyed that feeling, which often helped him relax, let down his barriers, and be the fun, happy-go-lucky person he often wanted to be but normally found hard to do. Cocaine was another matter. Most students, including Clark, looked down on cocaine as the drug of choice for the unemployed, homeless, addicts who lived in the train stations, or for bored housewives - mother's little helper as the Rolling Stones called it. LSD, on the other hand, held a strong allure for many students. Outrageous tales of weird experiences while on LSD spread daily through student unions and college pubs all over London. Students recounted stories of being in enhanced, outlandishly creative states while on LSD. The music and psychedelic art popular with university students strongly reflected this drug-based sensitivity. Being all the rage, it was hard to resist.

Clark had been invited to a gathering the second weekend after the Aberfan disaster. Gwen and Arthur hadn't returned from Wales, and Cynna had been unavailable since the night that Gwen found them on the couch. Mrs. Rovsek always answered their phone and said that Cynna was otherwise engaged. It was a scheduled off-weekend for rugby, which meant that they had gone two weeks without a game, and Clark missed it.

Erin lived in a flat in Kings Cross, just north of the university. Clark knew her from the creative writing course. He had asked Bernadette if she was going, but she had to work. His natural inclination was not to go alone, but he felt fairly comfortable around Erin. He had been assigned to read and critique her story, and he had liked it a lot. The female protagonist, an actress, reminded him of his sister. They shared a number of quirky personality traits.

As he entered the small, one-bedroom flat, he smelled the pungent odor of marijuana smoke mixed with the cigarette smoke. It hung visibly in the air. The room was crowded and loud, with people talking while Etta James played in the background. He recognized a few students from class, but many of the people were strangers. Most of them were women, and everybody seemed to be already drunk, high or both.

Erin, a cute second-year from Scotland, approached him, gave him a hug, which seemed like more than a simple friend-hug, and thrust a marijuana joint in his hand. He took a big toke and immediately began to relax. She left him with the joint and moved on across the room. Occasionally pausing to take a toke on the joint, Clark worked his way over to a table with soft drinks and wine. He noticed a man standing there, but as he got closer, he realized it was actually a woman with very short dark hair and dark-rimmed glasses, wearing a man's suit. She gave him a neutral stare and moved a half-step over to give him room to reach the table. He could feel her watching him as he poured a glass of white wine.

"The red is much better," advised the short-haired woman.

"Red often upsets my stomach."

"Probably the tannic acid. Happens to some people."

He turned to look at her and was met with a direct stare.

"Are you the Yank from Erin's writing class? The one with the story about the prostitute."

"Guilty." He put out his hand. This person struck him as someone you shake hands with. "Clark."

She took his hand with a very strong grip. "Micah, Erin's roommate, and lover."

Clark searched for a response. "Nice to meet you," seemed safe.

"I thought I'd get that out there just in case you were thinking of trying to jump her. She might come on to you a little because she said that your story makes her randy, but now you know what you need to know."

"Good to know. Thanks."

Before he could leave, she continued, "Most guys want to boff her because she's cute and sweet. But when they find out she's a lesbian, they get really turned on. It's a conquest thing.

They think they're so studly that they can convert her or save her. You know, bring her back from the heart of darkness."

Clark thought she might be trying to add a little humor, but it didn't really work. He took a sip of wine and looked for a way to escape. He wasn't completely surprised by the lesbian thing because the heroine in Erin's story was homosexual, and she had written a pretty graphic lesbian sex scene.

"You do think she's hot don't you? I mean completely fuckable, right? And I mean if you do prostitutes that means you'll put your knob in anything, right?"

Clark started to get angry, but then he realized that she was referring to his story and Tildi the laundromat housewife prostitute. "It's just a story."

"Well, we write what we know, right? I'm a writer myself, short stories and such. I've had a lot of stuff published in *Counter Culture*. You know that magazine?"

He didn't, but he nodded. "Hey that's cool," he said, and casually moved away. He didn't leave the party immediately because he had to admit that he did think Erin was pretty hot and that had been partly, or maybe mostly, the reason he had come to her party. The possibility that she might be interested in him, despite her normal sexual persuasion, made him stay. In her story, the main character had just decided to see what it would be like to have sex with a guy.

He had been in London - swinging, free-love London - for two months now and things were mostly great, but he remained a virgin. The one girl he had actually dated was a total enigma. The only reason that he hadn't become a sexual basket case was that he somehow had found a friend-with-benefits relationship with a beautiful young prostitute and her hot sister. And now here he stood, slightly high, in a flat full of lesbians. He didn't imagine that it could get any stranger, until it did.

Erin suddenly let out a piercing scream and started to race around the room, stripping her clothes off as she went. Her scream turned into a laugh and then a song that started off sounding like a Beatles song but then wasn't. After she'd shed her bra and panties, she stood naked in the middle of the room. She began to twirled around. Faster and faster she twirled until finally dizzy she crumpled on the floor.

Clark started to move to help her, but Micah grabbed his arm.

"She's tripping, she'll be okay. We got some radical acid. I dropped a tab two days ago, and I'm just coming down now. Fucking intense man."

Clark watched, mesmerized, as Erin stood up and began to rub her hands over her body in a very aggressive sexual way. All the while she reacted to and talked about things that weren't there. Shapes and patterns that she saw on the plain white walls. An animal horn growing out of one woman's head. And red lights flashing, like break lights on a car, from another woman's breasts. And penises, she saw them everywhere, particularly on the women. When she fell to her knees in front of one woman and tried to suck on her penis, she got very frustrated. That negativity grew quickly, and soon she yelled at Micah for hiding her penis from her. Then she saw Clark and began to paw at his zipper. He backed away, but she pursued him yelling, "Don't tease me Clark! Give it to me or I swear I'll bite it off."

"Her baby, here's my penis, suck on this," Micah said, thrusting a rubber dildo at Erin, who eagerly grabbed it and tried to bite it in half. Then she spat it out. "Ugh, that tastes horrible, no more penises for me." She disappeared into the kitchen and returned with a big knife. Everyone backed away from her as she swung it around. It had been a good show, but now the vibe had changed and many people quickly left the flat.

"No more penises, I'm gonna cut them all off, starting with mine." As she tried to cut off her imaginary penis, the blade cut the skin on her inner thigh, and blood started to drip on the floor. At that point, the few people who remained in the flat headed for the door.

Clark was going with them. But then he saw Micah trying to get Erin's attention and distract her from doing further damage with the knife. He quietly changed direction and moved around behind Erin and crept toward her. Just before she realized that he was there, he grabbed her arms from behind and pinned them against her naked body. She struggled, and the knife almost cut Clark and then Micah, who tried to get it out of Erin's hand.

The knife finally secured, Micah kept talking to Erin while motioning for Clark to keep holding her. "Erin baby, no more penises, just Clark's, and he has a nice one that won't hurt you. I'm going to put on some music you like, and we can listen to that, right? Do you want to put some clothes back on?"

Erin vigorously shook her head and then tried to turn around to see Clark. "Did you fuck your prostitute yet? Is that how the story ends? Would you like to get your leg over me? I'm not a prostitute. You don't have to pay me. And Micah would like to watch. She loves to do that you know, but she doesn't like to fuck men, just women…"

Micah finally found the right record, and Beethoven's *Fifth Symphony* blasted from the speakers.

"Oh I love this music. Do you want to dance? But no dancing in clothes silly, you have to take off your clothes. Right after I go pee. I gotta pee something terrible. Want to watch me pee? I like to watch men pee, pee from penis, ha that's funny. I'm gonna do that now, right now…"

Clark jumped back as Erin urinated on the floor. Micah grabbed her hands and began to move her away from the puddle of urine and toward the couch.

"Micah is mad at Erin..." Like a helium balloon, finally deflated, Erin collapsed on the couch. Her eyes were still open, but she was clearly somewhere else.

"Watch her while I get some antiseptic and a bandage," Micah instructed Clark, who tried to convince himself that Erin wasn't actually dead. Her eyes had no life in them. Her breathing had become so shallow as to be barely discernable. The wound on her thigh seemed to have stopped bleeding.

"Holy shit," he said to himself as he caught himself staring at her bushy hair. He knew he had to get out of here.

"I can handle her now, the worst is over, I only gave her a quarter tab," Micah said, as she knelt in front of Erin and used a washcloth to wipe the blood from her crotch and legs. Micah paused to look up at him. "Thanks for staying and helping. You're okay, right?"

Clark nodded and moved across the room and out the door. He found his car and just sat there for a while. He had never imagined that LSD would do that to someone. He hoped that Erin wouldn't remember anything when the drug wore off. He couldn't believe how vulnerable she had been. In a different setting, different group, she might have screwed every guy in the room and never realized what she was doing. He shuddered at the thought of what would have happened if this had been a college fraternity party.

Clark arrived in Creative Writing class the next Wednesday eager to see Bernadette, and was disappointed when she didn't show up. Erin wasn't there either.

It had been a painfully slow week. The news from Aberfan had migrated off the front page of the newspaper, but Gwen and Arthur were still in Wales. Clark continued his pattern as an official second-year student - he cut his classes. But he didn't want to miss Creative Writing. He also went to the Philosophy of International Law class even though he didn't expect Cynna to be there. More than two weeks had passed since he had last seen her, and she still wouldn't talk to him. Mrs. Rovsek always said that Cynna wanted to talk but that unfortunately he just kept missing her. He no longer believed it.

Thursday night he went to a performance of *The Mousetrap*. Agatha Christy's who-dun-it play that had been performed for over ten years in the same West End theater. This theater also offered the reduced rate student tickets on Thursday nights. He enjoyed the performances because the actors seemed to be having such a good time. But in the end he got terribly frustrated because it all turned out to be contrived and convoluted with the sole purpose of never letting anyone guess the identity of the killer. Simple logic and deduction were useless because Christy didn't divulge key information. He was angry because he felt manipulated, cheated.

The weather broke on Friday and the sun paid a welcome visit. Clark took his camera and was about to head for Cambridge when he paused, wondering whether Gwen had actually said, "We could go." He enjoyed her company. So instead he drove 80 kilometers southeast to Dover and walked along the top and then along the base of the beautiful white cliffs. Nature was maybe his favorite photographic subject because it didn't talk back at him and demand to know why he took its picture. He actually did like taking candid photos of people, but only with a medium telephoto lens so he could maintain some distance from the subject. One of his idols, photographer Ansel Adams, wrote that great photos of people only came with a close-up lens, but Clark couldn't make himself do that. After it got dark, he spent a few hours in a wonderful old pub in Dover before he drove home. He felt a little guilty about skipping rugby practice, but he had been there the days before in the rain, so he felt entitled to take a day off. And Arthur, the real taskmaster of the team, wasn't there to kick anyone's butt.

The good weather lasted through the rugby match against the University of Liverpool the next day. Clark had developed a solid comfort level with the game, the rules and strategy. He scored two tries and made a number of tackles. He knew he still had lots to learn, but he felt good that he had become a real contributor to their winning season.

In the locker room after their win, he overheard a couple of players talk about a team visiting England from the United States for a series of friendly matches. The UL might be invited to play. Before he got a chance to ask about it, Charles took him aside to make sure that he knew about the upcoming trip to Amsterdam and Paris. Charles said he thought that it was during a big American bank holiday, and he didn't know whether Clark might be going home. Clark realized that Charles referred to Thanksgiving, and he assured him that he was committed to the rugby trip and looking forward to it.

Later in the pub Clark realized that without Gwen and Cynna he felt bored with the after-game scene. There were plenty of unattached women; tarts and scrubbers as Gwen called them. But most of them were well on their way to being sloppy drunk. So he went home early.

His plan for Sunday had been to spend some time photographing on the Heath, but the weather turned foul again, and he spent a quiet day reading and working on a new story for class. He wanted to get inside the head of someone on an LSD trip, with psychedelic images and stream-of-conscious thoughts and dialogue. But he wanted to do it without taking the drug himself. The story soon became more of a poem, a beat-poem in the vein of Allen Ginsberg, and he thought that he would now have a better understanding of *Howl* than he had had in high school. After a while he paused and wondered if Erin had any recollection of that night and whether she really found him attractive. That led him to work on another poem that dealt with his frustrations over Cynna, but it then subtly changed to a series of images that were more about Bernadette, and then, surprisingly, a little about Gwen.

CHAPTER 11

Clark entered the student union on Monday and saw Nigel and Gwen sitting at a table, engrossed in the twenty or more black-and-white contact sheets, printed on 8x10 photo paper, that were scattered about on the surface. Each contact sheet contained all the images from a single roll of 35mm film.

Clark screwed up his courage. "Welcome back," he offered, as he got to their table but before they noticed him.

Nigel looked like he was bothered by the interruption, but Gwen smiled and seemed like she meant it. "Clark, hi, join us, we're just going over Nigel's snaps from Aberfan to make a selection for a photo-article for the paper, maybe even a booklet. He's got some wonderful images."

Nigel liked the accolade and then accepted Clark as an audience. As Clark sat down, Nigel handed him some of the contact sheets. They were full of powerful, sensitive, beautiful, and horrific images. Unlike Clark, Nigel was obviously perfectly comfortable getting very close to his subjects. And he also had a wonderful eye for composition.

Clark was overwhelmed by the photos even before any work was done to turn them into prints. He could tell that they would become striking images of tragic subjects. "These are incredible."

"They really are Nigel, I'm so proud of what you've done." Gwen tenderly touched Nigel's arm, and he blushed a little.

"Can I ask who printed these? I've been looking for someone with a darkroom where I can work on my photos. I heard that there's maybe a student who goes here who has their own."

Nigel looked at him for a moment, then replied, "There is." Then he added with a little smile, almost a smirk, "Me."

"That's so cool. Do you ever, you know, rent it out. I could pay a little bit."

"Do you have darkroom experience? I don't have time to teach anyone."

"Yeah, loads. I shot for my college newspaper for two years, and we developed and printed all our own stuff."

"What do you shoot with?"

"A Nikon F mostly with a 105 lens."

"Just the one lens?"

"Well, no I also have a fifty, but that's all I can afford. Besides, you only use one at a time, and I'm pretty quick at changing." Clark tried to make it a joke but couldn't read Nigel's expression well enough to know whether to expect a laugh.

Nigel did chuckle a little. "Sure, after all the lend-lease you Yanks gave us, it's the least I can do. My room's large enough that we can work at the same time, and then I'll see if I can let you in by yourself. But that's also up to my father. The darkroom's in our house in Mayfair." Nigel's attention suddenly shifted across the room to where another student stood in the doorway. Clark recognized him from the group that had been with Nigel in the Aldwych theater. "I've got to go. Gerald's going to catch me up on what Cohen has been doing so we can complete our petition to have him sacked. Meet me at number two Brooks Mews on Thursday at six o'clock, and we'll see what we see." As Nigel finished he had pulled his contact sheets back together, and then he rushed off to join Gerald.

Gwen turned her attention to Clark and asked cautiously, "Can you go Thursday evening? Isn't that when you and Cynna normally go out?"

"Well, actually I haven't seen her since you left. I call but can never reach her."

Gwen watched him and tried to determine how he felt about that. He didn't appear to be terribly upset, but she decided to drop the subject.

Arthur was also back, and he tore into rugby practice with a vengeance. He accused all of his forwards of slacking off while he was gone. He was tense and angry, and they attributed it to the stress of working in Aberfan. He had been digging in rubble for weeks with nothing but dead bodies to show for it.

At the end of practice, Arthur and Charles announced that they had filled the upcoming off-weekend with a friendly match against a team from an American university. A couple of guys groaned because they had made plans for the free weekend, but most of them were excited and eager to play after two weeks off. And then they all looked at Clark, who shrugged his shoulders. He had barely heard of rugby before he arrived in London.

"This team played here last fall and won a lot of games, beat Oxford, Cambridge and Greenwich." Then Charles added, "And they even sound like an English team, named after the bloody Earle of Dartmouth."

Clark blurted out, "Damn, that's my college. I didn't know we had a rugby team."

Clark worried about Bernadette and why she had missed another class. He knew she and Mags hadn't planned to go back home again so soon, but maybe something had happened to their mother. Something that might cause Bernadette to stay in Corsica for good.

Despite the miserable weather that afternoon, the upcoming game against Dartmouth motivated Clark to go to practice. The air felt saturated and wet and hung heavy on everything like a soggy, cold blanket. It seemed impossible that it wasn't actually raining.

Before and after practice, Arthur and Charles tried to get information from Clark about the Dartmouth team and seemed unable to believe that he didn't know anything. He tried to explain that most students at the small college would be equally clueless because rugby wasn't a varsity sport with a fan base, not like the football team.

Brooks Mews was situated in the block between Grosvenor Square and Claridge's Hotel, one of the finest and most expensive hotels in London. It was a short, narrow, cobblestoned street that would be called an alley in an American city. Nigel's house, a large stone mansion surrounded by a tall iron fence, was one of only four homes on the mews, and was by far the most impressive.

Clark double-checked the address before he pressed the button on an intercom at the gate. Its harsh buzzing sound alerted a formidable-looking security guard who appeared almost immediately and curtly demanded to know Clark's business. For a moment Clark feared that he had either stammered his explanation beyond comprehension or that Nigel had forgotten their appointment because the stone-faced guard didn't respond. Then, without a word or change of expression, the guard opened the heavy iron gate and allowed Clark to enter. The iron gate slammed closed behind him, causing Clark to involuntarily flinch. The guard gestured at Clark's bag, clearly intending to examine its contents. Satisfied that it contained only several dozen canisters of 35mm film and a new box of photographic paper, he motioned Clark toward the house. Clark headed down a short walk to a large wooden front door, which opened before Clark reached it. An elderly uniformed butler gave him a cautious examination before he motioned for Clark to enter. From a large center hallway, the butler showed Clark into a room immediately on the right. The first things that Clark noticed about the room were the antique furnishings, carved woodwork, and old leaded glass windows - all beautiful and obviously very old and expensive. Then he was struck by the incongruity of the modern artwork that hung on all the walls and sat on every surface, including two large metal sculptures standing on the floor. Clark's only exposure to modern art had been trips to the Museum of Modern Art in New York when he was fourteen and an art history course he took in college. But that proved more than enough to justify his impression that he was looking at an incredible collection of masterpieces by some of the most famous modern artists of the century.

"My mum was a modern art fancier," stated Nigel, who had quietly appeared behind Clark. "My da puts the best ones in here to impress visitors."

"Well, it certainly works." Clark smiled to try to counter the stoic, maybe painful look on Nigel's face. It didn't work.

"Come on, my darkroom's in the cellar."

Clark pictured a cellar as a dark, dank, place where the secrets of an English household were buried, not the warm, well-lit area he entered at the bottom of a wide staircase. They crossed a recreation room that put to shame any he had ever seen. Not one, but two billiard tables sat in one area, and a bar as large as those found in some pubs stood in another. Both a ladies and a men's bathroom were marked by signs in several different languages. At the back end of the room, a heavy black curtain hung across a doorway that led to the darkroom area.

Immediately behind the curtain was a small lobby with two chairs, a small couch, and a table. To the left Clark saw a room for developing film. On the right, Nigel showed him a larger room containing three enlargers spaced out along a counter top. Along the opposite wall there was a large trough-like sink that held trays for the developing chemicals, and several prints lay in the fixer and wash trays. Next to it was a drying rack that held five or six black-and-white prints. A single red safelight glowed from the ceiling in the center of the enlarger room. Clark couldn't believe that all of this was for one person.

Nigel hadn't said much except to point out the obvious as they made their way. Clark couldn't decide whether Nigel's tone of voice was condescending or maybe apologetic. "I assume you need to develop your film first."

Clark nodded and headed for the small developing room. He looked around and saw all he needed and turned back to Nigel, but Nigel had returned to the enlarger room and closed the door. Clark knew that he was being tested to see if he knew what he was doing. There were four developing reels and tanks, so he grabbed four canisters of exposed film from his bag and arranged them next to the reels and tanks so he could access them after he turned out the light. This first part of the developing process had to be done in complete darkness. He shut the door and turned out the light, then waited a moment for his eyes to adjust so he could confirm that no light spilled in anywhere.

Clark had developed hundreds of rolls of film, so the process had become automatic for him. As he waited for the developed film to dry, he wondered how Nigel's family had gotten so wealthy. The house and artwork were certainly impressive. Yet Nigel didn't dress or behave like a child of privilege. Even his often haughty tone of voice was common enough among Londoners of all backgrounds and income levels.

Clark debated whether to spend time developing more film or to work on some prints. Developing film was necessary but boring, while printing was creative and exciting. There had been many times when he had spent entire nights in the darkroom, so entranced that he felt like he had only been there a couple of hours. That had been one reason, besides the frat parties and trips to see Rebecca at Green Mountain Junior College, that his grades had suffered sophomore year.

He knocked on the door to the printing room to see if it was okay to enter.

"Just a second, I'm still in the develop bath," Nigel responded.

After a few minutes the door opened, and Clark entered to see more finished prints hanging up to dry and others in the fixer and wash baths.

Clark moved to the enlarger furthest from where Nigel worked.

"Use this one," Nigel said, as he pointed to the enlarger next to his. "It has a better lens." As Clark looked over the enlarger, Nigel handed him a pane of glass the size of the 8x10 photo paper. "You can use this for contact prints."

Clark made his contact sheets and then glanced at his images and tried to decide which shot to work on first. One roll had a lot of early tourist stuff; another was from the protest where he first met Gwen - including the out-of-focus shots of the bobbie who had grabbed her. He had been eager to see the shot of Gwen on the bridge at Oxford, but it wasn't on the rolls that he had developed. Finally, he picked an image, a dramatic shot of the cliffs at Dover, and began to work on it. Nigel periodically glanced over at what he was doing. Clark soon knew that he had picked the wrong image because, while it was a good composition, it had challenging areas of contrast that required special work. And for that he needed his hand-made burning and dodging tools, which he had left in the states. He ran a test strip for exposure and then was prepared to change images.

"Here you can use these," Nigel offered, sliding an assortment of professional burning and dodging tools over toward Clark. Another test.

"Thanks." Clark selected the burning tool and adjusted the opening to a circle of about a half-inch in diameter. The next test strip turned out okay but not great. Then he over-compensated on the next one before getting it right. Finally, he tried a full print, and a decent image began to appear in the developing bath. All the while Nigel worked on his own prints, clearly from Aberfan, but Clark knew that he was watching him.

"Nice photo. I always over-compensate myself," Nigel commented, his condescending tone almost gone.

Clark didn't know how much time passed until he glanced at his watch and saw that it was two o'clock in the morning. They had been there eight hours, and he and Nigel had formed a solid mutual admiration society, each appreciative of the other's artistic interests.

Besides his unique eye for news photos, Nigel obviously had strong feelings for the underdog, the underserved, and the underclass who lived virtually unseen on the fringes of society. And he wasn't afraid to get close to them. His photos were powerful statements, social and political commentaries that would make many people uncomfortable and maybe compel them to react.

Clark's photos, on the other hand, reflected his tendency to observe and not get involved. He loved design and context, both with larger objects, buildings and landscape but also with close-up detail. He didn't completely avoid people, but they were generally a part of the composition and not the central focus of it.

Clark didn't have any classes the next day, but he did have to go to practice so he stopped printing new shots and began to pack up while his final prints dried.

"I'll tell Reginald to let you in any time you want to come over and work," Nigel said, as he walked Clark to the front door.

"Your parents won't mind?"

Nigel shook his head. "No, it's fine. When he's home, he's always upstairs, except when there's some party or event going on, but that's not too often anymore."

Clark reached his car just minutes before it was going to be towed to clear the road for the overnight street sweeper. He struggled to stay awake as he drove home, but underneath the exhaustion he felt great, a satisfying sense of accomplishment.

The Dartmouth rugby players may have been rejects from the football team, as Clark imagined, but they were still plenty fast and strong. Their starting fifteen were easily a match for the UL starting fifteen, and the score was tied thirteen all at the half. A significant difference was that the Dartmouth team still seemed energetic and fit on their sideline, while many of the players on the UL team were tired and winded. Clark felt okay, but the English players' laid-back approach to fitness and their aggressive approach to drinking and smoking clearly affected them.

The UL players somehow found and expended a reserve of energy at the start of the second half and raced to a ten-point lead before they collapsed like wet ragdolls. Arthur and Charles tried to encourage them, but they were done. Dartmouth quickly made up the ten-point deficit and moved to a three-point lead. It was about to be a six-point advantage as the Dartmouth left winger got the ball and tried to get past Clark, who was in a good position to tackle him until he juked to the outside and forced Clark to lunge at him. They both fell to the ground, and Clark felt a sharp pain as his right ankle twisted, and the Dartmouth player rolled over on it. To avoid a penalty, Clark tried to get up and get out of the way of the scrum that had to form around the ball. But he couldn't stand on his ankle and collapsed back to the ground. The referee's whistle stopped play, and Charles ran up to Clark.

"It's my ankle," Clark barely managed to explain through his clenched teeth.

Charles helped him up and supported him so Clark could stand with his weight on his good leg. Leaning on Charles, Clark hobbled over to the sideline and collapsed on the bench. He felt light-headed from the throbbing pain, and then his body began to shiver in the cold air.

Gwen hurried over, took off her coat, and put it around Clark's shoulders. It was far too small, but it helped some. "Deep breaths. Slowly in and out," she urged. "There are some crutches in the athletic office, I'll be right back."

He didn't know how long she was gone, nor did he notice how the game had somehow ended with a UL victory.

The Dartmouth captain came over to Clark. "Your captain just told me that you're from big D. Sorry about the ankle. You played great. If you're back in Hanover next year, come play with us."

Just then Gwen arrived with the crutches. She had also found a blanket, which she wrapped around his shoulders in place of her coat. With help from Charles, she got Clark out to the street and into a taxi, which she instructed to go to the nearby Royal Hospital. Clark was in too much pain to do anything but let Gwen take charge.

"Hang on, we'll be in casualty in a moment," Gwen said, as she held his hand in the back seat of the taxi.

"It's not that bad, is it?" Clark responded, with a weak attempt at humor, not sure if he had heard her right. He didn't want to face his fear that his ankle was broken. The ramifications of that were too many and too awful to contemplate.

Gwen didn't respond because she concentrated on giving directions to the Pakistani taxi driver.

In the emergency room, Gwen never left Clark's side as he checked in, and then after a short wait, got an initial examination and was taken off for x-rays. When he came out of the x-ray room, they took him to a patient room. Gwen was already there. They didn't talk much, as he struggled to deal with the throbbing pain, exacerbated by the twisting and pulling done by the doctor and then the x-ray technician. When the pain killers finally began to take effect, he realized that she had held his hand for almost the entire time. Finally, the shock, the pain, the pain killers, and the warm blankets on the bed combined to drag him into a light asleep.

When he woke up, it took him a moment to figure out where he was. He didn't know how long he'd been asleep, but Gwen still sat on the chair by the side of the bed. "What time is it?"

"Almost nine," she replied with a poorly suppressed yawn. "You've been asleep over an hour."

"Thank you so much for helping. But you don't have to stay. You must be exhausted."

"Don't be daft. The doctor said that your ankle isn't broken, merely badly sprained and you should be okay in a fortnight. They're going to give you your own crutches and a walking boot."

"Wow, I missed all that?"

"They were going to wake you, but I told them they could tell me, that I was your sister."

"Well sis," he said, hoping that he smiled, but not sure that he pulled it off, "I don't know how I'm going to pay the bill. My wallet's back in the locker room. But I would love to get out of here. I really don't like hospitals."

"Oh, there's no bill. It's national health, and it covers you because you're a full-time student resident. You just have to come back with your passport to prove your visa status, but anytime in the next month is all right." Clark had grown so comfortable living in England that he had almost forgotten he was a foreigner on a student visa.

After a quick stop at the university so Gwen could run into the locker room and get his clothes and keys, a taxi deposited them at Clark's flat. Gwen helped him in.

Clark had been keeping things cleaner, or at least neater, after the embarrassing evening with Bernadette, and Gwen seemed impressed with the condition of the flat. Clark quickly explained who the flat belonged to before gently pushing her out to go home. He watched from the window as she got into the waiting taxi. Then he took another pain pill and struggled through a quick shower before collapsing on his bed. And despite the throbbing pain, he managed to fall asleep.

Ten o'clock the next morning, someone knocked on the door to the flat. He eventually heard it through the thick painkiller induced haze in his brain. He tried to hop on one leg, but cursed loudly when he fell against the dresser. Retrieving his crutches, he finally got to the door and opened it to see Bernadette.

She had the remnants of a large bruise on the left side of her face, her left eye still a little black and blue. "How's your ankle?" she asked.

"What happened to you?" he blurted out, not registering her question.

"Oh, just a bit of an accident," she replied with a shrug and a forced smile.

His imagination went into overdrive. "Did, did someone do this, hit you?" He couldn't stop the protective impulse from taking over. "My God, how can you…"

"Relax mate, it's not what you think. Yes, it was a client, but totally an accident, just an overly passionate Spaniard. I'm thinking of putting them on my banned list along with the Germans." She tried to make light of it and hoped that Mags hadn't been right to predict that Clark would overreact. But so far it didn't look good.

Clark struggled to keep control of his anger. He couldn't understand how she could be so nonchalant about getting injured. Fortunately, the lingering effect of the pain pills helped to keep his emotions in check. And then his brain realized that he had inadvertently stood on his bad ankle. The pain took over, and he would have collapsed if Bernadette hadn't grabbed his arm.

"Sit down," she said, as she guided him to the couch. "And put your leg up." She pulled the coffee table closer, then lifted his leg and placed it on the table. "Do you have pain meds?"

He nodded toward the bedroom, and a moment later she came back with his pills and got a glass of water from the kitchen. He took a pill and leaned back on the couch, closing his eyes. She gently lifted his leg and place a pillow on the table, under his ankle. They then sat in silence for several minutes.

He struggled with his reaction to her bruise. He hated to see her hurt and hated that it was an occupational hazard for her. But he kept telling himself that it was her choice. He knew that as a friend he should support her and not try to control her, but it was really hard to do. I'm not Nestor, he told himself, this is real life, not a movie.

"I'm sorry I overreacted," he offered tentatively, his eyes still shut. "I just hate to see you get hurt."

Hah! Mags, you were wrong! Bernadette silently rejoiced, and then she leaned over, gave him a kiss on his cheek, and took his hand in hers. "I don't like to see you get hurt either. And most likely you're hungry. I brought some food from Mags." She opened her bag and took out a fancy tin hot-food container. She took it to the kitchen and returned a few minutes later with a plate full of lasagna.

The great smell overwhelmed him, and he realized that he hadn't eaten in almost twenty-four hours. He quickly devoured several large bites. "For someone who's mostly French, she sure does know how to cook Italian food," he mumbled. After shoveling in more food, he remembered his manners. "Do you want some?"

She laughed. "Oh no, I ate earlier, that's all for you. And I put some more in your refrigerator for later. You'll just need to heat it."

The pain pill and the food helped him gain some clarity of thought. "So how did you know about my ankle?" He turned toward her in time to see her sheepish, guilty look.

"I was at the match and saw you get hurt."

"You were? I didn't see you."

"I stood on the other side." She paused, then confessed completely. "I've actually been to several of your matches."

"But why didn't you tell me or come on our side? Or were you cheering for the other team?" He tried to joke, but it fell flat.

"I wanted… I want to keep our friendship separate, apart from your, you know, normal life. I don't think your mates would really understand."

"But we're in class together, and people know we're friends."

Bernadette couldn't explain the apparent contradiction. She didn't have any sense of embarrassment about her profession. She knew what most people thought of prostitutes, and the images they had about them. But she also knew that their images didn't normally include people like her. She refused to have to explain it or justify it to anyone, and she liked Clark because she hadn't had to do that with him. But more importantly, she didn't want to put him in a position where he felt like he had to defend her reputation. And she was pretty sure that he would try to do that. "Yes, but it's different. And it also involves Cynna and Gwen, which makes it … difficult."

Clark acknowledged that and tried to accept it without completely understanding it.

Not normally a very good patient, Clark had plenty of motivation to take care of his ankle and get better. He desperately wanted to make the trip to Amsterdam and Paris with the rugby team. And more importantly, he wanted to play, not just hobble along as a spectator.

For the first week he struggled to fight off depression because it seemed like the ankle wasn't getting any better. He kept testing it by putting weight on it, but then he realized that the testing probably wasn't helping. So he resigned himself to spending hours on the couch with his foot elevated. He tried to look on it as a positive. He caught up on and actually got ahead in his reading for all of his courses - even for the two courses that he didn't attend anymore. And he finished his final revision of the story about the prostitute mom and a good first draft of his story/poem about the girl on LSD. He had accepted, with Bernadette's prodding, that he couldn't submit the LSD story/poem to class because of Erin. So he had begun another story about a reclusive photographer for whom photos appear in the darkroom - photos that he hasn't taken. Later he encounters the same scenes, same people, in real life. It was his first effort with fantasy and he liked the creative freedom it gave him.

For the first time since he'd lived there, he used Rita's television for more than just the news and weather on the BBC. He found a few shows that were entertaining enough to pass some time. He particularly liked the spy thriller *The Saint* with its Robin Hood-type character who stole from criminals. And even though science-fiction wasn't his favorite genre, he was captivated by *Doctor Who* and his space and time travel, world-saving, adventures.

He had frequent visits from Bernadette and a couple from Gwen. He worried about what he would do if they happened to arrive at the same time. Bernadette knew all about Gwen, but Gwen didn't know that Bernadette existed. And he sensed that Bernadette was correct when she advised him to keep it that way. One afternoon, Bernadette had just left when Gwen arrived. The timing was so close that he was sure that they must have passed each other in the stairway or on the front walk.

When Bernadette was there she took charge and pampered him like he was family. She chastised him for being a slob while she picked up and cleaned. After she finished cleaning, she was hot and casually stripped off her clothes and took a shower. Clark watched and admired her body and struggled unsuccessfully to avoid getting aroused.

When Gwen was there she seemed uncomfortable and unsure of what she should do. She never asked how he had been able to clean the flat or who had prepared the food she saw in his refrigerator. She always had an agenda like getting his passport information for the list she was compiling for border crossings and hotel registrations, or getting a progress report on his recovery to give to Arthur and Charles. It was all stuff that could have been done over the telephone, but Clark welcomed the distraction and never questioned why she made the trip.

When Clark woke up on Sunday morning, a week after he was injured, he finally felt a major improvement. He could stand on his ankle and walk slowly with very little discomfort.

Stir-crazy from being cooped up in the flat, he put on the walking boot and slowly walked to the store. He didn't need anything because Bernadette had done the shopping the day before. He just needed to get out. But he soon realized that he had overdone it, and when he got back home and collapsed on the couch, he swore at himself for being so stupid.

Bernadette came over that evening, and this time she had Mags with her. And with Mags came dinner. As they ate, he was thankful that Bernadette didn't chastised him too much for taking the walk. She clearly thought he was crazy, but she kept it light.

During dinner they discussed the rugby trip to the continent. They were scheduled to departed on Thursday. Mags had been to Paris several times but not to Amsterdam. Bernadette hadn't been to either city, but she quickly said, "no," when Clark suggested that she go with them. Mags teased Bernadette by complimenting Clark on how clean he kept his flat and how unusual that was for a single man. It was all very comfortable and family-like.

"You know Clark," Mags said. "I have to admit that I was wrong about you. When Bernie first brought you over, I didn't believe that a normal guy could be friends with her, with us, and not want to control us or reform us or take advantage of us. And I've had some unfortunate experience in that area. Remember the blowjob I gave you that night?"

Clark nodded. How could he forget that?

"Well, that was actually a test, a test to see if you would then try to take advantage of us and expect more of the same. But you didn't. And then your reaction to Bernie's injury proved you are a friend who can keep it all in perspective."

Clark didn't know what to say, so he just smiled and nodded. He realized that at some point Bernadette had taken his hand in hers.

"And now I need some help with the ending of my story," Bernadette said as she squeezed his hand and then pulled her story from her bag. They spent the next hour debating whether the DJ should regain his hearing or not. The bigger decision, however, was whether he would acknowledge and accept the love of the girl. Bernie leaned toward no hearing and love, while Clark pushed for hearing and love. Mags was ambivalent on the hearing decision but thought their love was unrealistic, hopelessly romantic.

The next morning Clark felt like he could run and jump on his ankle. But still wary of a relapse, he stayed off of it most of the day. He was sitting on the couch, reading, and listening to *Highway 61*, when he heard someone at his door, and then Gwen called his name.

"Well, you're certainly looking much better," Gwen commented with a smile when he opened the door. "I brought our final itinerary for the trip, and I need to get your check for the expenses. I'm going to buy our train and ferry tickets tomorrow. And I'll pay the Paris hotel as a group when we leave. Oh yes, big news, in Amsterdam we're not staying in a hotel anymore. The team has arranged for us all to stay with the families of their players. Evidently they do that with some visiting teams. Arthur doesn't agree, but Charles and I think it's a good idea."

"You're going with us?" he asked.

"Yes, I'm the traveling secretary. The one who stays sober."

He laughed. "So rugby players are drunks the world over?"

"Well, in Amsterdam it's probably getting high on other things as well, but yes that's the truth of it. Oh, Charles said that even if you're better, not to practice but maybe work out in the weight room."

Clark nodded. He had thought the same thing. What he really wanted to do was to go to Nigel's darkroom, but he knew that he shouldn't spend hours standing at the enlarger. "I went to Nigel's to use his darkroom, week before last. It's quite a set-up. Have you ever been to his house?"

"Fucking incredible isn't it. His father's a mogul in the jewelry business in England and a lot of the Commonwealth. But that also means he has to deal with the bloody thugs who rule South Africa, so he can access his diamond mines. Nigel has a lot of issues with that and some other aspects of his father's business."

"Yeah, I got the impression that he and his father aren't all that close."

"It was better before his mum died last year during the holidays. That hit him bloody hard. She was an artist and understood Nigel. His father doesn't."

"Oh, I didn't know about his mother," Clark said, remembering all the art in the house. "He said that I could use the darkroom any time, but I don't think my ankle would like that."

"That means he must trust you. He's very protective of that darkroom."

CHAPTER 12

Clark couldn't wait to begin the trip to the continent. On his recent trip to Dover he had seen an automobile-ferry getting ready to depart for France. He had fought a strong impulse to hop aboard and see some of the rest of Europe where things - the people, languages, clothing, buildings, food - would be more unique, more foreign, then in England. Once on the other side of the English Channel he could drive anywhere - France, Italy, Switzerland, even Asia and Africa. All incredibly romantic and exciting.

When he arrived at the St. Pancras Rail Station to join the team, Gwen met him and immediately took his passport and gave him his ticket for the train to Dover. "I keep all the passports for border crossings and hotels and give you the ferry and train tickets as you need them. That way none get lost."

"Tickets or players?" he joked.

"Ha ha, very funny. Sad but bloody true. This isn't my first trip with you blokes. Most of you plonkers are like my brother, wake with a hangover and no money, no passport, no memory of the last twenty-four hours. But then look at you, nice passport case."

"Thanks," he said, and smiled as he remembered Bernadette's kiss when she had given it to him on Wednesday after class.

Gwen put his passport in a folio that she carried in a dark blue canvas satchel, hung across her left shoulder. It looked like the bags that the motorcycle couriers used as they sped around London. Her efficiency and common sense reminded him of his mother and how she had kept his family together during their many moves. He then felt bad that he hadn't written home in a while and hadn't thought to do so when he had been sitting around the flat so much.

"Can I take your suitcase?" He gestured to the bag at her feet that looked full and heavy.

She stared at him as if he had sprouted wings and hovered up in the rafters of the station. "Uh, well, thanks, that's very nice of you. We're all in the third car from the last, number 5433."

As he got on the train, Clark looked around at the players who were already there. He had never seen them this early in the morning, and many of them looked extremely tired or painfully hung-over. Arthur looked the worse, but he didn't look like he was tired or hung-over as much as distraught. He sat alone by the window, and no one bothered him. It was Gwen who finally took the seat next to him, right before the train began to move.

Clark had found a seat next to Robert, who was naturally quiet like Clark and respected silence. Unfortunately, they were in the seat immediately in front of Heath, who kept making disparaging comments about the Negro players they would face in Amsterdam and Paris. Clark hadn't heard him say anything, but wondered if Heath had made similar comments about the black players on the Dartmouth team.

The dark, dull-gray morning light didn't enhance the view from the windows of the train as it passed through the bleak industrial heart of London and then into the congested commercial areas between London and Dover. Clark recalled the view on his recent drive to Dover, and marveled at how much better the country looked from the roadway than the railway.

As the team prepared to leave the train in Dover, Clark grabbed Gwen's suitcase and wouldn't let her carry it. "You keep us organized, and I'll be the bag-man."

The train station in Dover was only a few blocks, through the tourist area, from the ferry dock, but the process of moving the group required almost an hour. Twice Gwen had to pull a player from a shop and once from a pub. They finally managed to get on the ferry just as the final whistle blew. Because they boarded late, they couldn't find many seats together. Clark found one next to an old woman who smelled like mothballs and kept muttering to herself in what sounded to him like German.

Clark had done a lot of pleasure boating when he had lived in Seattle and Los Angeles, so he hadn't anticipated any problems with seasickness. There was only a moderate chop on the Channel, but the large ferry had a different motion through the waves than did the small boats that Clark was used to. The musty smell of the old woman, combined with the odor of diesel fuel from the engine room, added to the motion of the ferry and made his stomach queasy. He went outside to get some air. On the deck, near the bow of the ferry, he found Gwen who looked a little green. "Are you okay?" he asked, as he approached.

"Oh, hi Clark," she stammered, as she turned toward him. "A bit of the collywobbles. I really don't like bloody boats, never have. At home, father and Arthur love to sail, but I hate it."

"Just keep looking at the horizon, that normally helps." He followed his own advice and then did feel better. It seemed to help Gwen as well. They stood quietly while the sun strained to break through the clouds. It succeeded just enough to warm the air a little and help them relax.

"Cynna considered coming on this trip, but last minute decided she wasn't up to it," Gwen said tentatively, barely loud enough to be heard over the steady noise of the ship, the sea, and the wind.

Clark slowly nodded his head in response. He certainly hadn't forgotten Cynna, but he had moved on. They had nothing in common, and sex was obviously never going to happen. And he felt hurt that she had so abruptly and arbitrarily ceased all communication. Despite his best efforts to rationalize things, he couldn't shake the feeling that he had probably done something wrong.

He felt his stomach rumble and hoped it was hunger and not sea-sickness. If it were hunger, it would have to wait for their arrival in Ostend, Belgium. No way would he eat anything on the ship.

After a while, Gwen said that she felt better and went inside to try to get warm. Clark found a place out of the wind and sat on the deck with his back leaning against the bulkhead. He stayed there for the rest of the trip. He only went inside once to use the head, where the strong smell of disinfectant only partially covered the lingering odor of someone's vomit. He barely made it out of there without getting sick himself.

The Belgium coast and then the town of Ostend slowly came into view during the last hour of the trip. The anticipation helped make the time go by quickly, and almost before he knew it, they were at the dock and ready to disembark.

Gwen seemed fully recovered as she herded the team through customs and the small port town toward the nearby train station. The street signs all offered a combination of Dutch, French and English. The signs on the stores were in Dutch and French, but typically had a notice in the window that English was spoken there to accommodate the tourists. While in many ways similar to Dover, Ostend had enough differences in the architecture to begin to satisfy Clark's desire to have a foreign experience.

Because he carried her bag and liked being with her, Clark gradually stepped into the role of Gwen's assistant. He couldn't answer many questions, but he could hand out the train tickets. Once on the train, he felt a little disappointed that she again sat with Arthur and not in the seat he had carefully kept open beside him. He heard her converse with the train conductor in what sounded to him like fluent French. He once again regretted his inability to speak or understand a foreign language.

Now early afternoon, he joined several teammates in the dining car of the train for a sandwich and a beer. The Belgium lager came in a bottle, and the taste was great, but the heavy carbonation disagreed with him. The carbonation didn't get easily absorbed in his stomach, but tried to escape back up his esophagus. He noticed that it affected others the same way, as loud belches began to resonate throughout the car. Martin managed to say, "god bless the queen," as part of one long gastric eruption. No one on the team noticed that the other passengers were not as amused by it as they were.

Back in the passenger car, Clark sat and watched the Belgium countryside flow by. The farms and the small towns they passed had the same combination of familiar and different that he had seen in the English countryside. He took his camera and snapped some pictures of the landscape.

After a brief stop in Antwerp, the train came to the border outside of Rotterdam where it stopped. The customs officials for the Netherlands came on board, and the passengers didn't have to get off the train. He watched Gwen as she efficiently used a combination of English and French to deal with the customs official. Clark looked out the window to see if there was a border wall or fence, but didn't see anything other than a sign to officially mark the change from one country to the other.

A while later, after a brief stop in The Hague, Clark noticed that Gwen seemed to be nervous again. She got up and headed toward the dining car. After a few minutes, he followed, trying to act as casual as he could. "Are you okay, can I do something to help?" he asked her, as he took a seat next to her at the small counter.

"I'm having second thoughts about this bloody staying-with-families thing. I don't know why I agreed to it. Charles argued convincingly that it would be good for international rugby diplomacy, which could bloody-well use some help."

"I'm sure it'll be fine, and it could be fun to get to know a Dutch family. I assume they all have a rugby player so they should know what we're like."

"Yeah, I suppose, but..."

He waited for her to finish.

"Normally we go to Paris and Brussels on this trip, but last year there was a cock-up in Brussels, and we weren't welcome to return."

"What happened?"

"Arnold, a third-year, and Martin shared a hotel room, and they destroyed it. Almost burned down the whole bloody hotel, and to escape, they ran naked through the central town square with the two slappers they had in their room." She had to stifle a laugh as she remembered the absurdity of the scene. "We had to wake the British consul at three in the fucking morning to get them out of jail." She relaxed a little as she told the tale. "I'm surprised that they let us land at Ostend and travel through the country," she finished, with a small, rueful laugh.

"Ah, now I understand why Charles and Arthur spent so much time after practice yesterday discussing our behavior on the trip."

"Well, I hope it sunk in."

Just before seven o'clock they finally stood outside the Amsterdam Central train station. Clark admired its gorgeous neo-Renaissance architecture and took several photos. The others on the team looked around to see if they could find a pub.

"Beautiful isn't it?" Gwen asked. "There should be a bus here from the university, but I don't see it."

Moments later an all-white school bus arrived, with blue letters on the side that read 'University of Amsterdam' in Dutch, French, German, and English. It took them to the student center for the university where they met the Amsterdam team members and their families. Gwen and the Amsterdam team manager had assigned members of the UL team to particular families based on language ability. Many players on the UL team spoke French, some spoke German, and others Spanish, which did little good in the Netherlands. Clark was the only one who spoke only English. But when the families had heard about an American on the team, they all wanted to host him. The captain of the team, Isaac Rutte, had promptly claimed Clark for his family.

The Rutte family now stood and looked down at Clark. They were all tall, especially Isaac and his father who were easily six-foot-three or four. Mrs. Rutte was six-feet or a little more, and the two young girls, who appeared to be eighteen or nineteen and maybe thirteen/fourteen, were just a few inches shorter than Clark. He had never heard that the Dutch were considered to be the tallest people in the world.

"Welcome to our country, school and home," said Isaac, in English with an accent was a blend of Dutch, French and German influences - common for people in this area of the world.

As soon as everyone was set with a family, they dispersed. The plan was for the teams to meet the next morning for light practices and a joint lunch before the match at three o'clock. Clark watched as Gwen left with her counterpart, the male manager of the Amsterdam team, and his family who had expected to host a male and now had to quickly redo the sleeping arrangements. Clark had had a pleasant day with the group, and now he felt lonely even though surrounded by five very talkative and tall Dutch people.

The Ruttes lived in the Quid-Zuid area of Amsterdam, which was to the south west of the center city and just a few miles from the university. The area was known for its large, expensive homes and some of the best museums in the city, including the Van Gogh Museum. The homes were packed close together and no one seemed to have much of a yard. There was a lot of green space around, but it was concentrated in parks that seemed to be part of every block.

The inside of the Rutte home seemed very spacious because of the tall ceilings. The wood framed furniture had simple lines and looked much less comfortable than it actually was. Clark argued that he shouldn't have Isaac's room, while Isaac was relegated to a spare room in the back of the house, one that appeared to be designed for a live-in maid. But the decision had been made and was not to be changed.

They all sat down for a late supper. It was almost nine o'clock and late to eat by Clark's standard routines, but he didn't know if it was the same for them. The younger girl, Ellie, clearly a growing young girl, dug into the food as if she hadn't eaten in weeks. Isaac wasn't shy either, as he filled his plate and began to eat. Clark carefully considered each dish, and Wilhelmia, the older girl who they called Wil, watched him closely. Brussels sprouts, boiled potatoes and carrots - all things his mother made. The only thing that his mother would never have fixed were the fat sausages that sat in a pan full of gravy.

Clark was hungry and he ate a big portion of everything including the sausage. His appetite made Mrs. Rutte very happy, as did his repeated compliments of her food.

Mr. Rutte served a red wine that Clark wouldn't ordinarily drink, but he did so to be polite. Everyone drank including

Ellie, who Clark now thought was no more than twelve despite her height. The Ruttes were anxious to show off their English skills, and Clark was happy to listen and smile. He learned that Mr. Rutte, Maurice, had been on the Netherlands basketball team that played the very first year that basketball was in the Olympics - 1936 in Berlin. The games had been played outdoors on a converted tennis court. Mrs. Rutte, Antoinette, now a housewife, had been a tennis player, also on the Netherlands national team. Evidently Ellie had her mother's talent and already played in tennis tournaments all over Europe, including the Junior French Open the previous spring. Wil, however, didn't seem to have inherited the family's athletic gene or hadn't used it. She reminded Clark of the cheerleaders he knew from high school who lived in the world of sports but didn't participate. It was almost midnight when Mrs. Rutte reminded Clark and Isaac that they had rugby practice the next morning and a game that afternoon.

Nervous about a red wine hangover, Clark had just climbed into bed when he heard a soft knock on his door. He opened it to find Wil who wore a short cotton nightshirt that barely reached halfway to her knees. The top of her nightshirt was closed, but he could see that the buttons were undone. Without waiting for an invitation, Wil slid into the room, closed the door behind her and perched on the side of the bed. Clark stood at the door, wearing his boxer shorts and a t-shirt, unsure of what to do.

She patted the bed next to her and then repeated it when Clark didn't move. "Come here, I won't bite on you," she mocked, in her accent that he now found very sexy. "I wanted to talk."

He cautiously moved to the bed and sat, leaving plenty of room between them. It didn't take a seasoned diplomat to realize that the situation was fraught with the potential to be very bad for rugby international relations. Wil, with her vivid blue eyes and sharp angular features, was attractive and undeniably sexy. And yes, his radar was always alert for a way to end his virginity, but this didn't seem like a good time or place to consider it. Fortunately, she truly only wanted to talk about London and clubs and fashion and whether he had seen any pop stars like the Beatles or the Rolling Stones. He said he was exhausted, but she persisted. It was after one o'clock before he finally managed to get her out of his room and get to sleep.

Clark instinctively grabbed his small travel alarm clock and was prepared to throw it across the room before he remembered where he was.

Mrs. Rutte knocked on his door several minutes later and reminded him that it was nine o'clock and that he had to be at the university at ten thirty. He realized that he had actually gotten almost seven hours of sleep, and he should be okay, except for the wine. He gradually sat up and was relieved to find that his head felt okay and that his stomach seemed to be merely hungry.

After a substantial breakfast of eggs and the same sausage from dinner, Clark and Isaac rode with Mr. Rutte to the university. Isaac had his own car, a used Peugeot, but he didn't drive it on rugby match days. Evidently rugby parties were the same drunken events everywhere.

All the players on the team seemed to have had a good experience with their families, and they were all mostly sober, rested and ready to play. Craig teased Clark about whether he had scored with Wilhelmia, who everyone had noticed and thought was sexy hot. Clark had become somewhat of a legend on the team after he had started to date Cynna. They all referred to her as the ice princess because she had never acknowledged any of their attempts to come on to her. When Clark got his first date with her, they were amazed. But when they learned that she had been the one to ask him to go out again, his status reached Olympic heights. To them, Clark's conquest of a simple Dutch girl was a foregone conclusion.

Gwen looked exhausted as she recounted her problems with the team manager who had tried to grope her all evening. "I had to keep my bloody door locked," she laughed, even though she didn't find it at all funny. She had already made a reservation for the night at a hotel near the train station. And she kept a close watch on Arthur and hoped that he wouldn't over-react. In fact, everyone gave him a wide-berth because he seemed to be wound up tight, ready to explode.

After an enthusiastic but light practice and a good lunch, all the UL players thought they were ready for the match. Before the match began, Clark sought out the Ruttes and gave them all a friendly wave. He noticed that Wil stood on the sidelines with another girl, and they seemed to be closely examining and discussing all the boys.

The University of Amsterdam team had a very good reputation, and they expected a tight contest. They certainly got what they expected. While the players were almost even in terms of speed and strength, the height of the Dutch players was a significant advantage, particularly on the line-outs. All the Dutch families had come to the game to cheer for their boys, and they politely applauded the good plays by the UL team as well. Gwen did note that as being one positive outcome of the living arrangements.

After the hyper-intense, very physical nature of the Dartmouth team, everyone enjoyed getting back to the higher level of sportsmanship exhibited by European teams. After a very good tackle by Clark, the Amsterdam left wing jumped up and congratulated him. Clark saw the same thing happen time and again, all over the field.

With less than a minute to play and the game tied, Owen pitched the ball back to Clark, and he sprinted for the goal line.

Isaac suddenly appeared in front of him, ready to tackle him. Clark swerved to his left, which positioned him in front of the goal posts. Just as he neared Isaac, Clark suddenly stopped, dropped the ball, kicked it, and prayed. The ball wobbled over the bar like a wounded duck. Three points and a win for the UL team. During the backslapping and congratulations from the team, Charles laughed as he said. "A bloody drop kick, you're just full of surprises."

The University of Amsterdam pub lacked a lot in the way of charm, but made up for it in spirit and noise. The team didn't have a special room, so everyone - families, friends, and other students out on a Friday night - mixed with the two teams. The Netherlands and Belgium beers were on tap and much more agreeable that way. They were still much more carbonated than British bitter, but after a pint or two, no one cared.

It wasn't until after the first pint that Clark finally relaxed and reflected on how nervous he had been about whether his ankle would hold up. He had really dreaded having to spend the trip standing on the sidelines. Then he laughed that he had drop-kicked the ball without thinking of the impact on his ankle. Anything for the win, he kidded himself.

After an hour or so, most of the parents left. Clark noticed that several of his teammates were eagerly engaged with Dutch co-eds, speaking a mixture of languages. Then he saw Wil and her friend headed in his direction. She gave him a big, possessive hug before she introduced Astrid as her friend and classmate. Not nearly as attractive as Wil, Astrid proved to be more than her equal in personality. Both women had obviously been drinking and continued to do so over the next few hours. Wil refused to leave Clark's side even when he tried to talk to Gwen. Astrid tried to engage several players on both teams before she latched on to a random student. All the while, both women drank heavily.

Just before closing time, Clark went to the bar to get last drinks for him and Wil. Craig was there and offered Clark some condoms if he needed any.

"I'm good," Clark said, even though he wasn't - it had never crossed his mind to get any. Then he reconsidered as he wondered whether this could be it, with a hot Dutch girl. He turned back to Craig. "Hey man, maybe I will take one, I'm about out," he whispered, with a just-between-us-guys grin.

Jon, the guy Astrid had picked-up, had a car and offered to drive them home. As Wil and Clark climbed in the back seat of his Saab, she immediately jumped onto his lap and began kissing him. Over Wil's shoulder, Clark could see Astrid staring and grinning at them from the front seat. He felt curiously unaroused, probably because of the public assault and her cigarette taste. She hadn't smoked that many cigarettes during the evening, but they had been a very strong French brand, Gauloises.

Clark was drunk but not nearly as much as Wil. Immediately upon entering her house, she started to lead him upstairs, and he protested that her parents would hear them. She then pulled him toward the room where Isaac had slept the night before. She assured him that Isaac would spend the night at a university dorm with his girlfriend. Clark remembered seeing him with a girl, but he couldn't remember much of what she looked like, other than being blond and tall.

He carefully shut the door to the small bedroom and turned around to find that Wil had already begun to undress. With her shirt and bra off, he could see that her breasts were small. And as she got her panties off, she swayed on her feet, but then managed to reach him and claw at his shirt. He stopped her because he didn't have many shirts with him and would be in trouble if one got ripped. He knew he should be more excited about the possibilities that this situation presented, but he felt strangely uninvolved and conflicted. He wasn't too drunk to wonder whether this was really the way he wanted it to happen. As she reached for his belt and zipper, he pushed his doubts away. She had a hard time with his zipper, so he grabbed her hands and proceeded to do it himself. It felt good to let his stiffening penis escape the confines of his pants. She smiled as she grabbed it and pulled it toward her as she backed up to the bed. She collapsed on the bed still holding his erection but then let go as he began to remove his pants. He sat on the bed to remove his shoes so he could get his pants off. Having done that, he turned to her. She lay still on the bed, a smile on her face, completely passed out.

His reaction was more bemused than disappointed, which told him all he needed to know. He didn't want it to be a quickie with a stranger, particularly a drunk one. Then he realized that he had a much bigger problem. What should he do with her? It would look really bad for her parents to find her like this in the morning, even if he wasn't here. Could he get her up to her bedroom? He tried to lift her, but she was surprisingly heavy, and he was drunk. As he lay her back down, he couldn't resist feeling her breasts. They reminded him of a girl he had known in high school in Denver. Suzie had had breasts almost this small, and he had been fairly intimate with them a couple of times. He suddenly stopped because, even drunk, he realized that it was creepy.

It took him a while, but he finally managed to get her clothes back on her. Even during all the lifting, bending and pulling, she didn't move a muscle or otherwise react in any way. He knew he couldn't carry her up the stairs, but at least when they found her there in the morning, she would be dressed.

Exhausted, he stumbled upstairs and collapsed onto the bed. Thankful that their train for Paris wasn't scheduled to depart until one o'clock the next afternoon, his last though was to wonder how Gwen was doing at her hotel.

Clark hesitated before going downstairs the next morning - what would he find? Did Dutch fathers use shotguns like some American fathers reputedly did with boys who deflowered their daughters? But there had been no deflowering, and he was pretty sure that Wil was no virgin.

All seemed calm, however, as he entered the kitchen and returned Mrs. Rutte's cheerful greeting. Then he began to relax as she fed him breakfast and went on and on about the game and how proud she was of all the boys. Mr. Rutte and Ellie were at a tennis match and had said to say good-bye. When Mrs. Rutte said that she had to go wake Wil so she could go with them to the train station, Clark fought an impulse to race out of the house. He listened as she went upstairs and called for Wil, then knocked on her bedroom door and went in. He braced himself for her cry of alarm, but none came.

"Wil said she will be down after a shower," Mrs. Rutte told Clark, as she came back into the kitchen.

Clark concluded that Wil must have revived at some time during the night and gone up to her room. He waited nervously, but when Wil came into the kitchen, she was friendly but quiet, obviously hung-over. During Wil's quick breakfast and the ride to the station, Clark wondered how much she remembered of what happened, or didn't happen, the night before. As they neared the station, he asked her what she was going to do the rest of the day.

"I have to prepare for my birthday party," she replied. "It's tomorrow."

"Thank Gods she will finally be sixteen and can drive herself around," Mrs. Rutte offered as she turned the car into the parking lot of the train station.

Clark felt a huge knot tighten in the pit of his stomach. Oh shit, he thought. He cautiously looked over at Wil. Without her makeup, her hair undone, tired and hung-over, she did look that young. When Mrs. Rutte parked, he quickly thanked her for everything, nodded at Wil, and fled the car as fast as he could.

One of the first to arrive at the station, Clark found Gwen to see what he could do to help. She seemed tired and irritable as she curtly refused his offer, and he assumed that she must have had a bad night. But then as others arrived, he noticed that she acted happy and cheerful with them. He tried to take her bag to get on the train, but she wouldn't let him. Sitting on the train, he remembered that she had acted in a similar fashion when he first started going out with Cynna. Knowing he sucked at interpreting the inexplicable moods of women, he tried to forget it and began to play gin rummy with Robert.

A little while later, Owen, Charles, and Sean were looking for a fourth to play bridge in the club car. Tired of losing at gin, Clark volunteered. He generally got terrible cards in bridge, as he did in gin, but at least in bridge he had a partner and could still have some fun and maybe win a hand or at least foil the opponents. He had developed very good defensive bridge skills. After a while Charles wanted to quit and tried to get Gwen to take his place, but she begged off. Clark felt positive that he was the reason, but he still couldn't figure out why.

When the train stopped at the French border, the French customs officials were more diligent and Gwen struggled a little with her language skills. Clark could see her getting frustrated because she hadn't had a chance to hand out the French Rail tickets to the team. Ignoring her cold attitude, he went to her, took the tickets from her hand, and passed them out. The bridge game had broken up, so he went back to his seat and stared out at the French countryside. It looked so much the same as in Belgium and the Netherlands that he didn't bother to take any new photos.

"Thanks," Gwen said quietly, as she sat down next to him.

"No problem, happy to help."

After a few minutes of silence, she asked, "So did you enjoy yourself last night?" There was an edge in her voice, almost accusatory.

He could tell that it was a loaded question, but he wasn't sure how or why. "It was okay, I guess," he replied, seeking a safe answer.

More silence. He could almost feel her wrestling with herself, until she finally blurted out, "I know it's none of my business. But actually, in a way it is, for the team. Did you know how bloody young she was?"

It all suddenly became clear. "I found out this morning. Did you know?"

"I had a sense, and then I asked Rudi. But I wasn't trolleyed with a hard on." She couldn't help her attitude. She felt strongly about this, but wasn't completely sure why.

"Well, yeah I was drunk, but just to be clear, nothing happened."

"That's not what your mates think."

"Well, they weren't there, were they? Nor were you." He turned away to look out the window. He wasn't happy with this conversation, but he also felt a little guilty, knowing what he might have done if Wil hadn't passed out. He wondered why Gwen didn't leave, but she continued to sit there. They rode in awkward silence until the conductor announced that they would arrive in Paris in twenty minutes.

"Can you keep everyone together while I find the bus for the hotel?" she asked, very matter-of-factly, as she stood. She then moved to gather her stuff, which she had left next to Arthur. And when the train pulled into the station, she didn't object when Clark took her bag.

The Hotel Cluny Sorbonne was old and cheap, perfect for visiting rugby teams and starving artists. It was situated on the left bank, directly across the street from the University of Paris, the opponents for the match the following afternoon. The UL team had stayed there before and there hadn't been any incidents. Gwen attributed this to the fact that there were more than enough opportunities in the city for the guys to get into trouble without bringing it back to the hotel.

Clark had Robert for a roommate and silently thanked Gwen that he didn't have Heath. Robert was quiet, but that didn't mean he was dull. He knew Paris better than any of them because he often visited his older brother who lived and worked there. The previous year, Robert had taken the team to a brothel that his brother frequented. Translated into English as the Pleasure Pussy-Cat, it operated as one of the city's most genteel establishments of ill repute. It catered mostly to older tourists with money, bored pensioners, and foreign students with money and no illusions.

Given his reputation, everyone assumed that Clark would be eager to join the excursion to the Pleasure Pussy-Cat. He went along with the group, but he didn't really focus on where they were headed. He was just excited to be in Paris and not locked up in an Amsterdam jail for having sex with a minor.

When they got to the brothel, Clark couldn't translate the name, but the photos out front graphically told the story. Robert spoke passable French as did many of the others, and they were soon in a large parlor with bright red upholstered couches and love seats. Paintings on the wall depicted pretty young women in all kinds of sexual positions with faceless men. There was a small bar in the corner where the old bartender charged the equivalent of $10 for a beer, which was almost as much as the price for 30 minutes with one of the girls.

Clark wrestled with a major quandary. He had never been in a brothel, but he certainly had had recent experiences, both good and bad, with prostitutes. He would absolutely do it with Bernadette or even Tildi before any of these women. But equally important, he couldn't let the guys know that he was still a virgin. He struggled to figure out a suitable way to get out of there. He knew that he could just leave, but he liked the macho reputation that he seemed to have developed, even among the third-years. He didn't want to say that he couldn't afford it, because someone might offer to lend him the money. He thought he could linger in the lounge until everyone had gone off with a whore and then leave. But Robert seemed determined to wait to make sure that everyone was happily paired up with a girl. As several of the women tried to overcome his obvious reluctance, he felt his body respond to their entreaties. Strong hands started to massage his inner thighs. He looked up into a pair of sensitive hazel eyes that belonged to a tiny young girl who didn't look like she could be more than fourteen. She was, in fact, eighteen but looked very young. The madam of the brothel prized her young looking girls like they were crown-jewels. This particular prostitute wanted to be with her first American even if he was a student and probably couldn't afford a big tip.

Clark saw no good way out of his predicament, so he followed the young prostitute out of the parlor and down a long hall full of closed doors and sounds of sex. A little over half way down the hall they came to an open room, and she pulled him inside and closed the door. She smiled at him and spoke in French. It seemed to involve clothes because she started to remove hers and kept pointing at his. As her robe dropped to the floor, he saw that her body was tiny, but she had an enormous set of breasts that had been hidden under the loose robe. He had a hard time believing that they were real. Despite his determination not to have sex with her, he had to feel her breasts, and as he did so, she began to undo his pants. Nothing felt right - not her breasts in his hands or his semi hardness as she took him in her hands. She seemed confused that he appeared to be immune to her expensive breasts or her massage of his penis. She was astonished when he zipped up his pants and left the room.

Clark had almost reached the parlor when he heard her yell something down the hall. In the parlor, the madam tried to stop him from leaving. Suddenly, a very large man stood in front of him, effectively blocking his exit. He didn't realize that all the madam wanted was to get paid whether he had had sex or not. Through sign language and some familiar words, he finally got the message and paid. It took all the cash he had.

He walked along the Seine for a long time while his heart rate slowed and the tension dissipated from his body. Finally, as he stood in front of Notre Dame, he could laugh at the situation and at himself. He wondered how many crazy ways he could meet sexy women and still not have sex. Feeling better, he headed back toward the hotel. He was almost there when he saw a woman who looked like Gwen sitting alone in a café. As he got closer, he realized that it was Gwen. He thought about turning around, but she saw him through the window, smiled, and gestured at him to come in.

"Hi," he offered tentatively, as he sat down at her table and tried to get a sense for her mood. She was still smiling, which seemed like a good sign.

"Hi. What happened to the boy's night at the knocking shop?"

"Oh, not my thing really, that's not the place I want for my first-" he froze, afraid that he had said too much.

"First what?"

"Oh, first Paris experience, on my first trip to Paris, by myself…" He knew he was rambling so he stopped.

"So ideally what would be your first Paris experience? On your first trip to Paris. All by yourself, and fifteen randy teammates." She really liked to tease him and appreciated it that he took it well.

He tried to change the subject. "So what are you up to?" He had overheard her tell Arthur that she wanted nothing to do with any of them until the next day. Then he realized that Arthur hadn't been with the group at the brothel.

"I'm finishing my wine and then going to a poetry reading at a coffee house close to here." She carefully studied his reaction. She knew that the mere mention of poetry would cause all of the guys on the team, and most of the men that she knew, to experience an involuntary shiver of fear, followed by the impulse to run away, and then they would be gone. However, she saw none of that happen with Clark. In fact, to her surprise, he smiled and seemed to get excited.

"Cool, would you like some company?"

"You like poetry or you think there might be impressionable young women there?"

"Other than you?"

She laughed. She wasn't used to getting teased in return, and she enjoyed it.

They found the coffee house on a pointed corner where two streets came together in a V. It was about half full and the coffee aroma so strong that Clark didn't think he would have to drink any to get a massive dose of caffeine. Nor would he need to smoke a cigarette to get any nicotine because of the thick fog of smoke in the air - mostly cigarettes but also a strong smell of marijuana. A young woman dressed all in black sold wine and aperitifs from one end of the counter. Clark and Gwen found a small table by a window just as the first poet stepped up on the make-shift stage, a small riser on the far side of the room.

If Clark had been asked to create a picture of a French poet, this guy would have been his model. Tall and scraggily thin, with dirty black hair tied in a loose ponytail, he was dressed all in black, topped by a black beret and half-moon granny glasses. His gravely, tortured voice recited a poem with obvious drama. Clark listened for a while and tried to get a sense of the meaning of poem from the inflections of the poet's voice and his body language. But then he needed to know what the poem was about. "Do you mind translating?" he whispered to Gwen.

"I don't recognize all the words, but it's basically about his torment over his lover who had killed himself rather than suffer the humiliation of being exposed as a homosexual." After listening to the end, she continued, "He sees no alternative but to join his lover in death and cast a bright light on his shameful family and all those despicable bigots in the world."

"Heavy."

She nodded and hoped the next ones weren't so depressing.

The next two were more hopeful - concerned with the environment and the power of love. Then there was an intermission to allow patrons to re-caffeinate or buy liquor at the bar.

"Would you like some coffee or a wine or something?"

"Sure a wine would be nice," she replied, as she lit a cigarette.

Clark noticed that she had bought a pack of the Gauloises. "And, um could I borrow some money, I'm a little broke."

"Well, that's better than being a lot broke." She smiled as she pulled some francs from her bag.

Clark managed to buy two glasses of wine, one red and one white. He had gotten lucky with the red wine at the Ruttes, but he wasn't going to take a chance at this place.

The next two poets were women, and their poems were increasingly sexual and provocative. At one point, Gwen hesitated to translate a passage that described a large black penis thrust down the poet's throat as a metaphor for the need of African males to overcome the oppression of their European masters. The final poets were a couple who exchanged words of infatuation followed by words of love, then words of arousal and desire. They verbally brought each other to a climax and then froze in a tableau of orgasmic pleasure. The crowd thought it was over, but the couple didn't move.

Gwen shifted nervously. She had tried to be very calm as she translated the increasingly intimate and sexual words for Clark. She couldn't tell if they affected him or not, but she felt her body get increasingly warm as she translated and watched him.

People had started to stir when suddenly the couple sprang back to life, but this time with words of misunderstanding, then pain, and finally despair. They finished in another tableau, but this time of conflict, anger, parting. The crowd now had a sense for the performance and waited patiently. Just when it became almost too long, the couple started again as they were at the beginning, a new meeting, love and desire.

Clark thought the circular structure, the endless cycle of emotion, of life, was brilliant. It surprised him that many in the audience were not equally impressed. He couldn't tell what Gwen thought. He had noticed that she had grown increasingly uncomfortable translating the very vivid sexual imagery. He had tried to act calm, nonchalant, so as to not increase her discomfort, but it had been hard to do.

They walked back to their hotel. The night had grown much colder, and he had an impulse to put his arm around her, but he resisted. "So that was pretty intense, sorry you had to do all that translating. I always feel like such an idiot not knowing any other language."

"How did you manage that? We have to learn at least two in school to graduate and go to university."

"We only have to know one, and I did Latin." He expected her to laugh but she didn't.

"Many choose that as their second language, especially if they're going to be a solicitor or a humanities person."

They reached the river, which was beautiful and romantic, and they both felt a little awkward.

"It seemed like you enjoyed yourself," she offered.

"You're surprised?"

"Well, a little I guess. I really don't know you that well except for rugby and …" The ghostly image of Cynna hung visibly over the conversation.

He didn't know why he felt safe with her because she seemed too complex for him, but he did, so he opened up a little. "I actually write a bit of poetry myself. I would like to be a writer and live somewhere like here, or London." She didn't react negatively, so he continued. "I'm taking a creative writing course at Kings College on Wednesdays, and we're writing short stories."

She was still trying to process all of that information about him as they reached the hotel, stood awkwardly in the lobby for a moment, and then said goodnight. In her room, Gwen smoked her last cigarette of the day and struggled with the puzzle that was Clark - a randy jock wrapped around a smart, sensitive poet.

In his room, Clark couldn't figure out the enigma of Gwen. A very smart, sensitive, funny woman lurking beneath an austere, asexual, social crusader exterior.

The weather the next day made the UL players feel right at home in Paris. A cold rain pelted the pavement and kept all the sensible people inside any warm, dry structure. No one ventured out to the rugby pitch except for the teams. They were playing on a field that was part of the grounds in front of the Ecole Militaire or Military School, as Gwen translated. The structure next to them needed no translation. The Eiffel Tower rose majestically into the low gray clouds. Red aviation lights on top of the tower flashed an eerie warning to any pilot crazy enough to venture that way. It reminded Clark of a time in the fall of sixth grade in Washington, DC, when he had played peewee touch-football, and the games had been held on a field adjacent to the Washington Monument. That had been his only experience with football because they had moved the next summer to Seattle, where he fell in love with boating and water skiing.

The team from the Sorbonne was fast and sneaky. They had trick plays that Clark and the other new players had never seen before. Charles and Arthur had tried to prepare them, but they couldn't imagine it until they experienced it. Clark found himself caught off guard and out of position numerous times in the first half, and the Sorbonne team led fifteen to ten at the break. Then it turned out that the Frenchmen had even more tricks held in reserve for the second half, and they cruised to a fairly easy thirty to twenty victory.

It would have helped if the players on the UL team had been there mentally as well as physically. But most of them weren't completely there either mentally or physically. The main group had left the brothel the night before and then gone to a show at the Moulin Rouge. They had staggered back to the hotel as the dawn chased the darkness from the streets of Paris. Charles hadn't been with the group, but he also looked exhausted after a night with a French exchange student he had met in London the previous spring term. Clark and Arthur seemed to be the only two who had had a decent night's sleep and weren't hung-over.

Despite the best efforts of the French players, the party after the game never got beyond subdued. Maybe there actually was a limit to the abuse that the UL players could subject their bodies to and still function. It didn't help that the party room at the Sorbonne looked a lot like the parlor at the brothel and that the only alcohol being served was wine. Clark knew his teammates were exhausted when they didn't seem to get excited about the very pretty French co-eds who found the party room more to their liking than the soggy rugby pitch.

Clark stood nursing a glass of an uninteresting French wine and noticed that several teammates had already left. He assumed they had gone back to the hotel, which was right across the street, and he thought about joining them. He saw Gwen standing next to a French woman who would charitably be described as plump. She had a pretty face framed by hair that was a very unnatural bright red color. Her body carried too many pounds and most of them seemed to be in her two enormous breasts, easily visible under a very low cut blouse. Clark wondered what was it with French women and their big breasts. As he watched, Gwen introduced the woman to Winston. Clark fully expected Winston to collapse in fright at the sight of this woman, but he didn't. In the months he had known Winston, Clark had never seen him engage with any women. But he seemed to be immediately comfortable with her, and she seemingly with him.

"Well, they make a cute couple," Gwen teased sarcastically, as she joined Clark. "I had a feeling that they might be of the same persuasion."

Clark was confused and looked like it.

Gwen noticed and explained, "Both gay." She watched Clark struggle with this concept and had to tease him some more. "You know, you're surprisingly naïve for such a Casanova."

The next morning, as their train pulled out of the Gare Montparnasse train station, Clark marveled at the strong sense of camaraderie that he felt with the rugby group. They all seemed to like to be together, but they also mostly respected each other's privacy. They could joke and tease but seemed to maintain respectable boundaries. It had been a great trip, and he was sorry that it was over. He could have spent much more time in both cities, and he promised himself that he would return soon.

Most of the players fell asleep immediately. Clark knew that some of them hadn't been to bed, especially those who had returned to the brothel after the party at the Sorbonne. Charles wasn't there because he was staying a few more days with the French student. And Arthur looked terrible, but no one knew what he had been doing.

Clark had talked to a few French girls at the party, one of whom seemed very much into him and had invited him back to her room. He had declined and finally left alone because it had become abundantly clear to him that he didn't want to lose his virginity on an alcohol fueled one-night stand. It was, he realized, a logical corollary to his position on prostitutes, but he had never articulated it before this trip. He remembered something that Rita had said to him a few years before - that there's a big difference between sex and love. It didn't surprise him that he wanted both.

About an hour outside of Paris, Clark looked over at Gwen, who sat across the aisle and stared out the window. Arthur had been sitting next to her and they had been arguing about something before he got up and left. There was something about the way she looked that completely captivated him - strong yet vulnerable, hope traced with sadness. He quietly pulled out his camera and surreptitiously took a few photos of her.

On the ferry from Calais to Dover, Gwen again fought seasickness and went out on the deck. Clark followed her, and they sat and watched the horizon. Neither of them said anything, but she had sat close to him and their bodies casually touched. He thought that it was because she must be chilly, and he resisted an urge to put his arm around her.

The sun set with a beautiful array of colors behind the white cliffs as they approached Dover, and the light had disappeared completely by the time they docked and disembarked. Upon their arrival back in London, several players immediately set off to a pub. Clark, flabbergasted at their capacity to keep drinking, headed for home. He was eager to write down the ideas for stories and poems that he had had during the trip. The next time he traveled, he would remember to take a journal with him.

CHAPTER 13

Late Tuesday morning, Clark sat in the student union at LSE and reflected on the past three months. The trip to Europe had been an unequivocal success. He hadn't lost his virginity, but he had clarified a factor that he knew would be an important guidepost on his continuing quest - he needed a relationship. In the meantime, he could enjoy his friendships with two very interesting and unusual women. Feeling pretty positive, he then turned his attention back to his outline of a story about an underage sex maniac. He hadn't yet found the devise to make it real yet not be exactly like what had happened with Wil. He put that story aside when a new idea came to him for a good twist in the story set in a Parisian brothel. He was so intent on this that he didn't notice when Gwen arrived and stood in the doorway, glaring at him.

"You fucking son of a bitch!" she screamed, as she stormed across the room toward him.

Stunned, he looked up to see her stand over him, fists clenched, blue eyes bright with a hot fury. He couldn't find his voice to respond.

"How could you do it you arrogant selfish arsehole?!" She now had the complete attention of everyone in the room.

Finally, he managed to stammer, "What, what are you talking about?"

His denial only fueled her rage, and she really wanted to pummel him. "You know fucking well what I mean! When did you find out?!"

"Find out what?" he pleaded, instinctively leaning away from her and desperately trying to not give into his nervous laugh.

"Don't fuck with me, her father's taken her!"

There was only one connection that his brain could make. "Cynna? Her father?"

"Yes Cynna you bastard! She's pregnant! You knocked her up!"

Shock then relief almost simultaneously washed through him. If Cynna was in fact pregnant, he knew it certainly wasn't him. And then, suddenly, it all came together - her sickness, sore breasts, all the things that he had seen with Rita years ago and should have recognized with Cynna. It explained almost everything about her behavior, except for the kissing. But now he had to address the furious woman who stood over him, making them soon-to-be legends in the school. "Gwen," he said, as he started to get up, but immediately stopped because her reaction was a defensive stance that looked like a boxer with her fists poised to strike him. "Calm down please. I swear, I didn't get Cynna pregnant. I know nothing about it. Please believe me."

Gwen had been so positive that it was him. And so devastated that he could have acted so casual, even a little flirtatious, with her on the rugby trip, all the while knowing that Cynna was home pregnant. Yet as she looked at him now, she suddenly felt confused, uncertain. He looked genuinely shocked. As her anger subsided, so did her strength, and she collapsed on the chair across the table from him.

He watched her process things and wisely kept quiet. Finally, when she sat and seemed more in control, he tried again. "Please believe me, I did not do this. It's impossible."

"Clark, don't bloody bull shit me, okay, it had to be you, you were the one she was dating, staying out all night with."

It took him a few beats to process that. "Whoa, back up. Staying out all night? Never. The latest that we were out was maybe nine-thirty. She was always tired or sick. And now I know why."

"Come on, I live there, remember? She always came in around five or six in the morning on the nights you went out." Gwen was completely exasperated that he didn't just own up to it.

"I don't know about that, all I do know is that we never had sex, so I didn't get her pregnant."

"I saw her come in one morning, and she had definitely had sex." The volume of her voice started to rise again.

"Not me. Impossible," he replied, frustrated, his voice also louder.

"I don't believe you!" She was back to a shout, an assault.

"I'm still a virgin!" Exasperated. A defensive instinct. And his voice had risen almost to her level. He knew immediately and without a doubt that everyone in the room had heard his confession.

She looked at him and watched him wilt as he slumped down on his chair, stared at the table.

"Oh, my God," she whispered, and struggled to process it. "If not you, then who?"

"It was me."

They both looked up to see Arthur, who stood there looking like he had gone ten rounds in the boxing ring with the devil and lost everything. Neither of them could respond, and they just stared as he took a seat between them.

"We started dating secretly this summer, and then it got serious, and we had, we did it the first time right before we came back to school."

"In our house?"

He nodded, and Gwen seemed like she wanted to say something, but nothing came out.

Clark now put it together. "So she basically used me so she could see you. That's where she was until five in the morning."

Arthur nodded, but couldn't look directly at Clark. "It was a shitty thing to do, and I'm sorry, but that was the only way she could ditch her guard. She convinced Rovsek that you were... harmless."

Gwen looked at Clark and felt terrible for him, for thinking so poorly of him, for making him confess.

"Asshole!" Clark yelled at Arthur, as he jumped up. He desperately wanted to punch Arthur in the face, but he didn't. Instead he stormed out of the room, his shattered reputation and dignity floating like flotsam in his wake.

Arthur would have felt better if Clark had hit him. "What am I going to do Gwen, I can't live without her."

"Did you know while we were gone?" She wanted to be sympathetic and support her brother, but at the moment she found it very hard to do.

He nodded. "Yeah, she saw a doctor the day before we left and told me to go so she could have some time to think. I never thought he would find out and come get her."

"It was probably Rovsek. The signs had gotten pretty obvious, even though I completely missed them. And she would have known that she had fucked up. She did get sacked."

"Good." Arthur almost managed a smile. "She made it so bloody hard for us. And I really do feel bad about Clark. He's a good guy. Cynna thought he was very inexperienced, maybe even still a virgin, and I guess she was right."

Gwen just nodded her head.

Despite the cold air, heavy with moisture, Clark walked most of the way to Hampstead. He didn't even notice when it started to rain - it suited his mood perfectly. Clark wasn't by nature a violent person. Just because he liked to tackle people didn't mean that he wanted to hurt anyone. But he fantasized that the feeling of his fist crunching into Arthur's face sure would have felt great. Or maybe his hands around Arthur's throat as he struggled to breath and begged for mercy. But he knew that the best thing had been to leave.

He worried how he could ever face anyone. The guys on the team. They would laugh, call him a loser, a fool instead of a stud. "God, what a joke I am," he shouted out loud into the wind that drove the rain hard against his face. The only positive thing that he managed to cling to was the look of surprise and horror on Gwen's face, which meant that she obviously hadn't known what had been going on.

He tried to put Cynna and Arthur together, to figure out what they saw in each other. The fact that he couldn't imagine the attraction on anything other than a purely physical level only deepened his despair that he didn't know shit about women or love. And he was pretty sure that Arthur wasn't a prominent Greek. He finally noticed the rain. Soaked and cold, he stopped and hailed a taxi.

By the time he got home, dried off, and warmed up, Clark reached a point where he almost felt sorry for Arthur. It had been clear from his expression that he was genuinely devastated. He obviously had a lot at stake emotionally, and it had been snatched away from him.

That night Clark slept fitfully, tormented by dreams of indistinct frustrations. In the morning he had a hard time convincing himself that he should get out of bed. He could hide for a week, a month, or until they found his body. He had been disappointed by people before, but nothing like this betrayal. It would be a while before he could put it into perspective. But for now, he would deal with it as he had with crisis in the past - he would withdraw into himself. He would turn invisible. For a moment he thought he would go bare his pain to Bernadette. But he suppressed that impulse. He would eventually tell her and write about it, but not now, not while the pain and the humiliation were so fresh. No, he would leave. The University of Edinburgh rugby team was the last opponent of the fall season, that Saturday. No way on earth was he going to that match, but he had a car, and he could go to Scotland, to Edinburgh. A perfect place to escape.

He forced himself out of bed, showered, and went to a Royal Automobile Club travel shop on Hampstead High Street. They had maps and brochures that he used to plot a trip north to Scotland. He thanked the clerk for her concern that it would be very cold and could even snow there. That would actually suit his mood perfectly. He threw some clothes in his bag, jumped in his car, and headed for the A-1 north.

The travel clerk had said that the drive to Edinburgh should be ten to twelve hours by the A-1 and a little less if he took the western route through Liverpool, which offered a four-lane motorway. He had been drawn to the A-1 because of its history as the first through road from London to Scotland and because it went along the coast for the final two hundred kilometers from Newcastle upon Tyne to Edinburgh.

The driving conditions were terrible - traffic, rain, and road spray that covered his low-slung car. And driving on the left side of the car, he couldn't see a thing. If he hadn't been propelled by a tank-full of emotional energy, Clark would have soon given up and turned around. The A-1, a four-lane motorway leaving the city, soon changed to become a busy two-lane highway, full of large lorries and sedans that dwarfed his little MGB. He got stuck behind a slow moving farm-lorry, and impatient drivers tried to pass both him and the lorry; but they often didn't have enough time to pass both vehicles, so they had to dangerously swerve back in front of him. His energy flowed out of him with each tortuous mile.

His destination was York, an interesting walled city in Yorkshire, about halfway to Edinburgh. But after a couple of hours on the road, he knew that he would never make it that far and the conditions began to overwhelm him. He became desperate to find a place to stop, spend the night, but he passed small towns and villages that offered no accommodations. He longed for the ugly billboards along the highways at home that advertised hotels, restaurants and other attractions for the travelers - all very helpful information. He finally came to the cathedral town of Peterborough, which seemed large enough to maybe have an inn or a bed-and-breakfast. At a petrol station, he got the name of and directions to a local inn near the cathedral. He had only gone 135 kilometers in a little over four hours.

The Cloister Inn, small and quaint, had a room available with a single bed and a clean shared bathroom down the hall. All Clark wanted to do was collapse on the bed and sleep. But he knew he needed to eat something, so he found a quiet pub near the inn. The tension slowly began to dissipate from his body as he ate a steak-and-kidney pie and drank a pint of bitter.

Clark woke the next morning just as the first light spilled through the window and across his bed. He felt refreshed after a good night's sleep, one that had been surprisingly devoid of dreams about any of the women in his life. After a simple continental breakfast provided by the inn, he was back on the A-1, headed for Scotland. The rain had stopped. The sky was still overcast, but it had lightened considerably from the previous days, as did his mood. He gradually achieved a calm, no-agenda, touring/exploring, state-of-mind. He was a loner at heart, with a strong streak of wanderlust, and this suited him just fine.

The traffic diminished as he got further north, and he discovered a technique to pass a slow lorry on a two-lane road. He would hang back far enough that he could carefully ease out into the oncoming lane and see if there was any vehicle coming toward him. If not, his car had enough acceleration power that he could zip by the lorry and safely return to his side of the road. Unfortunately, this worked best when the road presented a nice, long straight stretch and that became increasingly rare as he went further north.

Six days later, Tuesday evening, Clark arrived back at his flat. Other than innkeepers, waiters, and barmen, he had barely spoken to anyone in days, and that had suited him just fine. He had seen what he believed to be the ugliest, most depressing place on earth - Newcastle, the center of the coal industry - unbelievably dark and sooty. Because of the driving conditions, he had to spend a night there. But ironically he discovered that it was also home to a wonderful beer, Newcastle Brown Ale. The east coast of England and Scotland had been beautiful. A westerly wind off the North Sea and the Firth of Forth had pushed the clouds back into the mainland, providing wonderful views of the coastline and small picturesque fishing villages. Edinburgh had lived up to his expectations as he wandered Castle Rock and the Edinburgh Castle, the Holyrood Palace, and the university. The highlight of his stay had been a Saturday night performance of *King Lear* at the Scottish National Theater. He had paid full price for a good seat.

The drive had been so strenuous that he hadn't really had time to dwell on what had happened with Cynna, Arthur, and Gwen. It had required all his energy to stay alert and alive on those roads, and also to enjoy the scenery, to explore new places. But despite all that distraction, he had been subconsciously dealing with the problem and had found a kind of peace with it. He dealt with most of his problems that way - quietly, alone. He didn't need to endlessly dissect a problem and talk about it ad nauseam, as did so many people. He was now sure that by the time rugby started again in March, he would be okay with Arthur. And he would never see Cynna again. Her father probably had her locked in a cellar or a convent. That image made him happy, despite knowing that it was mean. But thoughts of Bernadette and Gwen occasionally threaten his sense of peace. Okay, so the secret's out… what's the big deal? he asked himself, as he drank one of the Newcastle Brown Ales that he had brought home. Bernie already knew, and Gwen … he paused. That friendship, he realized, was much more complicated and important than he would have expected before the rugby trip.

He looked forward to the creative writing class and to seeing Bernadette. Last week he couldn't, but now he'd gained a sense of strength from having been virtually invisible for days on end. He would test it by going to class, which was the last one of the fall term. Maya should hand back their first stories with her comments and, he assumed, a grade.

His sense of strength increased when Bernadette gave him a big hug in front of the class. She whispered to him, "I was worried about you. Weren't you coming back last week? I thought maybe some Parisian sexpot had gotten her claws into you and made you her sex slave."

He smiled. "I'll tell you after class."

As the class ended, Maya asked Clark and Bernadette to wait a moment. When the room had cleared, she invited them to a party on Saturday night at her flat. She made it clear that they were the only students invited.

"Can you go?" Bernadette asked him, as they walked out of the building and headed for their usual pub for lunch. "No date with Cynna?" Then she added carefully, "Or Gwen."

Suddenly he was back in the LSE student union with Gwen screaming at him. "No," he mumbled, unable to articulate any more.

She waited patiently as they ordered lunch. She could tell that something had happened that he found difficult to talk about. Her intuitions were normally very good, and he had ordered a pint for lunch, which he never did.

"Well, it turns out," he started to talk quietly, "that Cynna was secretly screwing Arthur, Gwen's brother, and using me as a front, a smoke-screen to fool her commie chaperone." He took a drink before he continued. "And the real kicker is that she's been pregnant this whole time, with Arthur's baby."

"My God, you don't need any imagination to come up with material for a story," she teased lightly. "I mean you can't just make that shit up can you? You've got to live it." She smiled and was rewarded with his first genuine smile of the day.

"You're right, no way I could have imagined that storyline. Who the hell would believe it?"

The hard part now done, he told her about the trip to Amsterdam and Paris. She loved the parts about Wil and his attempt to run out of the brothel. "We have a big guy like that, Alfonzo, a former boxer and prison guard. No one stiffs a whore." They both cracked up when they caught her unintentional pun.

He casually mentioned his evening in Paris with Gwen, and she didn't ask him for details, but gave him a knowing little smile. She could tell that he was more than a little confused by that part.

As they finished lunch, she asked him if he would do her a huge favor and take portraits of her and Mags that they could give their mother for Christmas. It would have to be done soon, and she invited him for dinner on Sunday. He quickly agreed even though he had never done real portraits before, and he knew that the professionals used all sorts of fancy lighting. But it would be a good challenge that would keep him busy for the next few days.

The next morning, he went to a photo shop near the Hampstead underground station. The clerk tried to sell him some professional strobe lights, but they were far too pricey. So he settled for a simple 250-watt photo lamp in a parabolic-shaped metal frame and a reflector board. They had a free pamphlet about taking portraits, published by Kodak, which he took to study. He then noticed that a service of this photo shop was to develop black and white film, and it was a very reasonable price. Clark had taken a lot more photos on the rugby trip and his escape to Edinburgh, and he still had many rolls of exposed but undeveloped film from before. He hadn't been back to Nigel's darkroom since that first time and was very eager to go. But he didn't want to waste a lot of time developing film when he could be having fun in the darkroom. So he went home and returned with forty-two rolls of film.

He went to the Philosophy of International Law class in the afternoon because he liked that class, and it would be safely Cynna-free. Afterward he looked for Nigel around the school so he could ask him about using the darkroom. He didn't find him so he tried to ring him up later from the flat. Reginald, the butler, answered and informed him that Mr. Nigel was not at home, but that he had left instructions that Clark could use the darkroom at any time. Clark struggled not to laugh at Reginald's deadpan tone and haughty British accent.

Friday morning, Clark returned to the photo shop and was very surprised that they had managed to develop all forty-two rolls. He then headed for Mayfair. He knew that parking around Nigel's house would be difficult so he took the Tube. He arrived about ten o'clock, which he assumed would be an acceptable time - not too early and also during the day, like a business arrangement.

The same security man appeared when Clark approached the gate, and he opened it without a word. Reginald appeared at the front door within seconds after he knocked and showed Clark to the stairs that led down to the cellar. When Clark asked about Nigel, Reginald informed him that, "Mr. Nigel left earlier for an appointment." Clark didn't ask when he would be back.

Nigel had left a note for Clark that all the chemicals were fresh and ready to use. Clark unpacked his stuff and got right to work. He first made contact sheets of all his rolls of film so he could review the shots and select the ones that he wanted to make into prints. But with that many rolls, it was four hours before he was ready to work on his first print. He found himself mostly drawn to two shots of Gwen - the one taken on the bridge at Oxford and the other taken on the train from Paris to Calais. The focus on the bridge photo turned out to be too soft, but the train shot looked great. The light was perfect, and she looked serene yet intense, focused but lost in thought, ordinary and beautiful. But thinking about Gwen proved too much for him to handle at that moment, so he picked a negative that contained a nice composition of the architectural detail of the train station in Amsterdam along with a very bored looking porter, leaning against the wall. He stayed with various landscape and tourist shots for the next several hours.

At a little after five o'clock he heard someone in the lobby and expected Nigel to knock on the door to ask if it was safe to enter the room. But the door swung open, and an older man, dressed in a very conservative and undoubtedly expensive suit, stood in the doorway. The physical resemblance identified him immediately as Nigel's father. Clark was very glad that he hadn't yelled at the intruder who had ruined two prints when he opened the door and let light into the room.

Mr. Barrington glared at Clark, then looked around the room.

"My son's not here?"

"No sir. I'm Clark Westfield, a friend of Nigel's from school. He said I could use the darkroom."

Mr. Barrington inspected Clark. "Ah yes, the American. So tell me, Mr. Westfield, what kind of friend are you?"

Confused, Clark answered carefully, "Well, I don't know exactly, we have a class together, and some mutual friends, and we're both photographers." He saw Nigel's father process all of that and then maybe relaxed a little.

"Are you actually a rugger or did that come from Carnaby Street?" Nigel's father nodded at Clark's University of Amsterdam rugby shirt that Isaac Rutte had given him.

"Yes sir, I play right wing for the university."

"Well that's, that's good then. Sorry to bother. Carry on." He spun around on his heels and left without closing the door.

Clark heard him go up the stairs, and was curious what that strange encounter was all about.

An hour or so later, Clark debated whether he could or should work much longer. He didn't want to wear out his welcome by staying too long. And a rumbling in his stomach reminded him that he hadn't eaten since breakfast. So he finished up the prints he had been working on, packed up and left. He hadn't printed it, but the image of Gwen on the train kept coming back to him as he moved slowly with the mass of commuters headed into the subway. But his claustrophobia and impatience rebelled, and he turned around and pushed his way out of the station. It took several buses to get home, and they were all crowded, but at least they weren't underground.

CHAPTER 14

Clark picked up Bernadette at seven o'clock Saturday night, and they drove to Maya's flat in Golders Green, a town just to the north of Hampstead, not far from Clark's flat. That meant he drove all the way across town to get her, then all the way back to the party and planned to repeat the process to take her home. She had argued that it was silly for him to do all that driving when she could easily take the tube to Hampstead. He had insisted because it was the gentlemanly and friendly thing to do, and he loved to drive at night in London. London in the dark had a romantic charm that never failed to captivate him. All the modern, boring stuff faded into the dark background and allowed the older, architecturally impressive buildings and historical monuments to show off. It was like stepping back in time or into a dream. And all vehicles drove with only their parking lights turned on, so there were no annoying headlights ruining the scene.

Maya's building looked similar to Clark's, but her flat was one of two on the first floor rather than the entire floor of a duplex. Golders Green was nice but slightly less prosperous looking than Hampstead, and clearly populated with younger people. It wasn't an area where students could afford to live, but it was perfect for young professionals, professors, young families.

Maya had promised to have lots of food, and Clark and Bernadette were both starving. After Maya made some brief introductions to a few other guests, they made a bee-line for the food table. Carrying full plates, they found a couple of chairs to sit while they ate. Clark surveyed the room. There were probably thirty or so people, more than a third of them black, and most of them appeared to be intellectuals or artists, as evidenced by the styles of their clothing and the length of their hair. Clark and Bernadette were clearly the youngest people in the room. Maya was mid-thirties and most of her friends were that age or older.

"She's got some very interesting art work," Bernadette commented between bites of food.

Clark scanned the art on the walls, all of which seemed to be originals and very modern. Most were abstract paintings with designs and colors that obviously had meaning to the artists but completely escaped Clark. However, a series of paintings of a nude female figure attracted his interest. A black voluptuous figure, dramatically lit, posed in a way that screamed sexual power without being pornographic.

"I pretty sure that's her," Bernadette whispered to him, as she also studied the nudes.

"What's who?" Clark asked, confused.

"Those paintings, the model, I think that's Maya."

"Really? How can you tell? You can't see her face." And all that he had ever seen Maya wear were very loose fitting dresses that hid her figure.

"I just have a feeling, that's all. Let's ask her."

Clark hesitated. It seemed far too personal of a question to spring on a professor, even one who was as cool as Maya. But Bernadette grabbed his hand and pulled him over to where Maya stood talking to a much older woman who looked aboriginal of some sort, African or maybe Australian.

"Clark, Bernadette, this is my old friend and mentor Yvonne who's a fabulous writer from the Outback. Vee, these are those students I told you about."

Clark felt Yvonne's dark brown eyes peer into him, reaching down to his soul. Suddenly he felt naked and exposed; a nervous tremor flowed through him. He quickly looked down, closing that window, but not before she gave him a knowing little smile. She then looked at Bernadette and stared at her for what seemed to Clark like an uncomfortable amount of time. But it didn't faze Bernadette, as she calmly returned Yvonne's stare with her own.

"Maya has said such positive things about the two of you, I hope to read something soon," Yvonne finally said, as she broke off the staring contest with a flourish. "How's the food? I'm famished." Without waiting for an answer, she headed for the food table.

Maya laughed. "She's one-of-a-kind. Her stories are incredibly personal and powerful - growing up in poverty, facing brutal discrimination and abuse. So much so, that she can't get published in Australia."

"We love your art work, especially those." Bernadette pointed to the nude figure series. "And I told Clark that I have a feeling that that's you."

Maya's expression turned serious but not unhappy. No one had ever made the connection so quickly, and most didn't ever. She realized that clearly this young woman had some special gift, intuition, that helped inform her storytelling. "Well, I was much younger, about your age probably, just turned twenty-one."

Bernadette beamed, vindicated. Clark couldn't help but look at Maya's tent-like dress and wonder what was under there. Maya noticed Clark's look and was just about to tease him, when a loud noise came from across the room, near the front door.

Ezekiel, Gwen's drummer boyfriend, stood there with a set of bongo drums that hung on a strap around his neck. He banged on them with a flourish as he moved around the room.

It took Clark a few moments to remember him from the time in the pub when he had come to talk to Gwen. He finally made the connection as Ezekiel reached them and embraced Maya, who looked very pleased to see him.

"Ah, the party can now properly begin. Did you bring your special stuff, Batu?"

Ezekiel seemed to puff up even more and nodded. "Just as you requested," he said, as he handed her a small glass vial with maybe a dozen small white pills.

Clark immediately guessed LSD and remembered the scene with Erin at her party. Her bad trip had been caused by a strong batch of the drug according to Micah. Were these the same? Then it struck him - Ezekiel must be a drug dealer and Gwen was … He didn't have time to follow that train of thought because Maya grabbed his arm and Bernadette's and pulled them into a tight conspiracy circle with her and Ezekiel.

"I'm having a little after-party party if you'd like to stay and expand your mind a little. Ezekiel makes the purest yet mildest acid anywhere."

Clark looked to see Bernadette's reaction but couldn't read her expression. It wasn't negative, but it didn't seem positive either.

Bernadette had never tried LSD, but she did know that quite a few women in her profession dropped acid while working and had reported amazing experiences, ones that overcame the drudgery of their work. But there had also been bad trips such as the unfortunate instance when a woman on LSD confused the penis of her client for a cobra. The court had not accepted her drug-state as a defense in her trial for mutilation. And Bernadette also remembered Clark's story of the party at Erin's.

Ezekiel kissed Maya's cheeks and left, which made Clark happy because he didn't have to deal with the drug dealer and his association with Gwen.

Clark and Bernadette spent the next couple of hours drinking beer and wine and talking to some very interesting people. The beat poet from Romania who had escaped from the communists with his parents in 1954. The folk singer who spoke in whispers because her voice had been damaged by a venereal disease she had contracted while on tour. A writer of short stories who turned very defensive when Maya complemented Clark and Bernadette on their stories. The novelist who Clark had been sure was a woman until they talked. The deep masculine voice and flat chest gave him away, as did the large Adam's apple in his throat.

The group had thinned out by the time Clark noticed that it was after one o'clock. He didn't want to go, but he didn't like to be the last one at a party. He started to say something to Bernadette when Maya cornered them.

"Are you two having fun? I'm sure this is pretty tame compared to your parties. I remember my student days."

"Oh, I don't party too much, I'm usually working on weekends," Bernadette answered, and Clark looked at her, surprised that she had opened the door for the logical question from Maya.

"Oh, what do you do, waitressing?" Maya asked, as many glasses of wine overcame her normal aversion to making such stereotypical assumptions.

"Well, no, it's another service kind of thing, actually I'm a call-girl."

Maya looked and sounded completely stunned. "Really? I'm, I'm…"

Bernadette smiled. "I don't publicize it because most people don't understand, but I feel comfortable around you. You don't seem at all judgmental."

"Well, thank you, I try not to be. And are you two?" Maya indicated Clark who had been fascinated with the exchange, but now realized that Maya referred to him.

"Clark? We're very good friends, and he's become very cool in his own nonjudgmental style."

Clark smiled a little sheepish smile.

"Well, Bernadette, I think you have a real gift for writing, and I'd love to see you pursue it. I don't know what your long term plans are, but I think you could be a very successful writer." As Maya talked, she put her hand on Bernadette's arm and squeezed it. She then turned to address a very serious looking young man who Clark didn't remember seeing before. "Michael. Please come over and meet my friends. Bernadette, Clark, this is Michael who's my spotter when I get high. He's very good and keeps us safe. Would you like to join us?" She swept her hand around to indicate the small group of people who remained at the party.

It took Clark a moment longer than Bernadette to respond to the invitation. "That's cool, thanks, but that's not my thing really," Bernadette said, with a smile that conveyed no sense of judgment.

Clark quickly nodded in agreement. He didn't trust Ezekiel or his drugs.

Clark woke the next morning and couldn't believe that he didn't have a terrible hang-over. Then he couldn't believe that he was alone in his bed. Bernadette had been there when he went to sleep, or more accurately, passed out. They had both been dressed then, and he still was. When they had left Maya's it had been too late, and he had had too much to drink, to drive Bernadette all the way across London. So she had come back to his flat. She had refused to allow him to sleep on the couch, arguing that after all they had done with each other it was the height of hypocrisy to not sleep in the same bed. She suggested that they could keep their clothes on if it made him feel better. There had been a couple of very nice kisses, some cuddling, and then he didn't remember any more.

He got up and looked around the flat. Her note, taped on the refrigerator door, said that she had woken up early and had gone to get a taxi home, and would see him at six that evening.

As he ate some breakfast, he thought about the nude paintings in Maya's flat and whether he could take photographs like that - abstract portraits, or nude-studies, without seeing a face. Had there been a sexual relationship between Maya and the painter? he wondered. The paintings had seemed incredibly intimate as well as abstract. He sensed it, could feel it, but didn't quite understand it.

Bernadette looked great as usual. "I took a long nap this afternoon," she confessed.

Mags shared a strong family resemblance to Bernadette, but she wasn't as pretty. Normally she made up for it with energy and personality, but tonight she looked gorgeous. Clark thought she looked five years younger, but he was sure that that was not a polite thing to say.

"Clark, doesn't Mags look great, at least five years younger," Bernadette gushed.

He smiled, nodded, and continued to set up his camera on his small travel tripod. Although it wasn't very sturdy, he knew he needed a tripod for these shots because they would require a slower shutter speed and a more open aperture, both of which would increase the potential for a problem caused by the slightest movement of the camera. He had an inexpensive shutter plunger that would allow him to take a picture without touching the camera. He was determined to make these photographs perfect.

Bernadette hung a plain, dark blue, curtain on one wall as a backdrop. They positioned the backdrop so it was near a closet, and he attached the 250-watt light to the top of the closet door and aimed it down at the chair where they would sit. For fill light, he leaned a white cardboard reflector against a kitchen chair. He followed the suggestions and diagram in the Kodak portrait book to achieve what it called Rembrandt lighting. It was all very makeshift, and he tried to picture a young Ansel Adams doing it that way.

When everything was ready, he noticed that both women still wore jeans and fancy lace black bras but no shirts. That wasn't unusual for what they normally wore around their flat, but he didn't think that they would want to have their portraits done that way.

"Do you need time to get ready?" he asked.

They both looked confused, then concerned. "We are ready, is something wrong?" Bernadette replied.

"Oh, no, you both look spectacular," he quickly recovered. "Who's going first?"

After some spirited debate, the sisters decided that Mags would go first. She sat on the chair, and Clark could tell that she was nervous. She smiled, but it wasn't the Mags he knew, certainly not the one who teased him incessantly about his virginity and his love of blowjobs. He encouraged her to smile, and that just made it worse. She clearly thought she had been smiling and the additional effort only made her look more unnatural. It didn't help when Bernadette said, "Mags you can't look like that for your portrait, Momma will think you're hormonal or constipated." Bernadette told her a story from their childhood, then about one of her amusing clients, but nothing worked to get Mags to relax.

Desperate, Bernadette reached over and grabbed Clark's crotch. She pulled down his zipper and yanked out his penis, which immediately reacted to her touch. And as Mags watched, her face came alive, and Clark snapped some great photos.

When he had gotten enough, he started to stuff his penis back into his pants.

"Hey, what are you doing? What about me? I need a little inspiration too," Bernadette fake whined.

As Bernadette took the seat, Mags knelt down on the floor in front of Clark and behind the camera. She looked over at Bernadette, "I'll take care of little Yank here." Mags grabbed hold of Clark, and the sensation of her fingers brought him to full attention. He got distracted, lost in the pleasure. "Clark, are you watching Bernie and taking some pictures?!"

Clark hadn't been watching Bernadette or doing anything other than to enjoy the moment. He struggled to pull his attention back to the camera. When he managed to focus on Bernadette, he saw a wonderful look of concern and desire. No big smile, but a spectacular portrait of a caring, sexy, woman with more than a hint of the devil in her eyes. Classic Bernadette. Then he felt Mags put her lips to the tip of his penis and saw Bernadette smile. He knew it would rival the Mona Lisa for coy seductiveness. He was barely able to snap the photos as his body reacted to Mags. Then he went on auto-pilot, snapping more photos continually and trying not to give in to the pleasure.

"She's just showing off," Bernadette laughed. "She can keep a man dangling on the edge for hours."

After Mags finally brought Clark to a climax, it took him a while to recover. And by then they all realized that they were starving and decided to have dinner before taking down the curtain and the light. As they ate, Clark marveled at how he had gotten so lucky to have this relationship. At first he had thought that they were just playing with him, the silly virgin Yank. Then he had assumed they had some weird feeling of pity because he was so pathetic that he couldn't get laid except with a prostitute. But now he knew that it was a real and extremely odd friendship, one that he never in a million years would have believed to be possible. Friendly, and intimate, and also weirdly abstract. And suddenly Maya's nude paintings came into focus for him, and he understood them. He wondered if he could do that with Bernadette.

He hadn't said anything out loud, but Bernadette looked at him. "Clark do you remember those paintings of Maya in the nude, and do you think that we could do something like that with your camera?"

He tried not to look as excited as he felt. "I was just thinking of that, and I'd like to try if you want to."

"Absolutely. Let's do it. But I have an idea for them, if you'd like to hear it?"

"Sure."

"Okay." She started to remove her bra and pants as she spoke. "Her paintings are very abstract with the plain background, like we could do over there. And that would be good, but I'd also like to try some everyday sort of poses. You know eating dinner…" She posed with her arm over the back of the chair and her head turned seductively toward Clark. "Or reading the paper, watching telly, sitting on the toilet."

Mags cracked up at that one. Clark thought it was brilliant.

They started with Bernadette in front of the plain backdrop. She looked great but soon ran out of poses that seemed artistic and not pornographic. Then they tried a shot where she sat at the table with a glass of milk and read a textbook. Mags really got into it and soon had all her clothes off and took turns with Bernadette in most of the shots. Clark was amazed at how different they looked in the same setting, the same pose, both nude, but with very different personalities. He thought it probably also had something to do with his different feelings for them.

Creative sexual energy propelled them for the next few hours, as they moved around the flat and found poses that reflected ordinary-life kinds of things, but were also intimate and, of course, sexually exciting because of the naked bodies. Some turned out to be very funny - who knew how many things you could do with a big wooden spoon. Others bordered on the profound - a contemplative Bernadette lounging nude across the arms of a big arm chair with the light of the telly reflected on her body. Or Mags standing next to the window, peering into the darkness. They both kept joking about it, but neither was actually ready to do it on the toilet.

Finally, they were all exhausted and collapsed on the couch. Clark sat between two beautiful, naked women like it was the most natural thing in the world.

"That was incredible. I can't wait to see the photos. I loved looking at Mags through the camera," Bernadette said, and then she poked Clark. "Next time we get you naked, and I take some pictures,"

"Oh no, I stay behind the camera." He laughed, but he also wondered if he would be able to do that.

"And I want to do it again and have Maya over," Bernadette continued. "Some poses I have in mind would be uncomfortable with my sister, but they would be really cool with another woman. And I'm pretty sure that she's a lesbian or maybe swings both ways."

Clark was surprised. "Really?"

"Pretty sure. I got the feeling that if you hadn't been there last night, we would have been humping in her bedroom." She grabbed his leg and gave it a squeeze. "Or it could have been an exciting threesome if you ..." She felt her excitement grow, but stopped her hand just as it was about to reach for Clark's crotch.

"Sorry about that," he mocked. Clark was sure that would ever happen, but he did know that this was a night that he would never forget.

Clark knew that he couldn't give those rolls of film to the photo shop to develop. The portrait shots would be okay, but he wasn't sure which rolls they were on. So the next morning he called Nigel to arrange to use the darkroom. Reginald informed him that Mr. Nigel wasn't available, but Clark could come over at any time.

The security man remained expressionless despite Clark's friendly greeting, but Clark thought he got a glimmer of a grin from Reginald after Clark commented on his professional management of the household. Clark saw no evidence that Nigel had been working in the darkroom recently. The chemical baths were empty, and Clark had to mix fresh chemicals and fill the trays before he could develop any prints.

Clark felt a huge rush of excitement as he developed the contact sheets for the film. He had had images of Bernadette and Mags running through his head all night and morning. He forced himself to work on the portraits first because they were the priority for the girls. They were leaving for home on Wednesday and would be gone until after New Year. Thinking of that created an involuntary pang of anticipated loneliness.

He laughed out loud as he followed the progression of the night as reflected in Mags' expressions. When he saw her face come alive and remembered the impetus for it, he felt a reflex response in his genitals. In the excitement of the rest of the night, he had forgotten how many different expressions she had had. Serious Mags, nervous Mags, wild-eyed happy Mags, incredibly sexy Mags, and sweet not-so-innocent Mags. And there were several variations on each of them. It was a hard choice to narrow it down to three selections to print.

Interestingly, he found it much easier to choose the shots for Bernadette. He hadn't realized it, but he now knew her so well that it was immediately clear which shot captured her the best. It wasn't the overly sexy Bernadette, or the one with the crazy laugh, but the one with a slight smile and a twinkle in her eyes. Sexy, but also very sensitive, intelligent, wise.

He took a bathroom break while the last of the portrait shots sat in the fixer, and when he returned, he found Nigel examining the contact sheets.

It took a moment before Nigel realized Clark was there. "These are bloody brilliant. I didn't know you did stuff like this. Are these professional models?"

"No, just some friends of mine."

Nigel couldn't take his eyes off the shots of the nude women. "Smashing. So easy for these kind of shots to be trashy porno, but they're not, they're real art."

"Are you printing anything," Clark asked, as he grew self-conscious at Nigel's reaction to the photos.

"Oh, yes, I have some snaps from the anti-Rhodesia march on Saturday. Are you done in the developing room?"

"Yeah, it's all yours." Clark laughed as he realized what he'd said. "Of course it's yours."

Nigel seemed to get it and smiled as he reluctantly put the contact sheets down and left. Clark then got so absorbed in the nude-study photos that he barely realized when Nigel came back and began to work at his enlarger.

Clark had various photos in the chemical baths and the final wash. As he examined them, he realized that he was doing something that he knew wasn't good. He liked many of the shots and was impatient to see them come to life from the negative. So he rushed through them. Then, after the initial effort, he normally found it hard to go back and work more on individual shots. And he knew that it took that additional effort, sometimes a lot of additional effort, to turn a good photo into a great one. Clark worried that he was often too happy with good. But this time he promised himself that he would be diligent and go for great. But then he couldn't decide which shots to start with. He took them all out into the lobby area to contemplate.

Nigel watched him leave and then moved over to a metal cabinet in the corner where he kept the chemicals and photo paper. He pulled a large folio of prints from the top shelf and began to examine them. They were all nude-studies, somewhat similar to Clark's, but all of men. And more than a few of them were strikingly pornographic.

Clark had made little progress on his decisions when Nigel joined him. "I'm having a hard time prioritizing them," Clark said.

"I think those two have the most potential," Nigel re sponded, and pointed to the shots of Bernadette watching the telly and of the two women sitting cross-legged on the couch, facing each other, knees touching.

Clark smiled. They were in his top three, along with Mags at the window.

"Say, this Thursday some friends and I are going to the *Marat/Sade* at the National, and I know you like the theater, so I thought you might like to join us."

"Yeah, sure, I've wanted to see that."

For the next several hours Clark worked on the photo of Bernadette and the telly. He manipulated the composition by cropping it and that improved it a lot. But the more he got into it, the more he saw the problems of contrast that required very delicate burning and dodging adjustments. He was running low on photo paper, so he tore a sheet into long thin strips and used them to test different exposures. As Clark watched a new test strip develop, he noticed that Nigel's photo in the developer bath was a nice composition that featured Gwen with a bullhorn held by the side - the look of a real martyr, strong but beautiful. "So you've seen Gwen?"

"Yes, but she's gone home now. Probably until after winter break."

Clark realized that meant almost the end of January, and he felt disappointed.

"Did you hear about Arthur?" Nigel asked cautiously. "He went to Greece to try to talk to Cynna's father and convince him that they love each other and should be allowed to get married."

Clark hadn't thought about the fact that Nigel would undoubtedly know about his humiliation. He felt a sudden urge to finish up and leave.

"You got a raw deal with that," Nigel offered, with obvious compassion. "I never liked that bloody ice-queen. She sure has poor Arthur by the goolies. I just pray that her old man doesn't shoot him on the spot."

From what little Clark had learned from Cynna about her father, he could easily imagine such a tragic scenario. He then lost all of his residual feelings of anger at Arthur, replaced now with concern for his safety.

Later, as Clark rode the bus home, he couldn't wait to see Bernadette the next day. Happy with the portraits, he was really excited about the progress he had made on two of the nude-study shots. They weren't perfect yet, but he was determined to get there, or as close to perfection as it was possible to get with art.

It was Clark's first time in Harrods Department Store, and he wandered about, impressed, almost overwhelmed, by the ornate splendor of the building and the amount, variety, and cost of the merchandise for sale. The store was beautifully decorated for Christmas, but the holiday decorations were elegant and sophisticated, not fun and whimsical like those he remembered from New York City. No one did Christmas decorations like Macys or F.A.O. Schwartz.

He met Bernadette in the tearoom, which was quiet, being too early for the large crowd of elderly British ladies who normally came in for afternoon tea. He had never seen Bernadette wear anything other than very modern, colorful, stylish clothes that reflected the most modern fashion trends. But today she dressed very conservatively in a simple black dress that accentuated her wonderful curves and beautiful facial features. Wildly enthusiastic about the portrait prints, she pulled him into a serious hug and gave him a kiss that made his scalp tingle and his body vibrate. And then, after very expensive cups of tea, they walked to the section of the store where they sold picture frames. She caused a number of men and women to pause and wonder who she was - a celebrity or maybe royalty. And Clark felt incredibly happy and proud to be with her.

She carefully shopped for just the right frames. She planned to take all the photos, but she would only frame one each of her and Mags to give to their mother as gifts. Clark offered his opinion when asked, but he spent most of the time watching her. He thought about the fact that she was going away the next day and would be gone until mid-January. He was really going to miss her, and it must have been reflected on his face.

"Oh, Clark are you okay? You look so sad."

"I'm fine, it's just I'll miss you while you're gone."

"That's so sweet, I'll miss you also. I wish I could take you home but…"

He smiled and nodded, no explanation needed. He had hoped that maybe they could have dinner and hang out, but she couldn't.

"I'm sorry, but it's the holidays and the busiest time of year for … for our profession."

"Really?"

"Oh, you wouldn't believe how many men get depressed during the holidays. Even those who have wives or girlfriends or both. I read once that there are more suicides this season than any other time of year. Mags is booked all afternoon and night, and I'm..." She stopped because she could tell by his expression that he didn't want to get too many details on her professional sex life. And that was unfortunate because she really wanted to talk to someone other than her sister. Clark would be the logical choice, but he was so limited, no sexual sophistication at all. She knew he had gotten better, but he still had a long way to go.

He drove her home, and as he pulled away, he felt as lonely as he had ever been in his life.

The Royal Shakespeare Company had recently moved its production of *Marat/Sade* to the Aldwych Theater, where Clark had seen *US*. He didn't know much about the playwright Peter Weiss, but he knew that the play had been written in the vein of Bertolt Brecht. And Clark was a big fan of all of Brecht's plays, especially *Mother Courage and Her Children*, which his high school English teacher had called the greatest anti-war play of all time.

When he arrived at the theater, Clark found Nigel in the ticket lobby. With Nigel were several of the men who Clark had seen before, but there were also several women in the group, and many of the women looked like the men. Their hairstyles and clothes were masculine, but with small accents of bright color in a shirt or scarf or headband or, in one case, her hair.

"Clark, hi." Clark turned at the sound of a familiar voice to see Winston approach him with a cautious smile. "We missed you at the last game, but of course we expected, understood..."

Clark nodded, glad that Winston hadn't felt the need to spell it out. "How'd it go?"

"Well, without you or Arthur we sort of, well we were bloody awful actually," he said, as he laughed. "Twenty zip was the final. I hope you'll be back in the spring."

Clark nodded again. "I'm counting on it."

"Right then, here's your ticket," Nigel said, as he handed a ticket to Clark. "Let's carry on, shall we?"

Clark tried to give Nigel money for his ticket, but Nigel refused to take it. He muttered something about a bloody obscene allowance and helping friends, but Clark had a hard time hearing because of the noise from the rest of Nigel's group as they entered the theater. Clark noticed that the women all sat in one row and the men in another. He had assumed that at least some of them were couples on a date, but none of the women sat with any of the men.

The Persecution and Assassination of Jean-Paul Marat as Performed by the Inmates of the Asylum of Charenton Under the Direction of the Marquis de Sade presented a panorama of human suffering and struggle, set during the period of the French Revolution and the Napoleonic era that followed. Clark knew that the terms sadist and sadistic came from the Marquis de Sade, and there were plenty of depictions of him in the play which supported that legacy. Clark loved the intricate language and the play-within-a-play structure. But he wasn't so sure at first about the music. It didn't add to the plot or the character development, but like a Greek Chorus, it seemed to offer commentary on the themes raised in the play. The more he heard, however, the more he realized that the lyrics contained very much the same tone and feeling as many of his poems.

Several of the people in Nigel's group, including Nigel, seemed to know the words to the songs and sang along with the actors. They weren't loud, but Clark assumed that they could be heard up on the stage. He must have looked confused because Winston, who sat next to him, whispered, "Most of us have seen it five or six times and have the songs memorized."

As he came into the lobby with the group after the play ended, Clark didn't know what to do next. His instinct was to say good-bye and head home or to his favorite pub in Hampstead.

"Bloody brilliant play, don't you think. Most of us have seen it before, many times," Nigel commented. "Say, we're all going to Nelly's for a knees-up, care to join us?"

Clark was pretty sure that Nelly was the woman with the short dirty blond hair who seemed to be a little older than the rest and obviously the leader of the girl-pack. "Sure, why not." He suddenly felt ready for an adventure.

Everyone seemed to have a ride except for one young girl, Helen. Nigel asked Clark if he could give her a lift. Clark nodded as he casually examined Helen's cute but serious face and her slouching body that might be attractive if she stood up straight. Normally quiet and shy around people he didn't know, Clark was a jabberwocky compared to Helen. She pressed her body so hard against the door of his car that he feared she would force it open and fall out onto the road and into oncoming traffic. He tried to engage her in conversation but got nowhere. He took pity on poor Helen because he knew that there had undoubtedly been times when he would have come across to people that way. They rode in silence the rest of the way to Camden Town.

The Camden Town area didn't have a great reputation. Clark had had a couple of scary incidents there during his first weeks in London when he had walked through the area at night on his way home from the university pub. He hesitated, concerned whether to park his car and leave it. But then he noticed that Gerald had parked a few cars away, and his fancy BMW sedan was probably a lot more of a tempting target for thieves and vandals than Clark's MGB.

Helen jumped out of the car and immediately ran into Nelly's building, while Clark waited for Nigel who was in Gerald's car with two others. He thought their names were Robert and Howard, but he wasn't positive. None of them had shown much interest in talking to him, so it didn't really matter.

Nelly's flat was small, crowded, and very hot. Everyone shed their coats and many of the men completely unbuttoned their shirts. Clark dropped his coat on the pile but only undid one button on his shirt. He found a table with wine and some cheese and crackers but no beer or soft drinks. He spied Helen who sat alone in a corner gulping down a large glass of red wine. He felt sorry for her and wondered why she was there. She just didn't fit with the rest of the group - but of course neither did he.

"Clark, have you met Nelly?" Winston grabbed his arm and spun him around face-to-face with Nelly. Early thirties, she wore a lot of makeup to cover acne scars on her face. She wasn't that attractive, but Clark thought that she seemed interesting in a strange way.

"Jesus would you look at all that hair," Nelly shouted. Without warning, she grabbed Clark's shirt and started to unbutton it. He thought she might go right into his pants, but she stopped at his belt and then thrust her fingers into the hair on his chest. "Oh my god, it's so soft. Angela it's softer than your pussy!" she shouted across the room at a woman who looked to be Spanish and started to blush. "Come here and feel this. Does mine feel like this? I don't think so."

Nelly's outburst didn't impact the flow of other conversations, many of which seemed to be very intense. Clark then noticed a small glass vial in Nelly's hand. He knew those white pills, and he wanted no part of that with this group.

Nelly saw his interest in the pills. "It's great shit Clark, we're all getting crazy tonight. Aren't we Winnie?" Winston didn't seem bothered by her nickname for him, and his eyes widened with anticipation of the LSD trip.

"You know Clark that hair almost makes me want to try the other side tonight, wouldn't that be a fucking trip, haven't shagged a guy in so many years. Hey Angela, should we have a romp with Clark tonight? Have you ever fucked a guy Angela?" Angela turned her back on Nelly.

Helen, who had quietly joined them, reached for the vial of LSD. "Oh no, not you sweet cakes," Nelly said. "Mum would fry my ass if I let you trip." Then Nelly grabbed Clark's arm and pulled him close to whisper in his ear, "Clark, Helen's my baby sister, and I can't let her get high. You're not part of this scene, and I wouldn't really shag you, so would you be a good bloke and take her home? She lives in Hampstead. Do you know where that is? It's not too far." As she spoke, she carefully buttoned up his shirt.

Clark didn't tell her that he also lived in Hampstead. He would have driven Helen to Edinburgh to get out of this party and not look foolish. A small dose of Nelly went a very long way.

He didn't expect any conversation from Helen as they left and drove toward Hampstead, and he didn't get any. She sat up straight and stiff in her seat and played with the radio. The Rolling Stones, singing *Have You Seen Your Mother Baby?,* infused some life into her as she started to sing along and move her body. They pulled up in front of her house just as The Supremes began to sing *You Keep Me Hanging On.*

Unexpectedly, she didn't bolt out of the car, but slowly turned to Clark. "So, do you want me to suck your willy?"

Clark was too stunned to respond.

"I mean isn't that what you want?"

"Why would you think that?" he finally managed.

"My sister says that's what all men want, and that's why she prefers women. But I don't like women that way." She reached over to Clark's crotch, but he took her hand and held it away from him.

"How old are you Helen?"

"Sixteen. Almost seventeen. But that doesn't matter, Nelly says there's no law against a minor sucking a man's willy."

"Well, I don't know if Nelly's right about the law or not, but I know she's wrong about what most men want." He paused as he actually thought about that. "Well, I guess she may have a point about most men, but you shouldn't just offer to do that with a total stranger."

She seemed disappointed, but recovered quickly. "We could shag if you want. You'd be my first."

"I'm flattered, but I hope your first is with someone you know and like." He certainly wasn't about to tell her about his own lack of sexual experience.

"No, I'd rather do it with a stranger, and then I don't have to think about it every time I see them, you know in school or somewhere. And all of Nelly's friends are queer like her. I thought you probably were too at first."

"Well, Helen, it's not happening with me."

She didn't seem inclined to leave, so he got out, walked around the car, and opened her door. With a very pouty face, Helen slowly got out and trudged up the short walk to her front door. Clark had the car in gear and sped away as soon as she had the front door open. Poor little Helen, he thought, what a role model for a sister.

Clark woke with a start. It was early morning and still dark outside. He had been having a dream that Helen had pulled his penis from his pants and was sucking it while he stood in the middle of the crowd at Nelly's apartment. Then Arthur and Cynna appeared and pointed at him, laughing and yelling that he was still a virgin, that blowjobs don't count. That woke him up. He tried to get back to sleep, but memories of his series of women and sexual frustrations played out in his head like a bad kaleidoscope film.

He had had very little exposure to homosexuals, at least that he was aware of. Closets in his old world were still mostly kept shut, and if there were parties like Nelly's going on, he certainly wasn't aware of them. Confused as to why Nigel had invited him, he hoped that it had been just because they were friends, of sorts. Then he worried that maybe Nigel thought he was still a virgin because he was a latent homo. Clark felt very comfortable that he wasn't because he had never felt any kind of attraction to any guy.

He just couldn't understand why he kept having all of these odd and frustrating encounters with women. All he wanted was to establish a normal relationship with a nice woman and have nice normal sex. Instead it seemed like he was a magnet for every weird chick in the world. He added loud and crude Nelly and sad little Helen to that list.

He knew it would be impossible to get back to sleep, so he got up and got dressed. He made some coffee and realized that he had nothing to do. No school, no rugby, no friends. It occurred to him that he really had only one friend, and she was in Corsica at her family brothel. He would have laughed if he hadn't felt so pathetic.

Clark had grown up without the need for friends. It hadn't been an innate thing, but something that he had carefully developed over many years of moving and new schools and wrenching ends to early friendships. He had realized early-on that if he didn't make friends in a new town and new school, then he didn't have to be sad to leave them. It had worked very well until high school, and since then every time he had deviated from it, he had gotten burned. But here he was. He had again taken a chance, and his reward was to again feel like shit. The feeling centered mostly on Cynna and Bernadette, but it also had something to do with Gwen. She kept surfacing in his thoughts and often in his dreams. The pain and humiliation caused by Cynna and Arthur had dissipated, but he still experienced a sense of loss when he remembered Gwen's expressions the last time he had seen her. He knew that he needed to do something and not sit and wallow in his confused feelings.

Darkroom? No, Nigel had said that the house was off limits all weekend because his father had some business people staying there.

Laundry? No, it was Friday, and it would be packed with housewives and housekeepers getting things clean for the weekend. He had done that once and regretted it. Plus, Tildi might be there, and he certainly didn't want to interact with her in his current funky emotional state.

Cinema? Maybe an idea, and he looked around the flat for whatever newspaper he had. He found a week-old *London Times* and scanned the movie listings. *The Blue Max*, World War One drama - too depressing. *Cul-de-sac*, Roman Polanski, thriller, won the Golden Bear at the Berlin Film Festival - he wasn't in the mood for Polanski. *The Plague of the Zombies* - he hated horror films. *Fahrenheit 451*, Truffaut - he had wanted to see that, but not today, too much thinking required. *Alfie*, a good British comedy - perfect, but no matinee.

He looked outside. The sky was a typical light gray, and it was undoubtedly cold, but maybe it wouldn't rain. He hadn't wandered around central London for a while, so he decided to do that and then go to the seven o'clock screening of *Alfie* at a theater in Leicester Square.

He went down along the river at Westminster, but a stiff breeze coming from the west made it bitter cold. It wasn't windy in the Knightsbridge shopping district, and the crowds also provided some protection against the cold. He suddenly panicked when he realized that he hadn't thought of getting presents for his family for Christmas. His mother would surely send him something, and he'd probably get a check from his father. Sarah was hard to predict. So he looked in a lot of store windows for ideas for gifts. The windows were beautifully decorated for the season but rather than lift his spirits or get him in a holiday mood, they only heightened his depression.

He looked but didn't get any good ideas, and it dawned on him that he didn't really know what his parents needed or would like. That only added to his overall feeling of sadness. He found himself in front of Harrods and remembered the frames that Bernadette had purchased. The perfect solution. He would buy some frames, print some photos, maybe of Paris, put them in the frames, and send them early next week. He had no idea if they would reach Pennsylvania in time, probably not, but at least he would have done something.

Alfie had premiered in London the previous March, but after nine months it still drew big audiences on Friday and Saturday evenings. The large auditorium held almost three hundred and fifty people and was two-thirds full when Clark entered. The only aisle seat, which is what he preferred, was in a row almost at the very rear of the theater. Clark knew the film revolved around a scoundrel who mistreated women and eventually got his come-uppance. He had never seen the lead actor, Michael Caine, but he had heard Bernadette and Mags talk about how sexy he was. The actors were excellent, but Clark found himself increasingly uncomfortable with the main character's abusive behavior toward women and his cavalier attitude about several unwanted pregnancies and an abortion. But what bothered Clark the most was how eagerly and easily the audience, both men and women, laughed at each act of female humiliation. He couldn't understand why the women put up with it. He found himself depressed by the question and then more upset because he had no answer to, no understanding of, that dynamic. He certainly didn't consider the movie to be much of a comedy.

He left the theater and hurried to his favorite pub in the Piccadilly area, knowing it would be full of drunks and tourists. As expected, it was crowded, and there was a lot going on to divert his attention. Good people-watching normally lifted his spirits.

The next few days passed quietly, but not as quickly as Clark would have liked. Quiet days like those normally would be welcome, but he felt uneasy and out-of-sorts. He couldn't shake the feeling that he was treading water, going through the motions, and not getting anywhere. And the biggest problem was that he didn't know where he wanted to go. He had a strong sense that his destination wasn't even a physical place, and that didn't help at all.

He ventured to the university, but there were no students, and the pub and athletic facilities were closed. On a whim, he tried to check out one of Maya's novels from the university library. He had tried that months ago but couldn't because it was on a restricted list, which had increased his curiosity. The librarian was preoccupied with something else and didn't check the list as she glanced at his university identification card. Then as he read the novel, *Mountain of My Dreams*, he realized that it probably was restricted because of the content. Intensely and explicitly sexual, she used wonderful language and creative allusions to describe various sexual and metaphysical events. He tried to connect the Maya he knew from the classroom, and the image of Maya in the paintings in her flat, to Monique, the heroine of the novel, as she engaged in fascinating duels of wits and physical challenges, including a marathon chase on horseback across the Scottish Highlands. And then she took on two lovers at once, a male and a female. Maybe it wasn't Maya per se, but it certainly was her spirit. He had an impulse to go see her, but quickly squelched it.

Saturday night he went to the pub near his flat but left after one pint. There were too many cheerful couples, no interesting single women, and a lot of single, hungry-eyed men. He knew he wasn't a pick-up kind of guy even if there had been women who were available or looking for action. That was what had made the night he met Bernadette so unusual, and he really wanted to believe her that she hadn't been working.

Sunday morning, he went to the laundromat and ran into Tildi with her daughter. Some sexual innuendo enlivened their conversation, but Tildi made it clear that her husband was home for the holidays. As she left, she told him that her hubby would be gone right after the New Year and gave Clark a sly little wink. He wondered what she would think of his short story. Would she be amused or upset? He didn't intend to ever find out.

Monday morning finally came. Nigel had said that his house was off limits through the weekend. Clark hoped that Monday would be good because he had to do the prints for his family Christmas gifts, and he had been dying to continue working on the nude-study shots.

Reginald gave him the go-ahead over the phone, and Clark drove over, too impatient to wait for the underground or the bus. When he arrived and asked about Nigel, Reginald informed him that Nigel and his father had departed early that morning for Barcelona and Madrid, and would be gone a fortnight. He assured Clark that it was arranged for him to have access to the dark room at any time while they were gone. Clark asked Reginald if he was getting any time off for the holidays but didn't get any response.

From his contact sheets, Clark had selected a series of landscape shots to print for his parents as sort of a matching set. They could go in the family rec room or possibly his father would take one to his office. Clark had never been to his father's office, not in any one of the many places he had worked, but he tried not to dwell on that. For Sarah, Clark had a strong impulse to send her one of the nude-study shots. But he couldn't bring himself to do it, knowing that she'd open it Christmas morning with his parents there. That was something he didn't want to have to deal with on a long distance phone call. So he selected a picture he liked of a street kiosk along the Seine that had Notre Dame Cathedral looming in the background. The kiosk vendor sat with a bored expression while a pretty young French woman browsed through the rack of fashion magazines.

Satisfied with the prints for his family, Clark turned his attention to the nude-study shots. As he studied the photos on the contact sheets, he felt the influence Bernadette had on his life. It equaled the impact that his half-sister Rita had had on him when he was in high school. Rita had helped him break out from a very thick shell and take a chance on life and love. She had told him that being friends was the first step to being in love. He wondered if that applied to Bernadette. Was he falling in love with her? There was an undeniable connection between them, but he knew that he could never accept her profession if they were anything other than friends. Much better to keep it friends. Friends with unusual benefits, as Mags had said. He laughed to himself, and the memories of those benefits carried him through hours of work in the darkroom.

As he reached a point where his exhaustion thwarted any more productive work, he stopped and waited for the last prints to dry. He found himself looking at the contact sheets from the rugby trip. He had more shots with Gwen in them than he had remembered. Most of them weren't great photos, but they caused him to face the fact that he thought about her more than he realized. Are we friends? he wondered. He doubted it after the Cynna fiasco, even though it hadn't been his fault - he was the victim actually. But he wondered if they could get past it. Would she even have any interest in doing that?

Just before eight o'clock that night he finally got back to his car. James, the security man, had moved it twice to keep it from getting a ticket and then towed away. Clark was very effusive with his thanks, but James maintained his steady stoic expression. Clark had intended to drive straight home, but he found himself driving by Bernadette's flat, which was depressingly dark. Without making a conscious decision, he then drove by Cynna's and Gwen's flat - also depressingly dark. He expected his flat to look and feel the same, but when he pulled up, he noticed that a light was on. He didn't remember leaving one on, but maybe he had done it subconsciously. A light in the window for himself, the wayward traveler.

As he put the photos in frames and wrote notes for his parents and sister, he had to fight a strong impulse to grab his suitcase and head for the airport. He thought back to Thanksgiving the previous year, when he had planned to stay at school and catch up on school work rather than drive home. Initially he had enjoyed the quiet and the solitude of the empty campus, but that had gotten old very fast, and by late Wednesday night he had become so miserable that he had packed a bag, jumped into his car, and driven to Pittsburg. He had arrived home at six in the morning, just as his mother had come into the kitchen to begin preparations for the family Thanksgiving dinner. Her expression and warm hug had made the long drive totally worthwhile.

He briefly debated whether he should go home, but he knew he couldn't do that. For one thing, flying across the Atlantic was obviously different than driving across a few states. And what kind of message would that send to his parents, to himself? If he couldn't manage Christmas by himself, it would show weakness, a lack of maturity. But as much as his loneliness involved his family, it also involved Bernadette, and, he had to admit, Gwen. He would have to tough it out.

He paced aggressively around the flat and found himself in Melody's room, where he seldom went. For the first time, he really looked at the photos on the wall. They seemed to be from Ireland, or at least what he thought Ireland would look like. There was an enormous castle and a beautiful grassy cliff along the ocean. And a shot that someone had taken of Rita, Keith and Melody outside a place called The Dubliners Pub. He wondered if it was the actual place from the James Joyce stories.

Ireland? Rita's mother and her father, who was also Clark's father, were both pure Irish as evidenced by their brilliant green Irish eyes. And in Rita's case, by her dark red hair. Ireland? A wild idea raced around his head, and he made a spontaneous decision. He would go to Ireland for Christmas. It was the perfect destination, the perfect distraction.

CHAPTER 15

Wednesday afternoon, four days before Christmas, Clark stood on the deck of an Ireland Maritime ferry headed for Dublin. It had taken him an entire day to get ready. At the Royal Automobile Club, he had found out that he needed an insurance rider to drive in Ireland. Evidently the drivers there were worse than they were in England. He had left London early Wednesday morning, but the traffic on the M-1 motorway to Liverpool had been terrible and from there it was another 150 kilometers on two-lane roads to the ferry port at Holyhead, North Wales.

Eager to see the Irish shoreline, Clark squinted into the sun as it fell through the western sky toward the horizon. As they entered Dublin Bay and approached the city, he struck by the size of the busy port and the surprising lack of maintenance. Rusting cranes lurked over crumbling concrete docks, and ancient forklifts spewed black exhaust as they strained with their loads. It certainly didn't look at all prosperous.

Through the auto club, he had pre-booked a night in a hotel in Dublin. After that he intended to explore and take his chances on accommodations. He hoped he would find a network of independent inns similar to the ones he had found on his trip to Scotland. But in the spirit of adventure, he was willing to take his chances, and the auto club people had said that Christmas wasn't a big tourist season in Ireland. Their winter weather was as bad as and maybe worse than in England.

After checking into his hotel, Clark found the Dubliner Pub that he had seen in the photo in the flat. It was indeed old and Irish enough that James Joyce himself should have been at the bar. Irish men packed the public room. Most of them were drunk, loud, and pleased to meet an American of Irish descent. After his first pint, Clark didn't have to buy another one all night. He also got lots of advice on what to see and what to do. Opinions flowed as freely as the beer, and he soon learned that what one man lauded enthusiastically, another man denigrated with equal passion. They sang Irish ballads until the pub closed.

Clark woke the next morning with a throbbing hangover, his first since the rugby trip. He felt like staying in bed, but the sun shone brightly, and his wanderlust took over and eventually got him going.

Over the next few days, Clark wandered from Dublin to County Clare on the west coast of Ireland, then south through the counties of Limerick and Kerry to County Cork. He walked along the majestic grassy Cliffs of Moher that faced the Atlantic Ocean; toured a number of very old and interesting castles; visited the crystal glassblowing artists at Waterford; and saw a lot of spectacular scenery. He mostly kept to himself and found the people to be generally friendly but reserved. One night in Limerick, he stayed at a bed and breakfast and encountered a very friendly young Irish girl who worked there. He sensed that she was interested in him, but he hesitated, afraid that the only women who came on to him turned out to be either prostitutes or bored, over-sexed minors.

County Cork held special interest for him because both his father's family and Rita's mother were from there. His grandfather had come from the town of Cork, and Rita's mother had grown up on a small farm. He didn't know any specifics of where or what to look for, but he saw plenty of farms that looked pitifully poor. While in Cork, he toured Blarney Castle and kissed the Blarney Stone. He figured that it wouldn't hurt to be a little more loquacious. Late afternoon on Christmas Eve, he arrived back in Dublin.

Normally not a churchgoer, Clark felt a strong desire to experience the ambiance and hear the singing of a Christmas Day mass at St. Patrick's Cathedral. He barely found a place to stand along the rear wall. He thought of his parents going to their church in a few hours and wondered if Sarah would go with them. His sister questioned, more than he did, the Christian religious belief system that they had grown up with. Neither of them could understand people who took everything purely on faith and never questioned anything. He wouldn't call himself an atheist, but he felt comfortable thinking of himself as an agnostic. Or maybe a Buddhist like Rita, who had images and statues of the Buddha in the flat. He quietly left the cathedral when the priests began to offer communion.

He walked the almost deserted city for a couple of hours and then found a restaurant that had stayed open for tourists, single people, and couples without families. The restaurant staff went all out to make it festive, and that helped dull the forlorn feeling that came with eating Christmas dinner alone. Lonely and emotional, he knew that he could get really drunk, so it was fortunate that the Dubliner Pub, and all other pubs, were closed on Christmas day.

Clark arrived back in London in the evening, the day after Christmas. He wasn't sure what he was going to do with himself, but he had had enough touring for a while. He spent the next several days in the darkroom. He tried to keep a regular schedule of eight to ten hours each day. And every evening he fought off the impulse to drive by those dark, empty flats.

He had taken a lot of photos in Ireland that he was excited about, but he felt compelled to concentrated his time on the nude-study pictures, especially the five that he thought were the best. He experimented with different cropping and compositions and worked to get the contrasts just right. As time went on, it slowly became clear to him that he just wasn't a perfectionist by nature, and that applied to his writing as well as photography. He worried whether that would preclude him from ever being a real artist. Did all artists have to be tortured perfectionists? He hoped not.

Then on Friday morning, when he arrived at Nigel's house, Reginald informed him that he could not use the darkroom. Clark assumed that Mr. Barrington must be home and having another weekend event. He asked if it would be okay on Monday. Reginald gave him a blank look and repeated that the darkroom was closed, but didn't offer any explanation.

"Is Nigel back? Can I talk to him?"

"Mr. Nigel is not at home."

"When do you expect him? Is he also back from Barcelona?"

"I am not at liberty to say. Good day," Reginald replied, and cut off the conversation by firmly shutting the door.

Clark stood there confused and then upset because he had left his negatives, prints, a lot of stuff in the darkroom. Just as he reached to ring the bell, the door opened, and Reginald handed him a large Harrods shopping bag with all of his things in it. "I believe that is everything," the butler said brusquely, and shut the door again before Clark could respond. Clark had always thought that the setup with Nigel's darkroom was too good to be true, but he considered this unceremonious dumping to be very odd, even for the British.

Early the next morning, a loud knock on the front door of the flat woke Clark from a deep sleep. He had been up very late the night before, working on several stories, and he hoped that he could just ignore it. But then it came again, louder this time.

"What?" he shouted irritably as he neared the door.

"Clark, it's Gwen. I need to talk to you, it's important."

He only had on the boxer shorts that he normally slept in. "Just a minute," he shouted at the door, then rushed back to the bedroom for some clothes. When he opened the door, he found a very agitated Gwen.

She rushed into the flat before he could say anything. "Have you seen Nigel?" she demanded to know.

"Ah, no, I haven't, not since last Thursday, no wait, two Thursdays ago. Before he went to Barcelona with his father."

"Well, he's back and missing."

"Missing? Like police report missing?"

"No, missing like he ran away." Her energy dissipated, she collapsed on the couch.

Clark hesitated, not sure what to do. "Would you like some coffee?"

She shook her head and sat while he went to the kitchen to make some. When he returned with his coffee, she hadn't moved. She looked tired, worried, vulnerable. "Nigel and his father came back from Spain a few days ago. Then day before yesterday, it was his mother's … It has been a year since his mother's death, and I knew it was going to be hard on him, so I called. I could tell that Reggie was upset. He's been with their family since long before Nigel was born. And he finally told me that Nigel had been very emotional about his mother and had confessed to his father that he was a homosexual. And well, his father went crazy and threw him out of the house. I've been trying to find him to make sure he's okay."

Clark immediately thought of the strange interaction he had had with Nigel's father a few weeks earlier, and now his banishment from the darkroom made more sense.

"You haven't seen him or heard from him?" Gwen refocused on Clark.

"No. There's no reason I would have." He tried to remember if he had seen any sign of him having been in the darkroom. "Have you tried his friends?"

"Well, yes, of course I have, but they haven't seen him. One of them asked if I'd tried the bloody morgue. He was joking I think, but can you believe that?"

Clark didn't know those guys very well, but he wasn't surprised. "I do know one place we could try."

Clark drove her to Camden Town and pulled up in front of Nelly's apartment building.

"Who lives here?" Gwen asked.

"A woman named Nelly. She and Nigel seem close, and she's gay, but a woman, so probably not as complicated for him. Maybe."

"How do you know her?"

"He brought me to a party here the last time I saw him."

By now they were at the front door of Nelly's building, and Clark pressed the button for her flat. No answer, so he pressed again. Still no answer, but then the window above them opened, and Nelly stuck her head out. "Who the fuck's there?"

"That's Nelly." Clark grinned at Gwen before he responded to Nelly. "Hi Nelly, it's Clark Westfield, we met the other night, I drove your sister home. We're looking for Nigel. Is he here?"

"Fuck off, he doesn't want to see anyone."

Gwen stepped out to address Nelly. "Please tell him that it's Gwen, and I really need to see him."

Nelly frowned and pulled her head back in and shut the window. Then nothing happened for several long minutes. Clark was ready to go, but Gwen was rooted to the spot. "I don't think-" The buzz of the front door cut him off.

As they entered Nelly's flat, Nigel sat on the couch next to a pile of folded bedding. Nelly glared at them from just inside the doorway to her bedroom, and then she closed the door as they approached Nigel.

After some awkward attempts to be polite and several minutes of silence, Nigel finally broke down and told them about how he had come out of the closet and his father's reaction. "He wasn't violent, but he couldn't handle it, so he told me to leave. Nelly's been my refuge on several occasions in the past."

"I'm sure he'll settle down, and you can go home." Gwen attempted to be optimistic.

"He might, but I can't. There are just too many memories there." He lingered on the verge of tears.

"Can you stay here?" Clark asked, dubiously. The flat was very small and still hot, and Nelly's personality ate up a lot of room.

Nigel shook his head.

"Well, I have a spare room, you can stay there," Gwen offered. "I was going to post a classified for a lodger beginning of term."

Clark had an immediate and mixed reaction. Great deal for Nigel, but he couldn't forget the reason for the empty rooms.

After some wavering by Nigel, it was all settled. Clark drove Gwen home, each lost in their own thoughts.

"Thank you Clark, I never would have found him."

"No problem. I hadn't realized that you two were so close."

"Oh, I guess. We seem to feel the same about a lot of things, different causes. And in our first year we found ourselves alone at various events. He was much more in the closet in those days. And I had just started dating Ezekiel, well sort of dating, and he wasn't normally around. He's older and has never done the university thing. So Nigel and I got to know each other and became good friends."

Ezekiel the drug dealer, Clark thought, but caught himself before he said it out loud. Cautiously he asked, "So are you still dating Ezekiel?" He kept his eyes on the road while he waited for an answer.

"It's complicated," she finally responded, in a very quiet voice.

He wanted to but didn't feel like he was in a position to pry. So he changed the subject to lighten the mood. "I thought you were going to be home until the start of term."

It worked, as she laughed. "Yeah, but I was going stir-crazy with my parents. Normally I've got Arthur for a distraction but he's… he wasn't there."

"Have you heard from him?"

"Just a telegram a few days before Christmas. I hoped that he'd be back by now, after he realized that it's hopeless. But I guess we're both bloody stubborn and love lost causes." She tried to smile and make light of it, but it fell flat.

Later, as he drove home and turned on the radio, Clark heard people talk about their plans for New Year's Eve, that night. He considered for a moment whether to turn around and go back and ask Gwen if she had plans. But he assumed that she had to already be doing something, probably with the drug-dealer, so he continued home. He heard the phone begin to ring as he got to the front door of the flat and barely got there it in time to answer it.

"Hi Clark, I know this is kind of last minute and that I just saw you, but I wondered if you were doing anything tonight or would like to hang out," Gwen rushed and then paused expectantly.

It took him a moment to process, but that must have been too long for her.

"Oh, that's okay, never mind, I'm sure you've got-"

"No. No I'd love to hang out," he blurted out. "I actually almost came back after I left you to ask the same thing."

"Oh really?"

He could hear the surprise in her voice, and it sounded positive.

"Would you like to come here? I really hate going out on New Year's. But I understand if it's too awkward because of, you know, Cynna."

Neither had actually spoken her name until now.

"No it's fine. If I do happen to think of her, I picture her locked in a convent. I know that's mean but…"

She broke up laughing. "I'll remember that, it's a bloody good image."

He offered to stop and bring food, and she readily agreed, admitting that she didn't like to cook. He arrived back at her flat a little after nine o'clock with a bag of Indian food. He had picked Indian because he liked it and also because it seemed like the Indian restaurants were the only ones not jammed with people on New Year's Eve dates. He also brought her a gift - a print of the photo he had taken of her on the train from Paris, which he had put in a frame.

"Oh my God, I look terrible!" she exclaimed when she saw the photo.

Clark didn't agree. "No, I think you look … really nice."

"But I look so bloody serious." She peered intently at him. "Do I always look like this?"

He hesitated, knowing that it was a dangerous minefield of a female question. Should he reply with complete honesty - that she did look very serious most of the time? "I think you look great - confident, self-assured, as you lead a bunch of hung-over blokes back home."

She laughed and gave him a quick kiss on the cheek before putting the frame on the bookshelf in the living room. "I'm starved, let's eat," she said, as she grabbed his arm and steered him to the small kitchen table where she had set out plates, utensils and napkins.

Gwen's only complaint about the food was that it wasn't spicy enough, and she teased Clark for being a, "spicy-food Nancy." They sat at the table and talked for a long time. She enjoyed hearing about his trip to Ireland, especially the Blarney Stone. She went quiet at the mention of St. Patrick's. "I just couldn't do the church thing with my parents. They really wanted me to go, but it would have been too hypocritical."

Then they discussed some of Gwen's recent social and political events. She asked him why he didn't get involved in the anti-Vietnam movement.

"I'm definitely against the war, but I don't know, I just don't feel comfortable out there in public, trying to tell other people how they should think. They're either for it or against it."

"Quite the contrary, most people know bugger all to be one or the other, and we have to make sure that they know the truth."

"I guess. Like I didn't know anything about Rhodesia before I got here. It's not a topic in the States. I was actually a little surprised that Vietnam is such a big deal here, it's not your war."

"Any war is everyone's war, Clark."

He fell silent as he considered that.

"Let's see if they have any celebration stuff on the telly," she offered, trying to lighten the mood.

It was already after eleven o'clock, which surprised them as they sat on the couch, and she tuned to the BBC coverage of the New Year's Eve celebrations in Piccadilly Circus and at the Royal Albert Hall with the London Symphony. They sat carefully positioned with almost a full-body width of space between them.

"Wow, look at the crowd," she marveled. "All those desperate dates." Then after a moment, she asked, "You didn't think I was desperate did you? And I mean this isn't really a date, just hanging out isn't."

"No, hanging out is not a date. At least not in America."

"Corking. There's so much God damn pressure, particularly on a woman. You either have a date for New Year's Eve or you're a bloody wanker."

He wondered why she wasn't out with Ezekiel but knew not to ask. In the minutes of silence that followed, he thought of Bernadette and wondered what she was doing. Then he assumed that he didn't want to know because it had to be a very busy night in a brothel. He would have felt much better if he had known that the Ochera family brothel was always closed on New Year's Eve, a long family tradition. It was on New Year's day that they got crazy busy.

The festive activities at Piccadilly Circus gave them plenty to comment on as the time drew near to the stroke of midnight. As Big Ben rang the hour, they turned to each other and leaned in for the kiss that had been on both their minds. It was nice, and he barely noticed her cigarette taste. Neither one seemed compelled to break it off until they remembered that they were just hanging out. Then it started to feel awkward, and Clark soon got ready to leave.

As he started to close the front door behind him, she stopped him. "I wouldn't mind hanging out again, maybe a cinema, this weekend. Call me." Then she quickly shut the door.

The movie *Georgy Girl* had been playing at the Covent Garden Cinema since before Christmas, and Gwen really wanted to see it. The only things that Clark knew about it were that Lynn Redgrave looked very sexy on the movie posters plastered around town and that he liked the hit single title song by The Seekers.

On the drive from Gwen's flat, she reported about an anti-apartheid rally during the past week and that she had had a lot of trouble getting her friends out of jail. At one point she had been afraid that they were going to arrest her as well because she kept pestering the magistrate. None of them could afford to hire a solicitor, so they always argued their own cases. And in doing so, she had learned a lot about the laws of peaceful gathering, the anticipatory extraction of a perceived threat to the public, and the rules of retention without prosecution.

Clark was impressed and congratulated her, and also teased her, "Maybe you should become a lawyer."

"I just might do that."

"You might want to check out my Philosophy of International Law course, the professor is pretty cool." He paused, then asked, "So is it the custom to continue skipping classes during the second term as well?"

"Most certainly for us second years, but I don't know what you have to do for your school in the states."

Clark didn't either, and he had recently started to seriously worry about it. He had put it off during the fall, but now he knew he needed a plan. He would love to keep writing short stories and leave it at that, but he knew that those grades wouldn't be enough to earn credit for a full year of courses. He felt sure that Maya would write a recommendation letter for him, but he didn't know about the other professors, especially the two who obviously hated him.

Gwen insisted that, since they were hanging out, they should each pay for their own ticket, but she did let Clark buy her a small bag of popcorn. Soon after the film began, they both decided that they didn't like it. Clark got upset that the sweet but naive Georgina, or Georgy, could be so easily manipulated by an older man and then so casually jump into bed with her roommate's husband. Gwen was furious at the degrading portrayal of a supposedly intelligent woman. She saw it as an insult to smart women, and whispered to Clark, "Obviously directed by a fucking clueless man with a bloody hard-on." At the end of the film, when Georgy married the old man just to keep the baby that wasn't even hers, they were both disappointed.

"What a bloody waste," Gwen muttered, as they left the theater. "She's just throwing her whole life away."

"Well, at least the baby is lucky, I suppose. If they stay married, which I doubt. It's kind of Shakespearian in a way, except they don't all die."

"Don't insult bloody Shakespeare," she teased, as she picked up on his attempt to lighten the mood. "I still like the song though."

They stopped at a pub that she liked in her neighborhood. It had all the polished wood and brass of a typical pub, but there was something oddly different about it that Clark felt but couldn't articulate.

"Interesting that you notice," Gwen responded. "It's actually the first public house built and owned by a woman. 1908, but she had to hide behind the shirt of her brother because of the bloody sexist society back then."

"I'm not sure it's so different now," Clark observed. "It certainly was alive and well in that flick."

"My God, I was totally gobsmacked when that bloody roommate got knocked up again and again. What a trollop."

They shared a laugh and then sat quietly for a moment.

"I'm really sorry that I created that scene last month over bloody Cynna and caused you to… you know."

Clark hadn't thought about it for a while, and he struggled to decide how to handle this potentially awkward discussion.

"I'm sure people will have forgotten all about it," she continued. "And besides what's the big deal? So you're a virgin, there's nothing wrong with that."

"Not unless you don't want to be one."

"Well, why don't you do something about it?"

"It's not that easy. Not like for a woman."

"What's that supposed to mean?"

"For a girl, all she has to do is walk up to a guy she likes and ask him to go do it, and he's, of course, all for it, and presto it's done. If a guy does that, goes up to a girl he fancies, he gets slapped, maybe even arrested." He tried to keep it light, but he was absolutely serious.

"That's bloody rubbish Clark."

"No it's not. You don't think that if you were a virgin and you asked, that any guy in this pub wouldn't jump at the chance to, you know…?"

"Including you?" She instantly regretted saying it.

Clark hadn't expected that and nervously took a big drink of beer.

She tried to recover. "Sorry, not proper hanging-out etiquette. No more talk of virgins. Deal?"

He nodded, happy to move on.

"Except there is that bird over there." She pointed to a tall blond woman who stood alone at the bar. "I know her, and I'm sure she'd be happy to shag you if you asked. But you'd probably get a disease."

Clark felt completely at loose ends during the next week. It wasn't simply that he was unhappy with the interminable bleakness created by the wet, cold weather. Boredom had set in and dominated him. He had books to read, but… He had stories to write, but… He had lots of photos to print, but… For everything he thought of, he found a reason not to do it. So he moped around the flat during the day singing *Paint it Black* and *Ruby Tuesday* and a lot of James Brown. He got moderately drunk a couple of nights and then drove by Gwen's and Bernadette's flats.

He did have a bright moment when he received a letter from Rita telling him that she had arranged for him to meet with her old boss about a song that she and Keith had written using one of his poems as the lyrics. Clark and Rita and his old girlfriend Julie had created a song when he was a junior in high school. Keith and his band had recorded it, and the record had been a minor hit in England. It had even had some radio air-play in the U.S. They had collaborated on a few other songs over the past few years, but none had been as successfully.

He wrote a long letter to his parents after he received a letter from his mother thanking him for his gifts and telling him how quiet Christmas had been without him. He thanked her for the sweater she had sent him and was careful to not put anything in the letter that wasn't positive or that would cause them to worry about him.

Gwen had said she had a commitment on Saturday night, which he had translated to mean a date with Ezekiel. She never called them dates, nor did she ever refer to him as a boyfriend. She just kept saying that it was complicated. He couldn't figure out what that meant because it seemed so incongruous with the woman he had begun to know. All he knew was that it left an increasingly strong empty feeling in the pit of his stomach.

It was after midnight, and he had just gotten undressed for bed, when the telephone rang.

"Clark!" Gwen shouted urgently when Clark answered the phone.

"Gwen, is that you?"

"So sorry to bother, but I didn't have anyone else to call. I'm in a pay blower using my last shilling." She quickly explained that she was at a club and needed to go home, but her bag and purse had been stolen, and she had no money.

Clark didn't ask why she was alone, but got the address and left as soon as he got dressed. The Totem Club operated in a very rough part of Camden Town, not far from Nelly's flat. As he approached it, he remembered that he had been there several months ago to see Jimi Hendrix. He had left after the first set because it was just too loud and the guitar playing too frantic.

As he pulled up in front of the club, it surprised him that there wasn't a line of people waiting to get in. The only people he saw were a couple of men hanging around the entrance, and they looked drunk or high. He didn't see Gwen, and he began to worry. She had tried to be calm on the phone, but he could tell that she was upset or worried or scared. Just as he opened the door to get out of the car, Gwen emerged from the doorway of the building next door, rushed over to his car, and jumped in.

"Go! Please," she urged.

He started the car and quickly pulled off, headed across town toward her flat. She sat and stared out the side window. He didn't press for any information or even a greeting or a thank-you. He could tell that she was upset and probably high - a heavy aroma of marijuana drifted off her clothes and hair. They rode in silence all that way to her flat. When he pulled up and parked, she just got out and headed for her door. He respected a person's need to be quiet and private, but this was hard for him to accept.

At her front door, she paused and stood for a moment before she turned sharply and came back to the car. She sat back down. "You're a good friend Clark, thanks. And especially thanks for not getting all in my business."

He smiled carefully. "Sure. Are you okay?"

She stared at him for what seemed like forever until finally she said, "Yes and no. I wasn't, but now I am."

He waited. He was a good listener.

"Ezekiel had a gig there with this band, he's a drummer, bangs around with different groups. This one… well, let's just say they're fucking far out there. And they attract a dodgy crowd. I shouldn't have gotten high, but Ezekiel insisted. He wanted me to drop some of his acid, but thank God I didn't do that. It was a bad enough scene as it was. There were a couple of fights, and then I saw this one mean looking bloke with a knife. So I just had to get out of there, but my bag was gone from the band's dressing room, and Ezekiel was playing and…" Her voice trailed off.

"I'm glad you called me."

She smiled, not big but genuine. "Yeah, me too." She leaned over and gave him a quick kiss on his cheek. "Good night." And then she was gone.

On the drive home, he kept imagining her in a big threatening crowd. She was small, but yet he had seen her stand toe-to-toe with that bobbie at her protest rally. What really bothered him was the thought of her with Ezekiel, the drug dealer drummer.

CHAPTER 16

Clark had always had a love-hate relationship with school. Unlike most people, he loved the work, and it was the social aspect that he had seldom felt comfortable with. As the spring term began, he looked forward to some of his classes, but he dreaded having to face the aftermath of his confession in the student union. He knew that Gwen wasn't going to any classes, so he didn't even consider attending Modern Imperialism. He checked out Political Realities in the Middle East to see if Nigel would be there and if anything had been done about Professor Cohen. But the answers were both negative. There were only a handful of students in the room, and all of them were international students. He didn't bother to stay.

He didn't know exactly when Bernadette would return from Corsica. When he had driven by her flat the week before, it had still been dark. He had tried to call her on Sunday evening, but no one answered. When he arrived for the Creative Writing class on Wednesday morning, he didn't see her. Maya also seemed to look for Bernadette in the empty chair next to him, and he was pretty sure that he detected a trace of disappointment on her face.

Maya seemed distracted and not prepared to do anything except survey the students in the class to see if they had had any adventures over the break that gave them ideas for new stories. They were about half-way around the room when Bernadette poked her head in the door and sheepishly came in and took the seat next to Clark. He could see and feel a subtle change come over Maya, as she acknowledged Bernadette with a nod of her head.

When it was Clark's turn for a story idea, he described a simple farmer from Cork who touched the Blarney Stone and then couldn't stop talking, not even to eat or sleep. He knew it wasn't his best idea, but he didn't feel like sharing what he was really working on. Bernadette told a story of a lonely man from Corsica who discovers that he is the father of a woman who works in the local brothel.

"That's actually Mags' story," Bernadette told Clark later while they ate lunch in the pub. "My mother, whenever she wanted to have another baby, would pick one of her customers who she thought would have good genes to make a baby, a girl baby. Then when her time was right she would have unprotected sex with them to get pregnant. But the men never knew. Most of them already had families and wouldn't want to know. But this man, Mags' father, has recently lost his wife and son in a fire, and he was, he is, all alone."

"How did Mags know that he's the one, her father?"

"I don't know. She won't tell me. But I'm sure it didn't come from my mother. She only tells us the nationality. All my siblings are French from Corsica, except for me. I'm half-Italian. My mother says that's why I'm her most difficult."

"That's crazy." He laughed. "You're the most laid-back, easy-going person I know."

"Oh Clark, it's all an illusion for you," she half-teased. "My mother doesn't believe that women need an education to be good whores, and that's what Ochera women are bred to be. But I insisted on an education and drove her crazy until she relented. Then I almost blew it by insisting on going to America or England for university. I only won because of Mags. She agreed to accompany me and help me work while I went to school."

She had to leave right after lunch, and Clark fought his disappointment. He hadn't had a chance to tell her very much about Ireland or Gwen.

Clark remembered that Gwen had seemed interested in the Philosophy of International Law course when he described it to her, but he hadn't anticipated that she would actually show up for class on Thursday afternoon. She walked in right before class began and spoke to Professor Doctor. He nodded in agreement to whatever she said, and she took a seat next to Clark, the one he had always saved for Cynna.

He watched as Gwen immediately became engrossed in the lecture. He remembered the first time that he had seen her in a class and how he admired her ability to concentrate so intensely. At one point she asked a question that wasn't based on the reading, which she obviously hadn't done, but on her natural instincts for the law and morality. The professor was clearly impressed with her question.

At the end of class, Gwen jumped up, said, "Thanks again Clark," and rushed away before he could respond.

He remained disappointed and alone through the weekend.

Clark arrived at the EMI Record Studio on Abbey Road for his one o'clock Wednesday meeting with Terry Semple, Rita's former boss. He gave his name at the security desk and was directed to the third floor, where he encountered another security station. The guard there was much more vigilant and told him to wait. Clark wondered if all the security was normal, and he noticed a nearby recording studio where the red on-air light above the door was turned on.

As he waited, he thought about the poem he had sent to Rita six months or more before. He had written it about a young woman from an all-female junior college who goes to a dance, a freshmen mixer at an all-male college. She's forced to walk through a gauntlet of drunken upperclassmen to get from her bus to the gym, where the freshmen guys were waiting. She has to decide between continuing on to what is likely to be a lame chaperoned freshman dance or rebelling and giving in to the lure of wild fraternity parties as offered by the eager upperclassmen. Clark had been in the gym at such a mixer his freshman year in college and in the gauntlet his sophomore year when he was a pledge to a fraternity.

The red light turned off, and the door to the studio flew open. A small man with a wiry build and bloodshot eyes burst out, ran down the hall, and disappeared into the men's bathroom. Following him was an older, portly man. When he saw Clark, he came over and introduced himself as Terry Semple. He asked about Rita but didn't wait for an answer before he continued, saying that he was worried she would stay in Los Angeles. "But she'll probably be running the whole bloody studio by then," he finished, before he finally managed to catch his breath.

The small wiry man emerged from the bathroom, and Terry stopped him to introduce Clark. "This is Brian Epstein, manager of The Beatles. They're in there working on their new album. You can tell that it's going well because he's not screaming."

"Oh right, Rita's brother," Epstein realized. "It's a smashing good song really, but the lads aren't doing anything but their own material. They would like to meet you and asked if you want to sit in on the session." Then he ushered a very excited Clark into the studio to meet the Beatles.

Clark felt like he was in another dimension, floating in someone else's body. John Lennon came over, shook his hand,

and said that he remembered and liked Clark's song. He encouraged Clark to keep writing and suggested he contact Peter Noone of Herman's Hermits because they were working on a new album and might be looking for his kind of song. John told Clark to give his best to his sister whom he kept calling, "lovely Rita."

Clark sat in the control booth for several hours and watched and listened to the group work on a new song about a girl named Lucy who had diamonds in the sky. He had heard stories of the Beatles' growing difficulties working together and with producers. There were even rumors about a break-up. But he saw a casual, yet incredibly intense group that seemed to respond very positively to most of the suggestions from producer George Martin. Epstein spent most of the time talking on a telephone. At one point Clark thought about the Lucy he knew from home and the embarrassing reaction he had had the first time he met her, almost two years ago. He wondered what she was doing.

Clark could have stayed there all day, but the band reached an impasse on the second stanza of the song and left for an extended break. Terry smiled at Clark, shrugged his shoulders, and said, "They could be back in an hour or a fortnight." As he left the studio, Clark desperately wanted to tell someone about the experience, but that wasn't his style, and anyway he figured that no one would believe him. He went home and worked for the rest of the day and into the night on several poems that he thought might be suitable for songs. Rita had two albums of Herman's Hermits, and he played them both several times.

All weekend and the first days of the following week, Clark tried to keep busy. But he felt adrift. The only bright spot was on Sunday when the sun appeared through a break in the interminable rainy sky. He spent hours walking through

Hampstead Heath. At school he had by now run into a number of men from the rugby team, including Charles, and everything had been perfectly normal. There seemed to be no lingering effects from his virgin confession with any students he had encountered. He looked forward to Wednesday's creative writing class, but Bernadette didn't show up. He went to the Philosophy of International Law class on Thursday with the hope that Gwen might be there, but he was again disappointed. He had just left that class when he saw her in the hall, leaning against a wall, smoking a cigarette. She looked tired. She spotted him and immediately came over. "Would you like to go get a cup of coffee?" she asked.

He followed her to a trendy coffee and wine bar on the Aldwych around the corner from LSE. It was late afternoon, and the coffee crowd had thinned out. The evening wine and poetry crowd wouldn't arrive for several more hours.

Gwen kept silent, and he followed suit. They ordered coffee and found a table by a window in the front.

"How old are you Clark?"

That certainly hadn't been on his list of what he imagined she might want to talk about. "Twenty."

She nodded like that was the answer she'd expected. "When's your birthday, your twenty-first?"

"May ninth. Why?"

She didn't answer right away, then said softly, "Mine's today."

Momentarily confused, he recovered quickly. "Your twenty-first birthday is today?"

She nodded and didn't look very happy about it.

"Happy Birthday!" He tried to be upbeat even thought he could tell that she clearly had some major issues with it.

"Thanks," she responded with a weak smile. "I know it's this symbolic age, becoming a real bloody adult and all, but I just, I don't know, I just feel so fucking unsure, so... well, not lost exactly, but not fucking found either."

He nodded and hoped he offered a sympathetic look and rueful smile as he waited for her to continue.

"Ezekiel wants to have a big party on Saturday, but I'm not sure I want to."

Ezekiel the drug dealer drummer asshole, Clark silently mocked, then asked, "Why not?"

"Oh, I don't know." She hadn't yet touched her coffee but now took a sip. "I don't have many people I would want to invite. There's you, and Nigel. I don't want to invite any of my protest gang. Maybe a few of the ruggers - Winston, Charles. But Arthur's still gone, and I'm really worried about him. It'll turn out to be mostly Ezekiel's people, and I don't like them very much."

"Well, don't invite them."

"It's not that easy. He's hanging out with a bunch of new bloody people and some of them are... Ezekiel he's, well, he's gotten involved in some fucking stuff, and it's changed him."

Ezekiel the drug dealer drummer asshole. The refrain again ran through his head. He had never seen her this flustered and unfocused before. This was much different from the night outside the nightclub. "Do you want to celebrate? Would you like to go out to dinner?" he asked carefully.

"That's sweet Clark. Yes, I want to celebrate, and I'll probably agree to the party. But you have to promise me that you'll be there. I'll really need my friends around me."

"I promise."

She left soon after. She never responded to his dinner invitation, and he didn't repeat it.

Clark stayed for another coffee and tried to take his mind off Gwen by thinking some more about what he might propose to his LSE professors for some work product to prove that he had done what he was only partially doing. As he agonized over that dilemma, the weather seemed to respond to his mood. The sky darkened and then poured cold rain, sleet, and what looked suspiciously like snow.

Gwen called Clark early on Saturday morning to confirm that he was coming to her party. She sounded frazzled and emotional. He felt a little bit the same way because he needed to get her a present - the right present. But he didn't know what that would be. Despite the time they had spent together recently, he still felt that there was a lot about her that he didn't know that well. Finally, he remembered that Brian Epstein had given him an autographed photo of the Beatles. He assumed Gwen liked them because he had seen their poster and all of their albums at her flat. So he put the photo in a frame and wrapped it with leftover Christmas paper, which he hoped she would find funny.

Gwen's party took place in a large private room at The Star Tavern, a famous old pub in Belgravia, and was scheduled to start at eight o'clock. Clark arrived, as promised, at exactly eight. Gwen rewarded him with a very warm smile and quick embrace, which was immediately offset by a weak, cold handshake from Ezekiel. "Thanks for coming mate," Ezekiel offered in his very proper British East African accent. "Gwen talks a lot about you."

Clark looked for but didn't see a flicker of recognition from their brief meeting at Maya's party. Ezekiel's brown eyes were alive with intelligence and constantly darted around, looking for something - a friend, a client, prey. Clark also detected a touch of trepidation in his frantic demeanor and assumed that fear would be a drug dealer's occupational companion.

Clark got a pint and watched Gwen and Ezekiel as people arrived. The guests were mostly young. Some looked like musicians, and others were young enough to be students but they were dressed too expensively, too put-together in the latest fashions. He didn't recognize anyone from LSE. And then there were some older men with hard looks and uneasy eyes. The whole group made Clark nervous in a way he couldn't explain.

Clark could tell that Gwen was uneasy and didn't seem to know many of those people. He had never seen her smoke so much - one right after another. When Nigel arrived with Winston around eight-forty-five, she quickly left Ezekiel, went straight to them, and pulled them over to join Clark. It seemed like she would have been happy to stay with them, but Ezekiel soon grabbed her to introduce other new arrivals. Clark concluded that this was clearly Ezekiel's party, with Gwen's birthday merely an excuse to have it. What Clark couldn't figure out was why Ezekiel needed the pretense.

An hour or so later, as Clark talked to Winston, he noticed Ezekiel speaking with someone who looked vaguely familiar, and it seemed like they were staring at him. Then they both approached him.

"Jamie tells me that you're the bloke who wrote *No Tears for Me*," Ezekiel said, forcing a smile. "I played with Keith Malone's band a couple of times before he went to the states. The crowd always loved that song when we played it." Ezekiel now showed an entirely different attitude toward Clark. "And you got something going with the Beatles?"

Clark could barely stomach the sycophant. And now he remembered seeing this Jamie guy bring coffee to Brian Epstein. "No, that didn't work out," he mumbled, and hoped it would end the conversation.

"You met the Beatles?" Winston interjected loudly enough to stop conversations in the area around them.

Clark nodded and felt too many eyes on him. "My sister works for EMI, no big deal."

Just then Gwen came up and grabbed Clark. "I need your help over here if you don't mind."

He readily moved off with her to the side of the room and a table where people had put their birthday presents. "What do you need?"

"Oh, nothing, I thought you needed to be rescued," she smiled. It was the first hint of life he had seen in her eyes all evening.

"I did, thanks." They stood quietly for a moment. "There are a lot of people here," he offered.

"And I have no fucking idea who they are. A few are old friends of Ezekiel's, but not many."

Clark couldn't be sure but asked, "Is it just my imagination or do a lot of them seem high? But I don't see or smell weed."

She nodded. "Don't let him give you any little pills, not the yellow or green ones, and especially not the white ones."

Clark knew all about the white ones but not the others.

"He's been after me to drop acid, and I refuse. Have you ever done that?"

He shook his head.

"I can't imagine purposefully giving up control like that," she continued. "Everybody's got some bloody awful things inside them that they don't want to come out and run around dressed like fucking pink elephants or pink polka dotted hippos or some crazy shit like that."

Clark laughed uneasily, remembering what had happened to Erin.

Ezekiel appeared, put his arm around Gwen's waist and handed her a glass of wine. "Got someone I want you to meet love, excuse us Clark."

Clark found Nigel talking to several musician types and joined them. They were having an interesting discussion debating the influences and counter-influences of music from different regions of the world. It wasn't just the standard babble he heard at pubs or parties about the impact of British rock-n-roll on American rock-n-roll. He had gone to the bar for another pint when he heard Gwen scream.

"You bloody fucking arsehole! What did you give me?"

He had heard that tone before, and he was glad it wasn't directed at him. Then he became worried. He saw her, almost in the center of the room, clutching a fistful of Ezekiel's shirt and yelling in his face.

"You're turning pink you mother fucker, and next will come a trunk, a fucking elephant. I told you no elephants. Clark! Where are you? I need help!"

Ezekiel swung his head around to look at Clark, and it wasn't a friendly look. But his hostile expression turned to panic as Gwen continued to yell.

"Ezekiel you're such a fucking wanker! You doped me just to get laid. You pathetic piece of shit. Do all your friends know that? You got to drug me to get laid. Ha, not happening, no, no, that big pink trunk isn't going in me. I fucking hate pink. Clark, where the hell are you?" Her words were becoming more frantic, slurred.

Ezekiel pried Gwen's fingers from his shirt and backed away from her.

"Oh, the big pink cowardly elephant is leaving. And he's got what you all want, so don't let him go. Or go the fuck with him. I don't care 'cause I don't know you. All I know is Clark. Oh, there you are Clark. You're purple. Thank God you're not pink. Oh and there's Nigel who's pink, but that's okay."

Clark waited by her side and prayed that Ezekiel had slipped her the mild acid that he had given Maya. He had learned that LSD was a designer drug that reacted to the uniqueness of a person's personality and their individual body chemistry. So no one could predict what the drug's effects would be on a particular person. But he knew from the experience with Erin that he had to get Gwen out of the pub and safely back to her flat.

By now Ezekiel and all of his friends had gone, leaving only Nigel and Winston to help Clark get Gwen to his car. Fortunately, the noise of the crowd in the public room drowned out her comments about the colors of people and their assortment of increasingly exotic body parts.

At her flat, Nigel helped Clark get Gwen inside while Winston brought in the birthday gifts. One small package was clearly a bottle of pills, which he furtively slipped into his pocket. Gwen immediately began to pace around the room muttering about Cynna, Arthur, her father, and someone named Herbert.

"Do you want me to stay?" Nigel asked with very little conviction in his voice.

"That's okay, I got it."

Nigel looked relieved and immediately left with Winston.

Clark wondered if they were a couple, but he didn't have time to ponder the question because Gwen got more and more agitated as she paced around the flat. Then she complained that she felt sick as her world tilted on its axis and furniture started to lose form and substance. Every few minutes she would think that Clark had left and she would panic. Then she became desperate to leave the flat and run down the street. Clark knew that he couldn't let her go and used his body to barricade the door. Then he had to race across the room to stop her from going out a second story window. They went back and forth between the door and the windows for a long time before her focus shifted to music.

She started to sing as loudly as she could. He had long ago given up on trying to keep her quiet and just prayed that her neighbors were either not home, deaf, or stoned themselves. She found The Rolling Stones' *Aftermath* album, and ironically *Mothers Little Helper* came blasting out. Clark flashed back to the Beatles recording session and their song about Lucy with its psychedelic sound and subtext.

He heard Gwen in the kitchen and couldn't believe that she had moved so fast. He got there to find her at the stove with all the gas burners turned on and an empty kettle heating up. "Do you want some coffee? Will that help?" he asked, as he turned the burners off and went to the sink with the kettle.

She sat stone-still at the table, lost somewhere in her head. Her eyes were open but unfocused. "Did you know that Arthur is going to be a da? Oh fuck, of course you know that. Cynna the fucking slut. Father is so proud. I should be a da and make father proud. It's hot in here. Too hot." She stood and took off her shirt. Under her silk men's shirt, she wore a fancy beige lace bra that nicely accentuated her breasts.

Clark was too distracted to appreciate the view. "It's cooler in the living room. I'll open a window - but only for air, not for leaving." He didn't really want to touch her bare skin, so he gently herded her out of the kitchen and into the living room.

Then she freaked. He couldn't understand exactly what she said or screamed, but it had something to do with sex and her father and Arthur. One of them, or someone else, evidently planned to come in the window to get her. He tried to calm her down by closing the windows and locking them. Then he locked the door just before whoever-it-was could come through that. It calmed her a little but not enough to stop her rushing from the windows to the door, back and forth, over and over. He gave up trying to keep up with her and took a position midway between them so he could respond to any sudden change in her frantic movements.

For the next several hours, Gwen swung between euphoria at the brilliant colors and shapes in the air and terror over the threat of something related to her father or brother. Clark didn't know if he would be able to outlast her seemingly endless drug-fueled energy. He didn't dare sit because he knew he was exhausted and would probably pass out.

Finally, around three o'clock, she collapsed on the couch and began to shiver so badly that her whole body shook. Clark grabbed a blanket from her bed and wrapped it around her. Then he sat next to her and held her. He hoped it wasn't a mistake to sit because he didn't think he would be able to get up again if she revived. Without acknowledging him, Gwen snuggled close and passed out. Exhausted and uncomfortable, but not wanting to let go of her, Clark gathered her into his arms and pulled her down on the couch next to him, her body wedged up against the back. He promptly fell asleep.

It was early morning when Gwen woke and felt starved and confused, but very warm and comfortable. Instinctively, she snuggled up next to the person lying on the couch with her, her head resting on his chest. She was almost back to sleep when her eyes suddenly flew wide open.

Clark?! She confirmed that Clark indeed slept next to her, and then she noticed that her shirt was off. In waves, memories and images of the night began to flood into her consciousness, and she had to fight the urge to leap up and run away. Gradually her heart rate settled, and she focused on what she remembered about Clark and how he had helped her. Oh my God. He was there the whole time, she realized, embarrassed but also thankful. A burst of hatred for Ezekiel tore through her, and her body stiffened. Clark's body reacted quickly to hers, and he almost woke up. She calmed herself just in time, and he relaxed. She didn't want him to wake up yet, not until she could gather her wits. She didn't intend to, but she fell back to sleep.

An hour or so later, Clark woke up. It took him a moment to remember where he was and why it felt so good to have

Gwen snuggled up next to him. He didn't want to move, but he desperately had to pee, so he carefully extracted himself from her and went to the bathroom. When he returned, he found her sitting up, with the blanket wrapped around her shoulders.

"Sorry I woke you up," he said, and couldn't help but smile a little at the expression on her face. She looked confused but also very pretty in a tired, vulnerable sort of way.

She felt the urge to rush over and hug him but couldn't do that without letting go of the blanket. She returned his smile and noticed that he looked worn out and more than a little nervous. "Is my blouse around somewhere?"

Clark retrieved her shirt from the kitchen and handed it to her. He wondered if he should not look while she put it on, so he turned around while she dropped the blanked and put her shirt on. He remembered how sexy she had looked and wondered why she hid under those masculine clothes. "If you're okay, I can go and let you-"

"No! No, Clark please stay," she shouted, interrupting him. "I can make us some breakfast. I don't know about you, but I'm starved."

He sat quietly in the kitchen and watched her make eggs and toast. She kept saying how hungry she was and cooked enough for six people. "I may have made a little too much," she smiled sheepishly, as she set the plates down. But Clark was also very hungry, and they managed to eat most of it. Neither said much.

But now she lit a cigarette and looked intently at him. "I probably don't remember everything, but from what I do, I can't thank you enough for being here for me last night. You probably saved my life."

"Oh, it wasn't so bad."

"That's bullshit Clark, I do remember trying to jump out the bloody window, several times."

"Well, true. I didn't know if you were trying to get away from something or trying to get to something. Whatever it was, it was urgent." He tried to keep it light.

She remembered what it was, but didn't want to talk about it. As she remembered more about the trip, she realized that she had been in an incredibly vulnerable state, something that she had always tried to avoid. "Why didn't you take advantage of me?"

"What do you mean?"

"I obviously started to undress at some point. You're a virgin. You could have convinced me to solve your problem, and I might not have ever remembered."

"You don't really think that I would, that I would do ..." he stopped, upset.

"Oh no, no I don't think that. You're a nice guy, a really nice guy, and maybe too nice a guy. That could be why you're still, you know..."

That hit home as embarrassing and probably true. He thought about the old adage - nice guys do finish last. In high school, the ones who got laid were the jerky, aggressive guys who didn't care at all about the girls. Same thing in college. Now closing in on twenty-one and still a loser, it was like he was cursed.

She took pity on him and spoke quietly, "I am too."

It took him a moment to realize what she had said. "You're still?"

"A virgin. Yes, I am."

"But what about Ezekiel? And you just seem like a..."

"What, like a bloody slapper?" She tried to keep it from getting too heavy, but she did know the impression she made, her persona, because she had carefully crafted it.

"No, of course not. Just experienced. Mature."

"Yeah, I was real mature last night howling at the fucking moon."

"I can say with complete certainty that you didn't howl at the moon. Now, you did howl pretty loudly at the blue unicorn that flew by." He really wanted to move the conversation away from anyone's virginity.

They laughed comfortably. She got up to wash the dishes. He started to help, but she stopped him. So he sat back down and watched her. They had been spending a lot of time together, and it had been fun, comfortable.

Gwen could feel him looking at her, and she enjoyed it and felt glad that he was in her life. "Let's go sit on the couch," she said, after she finished the dishes.

They sat quietly. He faced forward, while she had crossed her legs under her and sat facing him. They were close but not touching. Suddenly she burst out laughing.

"What's so funny?"

"I just remembered the look on your face that night I came in, and you were here doing the slap and tickle with Cynna the slut. It was such a classic bloke kind of look. I'm so sorry that I misjudged you."

He nodded, not really wanting to talk about Cynna.

She scooted forward a little and took his hands in hers. After a moment she asked, "Do you remember what we talked about that night in the pub, after the movie?"

"I remember several things, school, Ezekiel's dodgy new friends."

"No, about the differences between men and women who want to lose their virginity. You said it would be easy for a woman because all she would have to do is ask a guy, and he would probably say yes."

"Yeah, it was a stupid thing to say."

"No it wasn't, and… well, I'm asking you." She watched him struggle with that and almost laughed.

"You want me to, us to?"

"Get this virgin thing over and done with, both of us. I like you, and I think you like me. We've seen each other in good moments and bad. I trust and respect you. We're friends, and we care about each other. If that's not the basis for a good fuck, then I don't know what the hell is."

He didn't respond right away, and she experienced a moment of fear that maybe he didn't want to do it with her.

Clark definitely wanted to, and the more he looked at her, the more excited he got. What she said made so much sense to him. He would have done the same with Bernadette a long time ago if it weren't for her occupation. He and Gwen definitely had a relationship of sorts. His only small worry was that there should be more of a sense of passion involved. But then he remembered where passion had gotten Arthur.

He turned his body around, and they both leaned in and kissed. It started out as a careful kiss but grew quickly into something more. Tongues got involved, and neither wanted to stop. Clark ignored her cigarette taste.

"You're a good kisser," she said, as they paused to take a breath. "What else are you good at?" She realized that there was only one way to find out. She got up, and still holding his hands, pulled him up and led the way down the hall to her bedroom. "I'm not doing it on that couch. Besides Nigel might come back, and he'd have a bloody heart attack."

He followed her, trying to keep his knees from buckling.

Once her bedroom door closed, they stood and faced each other.

He thought he should take charge, and he began to unbutton her shirt. She followed his lead and began to unbutton his. He reached around her to unclasp her bra, and she ran her fingers through his chest hair. He had her bra off and now concentrated on her breasts. They weren't large, but they felt perfect in his hands as he massaged them.

"Oh that feels good."

Because of their height difference, he had to stoop over to put his mouth on her breast. Her body reacted positively, and he used his tongue to play with her nipple. She realized that he must be uncomfortable stooping like that, and she didn't want him to stop. So she maneuvered them over to the bed, and they sat down on it. Then it struck her where they were, what they were doing, and she had a moment of panic, needed a diversion to slow it down. "Okay Clark, we need to have full disclosure here," she managed to say between spasms of delight emanating from her breasts.

Confused, he looked up at her. "What do you mean?"

"Well, we know that we're both virgins, but that's only the final act. I think we should tell each other how close to rumpy pumpy, the big deed, we've been. I can start if you like." He nodded, so she continued. "This snogging is actually as far as I've ever gone, and that was in no way as much fun as what you're doing to my jubblies."

Clark was surprised almost to the point of not believing her. "Really?" She nodded, and he paused and wondered how truthful he should be - whether she would be upset that he'd been so close, so intimate with a couple of women.

His silence made her nervous, so she interjected, "I saw this American film last summer and these teens were talking about sex as different levels. I think it was first stage, second and third stage and then… oh, I forget."

"Oh yeah, we call it bases, after our baseball game, where a player has to run to three bases before he can run home and score. So first base is kissing, second base is breasts, third base is down there, and scoring, coming home, is, well, you know."

"Oh great, so we're already to second base, that's fantastic. Have you been to third base?"

"Yes."

"More than once?"

He nodded.

"So how come you didn't score home?'

"It's complicated."

She could certainly understand that, after all here she was on second base for just the second time. Now she was calmer, ready. "Okay let's move to third base. I guess we have to get undressed." She said it, but then didn't move. And then it began to feel awkward. Too much light, she thought. So she got up and pulled the curtains closed to block out the gray daylight and create a more intimate ambiance. She turned to face him and stripped off her pants and panties in one motion, fueled more by nervous energy than sexual desire.

He stared at her, mesmerized by her body and how perfectly proportioned and gorgeous it was. "Wow, why do you keep that so hidden all the time? You have a beautiful body." He could see her blush rise from her breasts to her cheeks.

"I'll bet you say that to all the virgins." She grabbed his hand and pulled him off the bed. "Your turn."

With a small flourish, he undid his belt and pants and pulled it all down as she had done. He wasn't completely erect because of the strange process they were following. He could feel it growing as he examined her body.

She stepped to him and ran her hands over his hairy body. "My god it's everywhere." She got to his penis, which now stood fully erect. "Okay, so this goes in here," she gestured to her vagina but with more than a trace of disbelief in her voice. Slowly she got back on the bed.

"Are you sure you want to do this?"

"Yes, aren't you?" she replied quickly. "Come here."

Clark got on the bed and positioned himself over her and began to use his fingers to initiate some foreplay.

"What are you doing?" she gasped.

"What do you mean?"

"I think you should be using the other thing."

"This is foreplay, supposed to make it better."

"Just stick it in there Clark, before I lose my mind."

Clark moved up and positioned himself above her. She felt small under him, and he tried to keep his weight on his arms. He paused. She looked so vulnerable, so beautiful. "You're sure?" he asked.

She nodded quickly, and he tried to push inside her very tight opening. She flinched in pain. He started to pull back, but she grabbed his butt and pulled him toward her, then pulled harder until he finally pushed his way in and then trust inside her. She grimaced in pain but kept pressure on him to stay. He cautiously began to move and tried to thrust further. It felt good, but it also hurt a little because she was tight and dry. He closed his eyes; images of past girlfriends, all of them naked, came alive; then he looked into her blue eyes, felt her warm body beneath him; and without warning, it happened. The force of his orgasm caused him to lose all strength in his arms, and he collapsed on top of her. He knew he should be worried that he was crushing her, but he couldn't find the strength. He also knew that she hadn't had an orgasm, but he was incapable of doing anything about that.

As he lay on top of her, he felt her squeeze around him and saw her grimace in pain. She pushed him up and out of her, then quickly slid out from under him and disappeared into the bathroom.

It slowly dawned on him that he was no longer a virgin. But it felt so anti-climactic, so technical. He thought he should be much happier, but his concern about Gwen and how she felt overrode most of that.

She spent a long time in the bathroom. At one point he thought he heard her crying, but he wisely didn't intrude. He must have dozed off for a moment because he suddenly realized that she sat crossed-legged on the bed next to him. She had put her shirt on but hadn't buttoned it. She reached out and cautiously touched his shrunken penis. She smiled when she noticed that he was looking at her.

"Strange things."

"Yeah. Are you okay?

"Yes. But..."

"What?"

"Well, I don't see what all the fuss is about. I knew it would hurt the first time, everyone says that, especially my mum when we did the mum-daughter sex-talk thing. And I'm really happy that it happened with you and that you seemed to be so, so affected."

He nodded and tried not to look too happy because she didn't seem to be. He couldn't read the expression on her face, and he began to worry that she was going to kick him out. The whole thing had been perfunctory, like checking something off her list.

She seemed to reach a decision, announced by a little smile of determination. "I think that we're probably not doing it right, and that we need to practice."

Clark hadn't foreseen that.

"You probably think I'm daft."

"I think you're wonderful." He paused and considered for a moment. "I have a half-sister, Rita, and when I was seventeen she lived with us for a while, and she taught me a few things about foreplay, how to treat a woman's body. We could try some of that. That's what I was starting to do before we..." He didn't know what to call it without being crass.

"Before I made you jam your knob in me," she teased. "I'm sorry, I panicked and just wanted to get it over." Then she remembered his orgasm and laughed. "Although I think it hurt me more than you."

"Lie down here and I'll show you," he said hopefully.

"No, not now, I'm bloody and sore like a banshee. Maybe in a couple of days, if you still want to." From the look of desire on his face, she didn't have much doubt about that.

By then it was late afternoon and already getting dark. They dressed and went out to get a drink and dinner at the local pub where they had been before. It now had a special meaning for them. Their new intimacy danced around them like woodland sprites finally set free under a full moon. They were both quiet, lost in their own thoughts.

Clark's thoughts wandered back through his virgin past, and he catalogued the ways he felt different. It surprised him that there weren't that many, and he considered that virginity must be more of a state-of-mind thing than a physical one.

When they got back to the flat, Nigel had come in, and they resented the invasion of their privacy. He had been at a meeting with a group of Jewish college students who organized events to support Israel. The tension on the borders of Israel and its Arab neighbors had been increasing daily, and many thought that a war was imminent.

"You're not thinking of doing something stupid, are you?" Gwen asked.

Nigel evaded the question and soon went to his room.

As Clark left to go home, he paused and started to give Gwen a hug and kiss. She hesitated for a moment before she remembered that their relationship had indeed changed. She looked at the closed door to Nigel's room before she gave Clark a suitable hug and kiss.

As he drove home, Clark felt like a different person, and it wasn't just the sex. He didn't know if he could call it a relationship yet, but it felt good, strong, full of potential. And he didn't know how he could wait for even a day before seeing her again.

CHAPTER 17

Everything seemed off kilter to Clark during the next few days, like an emotional jetlag, as he struggled to keep Gwen and sexual desire from dominating his thoughts and messing with his body.

When he walked into Creative Writing class on Wednesday, Bernadette saw him and instantly she knew. Not even Maya's simultaneous arrival kept her from pulling him into a big hug and whispering in his ear, "Gwen?" He nodded and couldn't hold back his big Cheshire Cat grin.

"How'd you know?" he asked, as soon as they were in the hallway after class.

"It's so easy to tell with a man. You were one of the more challenging ones, but still. And Gwen, you may not realize it, but she's been a big part of your life for months now, and you talk about her a lot. Anyway, I'm so happy for you. And I can't wait to tell Mags. She wagered that you'd do it with me, but I told her that you'd hold out for a normal relationship."

"Well, I don't know if I'd call it a relationship."

"Clark, give me a break. Have you thought about anything else for the past…how many days has it been?"

"Three."

"Three days except for her? And not just her body, but being with her, talking to her, holding hands."

"Well, no, but-"

"There's no but about it. Please don't be another obtuse male."

They ate lunch, and he gave her a complete report on the party, Gwen's LSD trip, and waking up the next morning. He gave her a brief summary of the sex because he didn't feel comfortable giving details. She respected that because it was unusual for a man, most of whom wanted brag about it as often as they could.

"The problem is you're right. I just want to call her, drive over there and see her, all the time."

"Yeah, that's a problem and here's some free advice - don't." She waited for that to sink in. "Don't smother her. Yes, women like to be pursued. But we don't want to be stalked. It will either scare her off, or it will allow her to take you for granted. Do you have a date set up?"

"Friday night."

"Will you see her at school?"

"Probably not, but maybe in my class tomorrow afternoon, she audited it once."

"Okay. So if she's there, then that's maybe a sign to do something that night, maybe she can't wait until Friday. But if she's not there, then you have to be patient and wait. This is important information. Secret female stuff," she finished in a whisper, like a good James Bond MI-5 spy. She noticed that he looked crestfallen. "But it can, and it will change as things move forward. Blimey, at some point you'll be moving in together and then you'll wonder whatever happened to your freedom." She looked at her watch. "I've got to dash. I'm meeting Maya to work on my story."

Clark smiled. "I'll bet she wants to work on more than that."

Bernadette didn't deny it and teased him right back. "You could come also. But no, you'd be too conflicted over Gwen. You're definitely a monogamous kind of a bloke."

The next morning, Clark met with Professor Doctor to discuss his need to get a grade for something. He had decided that he couldn't approach the other two LSE professors because he never went to their classes, and they hated him because he was an American. Professor Doctor understood the problem and suggested a major research paper that would expand on a topic from the course. Clark had anticipated that. He hated research papers, but he knew it was the logical and probably the only solution. So he then went to the library to decide on a topic. He found it hard to concentrate because he kept wondering whether he would see Gwen later in class and then go to bed with her.

Gwen didn't come to the class that afternoon, and he struggled to contain his disappointment by reminding himself that she wasn't taking the course, so why would she be here. But now he worried that maybe she didn't want to see him at all and that it had been a one-time thing for her to accomplish a specific goal. She was kind of analytical that way. That line of thinking dumped him into real funk for the next twenty-four hours. When he arrived at her flat on Friday evening, he anticipated the worst.

Nigel opened the door. "Oh, thank the good lord you're here. That girl has been a blooming mess all week. Why doesn't he call or drop by? What if he forgets our date? What if he realized he doesn't like me? I told her to call you, but she said you'd think she was a stalker."

At that point, Gwen came out of her room and looked expectantly at Clark. She wore normal-girl clothes: a sweater and a skirt. The skirt wasn't as short as the modern style, but more than enough to show off her great legs.

"I've been going crazy all week too," Clark said to Gwen.

That was all she needed to rush across the hall, leap into his arms, and pull him to her for a very aggressive kiss.

"All right, no sex in the hall please. Sensitive roommate on the premises." Nigel tried to act stern, but then he laughed and retreated to his bedroom.

Clark and Gwen went out to dinner at a quiet French bistro a few blocks from her flat. They walked, each with an arm around the other, and ignored the light, cold drizzle. During dinner, they talked about what they had done and how they had felt during the week. They each had gone through a similar progression of worry and doubt based on a lack of information and erroneous assumptions. She had been consumed with the planning for a major rally to support the proposed plan by the Parliament to nationalize the British steel industry. And she had, in fact, planned to go to the Philosophy of International Law class on Thursday afternoon, but that had turned out to be when the student leaders from other cities started arriving.

"They're meeting right now, but I have a date." She smiled as she reached across the table and squeezed his hand.

He purposefully didn't mention his lunch and conversation with Bernadette.

"I have a plan," she said, as they were finishing dinner.

"Great, what is it?"

"We try again and this time go slowly and tell each other what we're doing and how it makes us feel. Then we keep doing the good things and eliminate the not so good things; that's assuming, of course, that there aren't any bad things."

Clark readily agreed with anything that meant they would get naked and in bed.

"However, there is one problem," she added, and his heart paused mid-beat. "Nigel and I reached this agreement that, out of respect for each other's feelings and sexual orientation, we wouldn't have lovers stay over at the flat."

As his heart re-started, Clark wondered what the problem was. "Well, that's fine, easy, we can go to my place."

"Perfect, I have a bag already packed."

Despite his nagging fear that his flat was a terrible mess, Clark enjoyed an incredible sense of anticipation as they drove across town. It had been hard to wait, but Bernadette had been right.

He graded the condition of his flat as moderately messy, but he didn't know what her standards were. In any event, she didn't seem to mind the dishes in the sink or the newspapers, books and magazines strewn about on the couch and coffee table. He offered her a glass of wine after he cleared the couch off. Knowing that she like the Beatles, he put the *Rubber Soul* album on. Then he sat, and they sipped their wine.

"I know that it's a little late to mention this, but I did get some condoms." He had realized early in the week that he had come inside her without any protection, and it had been a nagging worry ever since.

She appreciated his concern and smiled. "No worries, I'm on the pill."

"Really? Even though…"

"Even as a virgin? Yes, I wanted to be ready. And actually my mum insisted when I went to university. And I've heard that condoms can be a problem."

Clark knew all about that. His first experience with a condom had been at a party in junior high school with Julie Wells. He had come in the condom before he could get inside her. That became the first in his long series of sexual frustrations - a streak that had finally ended less than a week earlier.

He kissed her, but it felt a little awkward because she seemed tense. And he noticed her cigarette taste.

"I'd like to suggest that we skip first base and go right to second and third," she offered, not unlike planning an experiment in biology class.

He nodded agreement even though, despite the cigarette taste, he really liked kissing her. She casually lifted her sweater over her head and then undid her bra. He had been thinking a lot about those breasts, and his hands eagerly went for them. He gently massaged them and moved his mouth from nipple to nipple. It seemed like her right one was much more sensitive. So he sucked on that one while he massaged the other.

Gradually Gwen relaxed and allowed herself to enjoy the little shocks of pleasure that zapped through her every time he bit down on her nipple. It felt wonderful but she wanted to go further, faster. She finished her glass of wine. "Let's go to bed. Okay?"

He lifted his head from her breast and nodded. They walked into the bedroom, and she unfasten her skirt and let it drop to the floor. Wearing only her black panties, she hopped into his bed, while he struggled to get out of his shoes and shed his pants.

As he climbed in bed with her, he marveled at her body. It was even better than he remembered, and he had thought about it a lot. He hugged her and kissed her and felt heat surge through his body. He desperately wanted to be inside her, but he was worried - would it hurt her again?

"Clark, I'd like to find out what you meant the other day about foreplay, you know down there." As she spoke, she reached down and pulled off her panties.

He eagerly moved down her body, inhaled her musky scent and struggled to keep from losing control, not succumb to his urgent desire to release. His finger, then his tongue explored her and her moans and sounds of pleasure clearly indicated a good reaction. Then found her spot. Her body jerked in response. Her hands grabbed his head and pulled at his hair. It hurt a little, but that only excited him more. He didn't know how much longer he could last. He moved up and positioned himself over her, kissed her and paused. Would it be better fast or slow? He pushed slowly, but she was small.

She tensed up and then trust her pelvis toward him, and he finally entered her. She tightened around him. He pushed harder and further, and her firmness quickly pushed him over the edge, and he came in hard waves of pleasure… and guilt.

She felt him release and knew that wasn't right. She worried that it was her fault.

"I'm so sorry," they said simultaneously, and then laughed.

He rolled off to the side with one arm under her neck. The other arm lay across her chest, and his hand cupped her breast. It was still early, and he hoped that she would want to try again.

They lay there still for several minutes. Then he took his hand and traced the contours of her body with his fingers. She seemed to like it and reciprocated by running her fingers though his hair and gently pinching his nipples.

"How is it possible that you stayed a virgin for so long?" he asked her. "You're so beautiful and sexy."

"It's complicated." She gave him her standard avoidance phrase without looking at him and hoped that it would suffice. But a glance over at him told her clearly that it didn't. She turned back and stared at the ceiling. She could feel him give her time with his silence, and that was one of the things that she liked about him. It made her feel comfortable and able to trust him to the extent that she could trust anyone.

"You remember the other night during my acid trip, and you wondered what I was trying to reach for or run away from?" She knew without looking that of course he did. "Well, it was Arthur and my father, and I was trying to keep away from them." She felt him tense up and from the expression on his face she realized that he'd probable misinterpreted what she said. "Oh, no, not in a threatening or sexual sense, but… did you know that my brother was named Arthur after our famous

Welsh King Arthur of the round table? Well, he was, and I was supposed to be his Lancelot. But I fucked it up by being born a girl. We're only eleven months apart because my father was so anxious to have another boy. And then when that didn't work out, he wanted to get mum to have another go at it right away, but she refused. She told me, one night when she was a little tipsy, that she had told him that her vagina was closed. But it wasn't permanently closed because she did have my younger sister four years later. Is there any more of that wine left?"

She watched his naked body go into the living room, and soon he returned with two glasses of wine. She sat up on the bed with her back against the headboard, and he sat next to her. She was amazed at how comfortable she now felt being naked with him. And it had been a shock at first, but she was getting used to his hair.

He waited patiently for her to continue and tried not to jump to any conclusions, negative assumptions.

"So my father basically raised me as a boy, and I went along because I loved him and that was the only way to keep his attention. And Arthur went through these stages where he was jealous of me, then ultra-competitive with me. See this scar?" She pointed to a two-inch scar along her left side that he hadn't noticed before. "I could climb higher than he could in this tree in our back yard, and that made him mad, so one day he pushed me off. Then he cried and cried. And then his final stage was to be extremely protective - no one could bother me without Arthur beating them up. He even went after this one bint who was bullying me."

She went quiet for a while, and they sipped their wine. Clark tried not to anticipate where her story was going.

"So as I grew up, I was always more comfortable dressing and acting like a guy than a girl. And until I came to university, I didn't acknowledge how confining it had been and how much stuff I had suppressed. I had never learned to be feminine, and sexually I felt confused, ambiguous. If I had a willie to have sex, I would have used it long ago. I even had a fantasy about Cynna for a while, but I never acted on it… not like my brother did." She looked over at him for a reaction.

He had gone through a wild series of emotions as her story progressed - from fear to apprehension to relief to excitement as an image of her with Cynna made him smile.

"Okay, your turn, why did it take you so long to lose your cherry?"

He could feel himself turn a little red as he described the series of events that had begun with Julie Wells when he was seventeen. And continued with Molly, his girlfriend senior year in high school, and Rebecca last year in college. Without giving names, he told her about a girl in a dance club who turned out to be a prostitute and about a housewife with a baby. She knew about Wil in Amsterdam, and he described his adventure in the brothel in Paris. And, of course, she knew all about Cynna. As he talked, he began to come erect again, and she reached over and tried to help it along.

"What are we doing wrong?" she asked, as he was almost ready to play again.

"I don't know. But I'd like to try to give you an orgasm even if I'm not… you know in there."

"I liked what you were doing, but you're so far away."

So they tried several positions for their bodies until they finally found one where she lay on top of him and he used his fingers and tongue to bring her to a very satisfying orgasm. She was unable to move for quite a while. He felt good, successful, and he didn't mind terribly that she had stoked him almost to a climax, but never thought to put him in her mouth as he had hoped, and then seemingly forgot about him as she convulsed with her pleasure.

She finally rolled off him and snuggled up, exhausted, almost asleep. "Well, that sure was nice, but it's not really the right way, is it. We've still got work to do." She yawned, kissed him, and promptly fell asleep.

They tried again the next morning. It was easy because they woke to find that he already had an erection and it was pressing against her. Gwen was so eager that she told him to just push it in, slowly but steadily. But she was tight and dry, and he began to feel his skin get raw. After maybe a dozen or so thrusts, he winced as it grew increasingly painful, and finally pulled out of her.

"What's wrong? Did that hurt?"

"I think it's too much rubbing. I don't know if the skin gets tougher the more you do it. I hope so." He tried to keep it light even though he felt like a loser.

She sat up and examined his penis. "Oh blimey, it's rubbed red, bloody raw. You poor baby, I'm so sorry." Then she jumped out of bed. "Do you have any food?"

He didn't have anything, so they quickly showered, dressed, and went in search of breakfast. It was an unusually clear and sunny day for late January. The cold air felt good as they walked hand-in-hand to Hampstead High Street.

"I really suck at this. You must think I'm a total fucking loser."

He laughed. "That's exactly what I was thinking about myself. I'm the loser."

She stopped and pulled him into a hug. "I really like you Clark Westfield, you're an unusual man."

"I like you Gwen Thomas, you're a beautiful woman."

After breakfast, the nice weather continued, so they took a long walk through the Heath. She told him about growing up in Cardiff and the problems that had arisen when she was ten and still behaved like a boy. All the boys had started to grow taller and bigger, and she had slowly worked her way into her petite body. At fourteen she had become embarrassed by her breasts, which she felt were too big for her body. Clark assured her that they were absolutely perfect. She had developed a crush on Herbert McFadden at age fifteen and never got over the fact that he had thought of her as one-of-the-guys and proceeded to date and then shag Tina Wooster. Almost all the girls she knew had lost their virginity by the time they left school and quite a few had married soon after. In Cardiff, people commonly assumed that women were meant for the kitchen and not the university.

"My mum keeps hounding me that if I don't start looking and acting more feminine, like my little sister, I'm never going to get married. And then she's absolutely bloody horrified when I say that I don't want to get fucking married."

Clark recounted his history of moving every summer between school years and having to start every year in a new school with new people. He admitted that it had been hard and that it had made him a loner, reluctant to get close to people, which then contributed to his long term virgin status.

She asked him about his university in America and said it sounded like a beautiful place. But she also understood his feeling of isolation and his need to get away and live in the real world. "So are you going back for next year?"

"I don't really know. I'm supposed to, but I really like it here." He squeezed her hand to let her know that she was now a big part of that feeling.

It clouded over, and a light mist embraced the Heath as they made their way back to Clark's flat. He made some coffee and hoped that the day would never end. As he came into the living room with their coffee, Gwen sat on the couch looking at the nude-study photos, which he had forgotten were on his desk. Nervous, he tried to decipher the pensive look on her face.

"Are these your photos? Ones you've been doing at Nigel's?"

"Yes."

"Who are these women? I've never seen such incredible bodies. They're not perfect, yet they are. And the poses are so powerful, so empowering, these great naked bodies doing such ordinary things. My God, I'm so jealous."

"They're just friends really."

"I don't mean that, I mean I want a body like that." She continued to stare at them. "Friends like these and you lost your virginity with me? You're completely bonkers."

"It's complicated."

She laughed. "That's for bloody sure. I can't believe that you never wanted to fuck them, especially the younger one - she's so sexy, and what an attitude, unbelievable."

Clark hesitated. "Her name's Bernadette, and that's her sister Mags." He paused. "They're both call girls actually."

"Chippies? No fucking way." She looked at him as he sat next to her. "But now I'm confused."

Clark explained that Bernadette was the woman he had told her about from the dance club. He described their friendship as it developed, starting in the Creative Writing class. He carefully left out the sexual parts."

He could see her processing all of that, but he couldn't tell how she felt about it.

"Does she know about us?"

Clark looked away. He didn't know what to say because his natural instinct to be honest fought with his certainty that this was a loaded question that could possibly end their nascent relationship.

"Clark?" She pulled his face back to her and gave him her best sweet but totally serious smile.

Finally, he nodded, and held his breath, unsure of her potential reaction.

"That's perfect, I want to meet her."

"I don't know…" He was almost positive that that wasn't a great idea.

"Clark." She now flashed her most determined expression as she grabbed his hands in hers.

His resolve wilted. "I'll try."

Not satisfied, she narrowed her eyes and pursed her lips.

"Sure, next weekend if ... if she's not working." Then he relaxed as her face reflected her victory, and she followed up with a long, meaningful kiss.

They spent a quiet evening watching the telly. They snuggled on the couch and took turns rubbing each other. She discovered that he loved to have his back scratched. And she laughed at the way his body responded when she hit a good spot. She teased him that it would be a quick and simple way to give him an orgasm. Clark discovered that she was ticklish behind her ears and that gentle rubbing there made her laugh hard enough to almost wet pants. Later in bed, she began to rub his penis, and he flinched - it was too sore. So they kissed, explored each other until he produced another orgasm for her, and then finally slept.

As he drove Gwen home on Sunday afternoon, Clark asked when he could see her again. He got nervous when she turned and stared silently out the window. He was still insecure enough about their relationship to be afraid that she had come to her senses and was about to dump him.

"I can't this week. I'm sorry, but my father is in town for business meetings, and he expects to be able to see me at a moment's notice." There was more than a trace of bitterness in her voice. She then pulled a mockingly male voice from deep in her chest. "I'm very busy Gwen dear. Of course, I'll have time for you, but on my schedule because, after all, you're just a little girl in university,"

Clark didn't know whether to laugh or not. He didn't, which was good.

"I know I'm being a bitch, but ... well it's complicated." She tried to laugh.

When they arrived at her flat, Nigel greeted them and teased that they looked like they had been thoroughly shagged. He noticed that Gwen had the nude-study photo of Bernadette and Mags sitting on the couch, which was in a frame that they had bought Sunday morning at a shop in Hampstead.

"Oh, that's one of my favorites. And Clark, good news, I've arranged for my father to allow you back into the dark room whenever you want. Reginald spoke very highly of you and helped me convince him."

"Does that mean you're moving back home?" Clark asked cautiously.

"One step at a time. We had a civilized tea yesterday. We'll see what's next. I do have one condition however."

"What?"

"I have some 16x20 photo paper in the cabinet, and I want you to make me a print of that photo." He indicated the one that Gwen had now put on the bookshelf in the living room. "It's Nelly's birthday in ten days, and I'd love to give it to her as a present. She doesn't like my work - too political or the wrong sex - but she would love this. And you should sign it. She likes you because of what you didn't do with little Helen."

"Who's little Helen," Gwen asked, with a tone of mock-jealousy.

Nigel jumped in before Clark could answer. "Little Helen is Nelly's sixteen-year-old sister who is eager to suck any john thomas that comes near her. Evidently she's deluded to think that it will keep her from catching her sister's sexual persuasion, like it's the bloody flu or something. Well, Clark here wouldn't let her touch his willy."

"That's my Clark," Gwen chirped, and she then gave him a long passionate kiss. It was enough to make Nigel leave the room.

First thing Monday morning, Clark called Nigel's house to confirm he could use the darkroom. Reginald told him that indeed he could but only when the plumbers were finished with the repairs to the pipes that ran to the basement bathroom and the darkroom. There had been a leak. "I expect most of this week," Reginald replied when Clark asked him how long the repairs would take.

Clark tried to accept it with aplomb, but he was frustrated. He had foreseen working in the darkroom as a great way to make the week go faster. Good thing that Nelly's birthday was another week away.

Clark thought it was evident that Bernadette and Maya had actually spent some time on Bernadette's new story, because it had developed a lot since the last time he had heard it. When Maya asked him to report to the class, he confessed that he was stuck on his story and had made little progress all week. That elicited an understanding smile from Bernadette.

Later at lunch, Bernadette demanded, "all appropriate details."

Clark told her enough that she could see that he and Gwen had a problem. "So if I've got this correct, you've had intercourse, but only you come during it." She watched him nod. "And that's okay with her, with both of you?"

"No, not at all. We're still working on it. That's why my little yank got very sore, raw." He had struggled with Gwen's request, demand really, to meet Bernadette because he didn't want to jeopardize either of the relationships. They were both very strong personalities, likely to clash. He finally told her that Gwen had seen the photos, and that he had told her about their relationship, but with no mention of benefits. He then added cautiously, "She would like to meet you, this weekend."

Bernadette immediately turned serious. "Really? No, I don't think that's a good idea."

"Why not?" He agreed but wanted to hear her reasons, which would undoubtedly be better articulated than his.

She hesitated to make sure that she said it right, both the tone and the content. "Well, I haven't met Gwen, but I know that most women would be seriously threatened by the kind of relationship we have. They could never believe that we're just friends, certainly not given my profession."

Despite his dearth of knowledge about women, Clark easily sensed the truth of what she said. "Why then would she ask to meet you?"

"Well, I don't know, I guess it could be… I don't really know how to say this without sounding like a bitch." She took his hands in hers. "My guess is that she wants to check out what she perceives as the competition."

"But I told her that we're just friends and never…"

"And that's probably very hard for her to believe. Just a few months ago, I wouldn't have believed it possible myself."

He slumped back in his chair, feeling defeated. "Now I don't know what to do," he lamented.

"We need to talk to Mags."

They found Mags at the apartment ironing clothes, wearing only her bra and panties, and rocking out to *I'm Ready for Love* by Martha and the Vandellas.

"Hey Clark, congratulations on your leap into manhood," she teased him. "How's her blowjob? Not as good as mine I bet."

Clark laughed and knew that he should be embarrassed, but she just didn't have that effect on him anymore.

"Mags, we need your advice." Bernadette got right to the point and explained the dilemma. Mags turned off the iron, and they all sat at the kitchen table.

"So how big is Gwen?" Mags asked.

"Small, about five foot four or five, maybe." Clark instinctively put his hand at the level on his chest where the top of Gwen's head would be.

"Okay, but I really meant her vagina. And she was a virgin also? So probably pretty tight, hard to enter."

Clark nodded. "I don't have any comparison, but ..."

"And we know from some experience, that while you're normal, average length, you are thicker than average when aroused. So that's one problem. How much foreplay do you do?"

"I try some, but she gets impatient. Or she lets it go on and then comes without me."

"Mon Dieu, two virgins, such a problem, always ends badly."

Clark stiffened with anxiety.

Bernadette noticed and squeezed his arm. "Mags is right, usually, but it can work if you both want it to." She shot a look at Mags demanding confirmation. "Right!"

Mags looked slowly between the two of them and sighed. "Okay, we can help the problem with a highly lubricated condom. Put it on, do your best foreplay, get her really relaxed, and then be ready to go. Don't wait and then have to put the condom on.

"And if she gives you a blowjob first," Bernadette added, "then you would be ready to concentrate on her."

Clark smiled at her as he remembered the night they met. But he didn't know if Gwen was ready for that, or would even be willing to try it, or how she would know what to do. It was all a lot more complicated than he would ever have imagined.

When Clark arrived at Gwen's flat on Saturday evening he was a bundle of nerves and anxiety. She had called him Friday morning to say that she couldn't see him until Saturday, and he wanted to believe her when she said that it was because of her father.

She seemed happy to see him, but her enthusiasm was muted. Then in his car, she sat quietly and stared out the window at the lights of the city as he drove to a restaurant in Hampstead for dinner. She began to light up a cigarette, and he carefully reminded her that he didn't let people smoke in his car.

He then asked, "Are you okay?"

"It's been a long bloody week with my father." She didn't look at him or elaborate any further.

Clark hoped that she liked Italian food and was relieved when she replied that she loved it. Positano Italian Restaurant, on the eastern edge of Hampstead, had a classic Italian decor - red and white checkered table cloths, empty wine bottles used as candle stick holders on the table, and a fake wine arbor that covered the ceiling. It had good food and was only minutes from his flat.

Glen consumed her first glass of wine in two long gulps, smoked a cigarette, and slowly began to relax. He then asked about her father, which caused her face to scrunch in on itself like she'd tasted the sourest thing in the world. It took another glass of wine for her to begin to recover. So they stayed with casual, impersonal conversation for the rest of the dinner. She never asked about Bernadette, and he hoped that she had forgotten about it.

It was getting late when they arrived at Clark's flat. That afternoon, he had been careful to put all photos of Bernadette and Mags in his desk drawer. After a few awkward moments, they hugged each other, and he felt her body gradually start to relax. Another glass of wine led to some almost passionate kissing.

"I've been giving this a lot of thought, and I think we've put too much bloody pressure on ourselves," she offered.

Clark agreed, very glad that she had brought it up. "I got a special condom for us to try, not for the, you know, pregnancy thing, but to help me get in easier."

"Perfect. Why don't you pour us some more wine, put on some music, and I'll go get ready?"

Clark entered his bedroom to find Gwen already undressed and sitting up on the bed, leaning on a pillow against the headboard. The sheet and blanket were pulled up to her waist. He undressed and joined her, and they drank some wine as they casually touched and explored each other. Just before it got too passionate, he pulled on the condom. She watched, fascinated by the process.

After intense foreplay, the condom worked like magic as Clark easily pushed deep inside. As Gwen grew more and more excited, he struggled to keep himself from a climax. He was determined to last, to get her to climax first. It got increasingly difficult as he felt her body react, and her sounds of pleasure became louder and more frequent. It seemed like it was all working.

Gwen then opened her eyes and looked at Clark as his body moved on top of her, and she realized what was about to happen. It excited her, and it terrified her. Did she really want to give him, or anyone, that kind of power over her? To inflict his will on her, to impact her body so profoundly? Hopelessly conflicted, her passion wilted, her sexual energy ebbed, and her body stiffened.

Clark felt the change in Gwen and assumed that he had done something wrong. He tried a couple of strong thrusts as deep inside her as he could go, but he realized it was too late - the moment had gone. Frustrated and exhausted, he collapsed on top of her. What the hell happened? he wondered.

Neither one spoke, and after a few minutes, they got under the covers and held each other. Emotionally and physically spent, and unable to find the right words, they both drifted off to sleep.

Clark woke during the night and felt Gwen wrapped in his arms. He luxuriated in the warmth of her body. This was the feeling of connection that he had dreamed of, and he loved it. His positive feelings brought him to life, not with urgent passion but warmth and connection. He felt her stir, and then her eyes came half open. When she saw him, she smiled. It was sweet and tender and comfortable.

Still not fully awake, their bodies responded to each other in a sensual, instinctual way. Without thinking, Gwen moved her body on top of his, and his erection pressed against her now wet opening. With her eyes closed, she sat up on him. Her legs were spread wide across his body, and her pelvis was very relaxed from sleep. She pushed her body down onto him, and he moved easily into her. She began to move up and down in a steady rhythm. Her hands were pressed against his chest and grabbed his hair. Her eyes closed, she moved as if in a trance, lost in the pleasure, in her sexuality, her power. She was almost there when she opened her eyes, smiled down at him, and felt her orgasm tear through her body.

Her release gave him permission, and he quickly came also. Their orgasms overlapped and became one magnificent thing. She cried out, "Oh God, Clark! We did it! We fucking did it!"

It was morning when they woke again and realized that they were starving. It was a typical day for early February, cold, wet, and gray, but neither of them noticed as they made their way to a small restaurant in Hampstead for a late breakfast. On the way home, he felt his body quiver as he recalled the feeling of their combined orgasms.

The minute they were back in his flat, Gwen took his hand and let him back to the bedroom. There she took charge - undressed him and pushed him down onto the bed. She removed her clothes and climbed on top of him. He pulled her up along his chest to where he could tease her with his tongue. She quickly had an orgasm, and then with a wild look of satisfaction, she moved her body back and pushed down onto him. Up and down she moved, as Clark reached up and massaged her breasts. Soon another orgasm swept through her, and she almost collapsed down on his chest. He relaxed and allowed his own release to join hers.

Clark felt wonderfully tired and was content to just lie there and hold her. But she soon bounced up, energized, almost manic, and rushed into the bathroom. He heard the shower start and wondered whether he could join her - it was a fantasy of intimacy that he had had for many years. Just as he started to get up and do it, he heard the water turn off.

Without a word, she came out wrapped in a towel, gathered up her clothes, and took them back into the bathroom. A few minutes later, she emerged fully dressed and came over and sat down next to him on the bed. "Kosygin's coming to town, and I've got a planning meeting for our demonstration outside Buckingham Palace. The bloody queen is meeting with him. Can you believe it?"

Clark shook his head and struggled to hide his disappointment. He had anticipated spending the day together and some more sex.

"It's going to be a bonkers week, but we have to do this again next weekend." Without waiting for a confirmation or any response, she kissed him and left.

He waited and hoped that she would change her mind, even after he heard the front door close. But after several minutes, he accepted it that she had really gone, and he headed for the shower.

Emotionally and physically drained from the last eighteen hours, Clark stared out the window at the rain. He found it impossible not to obsess on the memory of Gwen and her look of pure joy and victory as she rode on top of him during her orgasm. Despite the success of their sexual quest, he felt a sense of loss, of frustration. He tried to convince himself that the loneliness was temporary, caused by emotions from the sex, but that didn't help much. Very seldom had he ever felt any compulsion to share his feelings with anyone, but today he did, and there was no one around. He walked to the grocery store, and as he passed his car, he fought off a strong impulse to get in and drive to Bernadette's.

CHAPTER 18

The plumbing was fixed, and Clark went to Nigel's house on Monday morning and made the 16x20 print of the nude-study photo that Nigel had asked for. He made several other large prints of the same photo, one for himself and one for Bernadette. For Gwen, he printed the same Parisian vendor scene that he had done for his sister's Christmas present. He certainly didn't want to remind her about Bernadette.

On Tuesday he forced himself to spend hours in the University of London library working on research for his paper. He had decided that his topic would be the moral dilemmas and conflicts between the rule-of-law as developed by the International Court of Justice and the religious laws or tenants of the world's dominant religions - Christianity, Judaism, Buddhism, and Islam. He had taken a course in world religions as a sophomore, and it had really fascinated him - particularly from the historical, sociological, and psychological points of view. He had tried to discuss this with Gwen, but she refused to talk about religion in any way. It frustrated him that he couldn't share his ideas with her.

He looked forward to seeing Bernadette in class on Wednesday and then talking to her at lunch. But she had to rush off right after class because of what she called an unusual business commitment. That darkened his mood as he thought of what that meant.

After considerable internal debate, he decided not to go to the protest at Buckingham Palace when Premier Kosygin met with the Queen. He had told Gwen that he would be there, and he wondered what her reaction would be, or if she would even notice. His only contact with her had been a short telephone conversation on Wednesday evening to make plans to get together on Saturday. Her tone had struck him as pleasant but professional, and a sense of uncertainty again embraced him like an old friend.

Clark arrived at Gwen's flat on Saturday evening and found Nigel involved in a very intense conversation with a man, probably in his late forties, who was dressed in a soldier's camouflage uniform, but without insignia or markings of any sort. They quickly ended their conversation, and the man left without acknowledging Clark.

When he handed Nigel the print for Nelly, Clark was gratified to see some of the anxiety dissipate from Nigel's face.

"Oh, wonderful, this is the bee's knees, she'll adore it. Thank you for signing it, makes it very officially artistic." Nigel left to put the print in his room, and when he came back it looked like his anxiety was back. "Gwen said to tell you that if she's not home, she'd be here soon. You can wait in the living room."

"Thanks," Clark replied, but didn't move because he sensed that Nigel wasn't done.

"Did you see my father when you were there?" Nigel asked cautiously.

"No, just Reginald." Clark couldn't tell if Nigel was relieved or disappointed.

"He thinks I'm insane to want to go and sign up, but I know it's what I need to do."

"Go where, sign up for what?"

Nigel seemed surprised that Clark didn't know. "Gwen hasn't told you?"

"Well, we haven't had much chance to talk."

Nigel gave him a sly little grin. "So I understand." When Clark didn't react, he continued, "I'm sure you know that there's a war about to happen between Israel and Syria, Jordan etcetera, and I plan to go there and enlist."

"Enlist, as in the army?" Clark replied, incredulous. Nigel would have been the last person he would have pegged for a soldier, but now the presence of the other man made sense.

Nigel had heard the same question from others but still asked, "Why not?"

Clark wanted to respond that Nigel was thin, weak, and a homosexual. But he actually said, "I thought you were a pacifist like Gwen, don't you go to all the rallies and demonstrations."

Before Nigel could respond, the door opened and Gwen burst in. Dressed in her typical masculine uniform, she was out of breath and red in the face like she'd been running for a couple of miles.

"Clark! Hi, you're here already."

Clark stepped toward her to hug her, but she backed away.

"Sorry, I'm a chronic fright, hot and sweaty like a bloody cow. I'm desperate for a shower. Be a love and get me a glass of wine will you." She smiled and then disappeared into her room before he could respond.

Nigel left to join his friends at the theater, and Clark felt a little jealous. When he had spoken to Gwen during the week, he had suggested that they go to the theater or a movie, but she said that all she wanted to do was have dinner and crash. Even assuming that crashing meant going to bed and having sex, he had been disappointed. He knocked on her door to give her the wine, and when she opened it, she kept her obviously naked body hidden behind the door as she took the glass.

Despite his misgivings, they had a very nice dinner, and Gwen was completely focused on him. They exchanged details about their activities during the week and maintained plenty of body contact that had begun with an intense hug and kiss when she had emerged from her bedroom. She wore a short skirt and a fitted sweater that nicely showed off her figure - the most feminine things he had ever seen her wear. They lingered at dinner, neither seemed to be in a rush. But the moment they entered Clark's flat, she grabbed him and pulled him to the bedroom. Without discussion, but clearly following her lead, they assumed their positions with her on top. It was a great success, and afterward they collapsed, hot and satiated.

"Christ, I've been getting myself wet all week thinking of that. I even managed to wank off the other night, first time ever."

"I would have been happy to come over and help you," he offered hopefully, as he was pretty sure that wank in this context meant masturbate. He had learned that this was a tricky slang word with several possible meanings.

"You're sweet, but I've been such a bloody bitch all week. Not fit to be around. You would hate me."

"I doubt that."

"Well, I get pretty fucking barmy. There are so many wankers who want to control everything and everyone. We're fighting for freedoms and personal justices, but these bloody little dictators... oh they just make me so fucking furious." By now she was sitting up, her body rigid with tension.

Clark moved behind her and began to massage her shoulders and then her back. As she began to relax, he moved his hands around to her breasts. He felt her relax and his penis stir.

They tried making love with him on top, but it worked for him and not for her. They fell asleep, and when they woke the next morning, they did it again, but with Gwen back on top, and it was the best yet. Gwen came alive, a completely different lover, different person, when she rode on top.

They followed that same routine for the next several weeks. Only once did they see each other during the week. She had asked him to take pictures at her demonstration against the Soviet nuclear test in Kazakhstan. He had watched her deal with the police, the press, and the other leaders of the demonstration, and he had had a hard time reconciling that aggressive person, who looked like a tough young boy, with the sexy naked woman who consumed him on weekends. She hadn't been exactly cold to him, but she hadn't been warm either. Twice she had barked orders at him to get a particular photo, and he had resolved to never do that again.

When he arrived at her flat on Saturday evening, he found her still dressed in her work clothes, cigarette in hand, and pacing around in a state of panic.

"I'm late!" she immediately shouted at him before she remembered that Nigel was in his room. She lowered her volume but not the intensity. "I'm bloody late. I'm on the fucking pill, but I'm late."

Too stunned to respond, he stood and stared at her. Her body language didn't welcome any physical approach.

"Sure, I'm not normally spot-on regular, but blimey I've got a bad feeling about this." She stopped pacing. "I can't go out like this. No, wait, I need something to take my mind off it. What can we do?"

Clark suggested a movie, the new spy thriller, or a play or going to a club and dancing. She shot them all down. They wound up going to dinner and then to his place where they sat, cuddled on the couch, occasionally kissed, and then went to bed. Neither one made a move to initiate sex.

When they woke in the morning, their physical desires got the best of them, and they had what felt to Clark like frantic sex, the kind he imagined people had when they thought it might be the last time, before going away to war or something like that. And afterward, he wanted to just lay there and hold her, but she couldn't stay still, even as he tried to massage the tension out of her body.

They returned to the flat after a late breakfast and sat on the couch reading the Sunday *London Times*. The unexpected ring of the telephone startled them both. Clark answered, and it was Bernadette who sounded like she was crying. She asked if Gwen was there and if he could come over to see her sometime that day. Clark didn't know what to do. Gwen stared at him, seemingly accusing him of something. One part of him, the coward, wanted to hang up, pretend it was a wrong number. While another part, the realist, knew that he had to face it sooner or later. Both women were a big part of his life.

"She's here now, and we haven't really talked about what we're doing today."

He knew something was very wrong, something had happened since he had seen her on Wednesday. He really wanted to help her, but he didn't say that because of the look he saw on Gwen's face. "Maybe later, I'll call you and let you know."

Gwen challenged him as soon as he hung up the telephone. "Was that her? What did she want?"

"She wants to see me. She's crying. I don't know why."

"Crying because you're fucking me and not her," Gwen replied, with a venomously sneer, which Clark tried to ignore. But he recalled Gwen's reaction the week before to the news that he had sold several prints of the nude-study photo to friends of Nelly, who had seen the photo at her birthday party. One of Nelly's friends had suggested that Clark contact a gallery owner she knew to inquire about a show. Clark had hoped that Gwen would be happy for him, but she had been caustically negative. "You don't want to be typed by that kind of work." Later in her flat, Gwen had pointed out the Parisian photo he had made for her, which hung in the living room. "Now that's a much better style of work for you." He had noticed that the nude-study print that he had given her weeks before was gone from the bookshelf.

Clark realized that Gwen was jealous, as Bernadette had predicted. "She's a friend, that's all. You're the one I love." The L-word poured out so effortlessly that it almost didn't register with him. But then her lack of a reaction made him uneasy.

"I can't control who you're friends with, but with a bloody …" She caught herself, but her anger and her frustration about her late period had taken control of her emotions. "I want to go home."

They were both quiet as he drove her home. He knew she was distraught, but he didn't know what to do about it. He had tried everything he could think of to get her mind off Bernadette and change her mind about going home. But she had insisted.

He walked her to her flat, and worried about her and the implications of her late period, he offered to stay. But she answered quickly and firmly, "I'm bloody shattered and need some time alone."

He sat quietly in his car outside her building for ten then twenty minutes in case she changed her mind and came running out to stop him. But she didn't. He debated whether he was being too passive and should he just go back and insist on … He didn't know what. He felt like the pull of the two women - one an angry lover and one a hysterical friend - was going to rip him apart. He remembered the anguish that he had heard in Bernadette's voice. His compassion and his curiosity finally motivated him to drive off toward Earls Court.

By the time Clark got to Bernadette's, it just after five o'clock, already dark. She answered the door and immediately embraced him. Sobbing, she hung on tightly.

"Bernie, what's wrong?" he asked.

"Oh, Clark it's my mother, she died last night. We found out this morning." She struggled to get the words out through her tears.

"Oh no Bernie, I'm so sorry." Beyond that, he was at a loss for words. He could feel some of the tension in her body flow out with her tears, and he hung on tight.

"Mags left for Corsica right away, and I've been getting some things in order and leave in the morning." She lifted her head from his shoulder and looked at him. "And I'm so sorry - I knew you were probably with Gwen, but I just had to talk, to see you."

"It's okay, I'm glad you called, really."

Neither of them had any experience in dealing with the death of a loved one or in the process of grieving. They stumbled around it for hours, alternating between tears and trying to make silly jokes to ease the tension. They ate some leftovers from the refrigerator and spent a lot of time just sitting on the couch, holding hands. They tried to find a distraction on the television but couldn't. It got late, and they were both exhausted - mentally, physically, everyway.

"Will you spend the night with me? I don't want to be alone."

"Of course. I can stay here," he replied, motioning to the couch.

"No, I need you in my bed. You can keep your clothes on, like we did that time at your place. But I have to get some sleep, and I can only sleep properly when I'm naked."

So they wound up in her bed, one naked and the other dressed. He was curled around her back, his arms around her, careful to avoid her breasts. She cried herself to sleep, even though she was sure that she had been all cried out.

During the night she woke to feel his very stiff erection pushed up in his pants against her back. She liked the feeling and was happy to let it go at that, but he woke up. He realized what was happening and immediately pulled his body back.

"Don't. It's okay. I like feeling you there."

He felt his body relax, but his erection actually stiffened. He was afraid that after tonight he might not ever see her again.

She turned around to face him and saw his desire written clearly on his face. Their kiss was different and seemed to ask for, demand more. Reaching down, she undid his pants and took him in her hand.

Electricity raced through his body, fried his inhibition, and obliterated his doubts. He kissed her with an intensity that he had never felt for anyone. She pushed his pants down as she pulled him on top of her. They moved as one body, and their emotions, their passions washed over them. Nothing existed for either of them but each other, the moment. Lost in feelings that overwhelmed them, they finally came together in a moment of pure ecstasy.

Bernadette had never had an orgasm as intense or as impactful. She clutched him tight and cried. This time tears of happiness dominated the tears of sorrow.

They fell asleep again before either one could consider the ramifications of their actions, their feelings, situations, relationships, jobs, or anything else. For that moment, they were both content to float along in a state of bliss. When they woke a few hours later, they made love again, slowly. They wanted to make it last, to remember each moment, to maximize the pleasure for the other.

It was only later, when Bernadette had gone to shower, that Clark thought of Gwen and whether this made him a terrible person. He felt successive waves of guilt, fear, and frustration. He knew Bernadette had to leave, probably for good, and Gwen was possibly, probably, pregnant. Only the wonderful lingering sensations of Bernadette's scent and warmth kept him from screaming.

After showering, he watched her as she finished packing. They were both quiet, each on their own emotional precipice - afraid to say anything that would cause themselves, or the other one, to break down. He drove her to the airport, but she refused to let him come in to see her off. She knew she couldn't deal with a long, drawn-out good bye.

As he drove home, Clark grappled with his feelings for the two women. It slowly dawned on him that he had little, if any, future with either of them. Gwen was obsessed with her causes and being able to control their relationship and their sex. They did have some things in common, but their approaches to them were very different, and she seldom seemed interested in his. Bernadette, conversely, shared many of his interests and was always supportive of everything he did. But there existed the not insignificant fact that he knew that he could never feel comfortable with, or accept, her profession, her family business, which would now probably keep her in Corsica. God, it's so screwed up, he lamented, as he remembered how he had always kept people and relationships at bay, never to be hurt. And although he knew that it was far better to have these connections with people, he wondered why it had to hurt so much.

Clark had almost no contact with Gwen for the next several weeks. Always too busy or too tired to see him, she kept their interactions limited to short telephone conversations that were very unsatisfying, at least for him. He would ask if her period had come, and she would curtly respond, "no", or "I don't want to talk about it". He tried not to dwell on the parallels with Cynna's behavior, and he worried that he had detected a change in her voice, ever since the Sunday night when he went off to see Bernadette.

He struggled mightily to keep from obsessing over Bernadette, but it was hard to do, very hard. He had reluctantly agreed when Bernadette insisted that they didn't call or write, that they accept their wonderful moment as just that and no more. She had promised him that she would contact him if she did come back to London, but she had no idea if that would happen or not. He knew that she was stronger and more sensible about it than he could ever be. He wrote several long, tortured, poems about both women and the fool who had longed to be a man and then found it so painful.

Clark was almost reconciled to the probable end of his relationship with Gwen. So he was surprised, encouraged, and cautious when she called and invited him over for dinner on Saturday. He asked her what she had been doing and how she felt, obviously alluding to the pregnancy, and she muttered, "It's my body, and I'll decide what to do."

As he parked in front of Gwen's building, Clark felt big butterflies fluttering around in his stomach. It would be so different, so easy if it weren't for the baby, one that he had helped create. He didn't think he could just walk away from that.

He entered the flat to find Nigel in the hall packing a very large backpack stretched out on a metal frame, the type used for long hiking and camping expeditions. Gwen was busy in the kitchen, and Clark gave her a quick kiss and hug. He noticed that under her apron she wore pants and a baggy shirt, the professional Gwen, not the sexy Gwen. He then turned his attention back to Nigel.

"Going camping?"

"Something like that."

"The bloody fool is hitchhiking to Israel to enlist," Gwen yelled from the kitchen.

"Really?"

Nigel just nodded and kept packing. He tried to roll a sleeping bag as tightly as he could so he could attach it to the bottom of the pack, but it kept unrolling when he tried to tie it up. Clark knelt down to help him.

"Thanks. It's the only way I can get there. My father cut me off when I told him what I planned to do. So I can't afford to fly, and I don't have a car."

"It's a long way to hitchhike."

"Five thousand kilometers."

"And to get there don't you have to go through, you know, the countries that don't like ... Israel?" Clark had caught himself before he said, "Don't like you."

"Yes, but my British passport should work fine."

"So, when are you leaving?"

"In a day or two. I still need a tourist visa from bloody Bulgaria."

Gwen called for Clark to test some spaghetti pasta, and he happily left Nigel to finish his packing. The pasta needed a few more minutes, and Clark sat at the kitchen table while Gwen fussed with a tossed salad. The table was set for two, and pushed together in one area were some maps of Europe and the Middle East. Clark loved maps, so he picked one up and examined it. He saw places that had always held romantic appeal for his wanderlust - Athens, Istanbul, Jerusalem, and Cairo. Then he saw Corsica, to the west of Italy and south of France. Gwen noticed his interest in the map, but didn't say anything. Her timer rang, and the pasta was ready.

Nigel yelled, "See you," from the front door as he left.

Gwen shook her head as she put the plates of food on the table and then sat down. "I've tried to convince him that they'll spot him as bloody homo in two seconds and as a Jew in three.

But the wanker is just too bloody stubborn. He's convinced that it's his fucking duty to go fight."

Clark only nodded, took a bite and complimented her on the dinner. They engaged in some small talk while they ate. She asked about his paper, and he asked about her demonstrations. He knew she had done one recently against the U.S. Army after it had been revealed by the *New York Times* that they were doing secret germ-warfare tests.

"Do you have any plans for the break next week?" she asked tentatively.

"Just working on the paper; spend some time in the darkroom. You're probably tied up with events?"

"No. So many students go home during those two weeks, we don't bother to plan any demonstrations." She paused before she continued. "I'm actually going to go home. I had planned to invite you to come with me before… but now…" Her voice trailed off.

He of course knew what she referred to, but he didn't ask about it. He was tired of getting blown-off whenever he asked, and he assumed that she would tell him when she was ready. They finished the dinner in silence. The unspoken thing lurked between them like a boogeyman behind a thin curtain. Clark, normally okay with silence, struggled to think of something to say that wasn't about sex or babies.

"Would you like to fuck?" Gwen broke the silence with an awkward but eager grin. She didn't wait for his answer, which she assumed would be yes. She took his hand and led him to her bedroom. Once she closed the door, she casually removed her clothes and then hopped onto her bed. She turned and looked expectantly at Clark.

He stared at her, looking at her stomach to see if there was a baby bump. It looked the same. As he took off his clothes, he struggled to remember, to regain, the excitement from the first time he had seen her naked. It didn't happen completely. He kissed her and started to massage her breasts, which he thought looked a little bigger. She stopped him, said they were sore. He had to struggle to get into the right mood despite his very eager penis.

Gwen was ready, impatient, her hormones on overdrive, and she popped up on top of him. There was no discussion of position, she was in charge. He again tried to touch her breasts as she moved up and down on him, but she winced and slapped his hand off. It almost caused him to lose his erection, but then the wild look of desire on her face kept him up. She climaxed faster that he remembered her ever doing before, and he realized that he wasn't trying to hold back. She kept moving even as she partially collapsed on his chest because she could tell that he hadn't come yet. She gave him an urgent look, equal parts curious and expectant and impatient. Finally, getting sore as her vagina became dry and tight, he faked an orgasm.

"Finally," she gasped, as she rolled off him and lay on her back. "God I needed that, when I'm not sick in the bloody loo, I'm God-awful horney."

He moved to cuddle her, hoping that now they could talk about it. But still percolating with energy, she jumped up and pulled her clothes on, panties but no bra. "I'm going to clean up. You rest, and I'll be back for more."

Clark knew that he wouldn't be able to fake it again and maybe not even get another erection. Is this a new Gwen, he wondered, or had he just not seen her clearly before? He fought against the uneasy feeling that he had just been used a little, maybe a lot. He got dressed and joined Gwen in the kitchen as she finished putting food away. The sink remained full of dirty dishes.

"I feel like I might be coming down with something. I should go home. I don't want to get you sick," he mumbled. He could see her process it and seemingly go from skeptical to resigned. She didn't try to talk him out of it or even see him to the door.

As he left, he saw Nigel's pack in the hall, ready for his adventure.

During his drive home, Clark vacillated between feeling like a fool for giving up perfectly good sex with a pretty woman and like he'd been a big coward for not forcing a discussion of the pregnancy issue. In need of a distraction, he decided to stop at a pub and have a pint. On the walk from his car, he passed the Royal Automobile Club travel shop and noticed a poster in the window for the Orient Express from Paris to Istanbul. Half way through his second pint, he put it all together in a plan.

He slept poorly that night. He tossed and turned, uneasy about his ambivalence toward Gwen and excited about his plan to have a grand adventure, and to maybe see Bernadette.

First thing the next morning, Clark called Nigel and arranged to meet him for lunch at the pub near Gwen's flat.

Clark got right to the point as soon as he and Nigel sat down, each with a plate of food and a pint of beer. "So I assume you have some money, just not enough for a plane ticket. Is that right?"

"Yes, why?"

"I propose that we drive to Israel in my car. I'll drop you there, and then continue to Cairo and Tunis, take a ferry to Rome and come back." He didn't mention his plan to take a ferry from Rome to Corsica. "So no hitching, but you help pay for gas. What do you say?"

"Can you drive from Israel to Tunis?"

"Oh yeah, along the coast of the Mediterranean. It should be beautiful."

"That's a long way to drive by yourself."

"I prefer to travel by myself." Clark noticed that Nigel's eyebrows lifted slightly. "Oh, but it would be great to have company for part of the way. And, of course, help with the gas."

Nigel didn't respond immediately, but Clark sensed that he knew it was too good of an offer to pass up. Hitchhiking to Israel would take weeks, a month, or more, and be fraught with potential trouble, while they could drive it, even with stops to tour, in a week, maybe ten days.

"I'm not a very good driver. I've never owned a car."

"No problem, I really love to drive. And I don't plan to go eighteen hours a day. I want to do some touring along the way."

"But you don't have any transit-tourist visas - Bulgaria has been a royal pain to get."

"I checked around this morning, and as an American I don't need them, even Bulgaria."

Nigel finally agreed. As they were leaving the pub, Nigel casually asked Clark if he intended to go back to the flat to see Gwen. Clark hesitated. He felt reluctant to face her. He tried to convince himself that he wasn't running away - just giving them some space for a few weeks. And besides, he reasoned, she had already made plans to go home for spring break without him. And he'd be back in a few weeks and would then insist that they talk. By the time he got back to his flat, he had almost convinced himself.

CHAPTER 19

The mid-March weather was so bad that it surprised Clark when the ferry departed from Dover for France. The waves outside the harbor looked to be two feet or more, and the wind gusts slammed the cold rain and sleet horizontally against the windows of the passenger lounge. Ship wrecked and drowned would be a fitting end for what had been an inauspicious beginning to the adventure.

Clark had tried to say good-bye to Gwen when he arrived to get Nigel, but she had refused to see him. Thankfully, Nigel hadn't commented other than to flash a sardonic smile. Then the frame of Nigel's fancy backpack hadn't fit in the small trunk of the MGB, and he had been upset to have to leave it behind. As it was, the small car was packed full with duffle bags, sleeping bags, and camera bags. And it turned out that Nigel wasn't a morning person, so he had grumbled and complained all the way from London to Dover.

"Lover's quarrel?" Nigel had asked, when they were safely outside of London.

"It's complicated."

"Everything with Gwen is complicated," Nigel had replied, and astutely left it at that.

Clark forced himself to remain positive as he stood on the ferry deck in the lee of the wind and rain and wondered if he had made a gigantic mistake. But as they now approached the mouth of the Dover harbor, the sky seemed considerably lighter and the waves substantially diminished. The captain's weather report or radar must have seen this clearing in the storm, Clark thought, and he managed to relax a little.

He hadn't asked Nigel whether he had any propensity for seasickness because he hadn't really wanted to know. But now he saw that Nigel seemed to be comfortable reading a book in the lounge. That was something that Clark could never do on a boat. He tried not to dwell on his memories of Gwen and her seasickness on their recent ferry rides.

A slash of sunlight broke through the thinning clouds and hit the water off the starboard bow of the ferry, generating a fragile rainbow. Clark eagerly took it as a positive omen. But that didn't completely assuage his feeling that he was maybe taking a coward's way out, running away from his responsibility to Gwen and the baby. The problem was that every time he tried to rationally address his feelings and imagine himself with Gwen and a baby, the image of Bernadette, lying naked in his arms, forced its way in and dominated everything.

As the ferry steamed eastward, the weather improved. By the time they docked at Calais, France, around noon, the sun had come out and burned most of the damp chill from the air. While not exactly convertible top-down weather, they did have the windows rolled down as they drove off the ferry dock.

The day before, Clark had spent several hours at the Royal Automobile Club office. He verified that his car was insured for anywhere he drove, even Asia, the Middle East, and Africa. And then he worked on a route to Israel and back. No one in that office had ever done a drive like that, and everyone had an opinion about how to go and what to avoid. The most direct route appeared to be through France, Germany, Austria, Yugoslavia, Bulgaria, Turkey, Syria and Lebanon. Someone suggested a slightly more northern route through Belgium and more of Germany with better roads, and then Austria, Hungary and Yugoslavia. Both routes came together in Belgrade,

Yugoslavia's capital, before proceeding east into Bulgaria. There was no alternative road through that eastern part of Europe. The best estimate seemed to be that it was definitely over five thousand kilometers from London to Tel Aviv. Various guesses on how long it would take ranged from five days to two weeks, depending on sightseeing, road conditions, political climate (border crossings at the Communist Iron Curtain countries were often closed on a whim), and the overall stamina of the driver and the car. No one in the office imagined that they would ever want to undertake such an excursion in a small sports car.

Clark had attempted to discuss the route with Nigel while they drove to the ferry, but Nigel's only input had been that he hated Germany. When Clark told him that they had to go through at least a part of Germany, Nigel had shrugged, "It's your car, you're the driver."

After a quick lunch in the tourist area of the port, they headed for Reims, France. Many of the cities they would pass had a romantic or an intellectual/historical allure for Clark, but he couldn't always explain why. The Royal Automobile Club had information on most cities in the western part of Europe, but very little up-to-date information to offer on the cities further east and behind the Iron Curtain.

Clark had anticipated that driving through Europe would be much different than his train trip with the rugby team, and he wasn't disappointed. Although he didn't have the same ability to leisurely examine the countryside as he had when sitting on the train, the experience of driving afforded him a much more tactile, immersive, and satisfying experience. And driving on the right side, the correct-side for him, of the road made him very happy - while at the same time it made Nigel quite nervous.

Nigel quickly proved to be a poor navigator. He couldn't read a map properly and seemed to have an abysmal sense of direction, even with the obvious clues afforded by the sun in the mostly clear sky. And he tended to daydream. The result was that Clark couldn't count on him to watch for signs or pay attention for any clues that might help get them to their destination. Nigel could, however, read and speak French, which proved very useful.

Clark had anticipated that they could cover the 275 kilometers from Calais to Reims in three or four hours. But he soon learned that driving in France was not the same as in the United States or England. Theoretically, many of the same traffic laws existed, but the adherence to them was substantially different. The highway, mostly two lanes, changed to four lanes and then back again with surprising frequency and without any discernable pattern. Many drivers tried to use the four lane stretches to speed past slower traffic, but they were often stymied when the slower drivers occupied both lanes and showed no inclination to move, despite the loud and insistent blaring of car horns. At first bemused, Clark soon felt the same frustration as the other faster drivers. Basically a safe driver, he did like to go fast. It was almost six o'clock and dark when they pulled into the city center of Reims and parked in the shadow of the Notre Dame de Reims, site of the coronation of many of France's kings. That crossed the first historical attraction off Clark's list.

After an uneventful night at a small youth hostel, Clark found the next spot on his list for Reims - the old Supreme Headquarters of the Allied Expeditionary Force where in 1945 General Dwight Eisenhower had accepted the unconditional surrender of Germany to end World War Two.

Clark's original goal for the second day had been to get all the way to Salzburg, Austria, 907 kilometers from Reims. After the first day he knew that that was far too ambitious. But that meant spending a night in Germany, which wouldn't make Nigel very happy.

"Doesn't bloody well matter, they're both Nazi countries," Nigel responded when Clark explained the situation. Clark forced himself back into touring mode and tried to relax - it was his adventure, in his car.

Strasbourg was the next big city, 350 kilometers from Reims, and Clark had two interests there: the shop where Gutenberg had invented his printing press in 1440; and the European Court of Human Rights, which had met in Strasbourg since its establishment in 1949. He didn't expect any elaborate location for the Court, but he just wanted to go there and be able to remember it when Professor Doctor referenced the court in his lectures, as he often did.

Unfortunately, Nigel had an altogether different frame of reference to Strasbourg because it had been the site of one of the first pogroms in Europe in the 1300s, when many Jews were burned alive. His mood only worsened as they subsequently drove over the Rhine River and entered Germany.

The architecture had begun to change as they drove through the Alsace region in France, so Germany didn't look much different, at least not right away. What did change immediately were the quality of the roads and speed of the drivers. As soon as they left the border control station, they were on a four-lane autobahn where speed and courtesy dominated. Clark soon revised his estimate that they would be lucky to make Stuttgart, which was 150 kilometers from the border and an industrial town without any allure for him. Now he set his sights on Munich, 233 kilometers beyond Stuttgart. For Clark, driving the autobahn seemed like driving the turnpikes and interstates at home. And similar to home, there was a lot of traffic and the pace around Stuttgart slowed and got more dangerous, as many drivers tried to maintain as much speed as possible despite the congestion.

Leaving Stuttgart, Clark realized he was tired and ready to stop. But Nigel refused to consider staying in any small German town. So, Clark pulled into a rest stop and then let Nigel drive, which he immediately regretted. Nigel drove carefully, too carefully, and much too slow for the German autobahn. With no posted speed limit, the pace, as Clark had found, often exceeded 120 kilometers per hour. The little MGB could cruise along nicely at 100 or even 110, but was still relegated to the slower right lane, while the Mercedes sedans and trucks raced past them in the left lane.

As they finally neared Munich, Clark consulted his *International Guidebook of Hostels* and directed them to a place close to the city center and near several famous beer halls. Clark looked forward to sampling the German beers, but Nigel only drank wine and refused to be in the same room with drunken Germans. Not to be deterred, Clark left Nigel at the hostel and found a warm, crowded, and very friendly beer hall. It wasn't tourist season, but there were enough foreigners there to make it interesting, and the bartenders spoke passable English. He got back to the hostel around one o'clock in the morning and found Nigel sitting alone in a small parlor, straining to listen to the BBC on a shortwave radio. He hadn't heard Clark come in and almost jumped out of his skin when he suddenly realized someone stood there.

"Just me mate. A little jumpy tonight?" Clark said, trying to keep it light.

"You do know what's just a few kilometers from here, don't you?" Nigel challenged.

Clark shook his head.

"Dachau, the first concentration camp. This is where the whole bloody mess started."

Clark had a hard time reconciling that with the fun-loving, beer-drinking, song-singing people he had met that evening.

But he did recall that Munich had been the first center of power for Hitler and the Nazis.

Nigel turned his attention back to the radio and turned it up slightly as the BBC Announcer reported, "Another incident happened today on the Israeli Syrian border. Troops from both countries exchanged fire near the Israeli settlements of Ein Gey and Gadot. And in related news, there were anti-Israel demonstrations again in Damascus and Cairo. And for the first time there was a small demonstration in Ankara. In other international news, American troops in Vietnam…"

The news jolted Clark out of his relaxed, vacation adventure frame-of-mind. "Okay, let's get some sleep, and we'll leave right after breakfast."

Clark knew that Austria and Germany were the same in Nigel's mind, but he really wanted to spend time in Salzburg. Like many, he had been captivated by the city as depicted in the recent film *The Sound of Music*. He also wanted to see Mozart's birthplace.

When they reached Salzburg, they had only come 140 kilometers from Munich, but it looked and felt like a different world. The baroque architecture, set against the backdrop of the Alps, was stunning enough to somewhat lift Nigel's dark mood. There were some tourists around, but the city seemed to be dominated by students, mostly Austrian but with a good mix of other nationalities. They found a hostel near the University of Salzburg and spent the day walking the streets of the old city, stopping at Mozart's birthplace and residence, and enjoying the flower gardens of the Mirabell Palace.

Nigel seemed relaxed enough that Clark felt comfortable to ask the question that had been on his mind for days. "I'm curious why you have this compulsion to go there and fight."

It took Nigel a while to answer. "Most of my mother's family were killed during the war, Auschwitz, and those that survived emigrated to Israel when the war was over. Military service is compulsory there and I… well, I think that it could have been me, it's my family, and it's something that I need to do."

Clark appreciated the passion and nodded.

That evening in a bistro, they met some Austrian students who spoke English. When Clark explained their trip, they all shook their heads in disbelief. No one had ever heard of such a thing. Clark noticed that Nigel didn't tell anyone about staying in Israel, but allowed the impression that they were both doing the entire trip around the Mediterranean.

The next morning, they headed south into the Alps, toward Yugoslavia. Everything had been easy and almost familiar up until then, but Clark knew that would probably change. The roughly 240 kilometer trip across the Alps took them over five hours because of the nature of the roads - steep, only two-lanes in most places, and busy with truck traffic. They also made frequent stops to take photos of the spectacular snowcapped mountains and quaint villages nestled in the narrow valleys. Clark had lived in Denver and knew the Rocky Mountains; and he had lived in Seattle and knew the Cascades. But the Alps were very different. He tried to explain it to Nigel. "It's like the Rockies have been pressed together and made higher, steeper, with much more narrow valleys. Like an accordion squeezed closed."

As they descended from the Alps, their apprehension grew. The Yugoslavian border loomed ahead, and they didn't know what to expect. Clark hoped that the absence of a traffic backup going in their direction and a steady stream of truck traffic moving in the opposite direction were indicators of an open border.

Clark tried to assure Nigel that most communist countries like Yugoslavia were not specifically anti-Jewish but were opposed to all religions - the opiate of the masses. Nigel knew that, but it didn't ease his anxiety very much. And Clark began to worry about how Nigel was going to deal with the countries in the Middle East that they had to travel through to get to Israel.

The border crossing into Yugoslavia turned out to be as easy as going from France into Germany. Marshall Tito, the ruler of Yugoslavia, had broken from the Soviet Union in 1948, and although he remained a communist, he had established cordial relations with the United States and England. Automobile traffic had a separate line and border post, so they didn't have to wait in the long line of trucks. The border guard gave their passports only a cursory glance and then a quick look to make sure Clark and Nigel matched the photographs.

They were almost to Ljubljana, but that city had no appeal to either of them so they pushed on to Zagreb, another 140 kilometers. They entered Zagreb as night fell. The entire city was dark, dirty, and depressing. Clark compared it to Newcastle but Nigel had never been there. Very few streetlights worked, and most stores were closed, or appeared to be closed because none of them had lighted signs. They followed the street signs for the city center, hoping that they could find a hostel or a hotel there. The hostel guidebook had no listings for any cities in the countries behind the Iron Curtain, so they were on their own until they got to Turkey.

Some stores and restaurants in the city center of Zagreb had lights on. They struggled to identify a building as a hotel, and when they did, they both felt reluctant to stop, but there didn't appear to be any other choices. The front-desk clerk in the hotel was cautious and very pretty in an unadorned way. She didn't speak English but knew French, which allowed Nigel to communicate their needs and understand the astonishingly inexpensive room rate. As they finished paying, Clark thought the clerk was smitten with Nigel, and he smiled at the multiple layers of irony.

About to fall asleep, Clark reflected on the fact that, other than the brief conversation in Salzburg, he and Nigel had had no meaningful conversations over the past days. Everything had been about perfunctory things like being hungry or tired or to comment on the scenery. Clark didn't feel a strong compulsion to really engage and get to know Nigel because they would split in a few days, and he would undoubtedly never see him again.

As they left Zagreb the next morning, Clark calculated that it was approximately thirteen-hundred kilometers to cross Yugoslavia and Bulgaria, reach the Turkish border, and get to Istanbul - so maybe a day and a half at normal speed. But it quickly became obvious that the communist leaders were not spending any money on the condition of their roads. If the autobahns were a ten on a ten-point scale, then the main highway that traversed Yugoslavia rated a five at best, and often less. And it carried a lot of traffic, mostly trucks. So Clark soon began to realize that they would need at least two days, and maybe three, to get to Istanbul, which was the next city that held any interest for him.

As it turned out, the communist leaders were spending some money on fixing their roads, but that meant construction areas, which caused long delays. It took them over ten exhausting hours to go the 380 kilometers from Zagreb to Belgrade. At the turnoff for Belgrade City Center, Clark thought he was hallucinating when he saw what looked like an American motel. Run down and depressing, it was clearly a motel, and trucks filled the parking area. At first the clerk indicated that there were no rooms, but when he realized that Clark was an American and not German, he found one.

Neither Clark nor Nigel slept well because of the constant noise of trucks on the highway, which was less than fifty yards from their room.

The road from Belgrade to Sofia was much the same, but there were fewer construction sites once they entered Bulgaria. Not that the Bulgarian roads didn't need the work. They spent several hours inching past an accident scene where two trucks had collided and no one seemed motivated to get them off the roadway. Clark had Nigel drive for some of that time because they weren't going anywhere quickly, and he had to shut his eyes for a while.

Sofia made Zagreb look like a western paradise. Virtual blackout conditions, no lights anywhere, no signs of a hotel, and the one restaurant they saw was packed with very unfriendly looking men. A petrol station on the highway had some prepared food in packages, and they reluctantly decided to stay in the station's parking lot and try to sleep in the car. Despite being very uncomfortable, they managed to fall asleep for a few hours.

The blare of a siren struck Clark like it was pressed up against his ear. His body jerked, and he hit his head on the metal strut that supported the canvas convertible top. A bright light from outside his window shone into his eyes and a loud voice yelled something. Startled, groggy, and more than a little scared, he tried to shield his eyes from the light so he could see what was going on. Then someone tried to open his door. By this time Nigel was awake, shouting and hyperventilating.

Clark reached over to start the car to get away from what he assumed were robbers when he saw a police car and its flashing lights. Cautiously, he partially rolled down his window. The light moved from his face, and he saw a uniformed policeman, who waved his flashlight and talked, fast and loud.

Clark's heart rate settled a little, and he took a deep breath. They soon established that the policeman didn't speak any English or French and that he was completely ill suited for non-verbal communication. Eventually, Clark thought he understood from the frustrated, but fortunately not angry, policeman that it wasn't okay for them to park there and sleep, even though there were probably twenty trucks and truckers doing the same thing. And so they drove off into the night.

The posted speed limit was 90 kilometers per hour, which only a fool would try to achieve on those roads, even in the daylight. Clark drove well under that because the police car had followed them.

Nigel turned around to look at it. "Bloody hell, is he going to follow us all night?!"

"Maybe," Clark replied fatalistically, as he adjusted his rearview mirror to keep the headlights out of his eyes.

After they had gone several miles, the police car's lights began to flash again, the siren sounded, and the turn signal came on.

"Christ, what now?" Clark mumbled, as he slowed down and looked for a place to pull over. Then he noticed that immediately ahead there was a wide turn off with a small sign that featured the drawing of a tent. He laughed. "He's directed us to a campground. Unbelievable."

Clark pulled into the small roadside campground and swerved to keep his headlights off two small tents that were set up on the grass, near some trees. The policeman turned off his flashing lights and sped off down the highway. Clark parked the car as far from the tents as possible and almost immediately fell asleep.

Unfortunately, Clark had parked the car facing east, so early the next morning the sun rose and blasted through the windshield into his face. He tried to shield his eyes, desperate for more sleep, but soon realized that it was hopeless. His body was stiff and sore, and he had to pee. Then he noticed that Nigel wasn't in the car, and he twisted around to look at the campground.

On the other side of the small area, Nigel sat next to a small campfire with four young men. They appeared to be in an animated discussion full of gestures and laughter. The tents had been taken down.

"Clark, these guys are French and love the story of what happened to us last night," Nigel said, as Clark joined the group. "They have coffee."

Clark accepted an old, chipped, porcelain mug offered by one of the Frenchmen and took a sip. "Merci, that's really good. Thank you."

"They don't speak any English, but they're on their way to Athens to find jobs on a cruise ship. They were working at a hotel in France that closed." Nigel was unusually casual and sociable with these men, and Clark wondered if they were gay and whether gay people had a kind of a signal to identify each other.

The Frenchmen told them about a decent roadside café a few kilometers back, and then they headed off south toward Greece. Clark and Nigel found the café, which was as good as advertised, and after breakfast they got back on the road. All the discussion of Greece had inexorably led Clark to think of Cynna and Arthur. He knew that there was nothing positive to be gained from that, but he had a hard time getting them out of his head. What would they think if they knew about Gwen and him and her… condition?

It was 311 kilometers from Sofia to the Turkish border, and the road got progressively worse but fortunately less crowded. Clark had to be extra alert so he would have time to react to the large potholes in the pavement, some of which could have easily busted an axle on the small sports car. They passed several sedans and small trucks that were seemingly abandoned on the side of the road with flat tires and one with a broken rear axle. And they had seen very few service stations, maybe one every hundred kilometers or more. Clark knew by then to fill up his gas tank any time he saw a functioning gas pump.

As they came over the top of a hill, they saw in the distance that the road widened into three lanes as it approached the border station at Kemel, Turkey. Each lane was full of trucks, and Clark estimated that there were thirty or more trucks backed up, none of them moving through the border checkpoint. There was a similar backup on the other side, traffic heading west. He saw only a few other cars and no special lane for them. As they approached, he decided to take the far outside lane and not get in between two lanes of trucks, many of them idling with thick diesel exhaust spewing out.

The lines weren't moving at all, and many of the truck drivers had left their vehicles and stood around smoking and talking. Bottles of liquor passed between them. Some of the men noticed the sports car and came over to inspect it.

Clark could see Nigel grow tense, as he slumped down in his seat and stared straight ahead. Clark rolled down his window despite the exhaust filled air and tried to smile casually. He struggled to maintain his composure as one man poked hard at the canvas top of the car.

Nigel jumped in his seat when a particularly mean-looking, probably drunk, old man thrust his face up to the passenger window and yelled something at him. He then gave Nigel a toothless grin as he backed up a little and pulled a revolver from his coat pocket. He waved the gun around wildly, and the other men gave him plenty of room. He pointed the gun at Nigel, who screamed and crunched down below the window, almost on the floor. That seemed to encourage the man to act more aggressively. Clark fought a sense of panic because he didn't know what he could or should do. He was sure that Nigel's reactions only made things worse with this drunken bully.

Suddenly, from the front of the lines came a long blast of a horn, and the trucks at the head of the lines started to move. The sounds of other truck horns followed and turned into an awful cacophony of noise. The toothless man put the gun away and ran with the others to their trucks. Nigel gradually unfolded his body and sat upright. Neither of them said anything as they slowly moved forward toward the border station.

Whatever had held up the lines had evidently been resolved because the trucks were now hustled through a quick inspection and then waved on. A haggard looking border guard perfunctorily stamped their passports and almost waved Clark through before he really focused on the car. He seemed to revive and looked closely at the passports, then at Clark and Nigel, and then back again at the car. The guard got out of his booth and called to another guard. They slowly walked around the car, talking excitedly. Clark began to get apprehensive and debated whether to say something. Nigel hadn't recovered from having the gun pointed at him and sat still and stiff, staring straight ahead. Both guards then laughed at something that one of them said. And then, still laughing, the guard handed the passports to Clark and waved his hand for them to proceed.

Neither of them spoke for several miles. Nigel was still too shaken up, and Clark had to concentrate on what was the worst road that they had been on. It was in terrible physical condition and crowded with old, beat-up, slow-moving cars. In addition, Clark had to carefully maneuver around rickety horse-drawn farm wagons, full of produce headed for market. And to make it even worse, there were lots of pedestrians, young and old, walking on the road. Clark smiled to himself despite the added stress. He was happy to finally be in what felt like a real foreign country and not the black hole that was Bulgaria.

255 kilometers from the border and over five hours later, they finally reached Istanbul. They entered the European section of the city that straddled the geographic divide between Europe and Asia. Much of this part of Istanbul still maintained the cosmopolitan nature that had begun back in the Middle Ages, when it had been the largest and wealthiest city in Europe, if not the world.

Thanks in large part to the English on most of the street signs, Clark didn't have too much trouble finding the hostel that they had picked from the guidebook. It was located on the western edge of the historical center of the city, on Bayazit Square and near Istanbul University. It had formerly been the palace of a minor sultan. The three large bunkrooms were crowded with European and Asian students and other young travelers. This included a large contingent from Australia. While they didn't travel as an organized group, the Australians had enough interaction and overlapping stays at different hostels to become familiar with each other. They eagerly welcomed Clark and Nigel because they were refreshing new distractions and because they encountered very few Americans in that part of the world. Nigel didn't have any interest in interacting, but Clark felt comfortable around them, particularly since many of the men wore rugby shirts, and the women were friendly and very down-to-earth.

The Australians had discovered a British style pub not far from the hostel, and Clark joined them for a beer. After several pints, they decided to make Clark an honorary Australian because they saw his journey to England and now Istanbul and beyond as comparable to their extensive, multi-year treks, which they undertook after university and before settling down at their careers. Almost all of them stumbled back to the hostel at one o'clock, just before the curfew when the building would be locked for the night. An Australian man and a woman stayed in the pub because they had hooked up with a Turkish woman and man from Istanbul University who wanted to practice their English and maybe get to know each other on a more intimate level. Clark felt a little envious because the Turkish woman was very pretty, exotic like Cynna, but a warm and friendly version.

Clark crawled into his bunk bed, exhausted but the happiest, most relaxed, that he had been in many weeks. He had tried on a new personality with the Australians - talkative and fun instead of his normal quiet and reserved self - and he was pleased with the attention it got him. Almost asleep, he felt someone sit down next to him. He opened his eyes to see one of the Australian women, Priscilla, wearing only a large t-shirt as she leaned in and kissed him. He had noticed her at the pub, and they had casually flirted, but he hadn't seen it going anywhere. Despite her strong cigarette breath, he didn't resist as she slid into his sleeping bag with him and initiated quiet, but very intense and satisfying sex.

When Clark woke in the morning, Priscilla was gone - really gone, he discovered later, as in checked out of the hostel and departed for Athens. It was his first one-night stand, and he didn't mention it to Nigel.

Feedback from the Australians had confirmed Clark's research that there were four things he really wanted to see or experience in Istanbul: Topkapi Palace, the sultan's former palace now a museum; the Hagia Sophia, once the world's largest cathedral, then a mosque and now another museum; the Blue Mosque, still a mosque and not a museum; and the Grand Bazaar, one of the largest, if not the largest, covered market in the world. Nigel was reluctant to go, but he felt more comfortable when Clark said that they could join a group from the hostel on an official tour that visited the sites along the eastern edge of the city, overlooking the Bosphorus. Clark normally liked to explore places on his own, but the tour included a bus, and he wouldn't have to drive and find places to park.

The Topkapi Palace, Hagia Sofia, and Blue Mosque were all near the shoreline of the Bosphorus Strait on the eastern end of the peninsula that was the historic city of Istanbul. There were no remnants of the original Greek settlements from the sixth century BC that had grown and become known as Byzantium. But there did exist vestiges of the time in the third century AD when the city had been the eastern capital of the Roman Empire and was called Constantinople. But the majority of the architecture reflected the Ottoman rule of the city, then known as Istanbul, from the mid fifteenth century until the formation of the Turkish Republic in 1922. The Hagia Sophia, their first tour-stop, reflected all of these influences with its huge dome of Byzantine architecture, its time as the largest catholic cathedral in the world, and then its conversion, including the addition of four minarets, to an imperial mosque during Ottoman rule.

Topkapi Palace, the second stop on the tour, had been the center of power for the Ottoman Empire, and at its peak had housed over four thousand people including the Sultan and his wives, consorts, and concubines. Part of the extensive network of low buildings had been converted into a museum, but most of the palace remained closed to the public. Clark had seen the heist film *Topkapi* during his freshman year at college and thought he recognized some of the exterior and a few of the courtyards of the palace from the film. He had been surprised that the director had ended the film with the heroes languishing in a Turkish prison, which looked pretty grim.

Most of the people on the tour seemed to be in no hurry and slowly moved from room to room and lingered over every exhibit. That was definitely not Clark's modus operandi in a museum. He normally made a quick overview, maybe focused on an exhibit or two, and kept moving. It drove his mother and sister crazy. However, he found a kindred spirit in Nigel, and they soon left the group behind and wound up on a bench overlooking the Bosphorus Strait. The Bosphorus separated Europe from Asia and was one of the busiest waterways in the world, carrying traffic between the Asian part of the city and the European side, and between the Mediterranean and the Black Sea. Below them and next to the water, they could see that Kennedy Avenue, a four-lane street named for the late U.S. President, was clogged with traffic.

"I'm glad we're not in that."

Nigel nodded in agreement.

"I'm going to take some photos, how about you?" Clark asked.

"No, nothing here that I'm interested in."

Clark left him and got so involved in capturing shots of interesting design patterns in the buildings that he almost missed the bus. They arrived at the last stop, the Blue Mosque, at afternoon prayer time. Nigel refused to go in, and it surprised Clark that tourists were allowed in during the prayers. Even more surprising, he saw tourists who moved around the mosque and took photos of the Muslims as they prayed. He couldn't imagine that happening in a church or cathedral. Cautiously he joined in, lost track of time, and almost missed the bus again.

By the time they got back to the hostel, Clark and Nigel had both had enough of the boisterous, energetic group, especially the Australians. Clark declined a return trip to the pub, and instead he and Nigel found a small restaurant near the university. They were the only foreigners there. They had just begun to try to decipher the menu when Clark noticed the same Turkish man and woman who had been at the pub the night before - the ones who had taken two Australians home with them. He looked away, but he had been spotted, and the two Turks came over and sat at their table.

"I am Deniz, and he is Emir. You are Clark I think," the woman said with a heavy accent, as she thrust her hand out to shake first with Clark and then with Nigel.

"Yes, I am Clark, and he is Nigel." Clark couldn't help but smile at the vivacious and attractive young woman with the firm handshake who had somehow remembered his name.

"We are brother sister and eager to English practice," Emir added, as he also shook their hands. "Our friends Australia left this today for Greek." Deniz whispered in his ear, and then he corrected himself, "Oh yes, for Greece."

"You are interested in Turkish food?" Deniz asked, as she looked at Nigel and tried to connect. She took his menu and begin to explain it. Nigel responded with a weak smile.

They all ordered and continued a get-acquainted conversation about schools and families.

"Are you two twins?" Clark asked.

Deniz and Emir looked at each other, thinking, then Deniz responded, "Oh, yes, twins born same mother and same day. I am older," she finished proudly.

"I am twin also," Clark said. "I have a twin sister. And I am older," he added, as he smiled at Deniz.

The food came, and Clark like the taste, but it was very spicy, too spicy for him. Nigel seemed to like his, and his mood brightened.

A group of Turkish men at a nearby table had gotten progressively more boisterous and loud over the past hour. Suddenly two of them started shouting at each other and the rest of the room went very quiet. Deniz and Emir looked at each other and then at Clark and Nigel. "Men get very upset over trouble in Palestine. Big war maybe. One man to peace and other to push Jews in sea," Deniz explained matter-of-factly without any indication that she thought that Nigel was Jewish. She didn't notice, as Clark did, how Nigel's expression immediately hardened and his body seemed to shrink into his chair.

"And Turkey is neutral, correct?" Clark asked hopefully.

"Yes on our own side, neutral," Emir answered. "But many follow strict ways of Islam and many hate Jews."

The commotion at the other table subsided, and Clark tried to change the subject. "We were at Topkapi today and going to the Grand Bazaar tomorrow." That succeeded in turning the conversation, but the night had been ruined for Nigel. He soon poked Clark. "I've got to get out of here," he whispered.

Clark thought for a moment of letting him go alone because he thought he wanted to stay with Deniz and see what might happen. But the worried look on Nigel's face convinced him that he should accompany him. He once again wondered how the hell Nigel was going to survive in the Israeli army. But he told himself that it wasn't his problem.

Later, as he lay on his bunk, unable to fall asleep, Clark couldn't help thinking about Gwen, really thinking for the first time since leaving London. She had certainly lingered in the back of his mind, especially during the long hours of driving. But he had managed to keep her at a safe distance, a vague longing, a distant rumble of anxiety and regret. But now he could no longer ignore the questions, the remorse, the guilt. It was easy, convenient, to blame her. She had been on the pill. She had pulled away. She had used him. But nevertheless, she was pregnant with his child, and he had fallen in bed, in love with Bernadette. Or was it love, he wondered. And he certainly hadn't resisted Priscilla, and tonight he could have easily hopped in bed with Deniz. He feared that it was evidence of a bad character flaw, one that had been hidden behind his virginity. Sleep finally overtook him before he found answers to the unanswerable.

At breakfast the next morning, Nigel announced that he didn't want to go to the Grand Bazaar, and Clark debated whether he would go anyway. But his sense of adventure soon took over, and he found himself on the fringe of the chaos that was the Grand Bazaar.

From its origins in the 15th century, the Grand Bazaar had grown into the largest covered shopping area in the world, with sixty-one covered narrow streets and almost three thousand shops. The abundance and diversity of goods for sale reflected the centuries of Ottoman Empire rule as an empire that had spread over three continents. And Istanbul had always been positioned strategically at the nexus of the trade routes between Europe, Asia, and Africa. The manager of the hostel had told Clark that the bazaar was one of the world's most visited tourist attractions and on an average day over two hundred thousand people would visit it.

Clark fought off his initial feelings of claustrophobia as he walked the narrow streets, full of an overwhelming crush of different types of people - all talking, many shouting. The small, one-story shops extended out to cover the sidewalks and spill into the street, creating narrow lanes for people to walk. Fortunately, the tiled roofs that covered the streets were arched and high enough to somewhat offset the potentially oppressive feeling created by the compressed walkways.

The people all wore colorless clothes - mostly black, brown, and some white. But the drab clothing was offset by a riot of colors in the shops - textiles, rugs, clothing for children, produce, and sundry goods. Unlike the rest of Istanbul, most of the women in the bazaar wore either the burka, completely covering their faces, or the hijab, that covered their hair. Far more traditional than the cosmopolitan part of the city, the marketplace presented a more realistic exposure to Turkish and Islamic culture, and Clark loved it. He found that, with only a few exceptions, people didn't mind his camera, and if they objected to a photo, they let him know in a friendly manner. When faced with the occasional vendor or shopper who spoke angrily at him, Clark quickly smiled, lowered his camera and moved on.

He wandered around the bazaar for several hours. He snacked at several kiosks - pastries and vegetable pies, which he liked, and yogurt drinks, which he didn't. He bought some small trinkets for his family including what appeared to be a ubiquitous souvenir that consisted of a dark blue circle with the shape of an eye in the middle. He had seen it on key rings, necklaces, and wall decorations. It hung in almost every shop, even those that didn't sell souvenirs. Finally, one vendor who spoke some English, explained, "Turkish good luck, nazar boncugu, the blue eye." He offered Clark one that looked very old, painted ceramic, strung on a leather necklace, which Clark bought and put around his neck.

Clark didn't return to the hostel until midafternoon. Nigel accosted him as soon as he entered, "There are big anti-Israel demonstrations in Antalya. We need to turn back."

Antalya was on their planned route along the southern coast of Turkey. But Clark didn't want to turn back and offered an alternative. "We can go east to Ankara and then south to Syria, stay away from that area."

Nigel considered and finally agreed when Clark suggested that they leave early the next morning so they could drive the 450 kilometers to Ankara, the Turkish capital, in one long day. Then they would reach Syria the day after. Clark refused to think about what it would be like when they reached the Syrian border.

CHAPTER 20

From the Topkapi Palace two days before, Clark had seen the ferries crossing the Bosphorus between Europe and Asia, and he had eagerly anticipated getting on one. People had been making the journey between Asia and Europe over this body of water for thousands of years. It was, however, easier said than done. Most of the ferries required an advanced booking and carried primarily trucks. The passenger car ferries that didn't require a reservation had long lines, and that was where Clark and Nigel were stuck.

After over an hour of listening to Nigel complain, Clark was ready to turn around and head back to London, and he might have done so if he could have gotten out of the line of cars. There were three lines packed bumper to bumper, and they were in the middle line with no place to back-up, turn around or do anything except to inch forward each time another ferry docked, emptied, and eventually began to load cars. When they were finally on a boat, the view of Istanbul from the water made the wait almost worthwhile. Unfortunately, it was almost noon and the light was flat, no shadows, so Clark could only imagine that in the early morning light it would be a spectacular view. Other than Clark and Nigel, there was no one else standing on the small aft deck. The Turks crowded in the passenger lounge, which was loud and hot and stank of Turkish cigarettes and body odor.

Clark had noticed as they traveled east that more and more people smoked, and the cigarettes got stronger, or at least they smelled that way. Priscilla's cigarette breath and taste when she had crawled into his bed and kissed him had been much worse than Gwen's. Nigel, who smoked a moderate amount of very mild English cigarettes, had tried a Turkish brand at the restaurant with the twins, but had coughed and gagged and quickly crushed it out.

By the time they were off the ferry in the eastern part of Istanbul it was early afternoon, and Ankara was still over four hundred kilometers away. According to the map they had found at the hostel, there didn't appear to be any place to stop before reaching the capital city. No big cities, and nothing in the hostel guidebook unless they got off the main road and went north to Karasu, a resort on the Black Sea, which did, in fact, hold some appeal for Clark.

Clark couldn't help but smile, thrilled to be officially in Asia. And the change in the city was fairly dramatic. The buildings, dominantly of byzantine architecture, seemed older and more run-down, almost decrepit. There were no traces of the cosmopolitan aspects of the European side of Istanbul: no modern buildings, stores or restaurants. Very few signs had an English translation, and while it didn't seem possible, the roads were the worse yet. They were badly in need of repair and crowded with the ubiquitous transport trucks and an array of barely functioning old cars, small battered trucks, horse-drawn farm wagons, bicycles, pedestrians, and stray animals.

They struggled down the crowded streets in the densely populated area for over an hour before they realized that they had made a wrong turn somewhere and were on the road to Izmir and not Ankara. The map they had was as useless as if drawn by a blind child with a crayon. By the time they doubled back, found the road to Ankara, it was mid-afternoon, and they still had almost the entire distance to go. They stopped for gas and something to drink at a truck stop.

"Let's turn back for Greece. The Australians thought that there was a ferry from Athens to Tel Aviv," Nigel almost begged.

"They didn't know for sure, at least not about a car ferry." Clark was not a turn-back person. "I think we should take turns driving and press on."

"We could be driving all bloody night."

Clark shrugged his shoulders. They had been sitting, waiting, for hours, and he was anxious to keep moving - forward. "I'll drive and you rest, then we'll switch up. Traffic should thin out eventually."

So they progressed eastward. The road actually did improve a little, but the traffic didn't diminish. They crept along with the local traffic for long stretches. They passed miles and miles of farmland where they could almost maintain the speed limit unless caught behind a slow moving truck. But then they would again come to a village where the local traffic increased, the road conditions deteriorated, and everything slowed to a crawl. That pattern played out for hours, well after it got dark. Then everyone seemed to disappear except for the trucks.

Almost every hour they alternated driving. Clark could rest his eyes but not sleep while Nigel drove. Driving on the right side of the road really confused him, and he was very cautious and hesitant to pass a slow-moving truck. To further increase their anxiety after it got dark, they saw a number of old trucks go by in the other direction without their headlights turned on.

Clark drove through a small village that had no signs of life. As they returned to farmland, they came up behind a slower moving car. Clark waited to see if it would speed up, but it stayed steady at just under the speed limit. Although Clark really liked to drive fast, he knew that it wasn't smart or possible on these roads, especially at night. He did try, however, to maintain a pace at the posted limit or a few kilometers above. Seeing a chance, he used his turn signals to indicate his intention and then sped up and around the car to pass. As he went by the car, he glanced over and saw that the driver wore the same hat and uniform that they had seen on a policeman at a gas station earlier in the evening. Oh shit, he thought. But he was committed, so he moved on ahead, used his signal, and pulled over in front of the car. The car didn't have the lights or any markings of an official police car, and Clark wondered if they used unmarked police cars in Turkey as they did at home. Or maybe the cop was off-duty and on his way home. Clark tensed as he maintained a speed just above the speed limit and waited to see if he was in trouble. The policeman maintained his slower speed and gradually faded from sight in Clark's rear view mirror.

It was almost eleven o'clock, and Clark realized that he had made a bad mistake with this plan. They had covered only about half the distance to Ankara, and he could barely stay awake. There were no radio stations. Nigel slept in the passenger seat. And it was a very dark, overcast night. Every ten minutes or so a large truck would roar past them headed the other direction, and he would have to avert his eyes from the painful blast of the truck's headlights as they swept over the little sports car. Then the air, compressed behind the truck, would pummel the car and try to push it off the road. Less frequently, he would come up behind a truck going their direction. And occasionally a truck would come up behind them and quickly speed past, going much too fast for the condition of the roads. Except for the policeman's car, he hadn't seen another passenger car for hours.

Clark had not seen any place where they could stop, other than to just pull into the parking area of one of the few gas stations they passed, most of which had been closed. But that hadn't worked out well the last time they tried it, and he hadn't seen anything like the roadside camping area that they had used in Bulgaria. As they entered a little village, he pulled over and parked in front of a small group of dark buildings. Exhausted, he turned off the engine and laid his head back, closed his eyes.

The silence and stillness soon woke Nigel. "What's going on? Where are we?"

"Sorry, I had to stop, I'm done. A couple of hours sleep and I'll be good to go."

Nigel looked around frantically. Adrenalin and fear forced him fully awake. "Oh no, you promised to push on, not stop somewhere like this. Ankara or bust you said."

"I know, I'm sorry, my eyes can't take it, the truck headlights… We'll be okay here for a few hours."

"I'm awake now, I'll drive," Nigel insisted, as he opened his door.

As Nigel steered the car back onto the road, Clark sat up straight, rolled down the window, and promised himself to help keep Nigel awake. He had loosened his seat belt a little so he could relax, and after a few minutes he fell asleep.

Clark began to dream of Bernadette. They were sitting on her couch, holding hands, and talking about Maya. She began to read a story that described making love to Maya, and it had a lot of very graphic detail. He felt himself getting excited. Suddenly an earthquake shook the room. Bernadette screamed and he flew off the couch, hitting his head. Something fell on top of him. Fighting panic, he struggled to get up. Waking up but disoriented, Clark realized that the car had stopped and that the screams came from Nigel. Clark's body had been thrown partially off the seat and up against the dashboard. The windshield was shattered, and the front frame of the canvas top pushed down into the car, almost on top of him. The car started to move slowly. Clark forced his body back onto the seat, then reached over and pulled up the emergency parking brake. He struggled to make out what Nigel was saying, something about lights and men and it not being his fault.

Clark smelled gas, so he turned the key in the ignition and the engine died. His instincts told him to get out of the car, and he yelled at Nigel to do the same. The collapse of the frame of the windshield had knocked the doorframe out of line, and it took all his strength, enhanced by his mounting panic, to force the door open. The crunch of glass and the squeal of metal on metal reverberated through the night, mixed with Nigel's histrionics. As he struggled to get out of the car, Clark again yelled at Nigel to get out.

Clark ran around the front of the car to help Nigel, but stopped when he saw the body of a person, a man, crushed against the windshield on the driver's side. Unable to process that immediately, Clark reached the driver's door and forced it open. Nigel no longer screamed but kept muttering, crying about lights and men and accident and death. Clark tried to get Nigel's attention but couldn't, and Nigel didn't seem interested in or capable of getting out of the car. Clark tried to pull him out, but his seat belt was still fastened, and he was a dead weight, stupefied. The interior car light had come on when the driver's door opened, and Clark saw what looked like blood dripping down from the windshield onto the steering wheel and Nigel. He looked more carefully at Nigel and saw more blood coming from a gash on his forehead. But he knew that didn't explain the other blood, which had to come from the man on the windshield.

Clark didn't want to face it, but he knew he had to check. The man was dressed in dark clothes, and from what little Clark could see of his face, blood came from his head where it had impacted the frame of the windshield. His breaths were very shallow, but Clark could tell that the man was breathing.

Clark no longer smelled gas but decided to check around the car to make sure there was no danger from fire. As he came around the rear of the car, he noticed the shape of another man, this one along the side of the road, about ten or twelve feet behind the car. He cautiously approached the man and then stopped when he saw the dark liquid pooling around the man's head. He didn't need the dim light from the car to tell that it was blood. He knelt down and tried to tell if the man was breathing, but he saw no evidence of it. He knew he could check for a pulse, but he couldn't bring himself to touch him.

"Oh, my God, he's dead. I killed him. Oh my God," cried Nigel, who had gotten out of the car and now stood staring at the man on the ground. His body swayed, losing strength, about to collapse.

Clark stood. "What the hell happened?"

"Two trucks went that way, lights blinded me, and these two just appeared in front. There wasn't time, they just hit and came over and…" Nigel started to sag, about to collapse, but Clark grabbed his shoulders to steady him.

"Okay, it was an accident. Now we need to find some help. I think the other one is still alive." As he spoke, Clark looked around and noticed buildings across the road and one of them had some interior lights on. There wasn't a sign, but it looked like some sort of restaurant or maybe a lounge/bar kind of place. He turned back to Nigel, but he was gone. He heard the car door and saw Nigel attempting to get back into the car. Clark ran over to him. "What're you doing?"

"We've got to get out of here. He's dead, we're in the middle of … and …" Nigel turned his attention to the man on the windshield and began to try to pull him off.

Clark grabbed Nigel and yelled at him, "Stop! He's hurt, we can't just dump him off and leave him. And we can't drive this."

Just then a speeding truck came up behind them, blew its horn, and barely managed to swerve around them. It didn't slow down or stop.

"But we better get the car off the road before we all get killed," Clark shouted at Nigel, over the receding noise of the truck. Clark couldn't get back in the driver's seat but reached in and undid the parking brake and popped the stick shift into neutral gear. He started to push carefully so the man on the windshield wouldn't fall off. Gradually, he got the car to move forward, then steered it off the road. He looked back at Nigel who had collapsed on the dirt along the side of the road, sitting with his knees pulled up to his chest, and his head collapsed on his arms.

Clark decided to head across the road to the building but noticed the dark shapes of several people as they came from the direction of the building and crossed the street toward them.

"Hello, we need help here!" Clark shouted at the approaching figures. "Someone call for help, an ambulance!" No response from any of them. "Does anyone speak English?" No response. He watched as three men now converged on the car and began to poke at the man on the windshield. "Hey, I don't think you should do that. He needs a doctor." Still no response. "Doctor. Do you understand?"

One of the men glared at Clark and muttered something in Turkish.

"English? French? Maybe someone in there speaks…?" Clark pointed to the building across the road.

The loud wail of a woman brought his attention back to the man on the side of the road. A small group had gathered around that man and had turned him over. One of them was an old woman in a burka who continued to wail, a high-pitched scream of pain and anger.

Clark rushed over to them. "I don't think you should touch him. Are you a doctor?" he asked the one man who continued to touch the dead man. The men and the woman then formed a circle, a barrier around the dead man so Clark couldn't get close. They spoke excitedly to each other in

Turkish. Clark didn't know what else to do, so he moved over and squatted next to Nigel.

"They're gonna kill us," Nigel sobbed. "They're his friends or family and that's what they do here."

Clark started to say something but then one of the men from the group at the windshield appeared in front of them and began to talk loudly. He gestured at the two men and the car. He didn't appear to Clark to be angry or that upset, but he was very serious and loud.

"I'm so sorry, but we don't understand Turkish," Clark interjected. That only got the man to speak more slowly and even louder. One of the men from group around the dead man shouted something. The man talking to Clark stopped, shook his head, and moved over to the dead man.

Clark's sense of frustration and uncertainty now began to turn to fear as he surveyed the scene and realized that he'd run out of ideas or options. He didn't know exactly what had happened. He believed Nigel that it had been an accident, but they couldn't communicate with these people, and the injured man needed help. He had no sense of how much time had gone by since the accident. It could have been five minutes or fifty. At least the woman had quieted down. Nigel continued to moan that they were going to be killed, and now Clark wasn't so sure that he wasn't correct.

Headlights approached from down the road, and Clark anticipated the roar of a truck and probably a blast from a horn, but instead the vehicle slowed down as it approached. A black Jeep pulled over and stopped behind the man on side of the road. Two men emerged from the Jeep. They were dressed in black clothes that looked like a uniform, but with no insignia. They each had a gun in a gun belt around their waists. Clark hoped that they were police, but he couldn't be sure.

One of the men-in-black went to the car and the other one went to the dead man on the ground. The group of men at the car was subdued while the group with the dead man was animated and the woman began to wail again. The man-in-black who had gone to the car returned to the Jeep, pulled a radio microphone from the dashboard and spoke urgently. Clark could hear a response come from a speaker in the car. He was encouraged to move over and try to talk. The man-in-black ignored him and moved over to the group by the dead man. Clark tried to communicate again and was met with a hard stare and a few stern words in Turkish. Clark backed away and went over to Nigel.

"They're vigilantes, that's how it happens in these countries," Nigel sputtered.

"No, I think they're cops," Clark responded, but wasn't totally convinced.

The one man-in-black who seemed to be in charge now approached them and started talking in a firm, matter-of-fact manner, which indicated no awareness that they couldn't understand him.

"We don't understand. We don't speak Turkish. Do you speak English, or French?" Clark asked.

Man-in-Black shrugged his shoulders, probably annoyed, and motioned for them to get into the Jeep. When neither Clark nor Nigel moved, he gestured more emphatically and raised his voice.

"We can't go with him or we're dead," Nigel cried.

"I don't think we have much choice," Clark responded, as he noticed that Man-in-Black had now placed his hand on his gun. Clark took Nigel's arm, pulled him up, and led him to the Jeep. He had to push Nigel into the back seat, and then he followed. Man-in-Black got into the driver's seat, started the car, pulled out and across the road, and headed back in the direction they had come from. They had gone less than a mile before they came to an intersection and took a right turn, north. Clark noticed a small roadside sign for a place called

Duzce, 2 kilometers away. They soon entered a small, dark, town - no streetlights or signs of life anywhere. Clark tried to be encouraged that they were in a town and not a field suitable for an execution.

The still night was broken by the squawking of a male voice from the radio on the dashboard of the Jeep. Man-in-Black responded as they reached a broad intersection that seemed like it could be the center of the town, and then pulled up in front of an old three-story building that occupied one corner. The building looked official but dilapidated and had a faded sign painted on the wall over the front door. The light inside the door was the first one Clark had seen in the entire town.

Man-in-Black got out and motioned for them to follow. Clark got out and pulled at Nigel. "Come on, I think this is okay, we should cooperate, not act guilty or anything."

Reluctantly, Nigel got out, and they followed Man-in-Black through the door into the building and then down a flight of concrete steps. The entered a room that had a couple of old metal office desks, some chairs along one wall, and two empty jail cells along another wall. An old man in a threadbare police uniform slept at one of the desks with his head lying on his arms.

Man-in-Black kicked the side of the desk. The loud noise caused Nigel and Clark to jump and startled the old policeman awake. Angry and ready for a fight, he cursed something in Turkish and then listened impatiently as Man-in-Black talked and motioned at Clark and Nigel.

Clark looked at the jail cells and had a bad feeling about them. Sure enough, the old policeman took a set of large keys from a desk drawer and went to open one of the cells. Man-in-Black then motioned for Clark and Nigel to get in.

"Wait a minute. No. It was an accident. We need someone who speaks English. We need a doctor," Clark said, as he pointed to the cut on Nigel's forehead, which didn't look too serious but was still bloody.

Man-in-Black repeated his motion, more emphatically. Nigel made a half-hearted move toward the stairs, but Man-in-Black caught him by the arm and steered him into the cell. Clark followed, having realized that there was no alternative. The loud clang made by the steel cell-door as it slammed shut caused Nigel to collapse like a rag doll on one of the two small beds bolted to the walls of the cell.

Clark looked around and remembered a ghost town in New Mexico that his family had visited years ago. The sheriff's office had had a jail cell just like this one. He remembered not wanting to go into it because of some irrational fear of being shut inside and how his sister had teased him about it. Now here he was in the middle of Turkey, locked in a real cell, with a hysterical friend and a very uncertain future.

Then he became aware of the terrible smell that came from the hole in the floor in the back corner of the cell. An old water pitcher sat next to the hole. He felt his knees get weak, and he sat heavily on the other bed. After a moment, he looked up and saw the old policeman staring at him through the bars. A cruel little smile broke across the old man's face and revealed the two teeth left in his mouth. Clark felt compelled to stare back and did so until the policeman finally shook his head and muttered something that sounded to Clark like, "Morte". Clark realized that that word sounded an awful lot like the Latin word for death or dead. Clark hoped the policeman referred to the man on the road and not their future. The old policeman returned to his desk and then promptly fell asleep.

Clark turned to Nigel to see if he had heard also, but Nigel sat with his back against the wall and stared blankly ahead. Clark had never seen someone in shock, but he imagined that that was Nigel's condition. At least he was calm and quiet, so Clark left him alone.

CHAPTER 21

Clark hadn't intended to fall asleep, but he was just too exhausted. He jerked awake at the sound of the cell door opening and through half-open, bleary, eyes saw that Man-in-Black had returned. He looked weary as he motioned for them to come out of the cell, accompanied by his command in Turkish. Clark hesitated. This isn't right, he thought. Why would the man-in-black take them out of the cell now? At two-thirty in the morning, according to Clark's watch. And Nigel slept, completely unresponsive.

Man-in-Black yelled something and that woke Nigel. He looked wildly around the cell as if seeing it for the first time. "What's going on?" he hysterically demanded of Clark.

"I'm pretty sure that he wants us to go with him. I can't tell whether he's angry or just tired, impatient."

"That's not good. No, I don't want to go. I think we're safer here."

Clark nodded; the same thought had gone through his mind. "I don't think we have a choice. They both seem like they could get rough," Clark added, as he indicated the old policeman who now stood next to Man-in-Black at the door to the cell. But the more he looked, they did seem more tired than mad, so Clark decided to go quietly. He grabbed Nigel by the arm and pulled him along. As they left the room, he distinctly heard the old policeman again say, "Morte."

Man-in-Black led them outside to the Jeep parked in front of the building. Once in, they sped off, headed down what appeared to be the main street of the town. Too dark to see much, Clark got the impression of a modest sized town that wasn't very prosperous. There didn't appear to be any industry that he could see, so he assumed that it was a farming community.

As they neared what appeared to be the outskirts of town, Nigel grew more fearful. "I told you! He's taking us to some field where they'll kill us and bury our bodies."

"Calm down, I don't-" Clark stopped as the Jeep braked and pulled into a gravel driveway that led to a building with a blue cross above the front door. In the circular drive in front of the building sat an old vehicle that looked like an ambulance. "Look it's a hospital," Clark almost yelled with relief.

Man-in-Black ushered them inside and into a dark waiting area that extended almost the entire length of the front of the building. Uncomfortable looking chairs sat along bare white walls. They didn't stop in the deserted waiting room but continued past an empty desk and through a set of double swinging doors that led into a dimly lit hallway. Clark saw light coming from a partially open door, down the hallway to their left, and they headed that way.

They entered a room that was brightly lit and looked like a combination of a hospital examination room and an operating room. A bright light hung over each of three examination tables, and cabinets of medical instruments and other paraphernalia lined two walls. On one table, a white sheet covered what appeared to be a human figure. The man from the windshield lay on another table with a bandage around his head and a cast on his right arm. Next to that table stood a middle aged man, wearing a white doctor's coat, who turned and approached them.

"This you work?" the doctor asked, as he pointed to the table with the sheet-covered body. Without waiting for an answer, he moved to that table and pulled the sheet back to expose the man from the ground. His head injuries were starkly evident in the bright light - the side of his head crushed, a horrible mess of blood, exposed skin and bone. Nigel started to gag and barely made it to a nearby sink before vomiting. Clark's stomach almost followed suit before his brain made a connection.

"You speak English?!"

"Little. I am Doctor Ataman."

"I'm Clark and that's Nigel," Clark responded, as he looked at Nigel who continued to lean over the sink. "What about that man?"

"Live, possibly. May be not. This one kill instant, I think." Dr. Ataman paused and looked at Clark. "You injured?"

"No. Well, Nigel has a cut on his head, maybe you could look at."

They both moved toward Nigel, but Clark stopped because of the smell. The doctor turned on the water in the sink and then looked at Nigel. "Can see head please?"

It took Nigel a moment to realize that he understood the question, and when he did the relief drained what little strength he had left. The doctor caught Nigel before he collapsed and led him to the third examination table. He examined and then cleaned Nigel's cut with an antiseptic that made Nigel flinch.

"Sorry. This not bad, no stitches. Fortunate but…" Dr. Ataman paused and glanced over at the other tables. "Unfortunate you stay. Now will be difficult for you."

"They were hurt, he needed help," Clark said, as he gestured to the injured man. "And my car is in no shape to drive anywhere."

"Bad, bad road. Accidents all time. People die, no stop. Good police came and these not local mens."

"Where are they from?" Clark asked.

"East Turkey, from clothing. Come here work in the fields. Bad, poor in east. May be lucky take long time news reach family."

"Why is that lucky?"

"Many peoples, many in east, follow holy ways. Sharia. Man kill your family, you kill that man or -".

The doctor stopped, interrupted by Nigel, who suddenly jumped off the table and bolted for the door. But Man-in-Black stepped in front of it before Nigel could get out. Nigel struggled and screamed through his tears of fear.

"Stop! Nigel!" Clark urged as he tried to pull him away from Man-in-Black, who managed to maintain his stoic composure. He didn't appear to see Nigel as a real threat. Clark finally got Nigel to sit on a chair. "Calm down! It's going to be okay, I promise." Clark didn't have any rational reason to believe that, but he just wanted to get Nigel under control before he turned his attention back to the doctor. "Can you ask him what they're going to do with us? They put us in a jail cell, but we don't seem to have been arrested. It was an accident. They ran across the road in front of us."

Dr. Ataman talked quietly with Man-in-Black, who appeared the most animated that Clark had seen. Then looks of concern swept across the doctor's face before he finally came back to Clark and Nigel. "Meeting today, not know called English, inquire maybe, local legal, local judge. He decision what happen."

"Can we stay here until then?"

The doctor spoke to Man-in-Black who shook his head as he replied. The doctor then reported, "No, not possible. He places you in jail for protection, not knowing these men."

"Can you ask him if there will be anyone there who can speak English?"

Man-in-Black shrugged his shoulders when the doctor asked the question.

"He know no one."

"What about you? Can you come to interpret for us?"

"That difficulty. Me only doctor, many patient."

"I understand, but if you don't, we're royally screwed."

Dawn had arrived and the early morning light shone on a town that rose early and went to work. The streets hummed with activity and most of the shops were opening. Man-in-Black drove them back to the building with the jail cells, the police station. The old policeman was just leaving the building as they arrived. He gave Clark his two-tooth smile and laughed as he said, "Bir morte."

Two young policemen now sat at the desks in the cell room, and one of them got up and opened the cell door for Clark and Nigel. Even though he had anticipated it, the loud metallic clang of the cell door again caused Clark to flinch. Nigel immediately collapsed on the bed.

Man-in-Black conferred with the two policemen for a few minutes. Clark thought that he must be on the verge of losing his mind because, as he looked at the two policemen, all he could think of was Laurel and Hardy, the comedy team. Like the policemen, one was very fat and the other ridiculously skinny.

Clark knew that he had to get some sleep, but he couldn't ignore the increasingly loud but indistinct muttering from Nigel, who now moved frantically, erratically, between the bed and the cell door. "Nigel, sit down and try to get some rest. We need to save our energy for the inquiry thing today."

"That's bloody bull shit Clark, and you know it. I'm never getting out of here alive. They're going to kill me."

"These cops aren't going to kill you. They would have done it last night if they were going to."

"I don't mean them. The relatives, the bloody relatives will come. You heard the doctor."

"We'll be long gone by then. When they realize it was an accident, they'll let us go. We'll get the car towed back to Istanbul and repaired, or to Ankara, and then continue."

"Oh, no, I'm done, I want to go home. I was insane to think I could do this. Once they find out what I did, who I am, what I am, I'm dead."

"Okay, Istanbul, you go home and I'll stay while the car is repaired." Despite everything, two strong images, desires, lurked in the back of Clark's mind - Deniz and a ferry to Corsica.

"Typical bloody American. Always an easy answer for everything."

The best that Clark could do was give Nigel a wan little smile before he laid down on the bed, closed his eyes, and tried to sleep.

All the town offices and the courtroom that served the town of Duzce and the immediate area were in the same municipal building as the police station and the jail. On the second floor, the courtroom was small and sparse with five rows of wooden spectator benches, like pews from a church. The spectator benches were set behind a wooden railing that separated them from two long wooden tables with wooden chairs - one table for the prosecutor and one for the defense. Everything faced the judge's table that sat on a platform, which raised it about a foot off the floor. The chair for the judge was the only padded, almost comfortable looking thing in the room. A Turkish flag hung limp from a pole that stood in a stand next to the judge's table. A black and while photograph of some stern looking man in a dark suit hung on the wall behind the judge. Two ceiling fans spun in a valiant, but unsuccessful, attempt to stir some air in the hot, stuffy room.

There were five or six men already in the room when Clark and Nigel arrived, escorted by the two young policemen, Laurel and Hardy. No one paid much attention to them as they were motioned to sit at the table on the left side, facing the judge's table. As he looked around, Clark was reminded of courtrooms that he had seen in movies of the old wild west. The only person he recognized was Man-in-Black, who now looked very tired. He didn't see the doctor.

A middle-aged man cautiously approached them. Like all the men, he wore a short-sleeved shirt and no tie. But his clothes looked particularly unkempt, shabby. He started to talk to them in Turkish. He spoke fast and mumbled.

"What the hell is he saying?" Nigel asked, as he poked Clark in the side.

"I don't know. Maybe he's our lawyer," Clark added, as he attempted to keep it light but failed miserably.

"Great. I told you, I'm fucked." Nigel then laid his head down on his arms on the table. Clark saw Nigel's body shake and felt the vibrations spread along the tabletop.

Shabby Lawyer stopped talking, and Clark couldn't tell if he was finished or had finally realized that they couldn't understand him. Clark got the strong impression that the man wasn't that smart. As he then took a seat next to them, Clark noticed that Shabby Lawyer didn't have anything with him - not a briefcase or a pad of paper or even a pen.

The clock on the wall indicated eleven-ten, but Clark's watch read eleven-thirty. He felt his adrenalin battle his exhaustion. He didn't know how much sleep he'd gotten, but it hadn't been much. The policemen had made no attempt to be quiet, and Clark thought that they had in fact been purposefully loud as they answered the phone, talked to each other and went about their business. Or maybe it had just been his raw nerves that augmented every sound. He had kept looking over at Nigel and hadn't been able tell if he was asleep or still in a state of shock. Clark had tried to be positive, but he couldn't avoid thinking that Nigel had every right to be scared. He was Jewish in a Muslim country. He had killed one or maybe two Turkish Muslim men. And he was gay.

At eleven-thirty on the court clock, a very elderly man wearing a black robe entered and sat at the judge's table. He adjusted a small electric fan on the table so it pointed directly at him. Everyone quickly took seats and the process began. The judge looked slowly around the room as he spoke and ended up staring at Clark and Nigel, who still had his head on the desk. The judge said something either to them or to Shabby Lawyer, who then tried to reach around Clark to poke Nigel.

Clark protectively pushed the man's arm away. "Nigel, you need to sit up. I think the judge is unhappy that you're not looking at him."

Nigel slowly lifted his head and tried to focus his vacant eyes on Clark. "What the fuck difference does it make? They'll kill me, or if they put me back in that cell, I'll kill myself."

The judge didn't look pleased as he again said something to Clark and Nigel. Then Shabby Lawyer urgently whispered something to them. They got the general idea and sat quietly.

A man at the other table stood and started to speak to the judge. Clark assumed that this was the prosecutor, as he watched him gesture at them and then at Man-in-Black who sat at the prosecutor's table. He was energetic and seemed somewhat professional in all the ways that Shabby Lawyer did not.

Clark kept looking around the room, hoping to see the doctor, and that seemed to make Shabby Lawyer more nervous. He grabbed Clark's arm to pull his attention back to the front of the room. "Don't touch me," Clark hissed angrily, as he pulled has arm back. "I'm looking for the doctor. Speaks English. Something you don't understand."

The prosecutor had Man-in-Black take a seat on the witness chair, which was on the side of the judge's table. Man-in-Black then gave what Clark assumed was a description of what had happened last night. But because it was very short and perfunctory, he doubted that it could have adequately described what happened. And anyway, he thought, how could Man-in-Black know what really happened? When Man-in-Black finished, the judge asked Shabby Lawyer what sounded like a question, but he just shook his head in response. Man-in-Black then got down and went back to the prosecutor's table.

"What did he say? What did he ask you?" Clark felt his frustration overwhelm him, and he spoke loudly, "We need someone who speaks English! Call Doctor Ataman. This is not fair!"

The judge looked exasperated as he said something that caused everyone to get up and prepare to leave the room.

"Is it over?" Nigel asked Clark.

"I have no idea."

The flashing lights indicated that they were near the accident scene. The pulsing beat had caused some backup of the traffic on the highway, and the black jeep, with Clark and Nigel in the back seat, edged forward. Man-in-Black drove, and they were at the head of a small procession of cars that carried the judge, prosecutor and Shabby Lawyer.

A very old police car, parked behind the accident scene, was the source of the flashing light. A uniformed policeman, sitting in the police car, had his late morning nap rudely interrupted by the blare of the horn of the black jeep as it pulled up behind the police car. The policeman jumped out of the car and nervously stood at attention as the cars parked in a line along the side of the road. The final car was another police car and it stopped in the roadway, its flashing light came on to mimic the first. Another policeman got out and began to direct traffic that now had to go in a single lane around the accident scene. The policeman from the first car then went to the other end and did the same. That started what soon became a massive traffic jam.

The court entourage spilled from their cars and ignored Clark and Nigel. Clark took a moment to look around. A freshly plowed field ran along the side of the road where they were parked. In the distance stood an old farmhouse and what looked like a small barn and two pens, one with a couple of pigs and the other with a large workhorse. Across the street were two buildings. He could see now that one was a garage and gas station with a Mobil gas sign and a very old gas pump. The other building, as he had thought, was a café/restaurant with a couple of rickety tables and chairs out front. Several old men sat there drinking from small cups or glasses. Clark assumed that the two men must have been eating or drinking there before they ran across the street. He wondered if they had been headed for the farm.

Clark now noticed several young boys circling around his car. They poked at it like it was an alien thing that could bite them. Several picked up pieces of glass and metal from the ground. One brave boy tried to reach in and grab something out of the car but was scared off by a stern shout from another policeman, who lingered near the car.

Clark hopped out of the jeep. "Are you coming?" he asked Nigel, who shook his head.

Man-in-Black took the officials to the spot where a marker had been placed to indicate the location of the dead man. And then they walked over to the car. The prosecutor asked a lot of questions, and the judge a few. But Shabby Lawyer hung back and kept quiet. In response to a question from the prosecutor,

Man-in-Black used a large tape measure to measure the distance from the car back to the marker for the dead man.

Clark couldn't hold back any longer and approached the officials. "We were driving along and trucks came from that way, bright lights, and then the two men ran from there, right in front of us. Accident." He tried some rudimentary pantomime to make his points.

They totally ignored him and focused on the prosecutor who now walked along the side of the road and mimicked a car driving off the road as it plowed into the men who were walking on the side of the road. Clark couldn't understand the words, but the pantomime was clear, and he knew it was very wrong.

"No! No, that's not what happened. We were out here on the road and we stopped here." He stood in the road where the car had originally stopped. He tried the same kind of pantomime as the prosecutor had used. But again he was ignored. He tried to grab Man-in-Black to have him measure the real distance, but Man-in-Black wearily shook him off. Clark then paced it off. And the car, where it now sat on the side of the road, was more than twice the distance from where it had originally stopped on the road.

"We moved it off the road to keep it, us safe," Clark said, as he stood in front of the prosecutor to get his attention.

The prosecutor replied by turning to Man-in-Black who came over and took Clark by the arm and escorted him back to the jeep where Nigel sat staring into space. Man-in-Black practically pushed Clark into the back seat.

"What's that all about?" Nigel asked in what was barely a whisper.

"Trouble," Clark replied.

The first thing that Clark noticed when they returned to the courtroom was that Dr. Ataman sat on the bench directly behind the prosecutor's table. Clark tried to go over to him but Laurel, the thin policeman, blocked his way. Clark did call out to him, and the doctor nodded his head in acknowledgement.

Soon everyone was back in their places, and the prosecutor called Dr. Ataman to testify. After the prosecutor had asked several questions, Clark wasn't surprised that Shabby Lawyer declined to ask any.

"Worthless piece of shit," Clark muttered, not caring if Shabby Lawyer could understand or not.

The prosecutor then addressed the judge with what seemed to be a summary statement. The judge then spoke to Shabby Lawyer. Clark assumed he was asking for some sort of rebuttal or objection or something, but he got nothing. After a brief pause, the judge then made a statement that seemed to make the prosecutor happy. The judge now looked at Clark and Nigel and said something to them. Everyone looked at Shabby Lawyer who shrank down in his seat. Obviously irritated, the judge turned back to the prosecutor, and they conferred for a moment before they asked the doctor to join them. Doctor Ataman listened, looked over at Clark and Nigel, and then asked the judge a couple of questions. Clearly uneasy, the doctor approached the defendant's table. Shabby Lawyer jumped up like someone had jammed a pin in his butt, and the doctor sat in his chair.

"What's going on?" Clark asked.

"The legal argue and judge agree, charge negligence death one man and injure other, who may live possible."

"That bull-" Clark caught himself. "That's crazy, we have to go back out there with you so they can understand what happened. They got it all wrong."

"Not possible. Judge decide. Not change."

Clark looked over at Nigel who looked like he was in a coma. His eyes were open, but there was no one home. Clark turned back to the doctor. "So what does that mean?"

"Judge not trial because person dead and you foreign, so big judge come from Bolu."

"When will that be?"

The doctor asked the prosecutor, then turned back to Clark. "He say one week, two start, many time here, two three month, maybe more."

"Months? We can't stay here for months. Where would we stay? I didn't see a hotel anywhere."

"Small hotel town, but driver stay in jail."

Clark didn't have to look to know that Nigel's body went stiff with fear. "That place downstairs? That's impossible."

The doctor exchanged more words with the prosecutor. "No, not here building. Prison of town. Little drive away."

Nigel tried to jump out of his chair, but Laurel, who was seated behind him, grabbed his shoulders and forced him back down. The thin policeman proved surprisingly strong, and Nigel was too weak to struggle.

"Judge know you understand?"

Clark heard the question but couldn't focus on it because he hadn't gotten beyond the implications of Nigel going to prison, a Turkish prison in the middle of nowhere. Ugly visions, stereotypes of prisons from films and literature raced through Clark's mind. A gay Jew in a Muslim prison. It was very clear to him that Nigel probably wouldn't survive long in such a place. When the doctor asked again, Clark nodded without thinking to ask the ultimate consequences of such charges.

"Judge know, who drive?"

Clark looked at Nigel who sat frozen with fear, barely breathing, his face chalky white, with beads of sweat formed on his brow and upper lip. His eyes were glazed over, ready to roll back in his head.

Clark made his decision.

CHAPTER 22

The prison in Duzce had been built by the Turkish Army during World War One for prisoners of war. But the Turks were not inclined to take many prisoners, so it came to be used for deserters and other violators of military laws. Between the world wars and then after the second one, the army continued to run the prison, but in a display of military and civilian cooperation, most of the inmates were people who had been convicted of civilian crimes.

A battered but clean police car pulled up in front of the prison and parked. Hardy, the fat policeman, emerged from the passenger side and opened the back door. Clark swung his legs around and awkwardly tried to get out. It was difficult to maneuver with the handcuffs on his wrists.

Clark had known when they demanded his passport in the courtroom that this was undoubtedly the stupidest thing he had ever done. Then they took the nazar boncugu, the blue eye, from around his neck. Some good luck charm, he had thought bitterly. But it had been the handcuffs that had really brought home to him the enormity of the decision he had made. He had almost shouted out that he'd been wrong, that he had thought they had asked who owned the car, not who was the driver. But it only took another look at Nigel for him to know that this had to be done. Nigel had gone catatonic when they took his passport. And while Clark had been led outside to the waiting police car, the doctor had taken him to the hospital for observation.

It had only been a short ride west down the main street to reach the prison, and Clark had tried to convince himself that he could deal with a cell despite his claustrophobia. And he expected that they had to treat him carefully because he had not been convicted of anything and he was a foreigner. That seemed to have been the situation up until the handcuffs.

As he got out of the car, Clark stared at the imposing stone walls of the prison. They extended almost seventy-five feet in each direction and rose up at least fifteen, maybe twenty feet high. On top of the walls, in each corner, was a wooden cupola and underneath that stood a uniformed military sentry with a rifle. They don't seem to be overly alert, Clark thought, as he stood in front of the large wooden front door, which was reinforced by steel struts that ran diagonally from corner to corner. There was no doorknob or handle on the exterior of the door.

Hardy pounded hard on the door and then again seconds later when no one answered immediately. He seemed annoyed, impatient, and he yelled something at the door. A small window opened in the center of the door and someone peered out. After a brief exchange of words, the window closed, followed by the sounds of locks being unlocked, iron dead-bolts moving. The heavy door swung open, and Hardy guided, practically pushed, Clark inside. There they encountered a heavyset man in an army uniform that had three stripes on the shoulders. The sergeant and Hardy exchanged a few words, then signatures on some paperwork. And then the policeman took the handcuffs off Clark and scurried away like he was afraid he might get stuck in there. The sergeant slammed the door closed, secured it and turned to inspect Clark, who rubbed his wrists and slowly looked around.

He stood on a barren courtyard of packed earth. To the right was a small building and directly ahead was a larger building that ran the entire width of the prison. Both buildings were one-story and made of the same stone as the exterior walls. And immediately on the left stood a flagpole, on which two flags hung limp in the still air. And beneath the flagpole was what looked like a failed attempt to establish a vegetable garden. A third building sat behind that, and several young men in army uniforms lounged on chairs in front of it. They all stared at Clark.

The sergeant didn't attempt to talk but directed Clark toward the large center prison building, where a door stood open, and a number of people, men and women, crowded in the doorway, watching them approach. Clark was surprised to see women there. So far he had not seen any in the courtroom or the city building, and very few on the streets. All of these women wore burkas. Maybe they work here, he thought. He noticed that a few of the men wore army uniforms but most of them wore civilian clothes.

As they reached the door, the sergeant yelled something, and the people moved aside to let them enter. From the bright exterior, Clark plunged into a dark, narrow hallway that was made more narrow by the number of people who stood there. All eyes were on him. No one moved or spoke. Again the sergeant yelled, and like a movie that had frozen on a single frame and then suddenly resumed, everyone sputtered into motion. The press of the bodies and the noise of voices, shouts and jeers cascaded over Clark like a physical thing, pushed him down, threatened to drown him. He was unable to process it - so far beyond his scope of experience, his rational-self struggled to cope with it. Like a drowning man seeing a life preserver, Clark focused on one face that appeared in front of him - a broad face, not unkind, with a flat nose and the overall appearance somewhat like a toad. Toad wore a non-military uniform and spoke a few words with the sergeant. Clark tried to keep his focus on them and ignore the activity around him. Two other men, wearing uniforms like Toad's, joined them, and they all seemed to try to decide something and had different opinions or maybe options. Toad smiled as a decision was evidently made, and the sergeant and the other two men turned and left. The sergeant went back outside, and the other men headed down the hallway that led further into the building.

Toad indicated to Clark that he should follow him, as he then turned and also headed down the hallway. They soon came to an intersection with another hallway that ran both to the left and the right. Blocking the hall to the right was a very stern looking older women who wore a headscarf and also a uniform like Toad's, which Clark now assumed meant a prison guard. She stared belligerently at them, ready to protect her turf. Straight ahead down the hallway, Clark could see the two other prison guards. The hallway to the left was empty, and at the end of it was another wooden door. Along the wall on the right side, five or six arms stuck out, waving around. It was a surreal sight, like the wall had sprouted arms. Clark then realized that Toad had been talking to him as he pointed down the various hallways. Toad now proceeded down the hallway on the left. As he came to the arms in the wall, he batted at them, more playfully than angrily, to make them pull back through a window with bars. He then turned and waited for Clark to catch up before he unhooked a ring of large keys from a clip on his belt and used one to unlock the wooden door.

Clark followed Toad through the door and found himself in a large open courtyard - approximately twenty feet square, with a concrete floor and walls that were the same stone. Along the wall directly opposite the main door there was an open doorway in the corner and in the middle of that wall was a large rectangular window with bars. There were then two solid walls and finally the wall with the window that looked out into the hallway. Overhead there was no roof or cover and the afternoon sun beat down, bright and hot.

But the only thing that grabbed Clark's attention were the men who filled the space. It seemed like a hundred of them - although Clark would later figure out that there were only twenty-two. With a few exceptions, they all stood and stared at him while Toad said something to them in a tone that alternated between friendly and stern. A short, wiry man, mid-thirties, maybe older, got up from a small table in the near corner and came over to them. As the man talked to Toad, Clark noticed that the left sleeve of his shirt was pinned up and there didn't appear to be an arm there. Seemingly satisfied, Toad left the courtyard and the main wooden door slammed shut. Clark involuntarily jumped at the sound, and many of the men laughed as they pressed closer to him.

Clark had been functioning on a survival autopilot ever since the handcuffs had been put on. He had followed the process, noticed the surroundings, and identified some of the people, all without internal comment or reflection. He hadn't made a conscious decision to do so; it was more like an instinctual survival mechanism that had tempered the fight-or-flight reflex that most people would have had in this circumstance. Neither fight nor flight had been a viable option, so he had methodically gone along and struggled to keep his emotions under control. That control was now about to be shattered as the reality of the situation hit him. This was not a solitary prison cell like he had assumed it would be. This was a gang and they weren't a bunch of traffic offenders. They all looked like hardened criminals. And no one spoke a word of English.

Clark felt a tug at his arm and spun around to face One-Arm, who motioned for Clark to follow him to the corner where two other men sat on chairs at a small wooden table.

One Arm sat on the one empty chair and there was no place for Clark to sit. One Arm turned to another man at the table, a large man with an intricate tattoo of what looked like a bald eagle on the bicep of his right arm. One Arm seemed to tell Tattoo to get up to let Clark sit, but Tattoo obviously didn't want to do it.

"No problem, I can stand." Clark didn't want to cause trouble or make Tattoo angry with him.

One Arm ignored him and stared at Tattoo until he reluctantly got up and left. Clark didn't want to sit, but One Arm pulled him down. "Chai?" One Arm asked Clark.

Clark knew from their few days in Istanbul that chai meant tea, and he nodded. He watched One Arm give an order to a frail looking young prisoner, who then went to the window that looked out into the hallway and yelled. Clark then noticed the third man at the table. He seemed to be in his mid to late forties, and he looked very tough, menacing. As Clark looked at him, he glanced up, scowled, and went back to reading his book.

"Ahmed," One Arm said to Clark, as he pointed at himself. He then pointed to the other man at the table and said, "Mohamed."

"My name's Clark, Clark Westfield," Clark responded to the obvious introduction. Ahmed didn't react. "I came from London in my car-"

"London!" Ahmed shouted as he picked up on a familiar word, repeated it, and then introduced Clark to the others as London. As some of the others crowded around the table, one prisoner who had very little hair on his head got too close to Mohamed. Without looking up from his book, Mohamed swung his arm out and knocked No Hair back into the wall. Laughter and excitement whipped through the group. Ahmed mimicked to Clark that Mohamed was a fighter and then used his fingers to make a pretend gun and shot it saying, "Morte."

That confirmed Clark's suspicion that morte meant dead or killed in Turkish.

Frail Boy brought two glass mugs of tea for Clark and Ahmed. Clark dug into his pants pocket to get some money. He placed some Turkish coins on the table. He wasn't very good with the denominations, but Ahmed pushed them away and indicated that Clark did not have to pay. Then Ahmed pulled out a pack of Turkish cigarettes and offered one to Clark.

"No thanks, I don't smoke," Clark said, as he also shook his head to communicate.

Ahmed shrugged his shoulders and lit his cigarette. He then kept up a steady stream of one-way conversation as Clark sipped the tea and struggled to contain the panic, the sense of terror that lay just below his stoic surface. The warm tea helped, and he cautiously looked around the courtyard. Some of the men continued to stare at him, but most of them had resumed other activities, which seemed to be mostly talking in small groups while either squatting or sitting on the concrete floor. A few of them paced back and forth across the courtyard.

Clark had barely finished his tea when Frail Boy came up behind him and used his forefinger to hit the back of Clark's right ear. It didn't hurt, and Clark was more confused than angry. He noticed that Ahmed stared at him, waited. A moment later Frail Boy did it again, and this time Clark used his arm to try to push him away. He wondered what was going on, as he tried to push down a rising panic attack. The courtyard had become very quiet, and all eyes were on Clark and Frail Boy. The third tweak got an angry response from Clark, desperate and on the verge of losing control. Everyone laughed, including Ahmed who subsequently motioned at Frail Boy to move away from Clark. Then they all went back to whatever they had been doing. Mohamed never looked up from his book.

A little later, Toad appeared at the window in the hall and said something, evidently to Clark. Ahmed jumped up and spoke to the guard. The only word that Clark understood was London. Toad opened the door to the courtyard and entered with Clark's duffle bag and sleeping bag, which he unceremoniously dumped on the floor. Several of the prisoners, including Frail Boy, immediately descended on the bags and began to try to open them.

Clark jumped up and went over to get his stuff. "Hey that's mine!" he shouted as he pushed Frail Boy away and turned his attention to another man. Immediately, Frail Boy was back, pawing at the bags. Clark was on the verge of losing it. "Back off!" he yelled.

Ahmed shouted something, and everyone retreated, laughing, having had great fun at Clark's expense. Ahmed motioned for Clark to follow him with his bags, and they went through the open doorway, across from the door to the hallway. They entered a narrow interior hall where pots, pans, and cooking utensils hung on nails that had been pounded into the mortar between the stones of the wall. An older man squatted in front of a large ceramic bowl and washed an old frying pan. Next to him sat two wire contraptions that looked to Clark like tripods with cans of Sterno at the bases and empty pans sitting on top.

Ahmed moved further down to the end of the hall and stood next to an open doorway to the right and a closed door on the left. As Clark caught up to Ahmed, the closed door opened and a man emerged. The smell immediately identified that room as the toilet.

Clark followed Ahmed into the room on the right. It was large, roughly the same size as the courtyard. A single bare light bulb hung in the middle of the room, on a wire that dropped down from the ceiling. But it wasn't on, and the only light came from the barred rectangular window in the wall that opened out to the courtyard.

Wooden shelves lined two walls of the room. Not bookshelves, these were six feet or so deep and contained bedding and other items, lined up, pressed next to each other. His senior year of high school, Clark had seen sleeping platforms like this in a film that showed the interior of the bunkrooms where the prisoners slept in the German concentration camps. The intimate communal nature and the other implications of that made his knees go weak.

Ahmed reached into the middle corner of the lower shelf and shoved aside some blankets and clothes to make a space for Clark's stuff. It was an awkward place to get to, around the wooden support strut at the corner. Clark squeezed in and tried to lay out his sleeping bag and stash the duffle bag at the back. That's when he realized that his camera bag was missing. He hoped that Nigel had it, but he grudgingly accepted the reality that it likely had been stolen. Normally that loss would have had a big impact on him, but it seemed trivial in comparison to his current situation.

Suddenly the face of an ugly old man loomed out of the darkness next to him. Clark instinctively jerked away and pushed out his arm in defense. Ugly Old Man shouted angrily, causing Clark to jerk up and hit his head on the bottom of the top shelf. Dazed, he barely heard Ahmed's angry rebuke to Ugly Old Man, who retreated like an awful apparition back into the darkness.

Clark rubbed his head as he followed Ahmed back into the hallway. Cook gave him a chunk of bread as they passed by. Cook gestured at the empty plates and shrugged his shoulders, seeming to indicate that Clark had missed lunch, which Clark's empty stomach confirmed.

"Teshek," Clark said, as he tried to thank the Cook. He had tried to learn how to say please and thank you from Deniz, anticipating it being useful as they traveled across the country.

Tattoo had retaken his seat at the table, but Ahmed again forced him to give it up for Clark. Clark tried to protest, but Ahmed insisted that he sit. While Clark devoured the bread, Ahmed continued a very earnest conversation with Clark, missing or ignoring the fact that Clark didn't understand anything that he said. But then Clark did pick up on the word otomobil and assumed that Ahmed was talking about the accident. When Ahmed held up two fingers and said, "Icki morte," Clark got concerned that maybe the other man had died, but then he wondered how Ahmed would know. Clark held up one finger and said, "One died, one morte." Ahmed smiled as he shrugged his shoulders in response. "Bir morte," he said, more as a question than a statement. "Bir," Ahmed said and held up one finger. "Icki", he held up two fingers, and then he continued through five. Clark caught on and repeated the numbers several times. Then with a big smile Ahmed directed Clark's attention to the window area where several prisoners stood and talked to people in the hallway. Clark wondered what he was supposed to notice.

Frail Boy hovered around behind the group at the window like a pesky fly. As Clark watched, he moved behind a prisoner who was not very big but had an enormous walrus mustache that dominated his face. Frail Boy suddenly tweaked Walrus' ear as he had done earlier with Clark. At first there was no reaction from Walrus, but as Frail Boy kept at it, Walrus finally turned and faced him. Walrus didn't appear angry but more amused as if this was an ordinary occurrence. Frail Boy and Walrus then moved to the middle of the courtyard, where other prisoners stepped aside to clear an open space. Some prisoners turned to watch the two men, but most didn't pay them any attention.

Frail Boy had an eager expression on his face as he crouched into a wrestler's stance with his knees bend and his arms out wide. He reached out with his hand and poked at

Walrus, who batted Frail Boy's hand away and took a similar stance.

His senior year of high school, Clark had been on the wrestling team during the winter term, and he recognized the initial moves of a wrestling match, as they tried to get into a position for a take-down, get the opponent on the floor. But that didn't explain why these two men were doing it. There didn't appear to have been an argument between them. They looked serious but there was no sense of animosity or anger. It reminded Clark of a practice match between teammates.

Ahmed pointed at Walrus and made a stabbing motion and said, "Morte." Then he indicated Frail Boy and pantomimed cutting someone's throat. "Bir morte," he said with a grin. Clark's despair deepened - he really was in a room full of murderers.

Walrus wasn't much bigger than Frail Boy, but the fight was soon over as Walrus charged and got Frail Boy easily to the ground. Walrus landed hard on top of Frail Boy who hit the concrete floor and winced in pain. Once on the ground, Frail Boy made a valiant effort to keep Walrus from pinning his shoulders and ending the fight. But it didn't take very long for Walrus to win and then jump up. There was very little reaction from the others. The few who had watched quickly went back to whatever they had been doing.

Clark turned back to look at Ahmed, who nodded his head, and as he spoke, he pointed at different men in the courtyard, like he counted them. There seemed to be a specific order that he used, and he finished by pointing at Mohamed who never looked up from his book.

The sound of the Muezzin reached the prison to call the Muslims to the sunset prayer. Clark felt a definite shift in the energy of the courtyard, as most of the prisoners including

Mohamed got their prayer rugs from the bunkroom. Most stayed in the bunkroom while some laid their rugs on the courtyard floor facing south toward Mecca and began to pray. The men who were not praying went about their business, but without the loud voices and physical jostling that had previously been prevalent.

Ahmed didn't pray, but he acted very respectful of those who did. He seemed to have gradually lost his fascination with Clark, or maybe he had grown tired of the one-way conversation. Clark was initially thankful for the respite from the struggle to communicate, but then he had to fight off the sense of terror that just wouldn't leave him. He felt utterly lost and knew it was crazy that he had thought he could do this. What the hell have I done? he screamed silently at himself.

Clark struggled to pull himself back to the moment and respond to Ahmed who motioned at the man standing next to him. Ahmed pointed at the man's arm, and Clark saw that he had a stump at the end of his right arm where his hand should have been. "Huzain," Ahmed said as he pointed at the man and began to pantomime. He walked up behind Huzain, distracted him and then pulled an old billfold from his pocket. He then shook his head, sat and put his arm on the table, while Huzain made a motion to cut off his hand. Clark got the idea. Huzain was a thief and his punishment had been to have his hand cut off. He knew that had once been a form of punishment but would have assumed that it had been a practice left in the Middle Ages. Sardonically, he tried to console himself that at least not everyone in the room was a murderer.

A loud bell rang through the prison complex. Clark pulled his watch from his pocket where he had stashed it to keep from obsessing over the time. It was six o'clock, but to Clark it seemed like forever since he had seen the sunrise outside the hospital or since the sunset outside of Istanbul only twenty-four hours ago. He was in a different universe, an alternate dimension, part of a cruel cosmic joke.

The bell was obviously a signal, because everyone in the courtyard started to move into the interior area. Clark hesitated, not sure what to do, and not eager to go back into the bunkroom. Toad had come back into the courtyard and now watched the men go inside. Finally, it was just him and Clark, and he made it clear that Clark had to go inside. As Clark entered the hallway, the door to the courtyard slammed closed behind him, and the shock waves reverberated through his body and psyche. He tried to focus on details to take his mind off the horrible big picture. Cook had the burners turned on under both wire-cooking stands, and pots full of food sat on top. He gave Clark a grin, and this time Clark noticed his dark, decaying teeth.

The bunkroom was crowded. No one had a chair but most squatted on the floor while others either sat or lay down on the sleeping platforms. Unlike the courtyard, the overall mood was subdued and almost quiet. Clark hesitated to sit on the platform because of the Old Man, but he couldn't squat on his haunches like the others, so he sat on the floor with his back against the wall. He noticed that very few men read, and none did it nonstop like Mohamed who had a great spot on the end of the top bunk. Many of them quietly worked their fingers on the same worry beads that Cynna had, but these beads weren't silver. Clark could hear the distinct click, click, click of the beads. Soothing, and he thought he might need to get some worry beads of his own.

A little later, Cook entered the bunkroom and placed three large platters of food on the floor along with three large loafs of bread. He spaced the platters apart so three groups of men could sit, each group around a bowl. Clark watched but didn't join. It seemed like everyone had a place, except for Ugly Old

Man who sat by himself and forced his way in to get some food from the bowl where Frail Boy sat. After a few minutes, Ahmed called, "London, London," and motioned for Clark to sit next to him. He sat and watched as the men tore off chunks of the bread and grabbed food off the platter using the bread and their fingers. Clark didn't remember anyone washing up and was momentarily put off by the lack of hygiene. But his hunger quickly bested his fear of germs, and he followed their example.

Half the platter contained eggs, scrambled hard and dry, and the other half had chunks of roasted meat, which Clark thought tasted like lamb, but he couldn't be sure. He barely got a few pieces before it all disappeared. Ahmed, with a big smile on his face, pointed to him and then at the meat. He said something to the others in the room, and they all nodded happily, while Clark only understood London as a part of the statement. It occurred to him that maybe they thought he had something to do with the fact that there was meat for dinner. If that were the case, he knew that that was a lot better than having the opposite effect.

After dinner, Clark again sat on the floor and observed. Frail Boy played some sort of card game with a young man with long hair cut in a mod rock-star style. Clark named him Ringo. Huzain played a game of checkers on an old checkerboard and seemed to be a very bad sport. He saw a couple of others look at what appeared to be Turkish magazines, and several talked intently but occasionally punctuated with laughter. On one level the antics, banter and activities were not so different from a mid-week evening in the living room of his fraternity at Dartmouth - except for the lack of a television, and of course you could leave whenever you wanted. But only a portion his mind observed, because the majority of it had shut down to protect itself from having to deal with the implications of his situation. He had always known intellectually that life could change course in an instant, but this shift in realities was far beyond his capacity to accept or even comprehend. Just over twenty-four hours ago, he had been in Istanbul.

Another bell rang through the complex, and all the men scrambled to their spots on the sleeping platform. Ahmed was at the end of the top shelf near the window, at the opposite end from Mohamed. Clark slowly followed and had just started to maneuver into his corner when the light went out. He looked around to see who had shut the light off, but there was no one there, and there wasn't a light switch on the wall.

It was pitch black under the shelf, and Clark hesitated, hoping that his eyes would grow accustomed to the dark. An extremely pale glow of light came in through the window that looked out on the courtyard, which itself was dark. The only source of light was across the courtyard and in the hallway of the prison - not enough for him to see much under the shelf. Resigned, Clark pushed forward carefully, felt his way along his sleeping bag. He could sense other bodies close to him on either side. One of those he knew was Ugly Old Man, and he desperately didn't want to touch him. The night temperature had cooled off, but it remained hot and very stuffy under the shelf. He positioned himself on top of his sleeping bag and used his duffle bag for a rough pillow. From having cursed the darkness, he now welcomed it and pulled within himself, trying to fall asleep. His exhaustion soon won out.

Clark dreamed of Gwen, which he hadn't done in many days. They were in her bedroom. He was very aware that he didn't want this dream for many reasons, but he couldn't pull out of it. She slept next to him in her bed. He could feel her naked body, and he felt compelled to reach over to rub it. That woke her, and she turned toward him and smiled - an ugly toothless smile. Ugly Old Man's face glared at him out of the darkness. Startled. Frightened. Repulsed. Clark sat up quickly and again hit his head, much harder this time, on the bottom of the upper shelf. He screamed, "Get the fuck away from me," as he struggled to get off the self. Suddenly a light burst into his eyes, overwhelming his dilated pupils. He again hit his head, this time on the support post, before he managed to stumble out into the open space.

Ahmed stood there and held his flashlight, now aimed at the floor. Ahmed smiled, and Clark could hear laughter coming from all over the shelving. Ahmed shone his light into the bunk and yelled something at Ugly Old Man, who cowered in the corner, his face full of hate. Frail Boy emerged from the other side of the Ugly Old Man and said something to Ahmed, who nodded in agreement. Frail Boy reached in and pulled out Clark's sleeping bag and duffle. He then put them back on the shelf next to him and away from Ugly Old Man. Clark thanked him and slowly settled down in his new spot. Although reluctant to sleep in case the dream came back, his exhaustion again overcame him.

CHAPTER 23

The sound of the prison bell was followed by the Muezzin call to pre-dawn prayer. Toad entered the courtyard and opened the inner door to allow the prayers to access the courtyard. A little later power returned to the light in the bunkroom, and the rest of the prisoners woke and slowly emerged from the shelves. Everyone ate breakfast after Cook placed three large old, chipped, porcelain bowls full of plain yogurt on the floor in the same places as the dinner. Breakfast was bread dipped in the yogurt. Through all of this, Clark continued to sleep, and the others didn't disturb him. Frail Boy wanted to wake him, but Ahmed told him no.

Clark woke almost two hours later, and for a brief moment, before he opened his eyes, he imagined that he was back in England, waking from a nightmare, an incredibly realistic one. He so desperately wanted that to be true, but the noises from the courtyard forced him into the reality of the present. As Clark struggled from the shelf, he knew that Ugly Old Man lurked there in the corner, glaring at him, but he managed to not look in that direction.

Clark crossed the empty bunkroom and headed to the bathroom, dreading the smell that arose from the hole in the floor. He emerged as quickly as he could and headed for the courtyard. Cook handed him a small bowl of yogurt and a chunk of bread as Clark passed him.

In the courtyard, Clark headed for the table in the corner where Ahmed sat with Mohamed and Tattoo. He anticipated that Ahmed would make Tattoo move again, but even though Ahmed acknowledged Clark with a smile, he didn't say anything to Tattoo. Clark didn't have the pantomime skills to question why, so he went and sat on the floor. He had never liked yogurt very much, and this was warm, which made it worse. He almost gagged, but he forced himself to eat as much as he could with chunks of bread. He knew he had to make do with what he got - there was no refrigerator or cupboard or … or any other normal, civilized convenience. He forced down any thoughts of, any contemplation of, what the day might bring, how he would manage to get through it. That would only lead to despair and maybe even madness. He would try to stay on survival autopilot.

It was late morning when Frail Boy sat down next to Clark and tried to direct his attention to a group of prisoners who squatted in a small circle and drank tea. Clark watched as No Hair came up behind Ringo and tweaked his ear. No Hair only had to do it once to get Ringo up on his feet and into a wrestler's stance. This fight drew scant attention from the other prisoners, and only a few formed a circle around the middle of the courtyard. Frail Boy jabbered away excitedly and pulled Clark up and into the circle. An older prisoner with a pinched face and wire rimmed glasses seemed to be taking bets on the fight. Clark watched as two or three prisoners made a bet with Bookmaker, but most didn't.

The fight that ensued was longer than the Frail Boy/Walrus fight the day before because it seemed more evenly matched. Eventually No Hair won, and it must have been an upset because Bookmaker didn't look pleased as he paid out money to several prisoners. The atmosphere immediately reverted to what Clark had begun to think of as prison-normal. Some of the men spent some time pacing the courtyard - six or seven paces, depending on the man, from one side to the other. Two prisoners could pace at a time in the small space. Clark noticed an open spot, and he started to walk, along with a prisoner who looked like a well-fed farm boy. Farm Boy had a quicker pace, but Clark had a longer one, and they soon fell into a workable rhythm without any specific communication. Clark continued to pace after Farm Boy quit and the thief Huzain took his spot. Huzain seemed to want to turn it into a race, but Clark refused to take the challenge. He was sure he was probably faster, but he didn't want to antagonize anyone, and there wasn't anywhere to run anyway. Huzain frantically made his turns as quickly as he could, and with a weird little smile of triumph, he soon lapped Clark.

Lunch was a mixture of rice with small bits of the same meat from dinner and a lot of cut-up carrots and some peas. And of course bread. Clark had seen two women and Toad come down the hallway to the door and give bowls of food to Cook, and he realized that Cook didn't really cook the food but kept it warm and then served it. He surmised that there must be a central kitchen somewhere in the complex. For this meal, Ahmed didn't invite him to join his group, but Frail Boy eagerly motioned to a spot next to him. Clark heard Ahmed again say something that sounded positive with London in it, and everyone nodded as they ate. Frail Boy pointed at Clark and then at the meat. "Yemek", he said. Clark pointed at the meat and repeated, "Yemek." Frail Boy smiled.

Clark heard Nigel before he saw him. There was a general hubbub in the hallway, and then Toad appeared at the window with Nigel in tow. Nigel looked around frantically and called for Clark who felt eager, yet also reluctant, to engage.

"Oh my God, this is an insane asylum not a prison," Nigel squealed as he saw Clark approach the window. Nigel liked his space, and he now had none, as people in the hallway crowded up next to him. Clark could see him struggle to keep control of himself. "I'm so sorry that I didn't get here sooner, they kept me at the hospital for ever and then you wouldn't believe the bloody awful little hotel room I have. They said it was all they had but what kind of business could they have in this godforsaken place, and ordering in the restaurant - truly a nightmare…" Nigel sputtered to a stop as he realized where he was and focused on the bars that separated him from Clark, who stood stiffly silent.

Before Clark could find words to respond to Nigel's callous rant, he felt someone tweak his ear. He had been expecting it all afternoon, and he knew without turning that it was Frail Boy. Clark had begun to realize that much of what went on in the prison - food groups, sleeping spots, and probably more - was based on an order, like a hierarchy, that seemed to have a lot to do with the wrestling. And Clark and Frail Boy seemed to be at the bottom of the order, except for Ugly Old Man who never came out from the shelf except to grab some food. So Clark knew that he had no choice but to fight. His first day had been special, and Ahmed, who seemed to be the leader, had protected him in a way, but today he was like everyone else.

Clark ignored Nigel's questions as he turned and walked into the middle of the courtyard to face Frail Boy. He noticed that everyone stopped what they were doing and most of them now formed a circle around them. Bookmaker seemed to be doing a brisk business, and Clark wondered who they were betting on. He was a good four or five inches taller and had much more muscle than Frail Boy.

Clark crouched into a wrestler's stance and heard a murmur of acceptance and anticipation run through the crowd. He slapped Frail Boy's hands away when they came at him and that energized Frail Boy to charge at him. Clark was ready with a step-aside and throw-down move that send Frail Boy crashing to the concrete floor. He tried to protect his face but was too late to stop his nose from slamming into the floor and breaking. Frail Boy thrashed out wildly as Clark tried to carefully pin him and end the fight. He knew he was getting Frail Boy's blood on him, but he couldn't back away, he had to finish it. He finally got Frail Boy's shoulders pinned against the concrete for what he thought was surely three seconds and then waited for five to be sure before letting him up.

Clark expected Frail Boy to be upset, but instead a big smile flashed across his bloody face as he jumped up and went to the window and yelled down the hall. He thrust his bloody hand out through the bars to touch Nigel who jumped away in disgust, causing the spectators in the hall to laugh. Soon, a man in an army uniform came with Toad, who opened the door, and they led Frail Boy out and down the hall.

Clark happened to glance over at Ahmed who smiled, held up two fingers, and said, "Ichi morte."

"Hey stop that!"

Clark heard Nigel yell and looked to see him swat at the hand of a man in the hallway who must have tweaked his ear. Clark didn't know if there was a similar hierarchical situation in other parts of the prison or if they were just teasing his nervous friend. "If you ignore him, he'll probably stop," Clark advised Nigel. He saw Nigel try to control himself. "Say, do you have my camera bag?"

"Yes," Nigel yelped as he jumped away from another tweak.

"Did you find a telephone to call anyone, the embassy?"

"No, the telephone in the hospital was out, which is evidently common, and there was no one at the hotel who spoke English." Nigel spoke quickly in between swatting at the man who continued to tweak his ear. "But there's evidently an American Peace Corps woman who lives around here, and I'm hopefully meeting her tonight. Maybe she can help us, talk to that judge." It had all gotten too much for him, and he swung around to leave. "I'll come back tomorrow," Nigel yelled over his shoulder, as he fled down the hall.

Clark saw Toad shake his head, seemingly amused, as he cleared the hallway of the glom of people who had come to see the spectacle. As Clark turned back to the courtyard, he thought he heard a siren approach and then stop nearby. Frail Boy on his way to the hospital.

The end-of-the-day routine repeated from the first night, with the evening prayer, the lock-down and then dinner, except now Clark ate with the third group in Frail Boy's place. A while after dinner Clark felt a stir of excitement go through the room. Ahmed called out something, and almost everyone formed a big circle in the middle of the room. Ahmed came over to Clark and talked and gestured while the fat man they called Askim moved into the middle of the circle. As he joined the circle, Clark felt some apprehension because the mood in the room seemed tense, but he couldn't decide if it was a bad tension or not. Ahmed had a dark blue bandana, which he handed to Tattoo, who wrapped it around Askim's eyes. Then Tattoo spun the fat man around until Clark was sure that he had to be dizzy. Askim swayed in the middle of the circle and then put his right arm under his other armpit so the palm of his right hand was exposed, facing away from his body. Ahmed pointed to the prisoner with thick glasses, 4-Eyes, who then snuck out from the circle and slapped Askim's palm as hard as he could.

The sound of the slap reverberated through the room and everyone laughed or cheered. 4-Eyes then spun Askim around once more and jumped back in the circle. Askim tore the bandana off and looked around. Everyone laughed and pointed at each other as Askim tried to identify who slapped him. He pointed at Farm Boy and everyone laughed louder. Askim rubbed his palm as Tattoo put the blindfold back on and the process repeated. This time Gimpy, the prisoner with a serious limp, hit Askim, who again guessed wrong. Everyone enjoyed themselves except for Askim whose palm was very red after losing a third round. For the fifth round, Ahmed pointed at Clark, clearly meaning for him to slap Askim's palm. Clark knew he had to do it but couldn't decide how hard to slap. It had seemed to him like they had all tried to outdo each other, and the slaps had gotten harder and harder. He couldn't get himself to do that and slapped Askim's palm hard, but not nearly as hard as even 4-Eyes had done. Whether it was the look on his face or the nature of the slap, but Askim immediately zeroed in on Clark as the slapper. Ahmed now indicated that Clark had to take Askim's place in the center. The room quieted with anticipation as Clark stepped into the middle, but just then the lights-out bell rang. With considerable grumbling, they all headed for the shelves. Clark knew he wouldn't get out of it that easily and that it would happen, maybe the next night, and he had to be prepared.

Just as everyone got settled, the door to the courtyard opened, followed by the door to the bunkhouse. Frail Boy came in with Toad. His nose was bandaged and one eye was turning black and blue. He looked weak but flashed a big smile as he clambered over to the shelf and crawled in next to Clark.

"Sorry about that man," Clark said, as he tried to ascertain Frail Boy's feelings toward him. It surprised him to realize that Frail Boy didn't seem angry but actually appeared to be happy. For the man at the bottom, it had evidently been far more excitement and positive attention than he had gotten in a long time.

The light went out, and Clark tried to relax and fall asleep, but he had a hard time ignoring the loud, open-mouth breathing of Frail Boy.

The morning routine repeated with the exception that Clark woke with the others and found that he could force down more of the yogurt when it wasn't warm. The morning fight occurred between No Hair and a short, very wiry built man who they called Zia. No Hair seemed energetic from his win the day before, but Zia proved to be too quick. Soon No Hair was out of breath and open for a quick charge by Zia that led to a pin and a win. This fight seemed to garner only modest interest from most of the other prisoners and not much action for Bookmaker. It appeared that they had all anticipated the result, that they had seen it before.

As Clark paced, he remembered a ranking that his high school wrestling coach had made. He had called it a challenge ladder, which determined who wrestled in the weekly matches with other schools. Each boy on the team could challenge the person ahead of him once a week, and if he won, he moved up the ladder and could then challenge the next higher person. The person he beat had to wait a week to challenge to regain his spot. Some of those challenges had been exciting and others were almost ignored because everyone knew what the result would be. Seldom were there any surprises. So far Clark thought he could identify the ones at the lower end of the ladder: Zia, No Hair, Ringo, Walrus and Frail Boy. Then he realized that he could insert himself ahead of Frail Boy. And they were all in the same eating group. Based on the fact that they had the only chairs at the only table in the courtyard, he figured that Ahmed, Mohamed and Tattoo must be at the top of the ladder. But how, he wondered, could Ahmed wrestle with one arm? Or Huzain with one hand?

Lunch was identical to the day before, and afterward Clark got a book from his duffle bag and tried to read. He had seen the film *Zorba the Greek* when it had come out a few years before, but he had never read the book and had picked up a copy when he had been trying to decipher Cynna. The only other person besides Mohamed who he had seen read a book was a quiet man with a fairly intelligent face. Clark thought they called him Aiden, and he seemed to read popular books while Mohamed always read what Clark had now decided was probably the *Koran*.

Clark hadn't been reading for very long when Frail Boy tried to pull him up and refused to accept Clark's pantomime that he wanted to sit and read. Finally, Clark got up and let Frail Boy pull him over to where a group sat in a small circle and played a card game. Frail Boy positioned him behind Walrus and tried to push Clark's hand toward Walrus' head. Clark knew what Frail Boy wanted him to do, but he hesitated. Did he really want to climb this ladder? Did he have any choice if he was going to survive in there?

Clark reluctantly put out his hand and tweaked Walrus' ear. He barely hit it and had to do it again, harder, to get a reaction from Walrus, who didn't seem thrilled as he looked up at Clark who was taller and probably thirty pounds heavier.

Clark was determined to not hurt Walrus as he had Frail Boy. He circled and parried with him as the crowd grew more animated and Bookmaker did a brisk business. It struck Clark that this was about more than just a pecking order of the prisoners. It also constituted their entertainment, as did the slapping game at night. He lost his concentration for a moment, and Walrus took advantage of it to knock Clark to the floor. He jumped cross his chest and almost pinned him. As Clark looked around at the crowd, he saw some expressions of amazement but many more looks of disappointment - disappointment that there wasn't going to be a good fight, that the new guy was a loser. Without making a conscious decision, Clark knew that he had to win and keep winning. Not an intellectual decision, it was pure animal instinct that had first emerged when the handcuffs went on his wrists, and it had blossomed and taken hold over the past 48 hours. He pulled his feet up to his butt and used his legs and neck to help thrust his back upward. At the same time, he twisted his shoulders and threw Walrus off his chest. As Walrus rolled on the floor, Clark grabbed him and forced him on his back. Clark then quickly pinned him. The other prisoners didn't cheer, but most nodded their heads at the outcome and then went back to whatever they had been doing.

Clark had to admit that he did feel a rush of excitement even though Walrus had really been no match for him. He looked over at No Hair. Or was it Ringo who should be next? He didn't hear Nigel the first time he yelled.

As Clark approached the window to the hallway, he saw Nigel and next to him was a young woman. She wore a headscarf, but Clark assumed she was English or American because of her fair skin, light blue/gray eyes, and a bit of blond hair that peeked out from under her head scarf.

"Oh Clark are you okay?" Nigel practically squeaked.

"Sure, why wouldn't I be?" Clark responded, as sarcastically as he could. He noted that the woman looked none too happy to be there. Then he saw that Toad and another guard stood as a barrier to keep the hallway empty except for Nigel and the woman. It had to be because of her, he thought.

"Well, you're bleeding," Nigel said, as he finally found his voice and pointed to Clark's forehead.

Clark reached up and touched his forehead with his fingers, which came away bloody. He hadn't felt his head scrape on the floor, but it must have done so when he had bucked

Walrus off him. Just then Frail Boy appeared at his side with a small wet cloth, which he handed to Clark and then motioned between his bandaged nose and Clark's head.

"Oh, just a little fun between friends." Clark laughed as he compared the big smile on Frail Boy's face and the look of horror on Nigel's.

Nigel sucked in a breath. "This is Joyce Edwards, she's in your Peace Corps and teaches English at the local school. She said she would help us communicate."

Joyce took in the sight that was Clark - bloody forehead plus four days unshaven and no shower. "Seems like he's communicating quite well on his own," she said, without changing her blank expression, and then she turned and walked away. Toad and the other guard moved aside to let her pass and then followed her, which allowed people to flood the hallway and crowd around Nigel.

"Well, she seems nice," Clark mocked, while Nigel stood frozen, unsure what to do. He felt that he should stay with Clark, but his lifeboat had sailed away.

"I'm going to Ankara in the morning on the bus, to go to the embassies, yours and mine. The telephones are bloody useless, never work. I'll be back with help as soon as I can. Joyce said I should be safe on the bus."

"That's comforting."

Nigel didn't register the sarcasm because his ears were getting tweaked again. "I'll be back, stay out of trouble." His feeble attempt at humor fell flat as he scooted away and left Clark at the window, shaking his head.

Clark was prepared for the hand-slapping game that night after dinner, but Ahmed didn't initiate it. Instead Ahmed sat in a corner of the room with Aiden who read what looked like a letter. It suddenly struck Clark that maybe Ahmed and some of the others didn't read because they couldn't. He knew that illiteracy was a major problem in this part of the world.

He felt someone poke his arm and turned to see Frail Boy who held out his hand to offer something to him - a simple set of worry beads. Frail Boy indicated that they were for Clark. He hesitated to take them, but Frail Boy looked so expectant and happy, that he did. "Thanks, chok," he said, with a smile. He tried to work the beads with his fingers as he saw other do, but it was surprisingly difficult. Frail Boy didn't laugh but he seemed to have fun watching Clark struggle with the beads.

Clark's third night in the cell was the best yet - a full night's sleep without any dreams that made him focus on the world outside. And he had moved over into Walrus' spot on the shelf, one more spot away from Ugly Old Man.

The morning fight was a big deal between Tattoo and Farm Boy for a position at the table. The betting seemed to be heavy on Tattoo who looked bored next to the eager, almost frantic, Farm Boy. Farm Boy had a clear advantage in size, but he had been in the prison for several years and had lost a lot of muscle. Other than the fighting and pacing, Clark had not seen anyone do any kind of exercising. He was already beginning to feel the effects on his body.

Tattoo effectively thwarted Farm Boy's attempts to get close to him. He looked like a cat toying with a big aggressive mouse. The casualness of Tattoo's efforts made Farm Boy more frantic and aggressive, and that led to a mistake as Farm Boy overextended his reach, and Tattoo used Farm Boy's own momentum to pull him to the ground. It would have been over except Farm Boy recovered in time to scramble away before Tattoo could establish a position on top of him. The spectators cheered for what now promised to be a longer, more violent match.

Ahmed came up and stood next to Clark in the circle. As they watched the wrestlers, Ahmed described and pantomimed that Tattoo had stabbed a man, "Morte." Clark got that part, but there was another piece of information that Ahmed tried to convey that didn't translate easily into pantomime. The only thing Clark understood was that it had something to do with the man that Tattoo had stabbed to death. Ahmed then pointed at Farm Boy, obviously getting winded and tired, and who, according to Ahmed, had strangled someone, "Morte." Zia stood on the other side of Clark, and Ahmed indicated that he had shot someone, "Morte." There was the same additional information about each of them that Clark couldn't figure out. Just as Ahmed seemed to get frustrated, their attention was pulled back to the fight. Tattoo had gotten inside of Farm Boy's arms and grabbed his body, which he then slammed to the floor. Farm Boy's head didn't hit the concrete, but his body did and that knocked all the air from his lungs. Tattoo then easily pinned him. The show over, everyone collected or paid their bets with Bookmaker and quietly went back to their business.

Clark noticed that Ugly Old Man stood at the window and looked out from the bunkroom to the courtyard. It was the first time Clark had seen him during the day, away from the shelf. Ahmed followed Clark's stare and saw Ugly Old Man just before he pulled back from the window. Ahmed made a motion with his hands that seemed to indicate a female figure and then thrust his hips in a sexual motion before finishing with his hands around his neck, "Morte." The look of repulsion on Ahmed's face clearly communicated that a rape and murder was a crime evidently considered the worst of the worst. The only other time that Clark had gotten the impression that a prisoner's crime was disturbing had been the day before when Ahmed had described a murder, supposedly with his fists beating someone, committed by the man with deep-set, dark eyes who looked like a wolf, a predator. Everyone evidently gave Wolf Eyes a wide berth out of fear, while they kept away from Ugly Old Man out of pure disgust.

Later as he ate lunch, Clark knew he needed to fight Ringo next. He struggled to put away his feeling that he liked the man with the long Beatle-style haircut who kept breaking into song and actually had a decent singing voice. Personal feelings had to be discarded in the world of survival. But he would again be careful and try not to hurt him. He had just decided to get it over with, when he heard his name being called. "London," again called Toad, who motioned him over to the hallway window. As Clark approached the window, Toad pointed toward the door and then moved that way. The door opened, and Toad stood aside and indicated that Clark should come out.

Clark struggled to keep calm. He desperately wanted to believe that this was the end of it, that he was about to get out of there. And as much as he warned himself to not get his hopes up, he did. Surely someone had come to their senses and realized that he didn't belong there.

Clark followed Toad to the entrance to the prison building where the sergeant waited. He nodded at Clark and guided him across the courtyard to the front gate where four soldiers stood, each one holding a rifle. Clark's knees went weak as an image of a firing squad dashed across his mind. No, he told himself, that's just not possible. But neither was the fact that he was in prison for something he hadn't done. As they reached the gate, the soldiers took up positions on four points surrounding Clark, their rifles now on their shoulders. The sergeant pulled a pair of handcuffs from his pocket and put them on Clark. After he fastened them, he said something to Clark that seemed to ask if they were too tight, and Clark responded by shaking his head. The sergeant seemed pleased and then opened the gate. They all stepped outside, and with the sergeant in the lead, they proceeded to march east into town. They marched in the road and traffic had to slow to pass them. A few drivers blew their horns in frustration or maybe just messing with them. Clark jumped each time a horn blew, and he could see that the soldiers were getting upset. What kind of idiot, he wondered, purposefully irritated a soldier with a rifle?

As they march through town, Clark noticed that people on the side of the road stopped and stared at them. He detected more of a sense of curiosity than of hostility, which helped keep his anxiety in check. They passed a plain looking building whose minarets identified it as the mosque. Several old men sat out front and smoked. As they reached the center of town, their destination became clear - the building with the police station and the courtroom. Laurel and Hardy, the same two policemen from the first day, waited at the front steps. And after the sergeant took the handcuffs off Clark, they led him inside.

The courtroom was more crowded than the first time Clark had been there. A different judge dealt with people at the two tables. The policemen indicated for Clark to sit on a chair along the wall near the defendant's table. Clark saw the Peace Corps woman who sat right behind the railing, but he couldn't remember her name. As he stared at her, she looked his way and unsuccessfully tried to force a smile. With a heavy sigh, she rose and moved next to Clark. Laurel started to object, but she said something to him that made him nod his head.

"Hi," Clark said, not sure about her but nervous and happy to have someone to talk to.

Joyce looked him over and clearly didn't like what she saw. Unshaven, dirty, hair uncombed, and the bandage on his forehead that reminded her of his behavior in the prison. Nigel had told her about one fight, and then she had seen the aftermath of another. The only thing that didn't bother her was his smell because all the men smelled. Neither baths nor deodorant were a part of their daily routine. The women didn't bathe that often either, but at least they sprayed themselves with some perfume to cover it up.

Clark could see her examine him and was pretty sure that her reaction wasn't that great. He needed her help so he tried to be polite. "I'm so sorry, but in the craziness of that place, I didn't get your name."

"Joyce, Joyce Edwards."

"Clark Westfield," he replied, as he stuck out his hand.

She looked at his hand but didn't take it. "As an American woman it would be okay to shake your hand, but around her I'm a foreign female on tenuous ground and to most people it would be improper for me to touch a strange man."

"I'm not so strange," he tried to keep it light. "So that's the reason for the headscarf?"

She nodded, gratified that maybe he wasn't totally an insensitive jerk.

"So do you know what's going on here?"

"All I know is that evidently this district judge," she nodded her head slightly toward the bench, "is here before his regularly scheduled date, just to hear your case."

"Well, that's good. We can get this all cleared up."

"Yes, but evidently there are others who have latched on, and I guess we have to wait."

Laurel stepped up to them and said something to Joyce.

"What did Laurel say?"

"Laurel?"

"Oh, yeah, those two remind me of Laurel and Hardy, you know the comedy team, one was fat, the other skinny, and-"

"I know Laurel and Hardy," she cut him off, and then reassessed her judgment about his sensitivity. "He says I have to sit over there and for you to be quiet until your case is called."

As Joyce retreated to her seat, Clark tried not to look over at her. Her expression reminded him of Gwen when she was stressed. Damn, he swore at himself. For several days now he had successfully kept her out of his head. He worked his worry beads and scanned the room to occupy his mind.

Shabby Lawyer was there, still shabby and without a briefcase or any other work prop. The same prosecutor was presenting something to the district judge who was a lot younger than the other judge and looked much more formidable, probably smarter. There were two men at the defense table. One clearly a lawyer and the other looked like a farmer who had tried to clean himself up for his day in court. This lawyer looked halfway professional, at least he had a briefcase and some files and a pad of paper. Clark was disappointed that this wasn't his lawyer, and he was even more disappointed that he didn't see Doctor Ataman in the courtroom. But I've got Joyce, he tried to console himself.

Clark couldn't tell what the legal issue was with the farmer, but it seemed to annoy the district judge who impatiently kept looking at his watch. Clark sat, happy to have it drag on. He even allowed himself to relax a little and almost enjoy the relative sanity and quiet of the courtroom. No one was going to tweak his ear. And he kept stealing glances at Joyce. The headscarf effectively neutralized much of the personality of a woman. But her facial features were very pleasing, and he tried to guess her hair color from just her eyebrows. In the prison it had seemed to be blonde, but in this light it appeared a light brown.

The loud bang of the judge's gavel snapped his attention back to the front of the room, where the farmer and his lawyer had stood and were now leaving. An older man, in a uniform that looked like a bellboy in a hotel, shouted something, and Shabby Lawyer reluctantly rose and headed for the defendant's table. Laurel stood and motioned for Clark to get up and move to the front. Joyce came with him and sat next to him at the table. He was in the middle between her and Shabby Lawyer.

"Alo," Clark said to Shabby Lawyer, who gave him a curious and not friendly look in response.

"Where did you learn that?" Joyce asked with an edge in her voice.

"At my country club," Clark tried another bad joke.

"The proper greeting is merhaba. That other one is vulgar slang used by the lower classes."

"And criminals," Clark added, wondering what he had done to make her dislike him so much.

The prosecutor began to address the district judge, and he spoke for several minutes before he put a hand-drawn chart on a metal stand so the district judge could see it. Clark could see that it represented the accident scene with crude drawings for the car and the dead man on the side of the road. The problem was immediately clear to Clark. The positioning of the car and the scale were based on the incorrect assumptions that the prosecutor had made at the scene on the first day. As the prosecutor spoke and motioned at the chart, Clark knew that what he told the district judge was all wrong.

"You've got to object," he demanded of Shabby Lawyer. Then to Joyce, "Tell him that he has to object, they've still got it all wrong. That's not how it happened!" Clark's voice had risen from a whisper to almost a shout, and the prosecutor, clearly annoyed, paused and turned toward them. The district judge then said something to Shabby Lawyer, who mumbled a response.

"The judge says that we will have our turn and to be quiet," Joyce interpreted for Clark.

Clark had no illusion that Shabby Lawyer would offer any defense and felt a renewed sense of dread overtake him - this wasn't going to end well. He expected to see Man-in-Black appear and then the doctor, but it was evidently only going to be the prosecutor. When he finished, the district judge turned his attention to the defense table. He asked a question of

Shabby Lawyer who just shook head and answered, "Yok," which Clark knew meant no.

"Come on you ass-," Clark caught himself before swearing at Shabby Lawyer and turned to Joyce, "Tell the judge that we object."

Joyce started to speak, but the district judge cut her off.

"He says that I am not allowed, I am an interpreter and not a lawyer."

"Well, neither is this jerk. But I can speak for myself. Just translate what I say." Clark stood and looked at the district judge. "Your honor, the prosecutor has it wrong. It was an accident. We were driving on the road and these two men ran across in front of us."

Joyce started to interpret, and again the district judge cut her off with a wave of his hand, then punctuated by a bang from his gavel. She was flustered and tried to respond, but the district judge held up his hand for her to stop. He then asked her a question.

Joyce looked at Clark. "He says he just wants to know what is your decision?"

"Decision? About what?"

"I believe he is asking… I'm so sorry but this vocabulary is unfamiliar to me. I think he asks whether you are guilty or not guilty."

Clark looked at the district judge who stared expectantly at him. "Not guilty, of course. It was an accident."

Joyce translated, and Clark saw the district judge react with a curious expression that seemed to combine surprise and annoyance. The district judge asked Joyce something, and she repeated what she had said. That caused the district judge to shake his head. Clark thought that he looked a little sad for some reason. Then the district judge spoke, seemingly something serious.

Clark almost grabbed Shabby Lawyer. He wanted to strangle him. "What the hell is going on?"

Shabby Lawyer leaned away and responded in his low voice. Clark turned to Joyce.

"Evidently you have been charged with one-hundred percent negligence in the death of one person and maiming of another, and that since you pled not guilty, there has to be a trial. The trial will begin in…" she paused. She didn't particularly like Clark, but she could feel his anguish. "It will begin in thirty days."

Clark struggled to control himself. "What about bail. Tell him to ask for bail."

Joyce spoke to Shabby Lawyer who reluctantly asked the district judge. The prosecutor said something to the district judge that caused him to shake his head before he responded to Shabby Lawyer.

"No bail. The prosecutor argues that you will leave, not stay for a trial."

The district judge banged his gavel and started to leave the room, but then paused and spoke again, this time looking directly at Clark.

"He wants to know if they are treating you well in the prison."

About to complain, Clark reconsidered and replied sarcastically, "Sure just like all the other murderers."

Joyce paused before translating and then didn't include the reference to murderers. The district judge nodded at her response and then quickly left the room.

"I'm so sorry." Joyce struggled, distraught, unable to look him in the eyes. "I don't know what happened or why."

"Hey, it's not your fault. It's been totally screwed up from the start."

Before they could say anything else, Laurel and Hardy arrived, took Clark by the arms and guided him out of the room.

CHAPTER 24

Twenty-two, twenty-three, twenty-four. Clark ignored the sweat that stung his eyes as he willed his aching muscles to do one more push-up. Twenty-five. He urged himself on. His goal was to do thirty, which would be five more than yesterday. He got to twenty-eight and collapsed on the concrete floor. Then he turned over on his back and started in on sit-ups.

He had begun to exercise the morning after the court hearing. It had been a long, awful night as his mind replayed over and over what had happened. He had allowed himself to hope, and as he had been paraded back to the prison, he knew that had been a heartbreaking mistake. It was a mistake that he couldn't allow himself to repeat. He had to survive in that cell, and to do so he had to be strong - mentally and physically stronger than any of them. Stronger then he'd ever been. And pacing and wrestling weren't nearly enough.

The other prisoners had given him a lot of space when he returned from the court. The grapevine had worked quickly, and they had known what happened before he got back. Ahmed hadn't expected Clark to return and had planned to sell his stuff the next day. It had been a nice diversion to have a foreigner in there for a few days, but no one imagined that it would last. Now they all watched as Clark finished two sets of twenty sit-ups and stood up to do squats. Most of them had been in the army and were familiar with the exercises, but no one ever did them voluntarily.

In the five days since the hearing Clark had easily defeated Ringo, No Hair, and Yagiz, the prisoner with the pockmarked skin. Today it would be the one they called Yusuf, with the one blue eye and one brown eye. And every evening after winning a fight, he had moved his bedroll and duffle bag along the bottom shelf toward the ends.

Frail Boy had become his tutor on the sequence of the challenges and on rudimentary words in Turkish. Ahmed and a few of the others helped with words, but it was Frail Boy who had the most energy and patience as well as the best imagination for effective pantomimes to convey definitions and meanings. Clark could already count to twenty, and he could order a tea from the prison kitchen and figure out the correct coins to pay. Frail Boy seemed to be picking up English even faster, as Clark reciprocated with English lessons.

Clark had stashed his watch deep in his bag and worked to follow the normal circadian routines of the prison. He also kept trying to master the worry beads but often fumbled and dropped them. Finally, Kerem, a younger version of Ugly Old Man, but not a rapist, took pity on him and gave him a few lessons on the proper technique. After that Clark began to really appreciate the beads and their function. He also found that for some odd reason his left hand was better with the beads than his right.

Clark once thought of Joyce when he mistook a young Turkish woman in a headscarf for her, as she passed by the hallway window. And he had almost managed to suppress any thought of Nigel and what had happened to him in Ankara and why he wasn't back. Did he leave? Clark wondered, and then didn't know whether he would blame him. He considered what he would do if the roles were reversed. But he stopped because it opened up too many painful thoughts and unwelcome feelings of freedom and home and …

Clark had been pacing for a while and his heart rate had settled when he heard Toad call his name. The guard smiled as Clark approached and then spoke excitedly. Clark looked around for Frail Boy, but he wasn't there. So he nodded in response to the expectant look from Toad. He thought that Toad would go away then, but he didn't. Frail Boy emerged from the inner hallway, and Ahmed yelled at him, which directed his attention over to Clark and Toad. After listening to Toad, Frail Boy said, "Banyo", which Clark already knew was bathroom, so he pointed toward the inner hall and the bathroom. Frail Boy shook his head and then started to pantomime taking a shower, "dus saganak."

"Shower?" Clark asked, as he repeated the pantomime.

"Evet, dus saganak, yes shower," Frail Boy said with a smile, as he pointed to Clark and then out into the prison hallway.

Ahmed yelled something that caused Frail Boy to ask Toad a question. Toad nodded. Ahmed smiled and made a motion of slashing his throat. "Morte," he said, as he laughed.

Clark got his toiletries kit and his towel from his duffle bag. He had wondered if, when, and how they would ever take a bath. He rubbed his face and felt his beard, which grew fast and was now almost full. After getting his last change of clean clothes, Clark followed Toad down the hall. They entered a small room with an old barber's chair, a small table with a porcelain basin of water, and an old man who energetically began to beat a straight razor along a strap of leather. Toad motioned for Clark to take a seat on the chair. Clark had never had anyone give him a shave before, and after Ahmed's gesturing, he looked apprehensively at the straight razor. The barber forced Clark's head to rest on the back of the chair and then used a small brush to put some warm thick soap on his face, which helped him relax a little. Clark knew it was a cliché that barbers talked a lot, but it certainly fit this old man. Toad interjected once, but otherwise the barber kept up a non-stop chatter as he carefully scrapped more than ten days of growth from Clark's face. When the barber held a small mirror up to Clark, he barely recognized himself. It wasn't the clean-shaven look. It was something about his eyes. They looked dull, almost lifeless, reflecting a resignation to prison life. He quickly looked away and pulled some money from his pocket. He had learned that everything in the prison cost money.

Toad led him down the main hall, away from the front door. After passing the hallway that would have led back to his courtyard, they continued down the center hallway and came to a small lobby space. Clark could see what looked like two more cell areas with windows opening onto the lobby. Then around to the left they reached the entrance to a room that looked like his high school shower room, only much older, and with no ceiling. Toad pointed out some wooden pegs that protruded from the wall, the water knobs and shower heads, and then he backed out of the room and stood outside with his back turned. Clark appreciated Toad's attempt to give him some privacy as he undressed and hung his clothes and towel on a peg. There was only one water knob per shower, and Clark didn't imagine that it would be for hot water, and it wasn't. The water started cold, but soon became lukewarm as he washed quickly. He didn't have any shampoo and had to use his soap for his hair. He began to feel almost human again and had a moment of panic that maybe that wasn't the best thing. *Why am I the only one getting a shower?* he kept asking himself.

His answer came after he finished and dressed. Toad led him to the front door where the sergeant waited. Then they walked across the dirt courtyard toward the one-story building adjacent to the front door. Clark had now passed it a couple of times and guessed that it was the office for the prison. As they entered, he saw that he was correct. They were in an open room with four desks, three of them empty, and at the other one sat a soldier pecking away at an old manual typewriter. The soldier looked up and used his head to direct him to a door on the right. Clark could hear voices coming from what looked like a small meeting room, and it took him a moment to realize that they spoke English. Nigel and Joyce.

Joyce saw Clark first. Influenced by her memory of him in the courtroom, she struggled to understand her reaction to this freshly shaven and showered person. At Nigel's request, she had asked to meet Clark outside of the cell complex, but she hadn't said anything about personal hygiene. All of this was tempered by the change in his face. Gone was any attempt at swagger or humor, replaced by a cold, hard stare. She noticed his worry beads moving quickly between the fingers on his left hand, and the phrase going-native came to her mind. She felt a little shiver run through her body as she forced a smile.

Nigel had his back to the door but followed Joyce's smile and swung around to face Clark. "Oh, hi Clark, good to see you, you wouldn't believe the trouble I've had."

Clark was way beyond sarcasm at this point and just shrugged, "Hey."

"You wouldn't believe what I had to go through at the embassies. It was a bloody nightmare, especially mine, bloody Foreign Service nits. I had to wait for hours in this crowded lobby. Then they said, 'Tough luck old chap, drive more carefully next time'. Can you believe that rubbish?"

Clark thought he saw Joyce flinch slightly and that stopped him from acting on an impulse to smash his fist into Nigel's face. "Yeah, okay, so what did they say?"

"Well they were more polite at your embassy and seemed concerned, but they're, you know, limited -"

Clark cut him off. "No, what did my parents say when you called them?"

Nigel seemed surprised at first, then he looked down at his shoes.

"You did call them, right?"

"The people at your embassy said that they would contact them and -"

"Damn it Nigel! They'll get a telegram from some bureaucrat saying sorry to inform you that your son is in a Turkish prison and… What the hell were you thinking?"

Nigel didn't look up from his shoes.

"You called your father didn't you?"

Nigel still didn't look up, but nodded his head.

"Sure you did," Clark lashed out, before he turned to leave. He paused at the door, composed himself and came back. "Okay, so what else is the embassy going to do?"

Nigel forced himself to look up but not right at Clark. "Well, they said that there's not a lot they can do other than make sure that you're being treated well and getting a fair trial."

"And how the hell would they know that? Will they get me a lawyer who speaks English?" He turned to face Joyce. "Joyce did her best to try to help, but she's not a lawyer. Something went wrong the other day, but all I did was say I wasn't guilty."

"They said because it's this kind of case, a local criminal matter, that they can't intervene." On the verge of tears, Nigel rushed on. "I'm really sorry, I tried my best, I really did." He finished and raced from the room.

Suddenly exhausted, deflated, Clark collapsed on a chair. He didn't look at Joyce, who shifted awkwardly on her feet, and after a moment, she sat also. Clark was good with silences, but she wasn't.

"You know after what you said the other day about being in here with all murderers, I was curious and checked around, and it seems like many of them are here for what they call honor murders."

He looked over at her. "What's that?"

"Well, you may know that Turkey thinks it's a secular state, at least in its head. But in its heart it's still very Muslim and many people follow the Sharia laws, even if they conflict with the secular ones. So if someone kills your brother or father or mother, anyone in your family really, then you are honor bound to kill them. It's an eye for an eye, and they willingly accept the official legal punishment even though according to their religious beliefs they acted honorably."

"That's kind of fucked up."

"Seriously."

"But it does explain a lot. Many of them don't seem like bad people, and I guess maybe they aren't."

Back in the prison courtyard, Clark again struggled with the depression that came from the abrupt change - being outside and having a brief semblance of normalcy and then thrust back into the maelstrom.

The others kept a distance from him for the rest of the afternoon. He gradually pulled himself out of his funk and began to try to determine which of them was a genuine bad-guy and which were there because of their religious convictions. He quickly assumed that Frail Boy, Ringo, Ayden, Farm Boy, and probably Tattoo were some of the honorable religious men and that Wolf Eyes, Yusuf, and certainly Ugly Old Man were bad-guys. Huzain was a thief, so bad guy, but not evil. And he still didn't know anything about Ahmed or Mohamed, who, despite the fact that he read the *Koran* all day, Clark assumed was more on the bad side than the honorable one. It then dawned on him that this must have been what Ahmed had been trying to communicate as he described some of their crimes - to tell him what caused them to have to kill for the sake of their religion. It did subtly change the way he felt about being there. It wasn't quite the den of evil murderers that he had initially assumed.

The Muezzin call for evening prayer gave him an opportunity to pay attention to who prayed and who didn't. He assumed that some level of devotion would coincide with the potential for an honorable murder. He then noticed that Wolf

Eyes prayed and considered that either he was wrong in his assumption, or that maybe religion had come after the bad deeds, or maybe that evil and religion could coexist in a person.

After dinner, Clark sat on the edge of the bottom shelf and tried to compose a letter to his parents. He had no illusions that they would ever get it or not for a long time, hopefully long after he was gone from there. He might not even post it, but he felt compelled to write it. He hesitated - could he tell them the truth? Would someone read it in the prison or the police? He did want them to know that he was okay, considering. And that he was determined to get through it and get home. Then a flood of emotions threatened to overwhelm him, and he had to put the letter aside. He pulled himself back into his protective shell by focusing on what was going on around him - on the present, not the past, or the future.

Clark managed to pass the next days by following the routine that seemed to work for most of his fellow inmates, except for praying five times a day. He continued his physical workouts and even got a few followers from those at the bottom of the wrestling ladder. Frail Boy was the only one who did it consistently, but he also followed Clark around like a puppy most of time. Clark paid close attention to all the fights, especially those that involved men he hadn't come to yet on the ladder. He studied their strengths and weaknesses in preparation for his match with them. He moved up the ladder one fight a day, almost every day. And every night after a fight, he moved his sleeping bag on the sleeping platform. He had reached the edge of the bottom shelf, and his next move would be up to the middle of the top shelf. He even thought that he had figured out why some didn't fight but had good spots on the shelf and an eating group. Some of them - Ahmed and Huzain - were physically handicapped. But some others such as

Aiden who read to people who couldn't read and Bookmaker - seemed to perform a service for the others that gave them some standing, a stature that kept them from the ladder. It wasn't a perfect theory yet, but he felt he was on the right track.

A big distraction occurred a couple of days after the meeting with Joyce and Nigel, when all of the men went to take a shower. There had been a lot of energy, joking and shoving all the way there, but once they got to the shower room, it got very quiet. No one seemed comfortable with their own nakedness or that of the other men in the room. They all kept their eyes to themselves as they quickly showered, dried off, and got dressed. In high school and college Clark had stood out because of his abundant body hair, but here he was not that unique. Several of the men, Mohamed in particular, were almost as hairy. But Clark didn't have the assortment of scars that almost everyone had. Mohamed had a particularly gruesome one that crossed his entire chest and was especially noticeable because hair didn't grow on the scar tissue.

Nigel visited a couple of times, but without Joyce he had to come into the prison and stand at the window. He never lasted for more than five minutes before people in the hall got to him. Clark had come to firmly believe that he had, in fact, saved Nigel's life. There was no way he could survived in the communal cell. That belief provided a foundation of strength for Clark, which helped whenever a wave of doubt or depression threatened to overwhelm him.

Clark had stopped keeping track of the days but guessed that it had been more than a week since he had been in the office with Nigel and Joyce. He had accepted the fact that it would be thirty days before his trial, and he certainly didn't expect Shabby Lawyer to do anything in the meantime, so he was curious when late one morning Toad took him for another shave and private shower.

Clark entered the office building, and the same soldier was there punishing the typewriter. But this time he indicated the door on the left. Clark entered what was the office of the commandant of the prison and saw Nigel and Joyce along with a very well dressed man who immediately approached Clark.

"Clark, Nathanial Streeter, U.S. Vice Consul from Istanbul. Duzce is in our area, and I got here as soon as I could. How are you doing my boy?"

Clark was immediately put off by Streeter with his faux aristocratic inflections, overly well-fed, out-of-shape body, and placid face.

"Have you met Commandant Bey?" Streeter continued, without waiting for Clark to answer, and motioned to a middle aged man who stood up from behind the only desk in the room and came around toward Clark.

Clark shook Commandant Bey's outstretched hand and returned his cautious smile. There were several rows of medals on the commandant's crisp clean Turkish Army uniform.

"Please welcome," the commandant said in heavily accented English, as he pointed to chairs around his desk. He moved back around behind his desk and sat as the others found a chair. Clark was on one side with Streeter between him and Nigel and Joyce. "English not well," the commandant said, and then continued in Turkish as he turned to face Joyce.

"The commandant apologizes for his English and would like to speak in Turkish if that is all right with everyone."

Streeter said something in Turkish that made the commandant smile and Joyce wince. They all paused as the soldier from the outer room entered with a wooden tray and glass cups of tea for everyone. The commandant smiled and gestured for them to take a cup.

After a perfunctory sip of tea, Streeter swung his attention back to Clark. "So I understand that we have something in common. I'm Dartmouth class of forty-three. My father was class of twenty-two. And my grandfather has a residence hall named after him. Streeter Hall, do you know it?"

Clark didn't live in that world anymore, and even if he did, he wouldn't have given this pompous ass the satisfaction of knowing that he had lived in Streeter Hall for two years. "Can you get me bail?"

"Oh, well, bail? No, actually, I'm afraid not. You see this is a difficult, a delicate situation. We've had these before, not too often thank God, but they take very careful handling, and there's not very much that we can do. Legally, it's an internal matter. We can only try to make sure that you're being treated properly. How are they treating you by the way?"

"Same as everyone else."

"Well, that's good, right? That's all we can expect, ask for, really."

"So how about a lawyer who speaks English and knows something about the law?"

"That's unfortunately not a function of our office. I will be happy to give you some names of people in Istanbul that you can contact."

"Sure, I'll have my secretary call them on my private telephone." Clark was frustrated and angry, but he didn't yell. "Listen, if you can't get me bail or a good lawyer, then don't waste my time." He got up and started to leave before he said anything worse. He noticed that Joyce hadn't translated that last part for the commandant.

"Your parents are coming," Nigel called out.

That got Clark's attention.

And Streeter quickly added, "Yes, and against our advice I must say."

Clark ignored Streeter and asked Nigel, "When?"

"In three days I think."

Clark then challenged Streeter. "Why?"

"Well, there's not much they can do really, and it might be difficult for them, you know, foreign country, the language, your situation. But it's their decision, of course, and we'll do our best to assist, make them comfortable. We have booked a suite for them at the Istanbul Hilton."

Clark had already tuned him out as he struggled to control his mix of emotions. It would be wonderful to see his parents, but it would completely upset his delicate balance between civilized and uncivilized, hope and fear, survival and giving up.

"Oh, by the way, the consul asked me to give this to you," Streeter said, as he reached into a leather satchel on the floor at his feet. "It was his daughters before she left for school in the states." He pulled out a small portable record player and handed it to Clark.

Clark took it with a blank look on his face that didn't reflect his internal reaction - what the fuck am I going to do with this, you asshole? He considered just leaving without the gift, but sensed that it was best to take it, which he did. He would have liked to have had a moment to speak with Nigel and Joyce, but he already felt overwhelmed by the news about his parents. So he politely thanked the commandant in Turkish, smiled weakly at the others, and left.

Everyone knew that Clark had been with the commandant and some big shot who had arrived in a fancy car with a driver, and they were eager to find out about it. But they quickly sensed Clark's foul mood when he returned to the courtyard, and they wisely left him alone.

Clark forced himself to eat some lunch even though he wasn't hungry. Part of him just wanted to sit alone and brood, but he knew that would be a mistake. At the beginning of the day it had been his intention to fight Askim and get to the top shelf in the bunkroom. But now he also used the fight to take out his anger and frustrations. Clark made one mistake that almost allowed the fat man to use his sheer bulk to win, but

Clark's exercises paid off, and he had enough strength to push Askim off and pin him.

That night the sound of a Turkish song competed with the normal noises in the bunkroom. Ringo sang along to a record that played on Clark's record player, which sat on the floor near the window. It was plugged into an old Army-green extension cord that Toad had given them and which ran out the window, across the courtyard and through the hallway window into the hall.

Clark sat on his sleeping bag with his back against the wall in his new spot in the middle of the top shelf. There was just enough headroom to sit up and not feel claustrophobic. It was clearly a spoil of battle and worth the sore shoulder he had suffered when Askim and all his weight had fallen on it.

Ahmed shouted something and the room got quiet. After a moment Clark noticed the quiet and peeked over the edge of the shelf to see them all standing in a circle, ready for the hand-slapping game. It had been so long ago that he had forgotten about it. He slowly climbed down and took his place in the center of the circle.

Ahmed nodded, seemingly pleased that Clark had remembered, wanted to play, and had taken his spot without being told to do so. Tattoo tied the bandana around Clark's eyes and said something to the others that caused them to laugh.

Clark heard the laughter, and it struck him as having a positive tone, not a negative one. He placed his right hand under his left arm and waited for the slap. It was hard, but not too bad and he slowly took off the blindfold and looked around the circle. It was very clear that Ringo was the slapper because he couldn't hide his smile. But Clark purposefully ignored Ringo and chose Huzain. After the laughter died down, the next slap was considerably harder and obviously came from

Askim - Clark could feel the chubbiness of Askim's hand as it slapped him. Again he purposefully chose incorrectly. More laughter, excitement. He couldn't have explained his actions, which weren't premeditated. It had something to do with proving himself - that he could take it and at the same time play a little game of his own. The third time, after a very hard slap, Clark really got into it. He made a fake move toward Farm Boy, who he thought had slapped him, then at Frail Boy, and finally picked Aiden, whom he was sure would have the weakest slap in the room. After the fifth slap, Clark's hand really hurt, and he was ready to finally move on, but the night bell rang, and they all scurried to their spots on the shelves.

It took Clark a while to fall asleep. He could feel the rhythm of his heart as his blood throbbed through his swollen hand. That made him remember Bernadette's story about the deaf DJ. He suppressed those feelings but that left him open to think of his parents. He tried hard but unsuccessfully to push thoughts of them out of his head. He loved his parents. His dad was an enigma to him, having been absent, always traveling for work, during most of Clark's formative early years. But he consistently proved to be a rock of support, with very few probing personal questions and an open checkbook. It was his mother he was really worried about. Normally so strong and sensible, how would she react to this chaos, to seeing her son in prison? And he agonized over whether he should or could tell them what really happened. Would they understand what he had done? Could they accept it, support it, and not try to correct it to get him released? He had made it this far, and he didn't want to see it all undone and have Nigel … he just couldn't imagine what would happen to Nigel if their positions were switched. It wouldn't be pretty. It would be tragic.

For the next several days Clark tried to suppress his anxiety over his parents' visit by keeping to his routine. It mostly succeeded, as one workout flowed into another, and one fight became the next fight: Zia, who had fought his way up to challenge Clark, to Kerem the ugly, to Farm Boy. He knew he had only to defeat Wolf Eyes to get to Tattoo and to win a seat at the table. He had only seen Tattoo fight once, with Farm Boy. And Wolf Eyes had recently defeated Farm Boy, but primarily because Wolf Eyes fought dirty, as evidenced by his teeth marks on Farm Boy's forearm. Tattoo, however, had not challenged Mohamed and didn't seem to have any inclination to do so. Clark knew that it would be very difficult to beat Tattoo, and if he did, he wondered whether he would feel compelled to fight Mohamed.

Clark was still puzzled by Ahmed, what he had done or why he seemed to be the leader, the boss of the cell. All he knew was that everyone called him Efe, which Joyce had said meant respected-one or big brother. And he seemed to have an inexhaustible supply of cash. He was always buying a tea for people for various reasons - if someone won a fight for example, or did something nice for another prisoner. Their clothes were cleaned by women who Clark at first thought were workers coming into the prison, but later he realized they were prisoners in the one wing of the building that he had not been to. The laundry service cost money, and Ahmed seemed to pay for many if not most of them including Clark. Clark also had the impression that Ahmed paid for them to have better food, meat on more occasions than the rest of the prison.

Some prisoners were allowed to roam the halls during the day, doing different jobs - cooking, cleaning, gardening. The telltale sign for a prisoner was the dull, vacant, prison-stare in their eyes. The same look that Clark had seen in his own eyes.

Nigel hadn't come to visit for days, and Clark worried briefly, but then realized that it certainly wasn't any fun for

Nigel to get harassed in the hallway, and that Clark usually didn't act all that pleased to see him. In different circumstances, he probably would have felt bad about that.

Clark was sure that it had been more than three days since the Streeter visit and yet no word about his parents. He tried not to think about it, not to worry, but he wasn't completely successful.

It had rained all afternoon, and the tension from twenty-three restless, bored, men made the bunkroom unbearable. Clark hadn't been able to stand it and now he paced alone outside in the rain. He welcomed the peace and didn't mind the slight chill that came through his soaked clothes. The courtyard normally got brutally hot in the afternoon sun, and this was a nice change. Clark went over his strategy for the fight with Wolf Eyes. He knew Wolf Eyes would cheat and try to bite or maybe knee him in the groin, so he was determined to end it quickly. He felt confident that he could do so, but that was based on seeing Wolf Eyes fight one time. It hadn't seemed like anyone who had been below him on the ladder had any interest in challenging the dirty fighter. Clark looked over at the window to the bunkroom and saw the wolf-like eyes follow him. Clark almost paused - what had he seen in those eyes… hunger? Or did it look more like fear?

The rain stopped, the clouds quickly moved on, and the sun began to bake the courtyard. Steam rose in fragile wisps around the men as they eagerly left the bunkroom. Clark waited for Wolf Eyes, and the others watched and anticipated. Few bet against Clark anymore, and Wolf Eyes was only feared for his bite. The anticipation grew thick as Wolf Eyes failed to appear. Frail Boy went back into the bunkroom and then could be heard crying out and shouting angrily. He emerged with red teeth marks on his hand and tears in his eyes. Clark got angry and even more motivated to beat Wolf Eyes, who stayed inside. Frail Boy said something, and a murmur went through the crowd. Ahmed got up and went inside. There was no crying or shouting, and he emerged a few minutes later and said something to the group before he took Clark's arm and raised it in victory. Clark didn't know the words, but he got the message that Wolf Eyes had declined to fight, and Clark won by default.

All eyes now turned from Clark to Tattoo, who sat at the table and watched.

Clark hesitated. He hadn't figured out a strategy for Tattoo yet. Tattoo was bigger than almost all the others, but he suffered from the common prison malaise of too little exercise. The crowd had been primed for a fight and this one had lots of possibilities. The looks on their faces told Clark that he had to do this now. Tattoo seemed to have gotten the same message. He stood and approached Clark in the center of the courtyard. They wouldn't insult each other with the tweaking ears routine.

Clark felt heavy and slow because of this wet clothes, so he took off his shirt as he and Tattoo cautiously circled each other. Tattoo seemed in no hurry, and Clark didn't want to get overly aggressive and careless.

The excitement grew with each tentative thrust of a hand. Clark noticed that the window to the hallway was full of faces including Toad's. That brief distraction almost cost him, as Tattoo tried to get past his hands and into his body for a takedown. Clark managed to break Tattoo's hold on his arm and spun away, causing the bigger man to stumble into the ring of eager spectators.

Clark focused his attention and tried to sense any tendencies of his opponent. Tattoo was patient and obviously had some skill. Clark tried to go for his legs and barely managed to get back upright after Tattoo effectively pushed him down and tried to get behind him. Clark mentally slapped himself to wake up and be patient. Both men had been moving counterclockwise, so Clark reversed direction and noticed that Tattoo didn't like that. He moved more aggressively clockwise, and Tattoo tried to force him the other way. In doing so, he allowed an opening for Clark to grab his arm and pull him off balance. Clark used his leg to further unbalance Tattoo and force him to the ground. Clark wasn't in a commanding position, but he had enough momentum and leverage to get Tattoo on his stomach with Clark securely on top. Tattoo struggled to get up and Clark managed to hold him down. Tattoo had to spend much more energy than Clark did and gradually Clark could feel him tire. Whenever Tattoo tried to rest, Clark made a move to turn him on his back to pin him. The first two times, Tattoo had enough strength to resist, and the first time almost got the better of Clark. But by the third time, Tattoo's strength was almost depleted. The fourth time, Clark got him on his back and pinned him.

The crowd went quiet. There hadn't been a change at the table for as long as most of them had been there. Then Frail Boy began to shout, "London, London," and many of the others joined in.

Clark jumped up and Tattoo stayed on the ground. Clark hesitated and then offered Tattoo a hand to help him up. Tattoo smiled and took Clark's hand. Once up, he escorted Clark to the table and offered him his chair. Ahmed already had glasses of tea ready for them. Mohamed didn't look up from his book.

That night, Clark took Tattoo's spot on the shelves at the end of the bottom shelf near the window. He noticed that no one spoke to Wolf Eyes, but then not many had done so before. Clark had been apprehensive because Wolf Eyes bedroll spot had been next to Tattoo's. But when he got into the bunkroom, Farm Boy was in that spot. Wolf Eyes had been relegated to the middle of the lower bunk next to Ugly Old Man. Evidently a coward was considered as abhorrent as a rapist. Clark knew that he needed to keep a careful eye on Wolf Eyes.

CHAPTER 25

Clark drank tea as he watched the morning prayer ritual. He had been studying it to decipher the routine and the words. But the only word he knew was Allah. He noticed Ahmed staring at him, and he smiled casually in return. He often had a hard time reading Ahmed's expressions, but this one seemed to indicate concern of some sort, for something. Clark debated whether to begin the exhausting process of trying to communicate feelings using pantomime when Toad appeared at the door and said, "Dus saganak". No one else reacted, so Clark knew Toad meant him alone. And that had to mean that his parents were there.

By the time Clark approached the office building, his anxiety had grown to surround him, press on him, a weight dragging him to the depths. He knew that this was going to be hard for everyone. He took a deep breath and vowed to be strong, especially for his mother.

As he entered the office, the same soldier sat there, and he stared at Clark, not making any pretense to be working. The soldier nodded at the commandant's office, but Clark was already headed that way. He could hear the voices, which sounded like a lot of people. He recognized Joyce, Nigel and his mother. And there were two men speaking in Turkish.

He stood in the doorway for a moment before anyone noticed him. His father, John Westfield, stood listening to Commandant Bey converse with a Turkish man dressed in a suit. His father also wore a suit. Joyce stood there and translated for Clark's father.

Clark saw his mother, Coleen, notice him and stand there quietly as she examined him. He could tell she struggled to keep her emotions under control. He knew he had changed, and that it was written all over him - certainly it had to be visible to a mother's eyes. He gave her as warm a smile as he could before she finally rushed over and hugged him. He could feel her fighting off tears. Then his father joined them. Reaching around his wife, he took Clark's upper arms in his hands and squeezed. Clark looked past his parents and saw the others staring at their little family tableau.

Clark's father pulled back and took control of the situation. "Clark this is Mustafa Burakgazi, he's a lawyer in Istanbul, and he's here to help us. And I know you have met the commandant."

Clark shook Mustafa's outstretched hand and nodded at the commandant who stayed safely behind his desk. His mother had herself under control and took comfort in standing next to him, with her hands firmly attached to his arm. He wasn't surprised. His mother had never been prone to hysterics.

As usual he found it hard to read Joyce's expression, and Nigel stared at his feet as they shifted nervously on the floor.

Mustafa spoke to Clark. "I was just about to tell your father that I have seen the prosecutor and that sorry excuse for a lawyer that they assigned to you. Miss Edwards told me what happened at the arraignment, and it was unfortunate that you pleaded not guilty."

"But it was an accident and not negligent homicide or whatever they called it," Clark argued.

"I understand, and I would agree if it were in an American courtroom, but we are not."

Clark's father jumped in. "Mustafa studied at Yale law and practiced in the States for several years before coming back home. His uncle is on the Turkish Supreme Court."

Mustafa nodded. "Here our system is unfortunately often based more on appearances than fact. We have a crazy blend of old Ottoman, British, and Muslim legal influences. And all of those operate, fight, in a system where money and influence often count more than truth or justice."

Clark didn't like the sound of all that, but it did resonate with what he had experienced as the results - his situation and some of the other men in his cell. He looked at Joyce who nodded her head, but kept her eyes down.

"If you had pleaded guilty," Mustafa continued, "the judge would have given you maybe a few years in prison."

Clark heard his mother gasp, and felt her grip tightened on his arm.

"But," Mustafa continued quickly, specifically addressing Clark's mother, "In our system that sentence is open to barter, sometimes with land or farm animals but mostly with cash." He turned to look at Clark's father. "It would have been several thousand dollars to pay for the release. Not so much in your country, but a lot of money in a district like this."

There was silence as that sank in with everyone.

"Okay, so I screwed up." Clark emphasized the I so Joyce wouldn't feel any responsibility. "What do we do now? Can we still pay and go?"

Mustafa slowly shook his head. "In some cases, involving locals, it might be possible. But not likely with a case involving a foreigner. I will go to see the district judge tomorrow and have a conversation with him." He finished with a half-smile that Clark appreciated. He could sense that the lawyer was trying to be straight but not too defeatist.

"If that doesn't work, then what happens? Will it be over at this trial in what, a little while now?" Clark had lost track of how many days had passed. He didn't like the expression on Mustafa's face, as he shook his head.

"That first trial date is in two days, but again we are a different system and this is a poor area. The district judge covers many towns, villages and many cases. Something like this, to try now to prove that… Let me put it another way. The prosecutor charged you with one hundred percent negligence, and the court will never find you completely blameless. That would mean too much losing face for the prosecutor. So to reduce the percent as low as possible could take many months, maybe even a year or more."

Every foreign knee went weak. Clark helped his mother to a chair where she collapsed with her face in her hands. Everyone sat except for Mustafa who had to wait for the soldier to bring in another chair. The silence was oppressive. The loudest noises, sobs and groans, came from Clark's mother and Nigel.

Clark couldn't look at anyone. He struggled to process a year in that cell when he had been keeping somewhat sane by the knowledge that it was only for thirty days and that was almost over. He took one of the glasses of tea that the commandant had ordered and the soldier served. He felt weak, as panic began to spread through his body.

"There has to be something we can do," Clark's mother pleaded.

His father tried to set a positive tone, a diversion. "I've already taken care of the car. As soon as the police release it, it'll be repaired and then shipped to the States. I had thought we'd just leave it here, sell it, but that's against the law." He shrugged as he looked at his wife and then Mustafa. "Can we get someone involved, you know, at a higher level?"

Mustafa carefully shook his head. "No, the best thing now is to, as you say, lay low. Tomorrow I'll speak to this judge and a new local lawyer who has been recommended highly, so we can be ready for the trial on Friday. The best we can hope for is for the judge to eventually give him bail."

Oh, so it must be Wednesday, Clark thought, not sure he really wanted to know.

"We can't just sit by and let him stay in here," Clark's father argued.

"There is unfortunately no choice, at the moment. The best thing is to keep a low profile for now. The fewer people who know you are in town the better. There are many things to see in Istanbul, there's the -."

Clark's mother cut him off. "I can't stay so far away, there must be a place here," she said, as she struggled to hold back her tears.

"I'm at the best place in town, and trust me, you don't want to be there," Nigel said, with his usual lack of tact. Fortunately, Clark was beyond caring about that. He did, however, notice that Joyce rolled her eyes, and that almost made him laugh because it reminded him of his sister who did that the same thing with her eyes.

"How's Sarah?" he asked his mother to change the subject. While he listened to her report about Sarah's small part in an off-Broadway play, Clark noticed that Mustafa, the commandant and his father were huddled in an intense conversation. At one point his father looked over at him with a curious look on his face. He saw Joyce also listening to the conversation, occasionally translating for his father, and she also looked at him with an unusual but not unpleasant expression.

Finally, it got uncomfortable in the room and everyone realized it was time to go. Clark could tell from his mother's hug that she didn't want to let him go. As they walked out of the building, Clark's father approached him. "The commandant was telling us about your activities in the prison, and that you've evidently made sort of a name for yourself. Are you sure you're okay?"

Clark wasn't surprised that the commandant knew about the fights. The guards certainly did, and they often bet on them. "I'm fine dad, don't worry. Just try to keep mom from obsessing over it." He noticed that Joyce had taken his mother's arm as they approached the front gate. Clark couldn't bear to watch them leave, so he turned and headed toward the prison building where Toad waited for him.

Clark spent a particularly difficult night as he tried to keep from thinking of his parents, and his mother in particular. The juxtaposition of the two worlds was simply too jarring, and instinctually he knew he couldn't let go of the calloused prison persona that had taken so much time, sweat, and blood to develop. It was good that everyone, even Frail Boy, gave him a lot of space because he was ready to fight anyone who got too close. That night he tried to get Ahmed to call for the slapping game so he could have a diversion, but Ahmed just shook his head, "Yok."

If anyone had expected Clark to fight Mohamed the next day, they were disappointed. Clark sat sullenly at the table and only got up to work-out or to pace. And he did both of those very aggressively. That night Ahmed did call for the slapping game, and Clark started in the middle and stayed there until his hand was almost bloody. He found it easier to sleep with the throbbing physical pain in his hand than with the emotional pain of thinking about his parents and life outside the prison.

Clark agonized over whether his parents would come back for his court date. He knew that he never wanted his mother to see him in handcuffs being paraded down the street with his little group of soldiers. He kept his eyes straight ahead and never looked at anyone. He stayed in his little isolation zone until he stood inside the courtroom and met his new lawyer.

"Mr. Westfield, I'm Mr. Ozturk, Mr. Burakgazi has retained me to represent you. I had hoped to see you at the prison first, but I needed time to get ready for this trial date. I apologize."

As he shook his hand, Clark examined this thin, middle-aged man with his narrow mustache and receding hairline. He wasn't very imposing, but at least he seemed intelligent and spoke excellent English. Clark nodded, "No problem. Is Mustafa here?"

"Oh no, we both agreed that it would not be good for appearances for him to be here. He, his family are very well known in Turkey. We want, as you would say, a lower profile."

Clark forced a smile. "Your English is very good. Too bad I didn't have you a month ago."

"Yes, I know Mr. Teke, your previous lawyer. It was an unfortunate choice by the court, but he is the local judge's son-in-law."

Clark felt his anger rising up to overwhelm him, so he looked around the courtroom and tried to keep it in check. If Shabby Lawyer had been there... Clark didn't want to think what he would have done to him - he was already on trial for one death. He saw Joyce and Nigel in the front row on the defense side, gave them a small wave, and carefully got himself under control before he turned back to the lawyer.

"Okay, so what's our game plan for today? Can I get bail?"

Mr. Ozturk very carefully shook his head. "No, that is not possible, not today, I would not even want to ask for it. My goal, our goal Mr. Burakgazi agrees, is to get a continuance for a week or two, so I can know the case and prepare -" the entrance of the district judge interrupted him, and everyone quickly took their seats.

Clark sat stoically as Mr. Ozturk addressed the district judge and then seemed to win an argument with the prosecutor. The district judge appeared to make a decision, banged his gavel and left. Mr. Ozturk and the prosecutor continued to talk privately, so Clark turned to face Joyce and Nigel.

"Your parents wanted to be here, but Mustafa strongly advised against it," Joyce said to Clark.

He nodded, trying not to let on how relieved he was that they weren't there.

Joyce noticed his red, swollen right hand. "Another fight?"

Clark looked at his hand, which still throbbed. "No, just a little game we play at night when we're locked inside." He meant to be jocular, but it didn't come out that way.

Joyce had to look away and bite her tongue. She struggled to reconcile this Clark with the one she had seen with his mother.

"Well, I wanted two weeks but the judge could only reschedule for one, so we have a lot to do, very quickly," Mr. Ozturk said, as he rejoined them. "The prosecutor has given us an office to use, so we should go now, Mr. Westfield and Mr. Barrington." He paused, as he looked at Nigel who had not moved or reacted to anything. He looked back at Clark, who could only shrug his shoulders.

Mr. Ozturk proved very thorough and wanted to know every small detail of the night of the accident. But Clark and Nigel had never talked about a story other than switching drivers. Clark told Mr. Ozturk that he needed some air and nudged Nigel to go with him. Laurel prevented them from going out of the building, but let them go back into the courtroom, which had emptied out for the day.

"I was asleep, but you need to say you were awake so you can provide details," Clark suggested to Nigel. "There may be something you can remember that will help."

"I don't know what that would be, I've been over it, second by second, every day since it happened. I can never get a decent night's sleep."

Clark wanted to make a snarky remark about trying to sleep on a crowded wooden sleeping platform with twenty other men, but he held back. He accepted it that, in his own way, Nigel was also having a bad time. He had actually been a little surprised when Nigel came back from Ankara. He imagined that Nigel could have gotten a replacement passport without too much trouble and gone home.

"They probably wouldn't believe you now," Nigel said quietly, almost whispered.

"Who believe what?"

Nigel never looked directly at Clark as he replied, "This has gotten so out of hand, I wouldn't blame you if you decided to change your mind, tell them I was driving."

Clark didn't actually know Nigel that well, and he had had many moments of considering him an insensitive, ungrateful prick, but he appreciated what he said. "No, I don't think they would believe it, and well, I'm okay, and I know …" He couldn't continue because he couldn't think of how to communicate, without being derogatory and mean, his certainty that Nigel would never survive in that prison.

"It's, it's so hard to express my gratitude for what you've done, it just seems so inadequate."

Clark nodded, and they sat quietly for a while. Then they spent some time coordinating their stories before they rejoined Mr. Ozturk.

By the end of the day, Mr. Ozturk had a plan, the first part of which he thought he could complete in a week. He carefully told tell them that it was only a first step, that things happened very slowly in this area of the world. He didn't want them to get their hopes up that they faced anything other than a long, slow slog through the arcane local judicial system. The biggest problem, he told them, was that Shabby Lawyer had not made arrangements to ensure that the injured man reminded in town to be available to testify as to what had happened that night. The man had been released from the hospital and immediately disappeared. He had probably gone home to Erzurum, a town in Eastern Turkey, where both men were evidently from. Mr. Ozturk quietly cursed the incompetent lawyer as, "a stupid goat herder."

"Can't we find him, subpoena him or something?" Clark asked.

"Mustafa is going to try, but it's probably… well, it's not very likely. We're not even sure what his name is. The hospital records are not very good and the police report only identifies him as the injured man."

Clark didn't get back to the prison until after the doors had been locked to the bunkroom. Cook had saved some dinner for him, despite the assumption by many of the prisoners that Clark wouldn't be back this time. The fact that he now had a fancy Istanbul lawyer had spread quickly through the prison grapevine. And the rumors and discussions of what had gone on in the commandant's office had kept them all busy for days.

Clark felt more exhausted from the day with the lawyer than he had from any day of exercising and fighting in the prison. It had been hard to keep up the story, but he was thankfully that he and Nigel had had a chance to talk.

CHAPTER 26

It had been days since his court visit, and Clark knew that he couldn't wait any longer to fight Mohamed. If he did, everyone would think that he was afraid of the big man with the perpetual scowl. There was a little fear involved, but mostly he was concerned that he had never seen Mohamed fight and had no idea how good he was or what he would do. He also knew that he felt some reluctance to try to depose the man from the top of the ladder. Clark had noticed over the past weeks that Mohamed got a lot of respect, not only from the prisoners in his cellblock, but from the guards as well. One reason might be his size. He was over six feet tall, slightly taller than Clark, which made him several inches taller than everyone else. And clearly he was very religious, but Clark wondered if that had been true before he became a murderer. There had never been any indication from Ahmed that Mohamed's crime had been the honor kind. Clark surmised that Mohamed, probably mid to late-forties, was of an age that he could have fought in the Second World War. Clark had never seen him fight or exercise except to occasionally pace, but he appeared to be in decent shape.

He could sense the anticipation pulse through the prisoners; he even felt it from the guards who seemed to stop by the window more often than usual. Clark was sure that Mohamed expected it. Sitting at the table, he occasionally caught Mohamed looking over at him. Was that a smile? Clark wondered. It certainly had been a small break of some sort in the man's perpetually stoic countenance. Clark told himself that he waited for the right moment. But he knew that he had to make the moment.

As Clark sat and agonized over his decision, he looked over at Mohamed and saw him stare right at him and then give him another little sardonic smile. Clark knew that it had to happen now or forever lose a lot of his painfully built reputation in the cell. He stood up, and Mohamed followed - no words were necessary.

An electric shock charged through the cellblock and spread out into the prison. Everyone gathered in a circle around Clark and Mohamed, and all of them shouted at Bookmaker to place a bet. The window to the hallway was packed with faces, all yelling, and some of them yelled, "London." Soon the door to the courtyard opened, and Toad and several other guards came in, followed by Commandant Bey.

Clark barely noticed the activity around him except for the arrival of the guards and the commandant. He hesitated, unsure if they were there to stop the fight. But it quickly became apparent that they had come to watch and to bet on the fight, not to stop it.

Mohamed took off his shirt, and his scar stood out angrily against his hairy chest. Clark did the same, and they looked like two wild animals preparing to fight for their territory. Neither man was in a hurry. They didn't want to make a foolish mistake. And in a competitive sense, they both enjoyed the moment.

Clark felt a strange sense of calm - it didn't matter if he won or lost. He still would have his seat at the table, and he didn't think it would be taken as a sign of weakness if he lost, as long as he put up a good fight. And Mohamed also appeared calm, as each man tested the other with quick thrusts, but neither one got too aggressive. The crowd, however, wanted some action, and the noise grew with the anticipation. It finally motivated Clark to make a move on Mohamed's legs. He barely escaped disaster, as the older man proved much quicker than Clark anticipated. All he got for his effort was a large raw abrasion on his forearm from scrapping along the concrete floor. Mohamed tried to take advantage of Clark's need to regroup, and he dove at Clark's legs and managed to topple him to the ground. Clark felt another abrasion on his other arm. Then Mohamed moved on top of him, and Clark barely got turned around, off his back. He thought he would let Mohamed tire as he had done with Tattoo, but the older man was cagey and used his weight to conserve his strength as Clack tried to get out from under him. Clark relaxed for a moment, then faked one way and rolled the other, managing to slide Mohamed across him and to the floor so Clark could scramble on top. Mohamed bucked his back up with surprising strength and flexibility, and Clark barely managed to escape to a standing position and face his opponent.

Back and forth they went. Clark didn't know how long it had gone on, but he had found no weaknesses to exploit and began to feel some fatigue. He hoped that it was the same with Mohamed, but it was hard to tell. Clark had gotten him to the ground several more times only to lose him, and Mohamed had done the same to him. The crowd grew more frantic. This had been the epic battle that they had anticipated. The betting moved back and forth, at first favoring Mohamed, then Clark, and now about even. There were no rounds or time limits to these fights, and Clark knew it needed to end soon, but he was afraid to be overly aggressive.

Mohamed charged at Clark, knocking him into the tight circle of spectators who pushed him back, right into Mohamed who caught him in a bear hug and dumped him to the ground. Clark's head hit the concrete floor, and for a moment he thought he would pass out. He refocused too late to prevent

Mohamed from getting him on his back and ready to pin. Clark arched his neck to keep his shoulders from the hard floor, but the pain in his head threatened to quickly sap his strength.

Time slowed and then paused for Clark. He saw Mohamed's sweaty face laced with effort and pain. He saw the faces of the prisoners, guards, and commandant, all shouting, but he didn't hear any noise. No disgrace in losing, he told himself, but that rang false. He had to win to survive. He had to be on top. He knew that if he won, no one would challenge him because they would have to go through Mohamed to reach him. But his strength ebbed, and his wrestling skills were tapped. It was over. But maybe not. Without thinking, purely on instinct, Clark pulled his right arm back, balled up his fist, and swung with all his remaining strength, an uppercut punch at Mohamed's jaw. He felt his fist connect and force Mohamed's head sharply backward. All the strength drained from the older man as he lapsed into semi-unconsciousness.

Clark quickly scrambled out from under Mohamed's inert body. As the crowd stood stone silent, Clark knelt beside his opponent and panicked as he realized what he had done. His instinct had won, but had he really? Had he cheated? Would Mohamed and the others be angry and hate him? Slowly Mohamed gathered his senses and took a moment to massage his jaw and look at Clark. Clark felt an impulse to apologize but didn't, instead he gave slight shrug of his shoulders and tried to keep calm, even as his body shook with exhaustion. Mohamed came to his knees and faced Clark. They stayed like that for a moment. Suddenly Mohamed reached out and grabbed Clark's shoulders, gave him big smile and yelled something to the crowd. He then took Clark's arm and thrust it up in victory.

The crowd grabbed both men and pulling them up to their feet. Not sure his knees would hold him up, Clark appreciated it when Frail Boy and Ahmed took his arms and supported him. Others did the same for Mohamed but with much more restraint. Slowly both moved to the table where Clark took the chair that Mohamed used, and Mohamed took Clark's chair. Clark shook the hand that appeared in front of him, and as he did he looked up to see the commandant smile at him. Clark barely noticed that it had gone completely silent and still in the courtyard. "London champion," the commandant said, and then quickly left.

That night they had what by prison standards would be called a feast. Plenty of meat, vegetables and even a sweet pastry made with honey and nuts. Mohamed and Clark had been allowed to shower, and the army medic had put some ointment on their numerous cuts and abrasions. Ahmed offered Clark something that looked like aspirin for his headache. Many of the prisoners made upper cut motions with their fists at each other and then laughed. Later, as he tried to fall asleep in his new position on the top shelf, Clark realized that if he ignored the walls and bars, he could almost feel comfortable in his surroundings.

The next morning Clark ached, stiff and sore all over. He sat quietly at the table and drank his third cup of tea, all of which someone else had paid for. When he heard Toad call his name he assumed that it was to make some comment on the fight, but the guard motioned him to the hallway door. In the hallway, Toad jabbered on, including making the uppercut motion with his fist, all the way to the front door. He paused there and motioned for Clark to go to the office building.

Clark hadn't anticipated guests, but then remembered that his parents were still around, and they might have come. He paused because he knew that the evidence of the fight was very visible on his face and arms, but he took a deep breath and entered the building. The soldier was not at his desk, and as

Clark approached the Commandant's office, it was quiet. He wondered what was going on. Then as he got to the door, he smelled something burning.

"Surprise! Happy Birthday!" shouted the group in the commandant's office. Clark's mother held out a small cake with three candles burning on it and tried to lead a spirited rendition of happy birthday. Joyce, his father, and Nigel joined her with varying levels of energy, while the commandant and Mustafa looked on, amused.

Clark had forgotten, or more correctly, suppressed any thought of his birthday. And as it now hit him where he was spending his twenty-first birthday, he realized why. The otherworldly juxtaposition of his parents in this place, his tired, sore body, and his bleak future overwhelmed him, and he collapsed on a chair. He struggled with all he had to keep his emotions from taking over. That resulted in a complete lack of any reaction, which caused his mother to be the first to come to tears. Joyce tried to comfort her, and Nigel turned to look out the window.

Clark's father didn't know what to do for his son or his wife and turned his attention to Mustafa who pulled him aside to tell him that he strongly suggested that they should go back to America. "There is nothing you can do here now, except to possibly cause a distraction that would not be good for the outcome of the trial." The lawyer then glanced at the commandant and continued, "And it is not completely safe for you to be here. Clark is safe in the prison, but you are family and have no protection."

"Protection from what?" Clark's father asked, as he noted the cuts and abrasions on his son.

"Our Muslim law, Sharia, would obligate someone from the dead man's family to take revenge on Clark, or not being able to reach Clark," he paused, "on his family."

"My God, does that still happen?"

"Yes, and this man was from the east where religion is very strong, stronger than the government." Mustafa watched John closely for his reaction and didn't see Nigel slump down and bury his head in his hands.

Clark meanwhile knew he had to help his mother, so he forced himself to put some life in his face, got up and gave her a hug. He felt Joyce's hand on his shoulder, and it lingered there for a moment. They all composed themselves and quietly had a piece of cake and a cup of tea. Clark managed a few smiles at his parents and Joyce and even Nigel.

Clark's mother couldn't stand the silence. "I remember when I turned twenty-one. It was during the war, and my mother couldn't find all the ingredients for a cake so we had a big fruit salad. Everything was so different then."

Joyce picked up the thread. "I had just graduated from college and been accepted into the Peace Corps. My mother didn't want me to go away."

Then Nigel found his voice. "Mine was six months ago in London, and I got royally pissed." He looked at Clark's mother and quickly added, "that means drunk in our version of English." She nodded and smiled. She had learned that phrase from her step daughter.

Clark heard the commandant say, "London champion," and turned in time to see him make an upper cut motion with his hand, as he recounted the fight to Mustafa and John. The lawyer hesitated before translating and looked at Joyce for support. She jumped in. "The commandant is telling us that Clark has had great success in getting accepted in the prison. He has a big spirit, and that they all consider him a winner in all that they do." She finished with a look at Mustafa that clearly asked him not to offer any more details.

"Oh, Clark, he knows how to fit in, he always has," his mother gushed, with more enthusiasm than she felt.

A heavy silence followed until Mustafa spoke up. "I've seen the district judge and unfortunately he feels that he cannot give Clark bail at this time because it would appear that he was bribed. That perception has unfortunately been created by my presence and yours." He indicated Clark's parents with a sweep of his hand. "The best he would promise was to accelerate the process as much as he could." Mustafa paused and then addressed Clark, "I have suggested to your parents that it would be best for them to go home and wait for all of this to work its way. I know that they must be a big support for you, but I think it is best."

Clark was torn. He could tell that his parents didn't want to leave him, but they were not only a distraction to the court but to him as well, to his ability to maintain his prison/survivor persona and mindset.

"Mr. Ozturk has worked diligently on the case and will be ready for the trial to begin next week, Wednesday."

"I thought it was a week which would be Monday," Clark's father observed.

"Yes, well, the judge spoke without consulting his clerk or his calendar," Mustafa answered with a shrug of his shoulders. "Let us hope that there is no further delay for Wednesday."

As they left the room, Joyce grabbed Clark by the arm and stopped him. She handed him a flat square thing wrapped in plain brown paper. "Happy birthday," she whispered, and then pushed ahead to take his mother's arm. This time Clark watched his parents leave through the exterior gate, and then wished that he hadn't because he couldn't shake the feeling, the fear that this might be the last time he would ever see them.

He threw himself into his routine and actually regretted it that no one remained on the ladder for him to fight. Slowly he managed to reestablish his inner and outer walls. That evening he tested it by opening the gift from Joyce - the Rolling Stones' album *Flowers*. He laughed out loud, and the room quieted as he pulled his record player out from under the lower bunk and put the album on. Frail Boy ran to the window and yelled for Toad to bring the extension cord.

Clark dropped the needle on his favorite song, *Ruby Tuesday*, and began to sway to the music. Ringo came over and listened intently, then tried to sing the words. Clark and the Frail Boy joined in, and the three of them entertained the others, singing and dancing. A few others joined in, and they continued until the light went out.

That night Clark couldn't keep images from his past out of his thoughts and his dreams. He saw Julie Wells from high school in Denver as she sang their song with Rita, and then she knelt naked on a bed and looked down at him. Julie then became Gwen as she sat on top of him and had her first climax. But mostly there was Bernadette. They were having lunch, riding in his car with the top down, taking photos with Mags. He woke and felt a level of despair that he knew would overwhelm him if he let it. He desperately wanted to get home, but he knew that the only way to survive was to avoid any thoughts of home or of anyone he cared about.

The next days were miserable for Clark. It must have been the birthday cake that made him sick because the rest of his food had been the same as everyone else and no one else was affected. He practically lived in the horrible small room with the hole in the floor and the pitcher of water to wash off. Twice it had been occupied when he felt the urge, and he almost hadn't made it through the wait. It sapped his strength and fed his sense of despair. Finally, the army medic offered him some unidentified pills, which he hesitated to take, but finally did after a particularly bad trip to the bathroom. Whatever they were, they were a miracle drug because almost immediately he felt better, and his intestinal system had a chance to settle down and recover. He had just one normal day before the trial began.

During his little one-man parade into town, Clark kept his eyes straight ahead and his mind focused on what might happen and what probably wouldn't happen with the district judge. He tried to push any thought of bail from his mind and to see this as just another step down a long, dark road with no end in sight.

In the courtroom, Clark sat at the defense table with Mr. Ozturk, who looked tired as he shuffled through a good sized stack of papers. Laurel and Hardy stood in their places along the wall. Nigel and Joyce came in together and sat behind him. He had a momentary feeling of jealousy for them, which he immediately suppressed. He knew that it was unhelpful. Nigel was ... he didn't go any further. And he struggled to deny himself any hint of any kind of feeling for Joyce. Nigel began to tell him that he had been helping Joyce at the school and how much fun the kids were, but Clark quickly tuned him out and turned his attention back to Mr. Ozturk and his papers. He could hear Joyce whisper something to Nigel that caused him to stop talking.

The district judge entered, and the trial began. Mr. Ozturk asked something of the judge who agreed, and Joyce was allowed to sit at the defense table next to Clark and interpret. The prosecutor went through the same routine with the same charts as he had at the hearing. Clark had expected Mr. Ozturk to object, but he kept quiet and let the prosecutor call Man-in-Black to the stand. Mr. Ozturk did ask a couple of questions of Man-in-Black.

"He asked him whether he or anyone else actually saw you drive on the side of the road as the prosecutor argues," Joyce whispered to Clark. "And there wasn't."

Doctor Ataman took the stand next, responded to the prosecutor's questions, and then left without a question from

Mr. Ozturk. "It is better to not focus on the details of the deceased," the lawyer whispered to Clark.

The prosecutor finished, and the judge called for a lunch recess before the defense started.

"Does that mean they're done?" Clark asked his lawyer. It seemed so quick, so perfunctory and he wondered how it could take a year.

"No, our system is different from yours. The prosecution can always come back and surely will with more witnesses, usually depending on what we do. It can go back and forth like that for a long time."

Mr. Ozturk had arranged for them to have the same office and lunch brought in. Clark, concerned about his recent illness, only ate the bread as he listened to Joyce and Nigel talk about a particularly creative girl in the school. Nigel wanted to show the kids how to take photos, but Joyce said no because they didn't have cameras, and even if they did, no one had money to buy film. Clark had never thought about taking pictures in the prison and didn't want to start thinking about it now. That was another world for him, and he had to keep them separate.

Mr. Ozturk gave Clark a sly little grin. "I think you'll be surprised by our first witness." Then he wouldn't tell who it was.

Back in the courtroom, Mr. Ozturk called a federal highway patrol officer to the stand. Clark laughed. During the preparation meeting, he had told the lawyer about passing a cop that night, and Mr. Ozturk had found him. The officer had been driving home the night of the incident, and he remembered that Clark had passed him. He testified that he knew immediately, even before he saw the car, that it was a foreigner by the way he used his turn signal to pass. With Mr. Ozturk's prompting, he told the court that Clark had been driving very carefully, not speeding, and he added that he had been concerned that a foreigner would drive on that road at night. It was very dangerous even in the daylight, and that night had been particularly dark, moonless. Mr. Ozturk finished, and then the prosecutor asked a question. "He wants to know if the trooper actually saw you driving," Joyce whispered to Clark, after the prosecutor pointed in his direction. "No, he says. Now the prosecutor is asking whether it is possible that the other man, Nigel, had been driving. He says it is possible."

Clark couldn't bring himself to look at Nigel.

Then Mr. Ozturk called a local man to the stand. "He's the owner of the service station and bar/restaurant near the accident," Joyce translated. "He remembers the two men, mostly because they were strangers. And he says that they had not been drinking, but they had run out of the bar without paying for their food. He wants to know if they had any money on them and if he can get paid." Joyce laughed at that, but Clark couldn't find the humor.

The proceedings moved very slowly, primarily because the prosecutor took a lot of time between his questions, repeated his questions, especially to the bar owner, and made a number of objections to stuff that seemed mundane.

"Are you going to ask for bail?" Clark asked the lawyer, when it appeared they were done for the day.

"No, we thought it best not to and have him deny it. At the next time I will ask and hopefully enough time will have passed."

"When is the next time?"

"We will know in a couple of days when the judge sets his calendar for June."

June! Clark knew it was about the middle of May because his birthday had been May 9. He forced down his disappointment, his anger, and his frustration, knowing that none of it would do him any good.

As Clark got ready to leave with Laurel and Hardy to meet his detail of soldiers, he stood silently and uneasily with Joyce and Nigel. They tried to be cautiously encouraging but didn't really know how to approach it, and they got no feedback from Clark. He knew he should be grateful for their support, but he just couldn't connect like that and at the same time keep his sanity for another month. He tried not to dwell on their confused, maybe hurt, expressions.

Clark didn't notice a middle-age man who had sat all day in the back of the courtroom and then seemed to follow him and his soldiers as they paraded down the street back to the prison. The man's clothing indicated that he was probably a farmer and not a very prosperous one. He was so intent on the soldiers and Clark that several times he bumped into other pedestrians on the road and almost got run over by an old pickup truck. As Clark and the soldiers entered the prison and the door slammed behind them, the farmer stood and watched from the vacant field across the street.

Clark stoically took his seat at the table in the courtyard and waited for the evening call to prayers and then the bell to send them into the bunkroom. No one bothered him, and he didn't respond to Frail Boy's cautious attempts to tell him about a fight between Zia and Fat Askim. Ahmed finally shooed Frail Boy away from the table. Clark noticed that Tattoo lurked nearby and wondered if he planned to fight Mohamed to regain his chair. He then considered whether Mohamed would want to fight him for revenge. Mohamed looked different. Clark couldn't describe it other than that the older man looked more relaxed. It was Mohamed's eyes, Clark realized - a lot of the old tension seemed to have gone.

After dinner, Clark watched as Ringo and Frail Boy sang and danced to the Rolling Stones. Frail Boy had no rhythm, but his energetic, frantic dance moves were amusing to watch. Mohamed sat on the edge of the shelf and watched, which he had never done before. He even seemed to smile as he followed Frail Boy's gyrations around the room.

Clark had not had any exercise for several days because of his intestinal problem and court, and he had a hard time falling asleep. Just as he started to doze off, he heard a loud noise in the hall. It sounded like the pots and pans that hung on the wall had crashed to the floor. Clark sat up and looked around the dark room. No one moved, and he wondered if he had been dreaming. He laid back down, and a minute later the whole shelf structure vibrated as someone stumbled into it. Clark sat up again and could now see a dark figure slowly collapse to the floor. No one else stirred, but Clark couldn't imagine that they hadn't felt the shock wave run through the wooden structure.

The figure lay motionless on the floor. Clark hesitated and then got up to investigate. He found Mohamed curled up in a ball. "Mohamed, are you okay?" No response. "What's wrong?" He tentatively shook Mohamed's shoulders. Then he shook harder as there was still no reaction. Just a deep sleep, Clark tried to tell himself, but he couldn't escape the feeling that the man's breathing wasn't right. It was slow, erratic, and very shallow, to the extent that it didn't seem like it could be very effective.

Clark went to Ahmed's spot, and after a pause to reconsider, shook him. "Ahmed, wake up, something's wrong with Mohamed." He pointed at the comatose man on the floor. "He might be sick, hasta, hasta bikin." He used the words that he had heard several people, including the medic, use with him when he had been sick.

Ahmed reluctantly got up and examined, poked at, spoke to, and shined his flashlight in Mohamed's face. No response. Ahmed shook his head and muttered something before he headed back to his place on the shelf.

"Are you just going to leave him there?"

Ahmed's only response was to shrug his shoulders.

Clark went to Mohamed's place on the shelf to get a blanket to put over him. As he pulled at the bedding, five or six prescription pill bottles rolled off and fell on the floor. Clark picked them up and took them to the window to try to get enough light to see what they were. It was clear that they were prescriptions, but they had different names on them. And they were all empty. He didn't want to face it, but it became obvious that Mohamed had probably taken all these pills, and the only explanation - he was trying to kill himself.

"Oh shit!" He rushed over to Ahmed and showed him the bottles. "We have to get a doctor. Mohamed is going to die. Morte!"

It appeared that Ahmed possibly understood, but he clearly didn't want to get involved. Clark couldn't comprehend or understand that and tried again. "Call the guards for help. The medic. We can't just let him die."

Ahmed shrugged again and turned away from him. Clark frantically looked around the shelves. Most of the other prisoners were now awake, but they also turned away.

Clark went to the window to the courtyard and yelled. "Help! Help! We need help. Morte! Morte!" He waited, sure that there would be a response from the guards. There had to be someone on duty during the night, although he had never seen or heard anyone. But no one appeared in the hallway. He shouted again, yelled as loud as he could. Nothing.

Something he had read in a novel, or seen in a film, told him that he had to keep Mohamed awake to keep him alive. He rushed over to the inert body and tried again to wake him. He shouted at him. He slapped his face several times, harder each time. No response. And he thought that Mohamed's breathing had gotten even slower and more shallow. But at least he was still breathing.

Clark grabbed him by the shoulders and tried to lift him up, but couldn't manage the man's dead weight. Then Clark began to pull him by the shoulders toward the hallway and the bathroom. The smell alone should have been enough to rouse anyone, but not Mohamed. Clark squatted and pulled Mohamed's head across his lap. He groped around in the dark room until he found the pitcher of water, which he poured over Mohamed's head. The man's body jerked in response, a reflex, but nothing more.

Clark took a deep breath and forced Mohamed's mouth open. He stuck his finger into the open mouth and had to pull it back quickly as Mohamed's involuntary reflex was to bite down. Clark grabbed Mohamed's jaw to keep it open as he again stuck his finger deep into his mouth and down his throat. No reaction at first, but then his finger hit the right spot, and Mohamed's body convulsed as he gagged and threw up a nasty mixture of dinner and drugs. Clark almost vomited himself as the odor hit him. He prayed that was enough because he couldn't stay in there, and he began to pull Mohamed back to the bunkroom.

Clark leaned Mohamed's body up against the wall and sat next to him, exhausted. He thought Mohamed's breathing had improved a little, but he still wouldn't wake up. Clark didn't want to, but he knew he had to get Mohamed up and keep him moving around. Twice he dropped the big man as he tried to lift him. Finally, he managed to get his shoulders under Mohamed's arm so he could shuffle around the room. At first he just dragged him, but after a while, Mohamed's feet began to move a little on their own, pure reflex but still alive.

Clark didn't know how long he walked, but eventually he knew he couldn't go another step. Just before he collapsed, he felt someone take Mohamed's other arm. Clark looked over to see Frail Boy, who give him a very nervous little smile. Together they kept Mohamed walking.

Early the next morning, Toad opened the door to the interior hallway and paused, confused because no one was there. Then he noticed the mess of pots and pans on the floor. Cautiously, he moved down the hallway and then peered into the bunkroom. All the prisoners were awake and sat on the shelves, staring at the corner of the room. Toad looked and saw three men collapsed on the floor, almost on top of each other. Before investigating, Toad yelled out for another guard, then he moved over and used his foot to poke at the figures. Clark, Frail Boy, and Mohamed barely stirred as Toad grabbed them and began to pull them apart. As another guard entered to help, Toad yelled at Ahmed to find out what had happened. Ahmed slowly got down and began to talk.

Clark jerked awake, disoriented, and then realized he was on the shelf, laying on top of his sleeping bag. His nightmare from the night before flooded back to him. It had to have been a dream. But his body ached and his head pounded. He struggled to sit up and look around. The room seemed empty, but then he saw a person on the lower shelf. Frail Boy slept in his spot in the center of the bottom shelf. It all flooded back to Clark, and he looked over at Mohamed's spot, but it was empty. He rushed out to the courtyard, where everyone milled around, almost normal but not quite. Mohamed's chair was unoccupied. Ahmed offered a cautious little smile as Clark collapsed on his chair and gratefully took the tea that Ahmed had waiting for him.

"Mohamed morte?" Clark asked softly and waited, afraid of the answer.

"Yok," Ahmed answered with a better smile. He made a pantomime of Mohamed being carried off. "Hastane," Ahmed said. It was a word that Clark recognized - hospital. He felt the tension release from his body, and he slumped back on his chair.

Clark would have preferred to go back to bed for the rest of the day but soon a guard appeared at the window. "Dus," he said.

As Clark moved down the hallways to the shower room, he glanced around for Toad but didn't see him.

The shower revived him, and he anticipated that it must be his parents who had come to see him because Mr. Ozturk had told him that they had agreed to return to America. He hadn't felt a need to say another good-bye, but evidently they did. But as he entered the office, the soldier indicated that he should go to the conference room and not the commandant's office. He heard voices, but they didn't belong to his parents or Joyce or Nigel. A little confused, he entered the room to find Mr. Ozturk huddled in a quiet but intense conversation with a heavy-set man with a bald head, who wore a suit that looked at least two sizes too small. It took them a moment before they realized that Clark had arrived. Mr. Ozturk introduced the man as Mr. Yilmaz, a representative and investigator in Turkey for the British insurance company that had issued the car insurance policy that Clark had purchased when he bought his car, and the rider he had added when he went to Ireland. They were going to take care of the car, and there was money for the dead man's family, but they were having a hard time tracking that down. They would also pay for Clark's legal bills, but only if it proved to be an accident.

"Mr. Yilmaz and I would like to take you out to the highway and have you show us what really happened and how this is incorrect," Mr. Ozturk said, as he pointed to a hand drawn diagram that looked like a copy of the chart used in the court by the prosecutor to show the position of the car and the dead man on the road.

As they walked out of the office, Mr. Ozturk told Clark that Mustafa had called him that morning to report that Clark's parents had gotten off safely for London. London? Clark wondered, why were they going to London?

"Are we going to get Nigel?" Clark asked as they approached the front gate.

"We didn't think that we needed him," Mr. Ozturk replied, "and I wasn't sure where to find him."

"Well, you sure know where to find me," Clark tried some humor but the lawyer didn't seem to get it.

Outside the prison gate, Laurel and Hardy waited in a police car and put Clark in the back seat. He had expected handcuffs, but evidently they forgot. No one paid any attention to the empty lot across the street from the prison where the farmer from the courtroom sat in the shade of an old stone wall that had once been part of a farm house, abandoned long ago because it was considered bad luck to live near a prison. There were a few other people scattered around the lot, using the wall and some scrub trees for shade.

Out on the highway at the accident scene, Clark showed the men where the car had been and how they had moved it off the road after the accident. He remembered the rough measurement he had made during the visit with the group from the court. Mr. Yilmaz made extensive notes and took some photographs, while Mr. Ozturk sketched in new positions on the diagram.

"How many people did you say were here that night?" Mr. Ozturk asked Clark.

"It seemed like a mob but maybe five or six, all men and one woman who screamed really loud." It seemed so long ago to Clark - almost another life.

"We'll try to find them, to see if they remember seeing the car before you moved it."

"Maybe Man-in-Black knows who they were." Clark noticed that Mr. Ozturk looked confused. "That's what I call the cop that showed up that night. They didn't wear uniforms and were dressed all in black. We thought they might be some sort of vigilantes come to kill us."

"There are such people, so you were lucky they were not," Mr. Yilmaz interjected.

Later, as they stood in front of the prison gate and waited for it to open, Clark noticed the lot across the street where there were now more people, including the farmer. "What are they doing over there?" he asked Mr. Ozturk.

"They are families of people in the prison, waiting to visit. It must be a visiting day. The guards will only let in a few people at a time."

Clark nodded. Some of the prisoners in his cellblock did have visitors from time to time. They had to talk through the window, as he had to do with Nigel. It struck him how unusual it must appear to everyone that his visitors got to use the conference room or even the commandant's office.

Mr. Ozturk looked carefully at Clark as the gate opened. He had noticed how tired Clark looked. "I heard from the judge's person this morning that we are on the calendar for June 13. That is less than thirty days. Are you okay until then?"

Clark absorbed the news, not fully processing it, not really wanting to focus on a particular date and how long it would be. He nodded slowly and stepped through the gate.

CHAPTER 27

It took Clark several days, but he finally got back into a routine that helped pass the time and suppress most thoughts of anything outside the prison walls. Mohamed had not returned, but the scuttlebutt was clear that he had survived and would soon be back. Toad and another guard had thoroughly searched the bunkroom and everyone's belongings for pills of any kind. Prisoners with valid prescriptions now had to get their medication from the army medic. The search had also uncovered three knives - two belonging to Wolf Eyes and the other to Bookmaker. Clark figured the Bookmaker might need protection, and he was relieved that Wolf Eyes no longer had any weapons.

Clark had just finished exercising and sat at the table trying to relax and let his body temperature come down. He had always been someone who perspired easily and his t-shirt was drenched. He would put on a dry one but not for a while, not until his body cooled off. Several weeks ago, he had been surprised to discover, at Ahmed's insistence, that the hot tea actually helped his body regulate its temperature.

No Hair stood by the window to the hallway and turned to Clark. "London," he said, as he motioned Clark over.

Clark hesitated for a moment. Nigel hadn't been to visit in a while, and Clark didn't really have any desire to see him, but that must be who it was in the hallway. Joyce and anyone else always got to meet him in the office. Slowly, somewhat reluctantly, Clark rose and walked to the window. As he approached, he looked out into the hallway, expecting to see Nigel.

No Hair stepped back from the window and the person he talked to. But it wasn't Nigel. The farmer stood there and stared blankly into the cellblock at Clark.

Toad had heard that Clark had a visitor that no one knew and thought it strange - strange enough to check it out. Halfway down the hall, he saw the farmer reach into his coat pocket and pull out an old revolver.

Clark had now reached the window and still looked for Nigel, not focusing on the farmer. As he looked around he saw the farmer raise his hand with the gun. It didn't register immediately because it was so unexpected, but then he could tell that it was aimed at him.

Toad flung his body forward and crashed into the farmer just as the gun fired.

Clark saw the flame from the gun barrel, heard the sound of the explosion, and felt a terrible punch to his body that spun him around and knocked him to the ground. A hot pain burned in his left side and quickly grew in intensity. He reached down and felt his wet t-shirt, and when he pulled his hand away, it wasn't covered in perspiration, but with blood. Oh fuck, was the first thing that went through his mind. Then he discovered that he couldn't handle the sight of his own blood, and his body shut down. Already on the ground, his head didn't have far to fall, as his eyes rolled back, and he lost consciousness.

This is so goddamn unfair, Clark thought, as he explored the darkness around him and desperately fought his fear. He couldn't believe that he had been killed as revenge for something that he hadn't done. And that had to have been what happened, who that person was, a relative of the dead man. Another and final ignominy caused by the curse of the nice guy. How many times had it backfired on him - not taking advantage of vulnerable girlfriends, dating Cynna, sex with Gwen, not pursuing Bernadette, and Nigel's driving. Images of all these people and more floated around him, whispers of light, fleeting. He wanted to reach out to them, but his arms were too heavy to move. At least there's no pain, he realized. But how am I moving? he wondered, before he realized that maybe he wasn't. He was floating, suspended somehow, like in the ocean but not wet. Limbo? Purgatory? Certainly not how I want to spend eternity, he told himself. Achingly tired, he wanted to sleep but feared that maybe he shouldn't. What if there really was a gate and an angel as some sort of gatekeeper. He certainly didn't want to be sound asleep and just drift past it, losing his chance for all eternity. But it was hard to stay awake in the dark. He tried to control the images but couldn't. That made him mad and that was better than being afraid.

Did it just get lighter? The images were gone and he searched the darkness that now seemed not as black but more like a deep gray. Then he heard someone, far in the distance, say his name. Is that Joyce? The voice was very faint and had a deep hollow echo. The grayness lightened a little more, and he now sensed a dim shadow moving, changing the intensity of the gray light that hit his closed eyelids. Was that really her and what was she doing in Purgatory? He wanted to see her, ask her, but he couldn't open his eyes. He tried to call out but couldn't get his mouth to work. Nothing seemed to work physically except he could hear, so he listened.

He heard urgency in Joyce's voice as she spoke in Turkish. She must be the shadow. There came a response from a male voice, and he heard, recognized, one English word - sedation.

Sedation. Drugs. Oh, thank God! Clark rejoiced without being able to express it in any way. Maybe he wasn't dead, and that Joyce was really there. That allowed him to relax, and he fell back under the drugs and his exhaustion. This time the darkness didn't scare him quite as much.

Clark recognized Nigel's voice. "I'm sorry, but I just couldn't stay in that room. That's where they were." Then Joyce's voice. "That's okay, there was nothing you could do anyway." Clark thought that maybe he could open his eyes if he wanted to, but he kept them closed and listened.

"You can go home," Nigel said. "I'll stay with him."

"I'm okay, but you look terrible why don't you go get some sleep?"

A door closed. Silence, but he could hear her breathing. Slowly Clark opened his eyes just enough to see a room, a small hospital room, and Joyce sat on a chair next to the bed. She appeared to be asleep. His eyes now opened a little more. He wanted to look around but his head wouldn't cooperate. He could move his eyes, so cautiously he glanced around and the first thing he noticed was a window and the darkness outside. The next thing he noticed were the steel bars on the window. Now he managed to turn his head slightly the other way and saw a door to the room. It was closed, and a small observation window in the door also had bars across it.

Suddenly, he desperately had to use the bathroom. He wanted to sit up but couldn't, he was too weak. He fought it, but the simple exertion caused him to pass out again.

The next time he woke he was alone in the room, and daylight streamed in through the window. Then he remembered having had to pee and steeled himself that he must have wet the bed.

But it all seemed dry. Then he noticed a strange sensation in his penis, and he cautiously reached down to feel a tube stuck up in there that led to a bag that hung off the bed, full of yellow fluid. Interesting but gross, he thought, and then wondered why the tube stuck up his penis didn't hurt like crazy. That's when he noticed a metal pole next to the bed with two other bags hanging on it, each with a tube that led to one of two needles that were stuck into his arm and secured with tape. Those should hurt also, he realized. The last thing he felt before he passed out again was the tape on his stomach that pulled at his skin but not at his hair. Where's my hair? he wondered, as the darkness enveloped him again.

The pain and the voices woke him the next time.

"Practice English yes?"

Clark recognized Dr. Ataman's voice and then Joyce's.

"Of course."

"I cut morphine will feel pain now, but necessary to get not added to the drug."

"I think you mean not get addicted. Is it all right if I stay here for a while?"

"Okay with police, okay with me," the doctor responded. "Doing well, but…"

"But what?"

"Heart is fine, strong, but other signs weak."

"I saw him a little while ago, and he was exhausted. They fight in that prison you know."

"Yes, I see results. But is what you say ironing, no?"

"I'm not sure what you mean."

"Days ago, this other prisoner, made to kill himself with pills. Alive only because one prisoner save him, made sick, kept awake all night guards sleep and all other prisoners afraid get involved."

"Is he all right?"

"Yes, back prison two days before… make room open for this one. This same one is one who saves him. And he saves by other one's cousin, prison guard."

"Clark's the one who saved that other prisoner?"

"Yes. Moral debts seem go many ways."

Clark struggled to process this information - had he followed that correctly? Toad had saved him, and he was Mohamed's cousin?

He heard someone, he thought Joyce, move around, maybe over to the window. He didn't want them to know that he was awake.

"What do you know about him"

"This one, not much, bad luck you Americans say. Why?"

"Oh I don't know. He drives negligently, hits those men and then tried to drive off. He fights in the prison and seems to enjoy it. Then he saves someone. Does that make any sense to you? It doesn't to me?"

"May you like him?"

"I guess I do, that's the strange thing. I don't know why or if I should."

"Simple doctor not head doctor, but possible you think too much."

It was quiet for a moment and then Clark heard the door open and close. He decided to wait for a few minutes before waking up to talk to Joyce, but instead he fell back asleep.

Clark opened his eyes. It was dark, and he appeared to be alone in the hospital room. The only light came from the small observation window in the door. He still had pain, but it felt manageable, and he tried to pull himself up to a sitting position. He immediately found that he couldn't use his stomach muscles. When he tried to tighten his core, it hurt like crazy. So he relied on his arms and felt good when he finally managed to rest his back against the metal bed frame. But that didn't last. The bedframe dug into his back, and the pain from his wound screamed at him and his back ached like crazy. So he slowly lowered himself back down and then collapsed, exhausted, and slept again.

Clark felt someone tug at his bandages. He winced in pain as the adhesive tore at his new hair. He eyes flew open to see Dr. Ataman.

"Sorry. Much hair. Have to change dressing. You manage? I increase pain killer?" Dr. Ataman asked, as he motioned to the bags on the pole next to the bed.

Clark shook his head. "No, I'm okay, just do it quickly. Slow is bad." Clark knew that from experience. But the doctor had used a really strong adhesive, and Clark couldn't help let out a yelp of pain as the doctor pulled it off.

The doctor removed the dressing from the wound and Clark saw very little blood on it. He debated whether he wanted to look but then had to. There was a surprisingly small wound with tight stitches. The doctor saw him look.

"Not big, bigger on back bullet came out."

Clark hadn't thought of that and now realized where the pain in his back came from.

After the doctor finished with the wound on Clark's back, he checked his vitals and seemed pleased. "You better. Are hungry?"

"Starved." Clark suddenly realized.

"I bring some food."

"Don't you have a nurse or someone who can do it? I know you're busy." The doctor gave him a weary look, but didn't say anything.

Clark had almost finished his lunch when he heard the door open and looked up to see Joyce enter. Hardy stood guard in the hallway.

Joyce smiled. "Well, you're awake. How do you feel?"

"Like I've been shot." Sheepish smile.

"Well that's appropriate I guess." Cautious smile.

"But I need coffee."

"I'll ask the doctor."

"He already said no," Clark confessed.

"Well, here, pretend," she teased, as she handed him the cup of water from the tray on the small bedside table.

He sipped his water as he watched her pull the chair into the place where she sat before. He thought it had been the previous night, but he wasn't sure.

"I guess I've been a bit out of it."

She nodded with a smile. "Just a little."

"So how long has it been, have I been here since, you know?"

"It's been almost three days."

That took him by surprise. He thought he'd been aware of a lot, but he had obviously missed a lot more. "Wow, that's a…" He paused, not sure what he meant. His brain still felt a little fuzzy.

A commotion in the hallway diverted their attention. Someone talked fast and loud. Joyce went to the door to investigate and then tapped on it to get Hardy's attention. The door opened to allow Nigel to enter.

"Bloody hell, he sure takes his job seriously. You'd think he'd know me by now," Nigel said, as he looked over at Clark. "Well mate, you're looking good. How do you feel?"

Clark gave Joyce a quick glance, but didn't bother to use his same line. "Okay, been better."

"Has the doc been around," Nigel asked Joyce.

"I haven't seen him since last night."

Nigel squirmed a little. “Oh, I didn’t know you were here last night. I could have joined you.”

Joyce just smiled and turned back to face Clark.

Nigel looked around, but didn’t see another chair so he stood uneasily. “I finally got a call in to Mustafa this morning to tell him what happened. He’s going to call your parents.”

“What! Why the hell did you do that?” Clark yelled, and would have leapt out of bed and strangled Nigel, except it hurt too much and he still had the IV needles in his arm. “Call him back right now and tell him he can’t call them!”

“I thought you’d want -”

“Stop thinking and do it. God damn it Nigel, how do you think they’ll feel knowing that they left, and I get shot? Go ask the doctor to use his phone.”

Nigel backed quickly to the door and pounded on it. Hardy looked exasperated as Nigel rushed past him.

Clark looked at Joyce who looked concerned, unhappy. “Do you think I’m wrong?” he asked, challenged.

“Oh, no you’re right about your parents, but you could have been easier on Nigel. He’s been loyal to you all this time. He’s stayed here, even though his father has been pressuring him to come home. Somehow he got the British Embassy to agree to issue Nigel a new passport.”

Clark was unable to respond to all that, so he just stared out the window.

Clark held his breath and grimaced as Dr. Ataman prepared to pull the adhesive tape. The doctor had tried to vary the places he put it, but by now all the skin around the wound was bright red.

“Looks good. Use smaller bandaging today.”

“No sign of infection anywhere?” Clark asked.

“Sound disappointment?”

"I know where I'll have to go as soon as I'm better."

The doctor nodded slightly. "Well, will see." Then to change the subject, he asked, "Miss Edwards here today?"

Clark shook his head. "What do you know about her," he asked cautiously.

The doctor smiled. "Well, not much. Very hard for woman like her. Not married. Looks good. Many traditional people who not approve, refuse children education. She has be strong but quiet, modesty so survive. Not sure it good that she here so many times, alone."

Clark looked quizzically at the doctor, he vaguely remembered Joyce being there a lot.

"She here every minutes you were surgery and later. Many, many hours. I assure her you safe, then her go home."

Clark had just begun to eat dinner when the door opened. He looked up eager to see Joyce, but it was Nigel. He tried to hide his disappointment.

"Hey, that looks good." Nigel had seen Clark's disappointment and wanted to get past it.

"Yeah, a lot better than I've had the past seven weeks"

"Trust me, the food out there isn't that much better, not like that anyway"

"Joyce told me that the doctor's wife makes it."

"Has she been here lately?"

"The doctor's wife?"

"No, you twit, Joyce." Nigel was seldom comfortable with Clark's sense of humor, but he tried to keep positive.

"Don't you see her at school, helping her?"

"No, not anymore. Some of the parents complained. It does get bloody boring I'll tell you." Nigel stopped as he recalled the cuts, bruises, abrasions and now gunshot wound on Clark.

"Happy to switch places, any time."

Nigel stared at the window. "Believe me, if I could, I would trade places." He seemed to be on the verge of tears, and Clark now felt bad. After all, it had been his decision. Nigel hadn't asked him to do it.

Now night, the room was dark except for the small lamp on the table next to the bed. Clark sat up in bed and wrote on some paper that the doctor had given him. Not a letter but an outlet for a flood of emotions that he couldn't contain now that he been away from the prison for almost a week. He tried to address his feelings for Gwen and the baby. He had no idea whether she would want to keep it. She seemed so much like a woman who wouldn't want to be tied down to a kid. He knew that she probably wouldn't consider his desires, and anyway, he couldn't say for sure what they were. She didn't seem to want him around, but he admitted that he had run away. He didn't believe enough in a supreme power to think that he was being punished in some way, but there had to be some seriously messed up karma at work. And then there were his feelings for Bernadette, and he knew that he had to force her back into the friend category. He worked on the rough beginning of a poem and then fell asleep with the papers on his lap.

He woke up hours later, just as the dawn began to illuminate the world outside the window. He saw Joyce, who sat on the chair, which she had pulled over to the window. She had his papers and was reading them. His first impulse was to yell at her to stop, but he caught himself. Instead he made a little coughing noise in as non-threatening and non-judgmental way as he could. But even then it startled her, and she jumped off the chair. The papers scattered across the floor.

"Oh my god, Clark, I'm so sorry. I don't know why, I would never, but I glanced at them when I helped you get comfortable. I read a little bit, and then I just couldn't stop." She appeared to be on the verge of tears as she scrambled to pick up the papers.

He couldn't let it go that far. "Joyce, Joyce, it's okay really. I'm not upset." He vaguely remembered her helping him straighten out and get comfortable, after he had fallen asleep. Then it hit him. "What were you doing here then? It must have been…"

"A little after four in the morning," she finished for him. "I couldn't sleep, and I don't know, I just feel safe here. Strange huh. Maybe it's the twenty-four-hour guard," she said, and tried to laugh.

"Is it Laurel or Hardy?"

"Laurel, he understands better than Hardy." Now she started to relax as she pulled the chair next to the bed. "He won't go run and report to the local Imam. I hope you don't mind me using your hospital room as a refuge."

"No, I feel the same way about it."

They sat in silence for a while. Then she remembered and reached into her bag and pulled out a small paper bag, which she handed to Clark. He raised his eyebrows but didn't say anything as he opened the bag and pulled out a set of worry beads. They were much nicer than the ones he had in the prison.

"They're nice, thanks." He hoped that his eyes didn't contradict his smile. It was a simple gift but also felt very personal. He put them in his left hand, and his fingers quickly found the rhythm.

It made her happy to watch him. "I've just never gotten the hang of that." Finally, she had to ask, "Do you love them?"

He almost made a bad joke that yes he loved the beads, but she looked so conflicted, so uneasy, that he didn't say anything.

That made her fidget even more, and he felt bad and had to answer. "I don't know. They were both friends and then ... something else.

"What happened?"

"It's complicated." Clark stared at the bars on the windows and knew that this was dangerous territory. "I don't really want to talk about it."

"Okay. Do you want to talk about anything?"

"I don't know."

"Do you want me to go," she asked, as she tried to find a guideline to help her. She didn't have a lot of experience with men and certainly none as complicated, as difficult, as this one.

"No, but you can if you want to."

"No, I want to talk, actually."

"Okay." He smiled, happy with that.

She wanted to remind him that talking was normally a two-way proposition, but she decided to take what she could get for now. "I've been here over two years, and it's very lonely. I don't mind being by myself, that's not it. But I do miss talking to someone, someone who can understand more than just the words, but who also gets the subtleties, the context. Another American. Not a Brit," she added with a careful smile.

Clark watched her carefully as she described the Peace Corps meeting three times a year in Ankara and her need for that contact. Clark had always been a good listener, and he didn't have to try hard with Joyce because she was eager to talk. She told him about her childhood in Virginia, growing up in the same house her whole life. The stability. Her father had taught science at the high school and her mother ran a day care center.

"Your mother told me a little about how you grew up, and I don't know how you did it. I would have hated it, moving every year, all those different schools."

"You get used to it; we had no choice. Where did you go to college?" he asked, to put the conversation back on her.

"Oh, Northwestern in Chicago, pre-med," she answered, but without enthusiasm. Her mind seemed to wander to another place, another time, and it wasn't happy. "My dad died my freshman year, heart attack, and well, I guess I sort of lost my way for a while. I was young, only eighteen."

"I'm so sorry about your dad."

Another period of quiet. "My dad was so important to me that I tried to replace him with this, this professor who… well truth be told, the shit took advantage of me. I was vulnerable and a virgin. We had a sordid affair, and when his wife found out, she made life unbearable for me, and I dropped out."

Clark hesitated but then followed an instinct to reach out to her, he took her hand. "That's…"

"Yeah, exactly," she agreed with a bitter laugh when it became obvious that he couldn't complete his thought. She sensed what he wanted to say - compassion was clearly written on his face. "So I finished at a local college, George Mason, where I found that I have a strong facility for languages, and then joined the Peace Corp. So I guess I ran away also," she said, as she indicated his papers. "And this town is my prison even though there aren't any bars."

He nodded, and they sat there in silence for a while.

"Can I ask you a question?"

"What?" he replied, and hoped that he hadn't sounded too defensive. He squeezed her hand to counter it if he had.

"I know that you've managed to pick up some of the language, more than just the slang," she teased him. "But it seems like you've been able to communicate very well without the language, well enough to survive, if not even to thrive in a weird way."

He laughed. "Yeah, it's like I'm the first chair in the orchestra." He noticed her confusion. "I'm not sure I can explain it. We're not discussing existential philosophy in there. It's personal conditions, needs, and most of those are physical and not too hard to pantomime. I don't know most of their names, but I have my names for them - mostly based on appearance. And they call me London because on the first day I mentioned that I lived in London, and it was a word that was familiar to them. And then eventually it became almost normal, and I can sense some of their emotions and feelings. Not all of them for sure, but many of them."

"I guess emotions and feelings are pretty universal," Joyce added, and gave him a very warm smile, squeezed his hand, trying to solidify a connection.

Clark felt it and tried to categorize it - friend? More than a friend? All the emotions he had bottled up and corked for almost two months threatened to explode. He felt this terrible need to hug her, kiss her. But then he focused on the bars on the window, on the door, and reality hit him, and alarm bells resounded through his head. No way could he go back to the prison and survive with that sort of feeling for her. He had to push it away, deny it, kill it. Abruptly he dropped her hand and went to the window, stared out at the parking lot and the street beyond. The real world was out there, and it sucked.

Joyce came over and put her hand on his shoulder, but he shrugged it off. She started to speak, to ask him what was wrong, but the hard, cold, look on his face stopped her. Embarrassed and uncomfortable that she had opened up, she turned and left.

The door to the room slammed shut, and with it Clark tried to close a door inside that he knew he had to keep locked. He took his papers and torn them until they were small and unreadable. Then he sat on the chair and stared out at the coming day. Occasionally a car or truck passed on the road, but it was still mostly quiet. He used the worry beads that Joyce had given him, but suddenly he stopped and in a fit of emotional frustration pulled the string until it began to cut into his hand. And then the string broke, scattering the beads across the hard linoleum floor.

CHAPTER 28

Mustafa stepped back from the partially open door to Clark's hospital room and faced Nigel and Joyce who stood with him in the hallway. "It appears that he is asleep. I must go soon, so you will have to report to him what the judge said to me."

"But I just can't believe it. It's so, so..." Nigel had the words, but he wasn't sure he should use them around the lawyer, Joyce, and Hardy, who sat near the door and seemed disinterested, but maybe wasn't.

"The judge is firm on this. A few years ago they had a similar case that involved an American soldier from the base in Izmir, who was on leave and had an accident on this road. The judge gave him bail, and the U.S. Army promptly flew him out of the country."

"But to have to stay here for ... how long will this bloody thing take?" Nigel asked, as his voice rose, no longer concerned about who heard.

"To get the percent of negligence down to an acceptable level, it could take six months to a year. The court would no longer make it a priority if Clark is on bail. Their docket is very full."

"Oh, hell no, I'm not staying in this bloody country for a year."

"It's not you that they're worried about," Clark shouted from his room.

They entered the room as Clark struggled to sit up on the side of the bed. He had slept poorly and his back wound throbbed with a dull pain.

Joyce approached him to help, but he abruptly waved her away. She tried to keep the hurt from her face and hoped that no one noticed. Nigel didn't, but Mustafa did.

"So they'll give me bail," Clark summarized what he had overheard. "But I have to remain in the country for the trial to finish."

Mustafa nodded. "It's the best I can do at the moment. I cannot guarantee even that, but the judge is now concerned about your safety. He has not decided, however, whether you are safer inside the prison or outside."

"Well, clearly inside isn't that safe," Joyce observed caustically.

"What about now, until the next court date?" Clark asked.

"It will be up to the doctor. If he says that you should stay here, the judge will listen," Mustafa added carefully.

"Won't he do that?" Clark struggled with what he knew was likely false hope.

Joyce offered cautiously, "He's under a lot of pressure."

"What kind of pressure?" Nigel questioned.

"Let's just say that not everyone, or maybe not even most people in town are happy that Clark survived."

Clark looked away to consider that.

"The next court date is in approximately twenty days, and my guess is that you will have to return to the prison for some or maybe most of that time. And then we will see, we will hope for the best," Mustafa concluded, and then turned to leave. "I will be back in a few days."

Clark watched Mustafa leave. Then he glanced at Joyce and Nigel who stood nervously and waited for him to do or say something. Unable to deal with any of it, he plopped back on the bed, turned on his side with his back to them, and pulled the sheet up over his head.

Tempted to call him out on his childish behavior, Joyce thought better of it. As she turned to leave, she noticed the broken string and a few of the worry beads on the bedside table.

There was a pretty sunset out the window, but Clark refused to notice. He focused on Dr. Ataman as he checked the stitches and rubbed the wound with disinfectant. Then the doctor moved to the stitches in the larger exit wound. That area was more tender, and Clark couldn't help but wince a little.

"Sorry," the doctor said. "A little redness here keep an eyes on. You take antibiotics?"

"Yes." Clark nodded as he replied. "How come you're the only person I see? Don't you have any other help here, another doctor, nurses?"

"No another doctor. Have nurses, but they …"

Clark waited for him to continue.

"Feel uncomfortably here."

"Because of me?"

The doctor nodded but clearly didn't want to continue that line of conversation. "Will be scars but little one here." He motioned to the front wound as he put a fresh bandage on it.

"Does that mean you will release me soon?"

"Very small town," the doctor spoke slowly, carefully. "Many people cannot read write. Farmers. Simple peoples. Religious peoples. Enjoys distract in lives, but soon, soon go back to what they used to. So take in or … drive it away."

"Or kill it," Clark added, and watched the doctor nod, a very slight motion, but enough.

"Is means to survive. Do you understand?"

"Better than you can imagine."

Clark had shed his hospital gown for real clothes, retrieved from the prison by Mr. Ozturk. He stood by the window, stared out without seeing. He was frustrated, bored and anxious. In many ways this small room had become more oppressive than the prison. He heard but didn't react to the sound of the door as it opened. Nor did he react as Joyce came to stand next to him - not close, but closer than he wanted.

"Maybe I can get Laurel to let you go for a walk around," she offered.

"I'm good."

"I brought you a simit," she continued, holding out a small paper bag. "It's a breakfast pastry with sesame seeds. I could try to get you some coffee."

"You don't have to wait on me."

"What's wrong with you?"

"Nothing."

"Why can't you just talk to me like a normal person?"

"I can't."

"Clark, you seem like… I think you're basically a nice guy, but why can't you just relax? You did the other day."

"I just can't, that's all. If you don't like it, then …" His voice was cold, distant, but not angry.

Joyce took a deep breath and considered what to do. They had connected, and even if it had only been for a moment, she didn't want to give up that easily. But the tension in his body was palpable, and so she finally turned and left. As she entered the hallway she encountered Mr. Ozturk, who smiled like he had positive news, so she paused as he went in to see Clark, and she listened.

Clark had started to pace across the room and didn't stop when Mr. Ozturk entered and began to speak. Neither of them noticed that the door hadn't shut completely.

"The judge has confirmed the schedule for June, and I'm hopeful that things are favorable for your bail. But I don't want to get your hopes up too far."

"Yeah, no more of that." Clark's sarcasm was either lost on Mr. Ozturk or he ignored it. He noticed that the lawyer seemed to be very intent on something so he stopped to listen.

Mr. Ozturk continued, "I also spoke with the doctor, and he will release you tomorrow to go back to the prison until the court date."

"I figured that was coming."

"Can you manage that?"

"What choice do I have? I'll survive."

The lawyer chose his words carefully. "I know it's difficult, but you have done very well so far. You surprised many people."

"Including myself." Clark's attention seemed to drift off somewhere. "When I entered that cell for the first time, all the people, the noise, smells, something inside me changed, switched, like an on/off light switch. I knew, without thinking, without any real decision, that I would do whatever it took to survive. I would live by their rules."

"Living by their rules would not have saved the prisoner Mohamed."

"No? Maybe not."

"I was in the army for two years. All of us have to do compulsory military service. And almost didn't survive because I didn't have that switch of yours, or at least I couldn't find it. But at least you have gotten away from it for a little while."

"That's not really a positive," Clark responded almost vehemently. "I switched back and allowed myself to begin to feel something for someone. And now I don't know if I can do it again. What if I can't find that switch this time? I've been trying for days now but …"

In the hallway, Joyce smiled, but was also on the verge of tears. She had to walk away before Laurel noticed or Mr. Ozturk emerged.

In the room, Mr. Ozturk now used a conspiratorial whisper. "Well, here is the most important thing. We have petitioned the judge to give you bail and your passport. Now, if he does that, and if he sets the bail at a high level, then that will be a signal to us that it is okay for you to leave the country."

That got Clark's attention. "How would I do that?"

"Leave that to Mustafa."

The next day outside the hospital, an empty police car idled as Clark emerged with Laurel and Hardy as escorts. Joyce and Nigel stood to the side and watched. Just as Clark got to the car, Joyce came over and handed him a small book. With as much disinterest as he could muster, he looked at it - an English/Turkish dictionary. A very quiet, "Thanks," and a small nod of his head was all he offered before he stepped into the police car. Laurel closed the door behind him.

As the police car drove onto the main street headed for the prison, Nigel noticed the intense emotion on Joyce's face. "Are you okay?"

"He just makes me so furious."

"Join the club."

"For a moment the other day I thought we were getting close, beginning to communicate. Then ..." She noticed Nigel's curious look. "I'm sorry, I know that I shouldn't let it bother me. I hate what he did, yet somehow I ..."

Nigel didn't realize what she referred to. "What did he do?"

"The accident," she replied, incredulous that Nigel didn't get it. "He had to have been negligent. And then he tried to leave."

Nigel now shifted nervously and looked down at his feet.

"But then he saves that man. And all those fights, and he seems to actually enjoy it." She couldn't stand still any longer, she had promised herself not to cry. "I've got to go. I'm sorry."

As he watched her leave, he debated, then knew what he had to do. "Joyce, wait. Can we go somewhere private and talk?"

A hush fell over the crowd that had gathered at the entrance to the main prison building. Clark approached with the sergeant and nodded to Toad who waited for him. The quiet continued down the hallways to the cellblock. All the prisoners had stopped whatever they had been doing when news of Clark's arrival raced ahead through the building. Anticipation, tension filled the air. Clark could feel it, and it put him all the more on edge, a keg of blasting powder ready to explode.

As he entered the courtyard, he looked around at all the familiar faces. Not friends and not enemies. He stood still, not sure what to do. "London!" Frail Boy broke the silence in a loud, very positive tone. A shout, "London," followed from most of the others, who then immediately went back to whatever they had been doing before. The courtyard quickly fell back into its familiar rhythm.

Clark approached the table and his empty chair. Mohamed sat and read his Koran as if nothing had changed, but he did then look up as Clark sat. And as their eyes met, he gave him a barely perceptible nod of his head, which Clark returned.

Ahmed began a stream of talk, gesturing around at various people, and that allowed Clark to sit quietly and begin to try to find his prison groove. He had done it before, but he couldn't remember how. So much then had been driven by the fear of the unknown, a fear that had had so many levels. He tried to convince himself that things were different now. He was the champion of the cell. He had a seat at the table. He didn't have to fight. He looked around, and the faces that had been so terrifying the first time were now just men that he knew on some level. He saw Frail Boy lurking nearby, so he smiled at him and was rewarded with a huge grin. I can do this, he thought, and felt his body slowly begin to relax.

CHAPTER 29

For the next twenty-three days, Clark struggled not to obsess over the approaching court date. The date got pushed back twice for unknown reasons, and he managed to not get upset. The routine of the cell with its mind-numbing sameness helped the time flow by. Clark tried, mostly successfully, to keep from thinking of home, his parents, Gwen, Bernadette, Joyce, or anyone, or anything outside the stone walls of the prison.

He made it known through Mr. Ozturk that he wanted no visitors other than the lawyers. The only exception had been Mr. Yilmaz, the insurance man, who informed him that the insurance would not pay for his legal fees and living expenses in Turkey unless his percentage of negligence was determined to be less than twenty percent.

Mustafa made a big production, during one visit in the commandant's office, when he brought brochures from the University of Istanbul and had Clark signed an application form. "A mere formality," he said, because he had already secured spots for them when the new term began in the fall. It was during that visit that Mustafa said to him, "I don't know if you get any news in here, but I believe that you and Mr. Barrington were headed for Israel."

Clark tensed, "Oh sure, we had to go through there to get to Egypt and Tunisia."

Mustafa gave him a curious look, and Clark had a strong feeling that he somehow knew about Nigel, his religion and his intentions. "Yes, of course, but good thing that you aren't there now, a war broke out three days ago. It's bad, but Israel seems to be on the verge of a very quick and decisive victory. It's almost like they welcomed it." Clark couldn't figure out what to say so he just nodded and tried to forget it.

Clark amassed a group of seven or eight prisoners who followed his daily exercise routine, and engaged in spirited, and occasionally violent, challenges of strength - arm wrestling being everyone's favorite. The prisoners still wrestled, but Clark also instituted a new challenge ladder with a game that he remembered from his childhood. Two men stood with their right feet touching and planted on the floor, and they then tried to use their hands and bodies to force the other to move that foot. The left foot could move, but if the right foot moved other than to pivot in place, then that person lost. It quickly got aggressive, and Tattoo climbed the ladder and emerged as the undisputed champion of the cell. Clark then convinced Toad to find another chair to put at the table for Tattoo. He wasn't sure, but it was possible that Ahmed had paid for it.

Clark spent a lot of time with Frail Boy and the dictionary that Joyce had given him. His motivation to learn Turkish paled beside Frail Boy's eagerness to learn English. Frail Boy could be released in another two years, and he assumed that speaking English would be a valuable skill. Clark knew that if he got bail he would leave the dictionary for Frail Boy.

The first time they had a group shower, Clark was amused to notice that the others discretely checked out his scars. He really was one of the guys now.

On the day the trial resumed, Clark had a shower but refused a shave. His beard had grown in and he didn't want to make any special deal about the day because he didn't want to get his hopes up. He didn't pack anything or prepare anything. He did nothing that would indicate an assumption that he would get anything other than the total frustration that he had experienced every other time he had put a foot in that courtroom. Other than a look from Ahmed and an unexpected handshake from Mohamed, the others cooperated to make it an ordinary, nothing special day.

Laurel and Hardy picked him up at the entrance to the prison and transported him in a police car. He assumed that for security reasons there was to be no little parade to the court.

The courtroom was almost empty when Clark entered. Mr. Ozturk had requested to be the last case for the day. They wanted to do everything they could to allow attention on the case to subside, to ease the pressure on the judge.

For the first time since leaving the hospital, Clark saw Joyce. She sat with Mr. Ozturk at the defense table. And Nigel was in his normal spot on the bench behind the railing. They both gave him a cautious smile as he approached and sat.

The district judge had stepped out of the room after the last case, and so they waited. Clark stared straight ahead. In the past he had appreciated the wait, but this time it felt like torture.

The district judge came quietly into the room and everyone stood up. The judge held a piece of paper in his hand as he sat, and he immediately began to read.

Clark watched the prosecutor and thought he saw him grimace. That was probably good. Then he looked at Mr. Ozturk, who struggled to keep his face passive. Finally, he could no longer contain himself and turned to Joyce. "What's he saying?"

She motioned for him to hush while she listened some more, then she turned to him with a tight, compressed smile. "The judge reviewed the facts of the case so far and has decided to give you bail."

Clark struggled to contain his feeling of relief. But there remained another, more important, piece to this puzzle. The judge called the prosecutor and Mr. Ozturk to his table. Clark turned back to Joyce. "How much is the bail?"

"Forty-five thousand lira. My God, that's an awful lot, almost five-thousand US dollars."

Clark knew the larger the better. He held his breath as the district judge left the room, and Mr. Ozturk returned to the defense table with some typed legal papers. Clark couldn't read his poker face.

"The judge has agreed to the conditions that you will remain in Turkey for the rest of the trial. But he has also agreed to give you your passports. Mustafa has wired the money to the court. You must sign these papers, and then you can go." As the lawyer finished, he could no longer keep the smile from his face or the excitement from his voice.

Clark glanced at the documents. They were in Turkish, but he did notice one signature of the several that had already been made at the bottom. "What's Streeter's signature doing here?"

"Vice Consul Streeter has officially guaranteed that you will remain in the country under the auspices of the U.S. Consul in Istanbul," Mr. Ozturk explained.

"Guaranteed?" Clark asked. "How?"

"I do not know. Mustafa worked that out as part of the deal with the judge. Please just sign so we can go."

Clark pushed away his feelings for Streeter and eagerly signed all four copies of the document. Then he jumped to his feet but had to pause because the emotional release had suddenly sapped all his strength. His body wavered. Joyce took his arm and whispered in his ear, "I know the truth about what really happened. I'm so sorry that I thought you could -"

Mr. Ozturk interrupted her. "We must go," he said, as he pushed them out of the courtroom and into the hallway. Mr.

Ozturk then left them to take the papers to the court clerk. He returned in a few minutes with their passports. He also had Clark's blue eye Turkish good luck charm. Clark didn't feel comfortable putting it on, so he put it in his pocket.

Clark shook the lawyer's hand. "Thank you so much. You were fantastic."

"You are welcome. I will see you in Istanbul in a few weeks. The trial will now move to Bolu, the district center. Mustafa is waiting for you outside. I have a few more things to do in the office."

Clark had to hold on to the railing as he went down the stairs. It was real, yet surreal, and he still feared that it would soon prove to be a cruel hoax; that Laurel and Hardy would be waiting for him at the bottom of the stairs to take him back to prison. But the stairway was empty, and as they emerged from the building, he didn't see Laurel or Hardy or Mustafa.

The first shot rang out and the bullet hit the side of the building about a foot from Clark's head.

He felt like his feet were encased in concrete as he struggled to process what was happening and tried to spin around and get back inside. He pulled Joyce with him and saw Nigel on the ground. Oh my God he's shot, Clark screamed at himself. He followed his instinct and got Joyce inside and started to go back for Nigel. But then Nigel scampered through the door on his hands and knees.

Another shot hit the door and embedded in the solid wood.

"I thought they got that guy. Where the hell did he come from?" Clark shouted.

"Who?" Joyce asked.

"The brother. It must be him, the one that shot me."

"He's in jail," Nigel responded.

"Then who else could it be?"

"They have large families," Joyce offered.

"Where the hell is everyone? Help!" Clark yelled, as he looked around the empty stairs and hallways.

Out on the street, a car horn blew, loudly. It repeated urgently. Clark opened the door a crack to look out, and he saw a large black Lincoln Continental sedan parked at the bottom of the stairs. It had come up on the sidewalk to get as close to the stairs as possible, maybe ten feet from the door. Mustafa yelled out from the driver's seat, "Come on, get in."

"It's Mustafa in a car, I'm gonna run for it. You two stay here, it's me they want." He didn't wait for an argument or discussion and bolted from the door and raced down the steps. Mustafa had opened the door to the rear seat, and Clark dove in just as another bullet whizzed over his head and hit the wall of the building. Then a bullet hit the window of the car. Clark flinched and ducked, but the window was undamaged.

"Bulletproof," Mustafa yelled from the front seat. "My uncle's, a present from the Americans."

Clark flinched again as another bullet hit the side of the car. He was fixated on that and didn't notice Joyce, and then Nigel, as they ran from the building and leapt into the back of the car with him.

Mustafa stepped on the gas, and the car roared off the sidewalk and onto the street. The sudden acceleration and maneuver almost caused the car to spin out, but Mustafa managed to keep control of it. They raced down the street as Laurel, Hardy, and another policeman emerged from the building with their guns drawn. Clark couldn't see the shooter through the rear window, but he saw Hardy and the other policeman as they ran down the street. Laurel headed the other direction. Their car turned a corner before Clark could see if they caught someone or not.

Mustafa slowed down a little - he didn't think the shooter would have a car. The three in the back seat tried to relax. Even though the car was large, they were pressed close together.

Clark noticed that Joyce had taken his hand and held it tight. He didn't mind.

"My God, that was amazing Mustafa, thank you," Clark said, as the others nodded and then added their thanks.

Clark now focused on Joyce. "What about you? What'll happen?"

"I don't know. I didn't think it through, I just reacted."

Mustafa chimed in, "I think you should come with us for now. I can ask Mr. Ozturk to gauge the reaction in the town before you return or…"

"Or if I return," she finished his sentence, not sure how she felt about it.

"You can stay with my sister in Istanbul for a while until we sort things out," Mustafa offered.

Joyce nodded and tightened her grip on Clark's hand.

"But what about our stuff?" Nigel asked. "My camera, our cameras are in my hotel room."

Mustafa laughed. "Do you want me to go back?" He let up slightly on the accelerator.

"No! No, that's okay, not worth it," Nigel shouted, and then he slumped back as Mustafa hit the gas again.

Clark turned his attention to the passing countryside. He felt for his passport in his pocket, reassured himself that it was still there. Then he touched the blue eye - had it brought bad luck again or had it meant good luck that they had survived? Maybe it had been the same with the accident - he and Nigel could have been killed that night. Luck can certainly be very relative he realized.

He was happy that Joyce sat next to him, but he felt bad that they had maybe messed things up for her with the Peace Corps. He didn't mind listening to Nigel's tortured recount of all the photos he had taken and would now never see, or the leather jacket that he loved, back in his hotel room.

Clark silently said good-bye to all the prisoners, Toad and the commandant. He struggled against a sense of hope that he definitely didn't want to overwhelm him. He knew he couldn't relax. It wasn't over, not yet.

The traffic was typically bad, and it took over four hours before they were on the ferry and left Asia behind. Clark stood on the fore deck of the ferry with Joyce and watched the lights of Istanbul. The time had gone so slowly, often painfully, but now it felt like just the other day when he had seen this view in the daylight.

Eventually they reached Nathaniel Streeter's flat in the tony section of the old town where many of the foreign diplomatic corps lived. After ringing them in, Streeter answered his door and looked upset, then surprised when he saw Joyce. "I expected you hours ago, but not..."

Mustafa jumped in for Joyce. "She got caught up in the crossfire, and we had to bring her. It wouldn't have been safe for her to stay there."

"Crossfire?" Streeter questioned, not sure if it was just a figure of speech.

"Someone shot at me, as we came out of the courthouse," Clark clarified. "Mustafa saved us."

Streeter immediately changed his approach and ushered them into his spacious flat. A duplex with a large window in the living room, it had a spectacular view of the Bosphorus. Stairs led up to a second level with two bedrooms, each with a bathroom. He showed the boys to the guest room and started to show them where to put their stuff when he realized that they didn't have any. "I can take you to the commissary tomorrow for some clothes and things. There are some toiletries in the cabinet over the sink."

Mustafa interjected, "Thank you, but I've already made arrangements to take them shopping tomorrow. We don't want to impose on your busy schedule. And then they will have dinner with my family." He emphasized the last part because he knew that Streeter was aware of the political position of his family.

Streeter offered them some leftovers from his refrigerator, but Clark was physical and emotional exhausted, and he just wanted to go to bed. Before Mustafa left with Joyce, Streeter insisted that they all go over the conditions of the bail agreement that he had signed. He made it clear that he didn't like putting himself out there like that, and that he had only done so at the insistence of his boss. "We can find you a flat of your own, and I understand that Mustafa has enrolled you in the university."

"Sounds great." Clark's sarcasm was completely lost on Streeter.

As she was leaving, Joyce hugged Clark and kissed his cheek. "See you tomorrow," she said with a lot of feeling and anticipation in her voice. She handed Clark a small package and left.

Later, Clark opened the package and found new worry beads. But these were nicer, more expensive, than the ones he had destroyed. He smiled and immediately began to work them.

Clark woke up many times during the night, often disoriented, occasionally scared that it had all been a dream and that he was really back on the shelf. But Nigel's heavy breathing couldn't compare with the sounds of over twenty men. And the constant city street noises from outside Streeter's flat were a welcome counterpoint to the nighttime silence of the rural prison.

Already awake, he pretended to be asleep at eight o'clock when Streeter poked his head in the room to check on them before he left for work. As soon as Clark heard the front door close and lock, he jumped up. In the bathroom, he shaved off his beard before taking a shower. The hot water felt wonderful, but he knew he couldn't linger.

Nigel had just come into the living room to join Clark when the intercom buzzed. Clark went to the window and looked down at the street where Mustafa stood next to a different black car, one with no bullet holes.

The boys left the flat and got into the car. "Where's Joyce?" Clark asked, as he sat in the front, Nigel got in the back.

"It's better that she does not know or have any participation in this," Mustafa responded seriously. "She can then say truthfully that she does not know what happened."

They rode in silence for a little while as Mustafa navigated the traffic and headed south out of town on Kennedy Boulevard. "Here are your tickets," Mustafa said, as he pulled two Pan American Airlines tickets from his coat pocket. "Pan Am flight number one, departs at twelve thirty for Athens, Rome, Paris, London and New York," he spouted off the itinerary like a seasoned travel agent. "I am sorry that we have to do this to the vice-consul, but there is no other way".

"I'm not, he's a total asshole," Clark rejoined, and Nigel laughed.

"Well, they could make trouble for you back in the States."

"I'll burn that bridge when I get there," Clark said, with his new fatalistic, prison-fueled philosophy.

Fifteen minutes later, the car pulled up to the international departures terminal of Istanbul International Airport. Mustafa turned to them. "I cannot come in or wait. You are on your own if you still want to do this."

Clark nodded. "Absolutely." He didn't look at Nigel for confirmation, but assumed that he could object if he wanted to.

"All right, then you know what to do?" Mustafa asked.

"Yes, and tell Joyce I said goodbye and hope to see her in America." Clark paused. "I don't know how to thank you. You've done so much for us."

"You are most welcome. I hope that I will see you one day in America, not Turkey."

Mustafa got out and went to the trunk where he grabbed two suitcases that he had filled with old clothes that his family no longer used. "Here," he said, as he handed them to Clark and Nigel, "no one travels without a suitcase."

As Clark got to the terminal door, he turned around to wave to Mustafa, but the car was already gone. Once inside, they looked around the crowded departure area and saw a large board with flight information written in chalk. Pan Am flight one was on schedule to depart in two hours. Per Mustafa's instructions, they immediately checked in, deposited their suitcases, and got boarding passes. They then they headed for the border checkpoint.

"What if he's wrong, and the court did send a notice to the border police?" Nigel whispered as they approached the end of the line.

"Only one way we'll find out," Clark teased, but then quickly relented when he saw the look of fear on Nigel's face. "He was sure it's extremely unlikely given the amount of the bail."

"I've got some money, maybe you should, you know, put it in your passport."

"Great idea Nigel, then I get arrested for attempted bribery. What the hell are you worried about anyway? It's not your name that would be on the list." They had now joined the line and stayed quiet.

Clark sorted through the probabilities in his head. There had been the arrangement or understanding with the judge and the amount of the bail. It had been late afternoon and unlikely that they would rush to telephone or telegraph the airports and other border crossings. And there had been a lot of excitement with the shooting. They might wonder if he was hurt or even still alive.

As they neared the booth with the border officer, Clark watched him carefully. He seemed very casual in his work, but he had something, a list, that he looked at with each passport. Clark almost changed his mind and asked Nigel for the money, but realized that that could lead to a real catastrophe.

The border officer took Nigel's passport, found the page with the entry stamp and then looked at him for a long moment. "Long time," he said, part statement and part question.

Clark could sense Nigel start to panic. "We really like it here," Clark said, as he squeezed up next to Nigel and addressed the officer. He held out his own passport, which the officer took and examined. The border officer took a moment, which seemed like forever to Clark, as he scanned a list that appeared to be many typed pages stapled together. He glanced up at them, and Clark recognized the look. Prison guards and prisoners, all had the same disinterested, almost vacant stare. Clark didn't flinch or look down, but he also didn't look him directly in the eyes. Nigel flinched, but Clark didn't, as the thud of the exit-stamp hit the first passport and then the second one.

"Have a nice trip," the officer muttered in perfunctory English.

"Chok teshekkurler ederim," Clark thanked him with a pretty good accent, as he grabbed the passports and pushed Nigel forward.

As they entered the departure lounge, Nigel was vibrating with excitement. "We're out!" He almost shouted.

"Quiet," Clark warned. "This is still Turkish territory. Just keep calm."

The next hour passed as slowly as time had ever passed for Clark. He tried to distract himself in the duty-free shop, but didn't buy anything. They both had a coffee, which only made Nigel more anxious. Clark wished he had a sedative to put in Nigel's drink. Then about fifteen minutes before the scheduled departure time, a public address announcement over the loudspeaker said in Turkish and then English that Pan Am flight number one for Athens was going to board in twenty minutes. At the same time, two heavily armed soldiers entered the lounge and took up positions by the two doors - the one back to the border control and the other out to the planes.

Clark grabbed Nigel's arm as he started to jump up. "Stay calm," Clark whispered urgently. He held his breath as he watched the soldiers without looking directly at them. After a few minutes the soldiers hadn't moved, and Clark began to hope that this was some sort of a standard security protocol and that they weren't there to detain anyone - him specifically.

Finally, the disembodied voice on the loudspeaker announced the boarding of their flight. Nigel jumped up, ready to run to the door, but Clark again took a firm hold on his arm. "Don't rush, blend in."

Clark and Nigel walked in the middle of the crowd of passengers as they filed across the tarmac to the gangway stairs that had been rolled up to the front door of the plane. Clark saw the American flag painted on the tail of the Boeing 707 and had to remind himself to breathe.

More heavily armed soldiers were stationed around the plane and at the various entrances and luggage bays in the terminal building. Clark didn't know it, but they were on alert because of a threat from an Armenian extremist group and not because of some random American bail-jumper.

Clark and Nigel found their seats. Clark had the aisle with Nigel between him and a large man by the window who had an unlit cigarette in his mouth. There had not been that many people in the departure lounge, but the plane was almost full with through passengers, who had been in a separate transit lounge and were headed for somewhere other than Turkey.

His seat belt buckled, Clark put his head back and closed his eyes. His fingers furiously worked his new worry beads. They were so close. It seemed like a dream, but a dream that could still turn into a nightmare. He heard the airplane's door close and felt the pressure increase in the cabin. Then the roar of the engines proceeded a jerky movement as the plane pulled away from the terminal and began to taxi. The head steward's voice came over the speakers, "We have now been cleared for departure. Please remain in your seats until the captain has notified us that it is clear to move about the cabin. Our flight to Athens will be one hour and fifty-five minutes." The steward went on about seat belts, emergency exits, smoking, and duty free, and Clark silently urged him to hurry up. He knew they couldn't takeoff until the steward was done with the pre-flight safety instructions and announcements.

Finally, the plane reached the end of the runway, where it turned and then began to race toward takeoff speed. Clark felt the power of the engines vibrate through the plane and knew it meant freedom. He also knew he couldn't deal with all the emotions, so he put his head back on the headrest and promptly fell asleep.

CHAPTER 30

Midafternoon the next day, Pan Am flight one finally landed at London's Heathrow airport. There had only been three stops, but all of them included long waits in the transit lounges. In Rome there had been an additional delay because the fuel truck drivers were on strike. Clark didn't mind any of it. He was free and nothing could bother him, not even Nigel's growing impatience and his continued anguish over his cameras.

Clark tried to ignore the newspapers in the transit lounges but couldn't miss the headlines about the Chinese testing of their first hydrogen bomb. He didn't ask Nigel what had happened with the war in Israel and there wasn't any mention of it on the front page. They didn't talk much at all.

It was harder for him to resist thinking of Joyce and what would happen to her. Would she go back to Duzce? Would it be safe for her? Would he ever see her again? There had been an undeniable connection, but was it real, sustainable, or had it been based solely on their mutual needs of that moment, of that place? He could already feel himself compartmentalizing her and the whole experience as he had done so many times before - every time his family had moved.

Nigel's father met them outside the customs area at Heathrow. Clark hoped that Mr. Barrington's exuberant hug of his son indicated that all was forgiven. And then he was very surprised when Nigel's father embraced him in a hug also. Evidently Clark's parents had stopped in London on their way home, where they had met Mr. Barrington and reported on what was going on in Turkey. That had earned Clark the status of what Mr. Barrington called, "Nearly family".

As he entered the flat in Hampstead, Clark couldn't remember how he had left it, but he knew it hadn't been as clean as it was. A note from his mother explained it. They had been there as well. He had a moment of panic until he found that all the photos of Bernadette were still in the desk drawer and didn't look like they'd been disturbed. He quickly showered, changed clothes and went out to a pub to get drunk.

It took Clark a few moments the next morning to orient himself at the flat. He didn't know the time or what time zone his body was in. He was hungry but not hung over. It had only taken one pint the night before to make him feel lightheaded, and he hadn't wanted to lose control. And there had been a young woman in the pub who reminded him too much of Gwen. The memory of her sitting on top of him popped into his mind, so he quickly jumped out of bed and headed for the shower. He wasn't ready to deal with that yet.

Later, as he took a better look around, Clark noticed a neat stack of mail on the desk. He seldom got mail, but he scanned through it quickly. The mauve envelope with the foreign stamps caused him to freeze, hold his breath, as he noted the return address: Bernadette Ochera, House of Ochera, Chemin de Torreta, Ajaccio, Corsica. The postmark was in French, but the date was clear - May 19, 1967 - over a month ago. He took the letter and put it on the coffee table as he made coffee. He had to compose himself. He wasn't sure he could deal with this either, but there it was, right in front of him. What had she written? The possibilities overwhelmed his imagination, as he tore open the envelope and read.

My Dearest Clark

I despair that this will not reach you and that I will never know what has happened to you. I am so worried. I was in London this past week to pack up our flat, and I tried to contact you so many times, telephone, stopped by your flat. I even tried to contact Gwen, but no luck. Maybe you are together?

I am staying in Corsica now and I will be going to the University of Corsica to finish my degree. My family is eager for me to do that because of the prize. Oh yes, I won the Smithson Prize for Short Fiction. I didn't know that Maya had entered my story - and yours also. It is a big honor and also had a two-thousand-pound sterling award. I will, of course, still work for the family but only on weekends.

I pray that you are okay and know that our night together was the best thing in my life and if I were not on this path I would want to be with no one other than you.

With love

Bernie

So, after learning of Gwen's pregnancy, sex with Bernadette, almost three months and his twenty-first birthday in prison, getting shot, escaping… Clark finally cried. It all poured out, and it felt good. But then it didn't stop, each memory brought a new wave of emotion, and he had a moment of real fear. Finally, he managed to corral his feelings. He wanted to call her in Corsica. Bad idea, he convinced himself. He knew he had to get out of the flat.

The weather in London had improved a lot in the months he had been gone. It was summer, mild, almost hot, but pleasant compared to the heat in Turkey. He bought a steak and egg sandwich and a cup of coffee at the little commuter food stand at the underground station and sat on a bench on the Hampstead High Street. As he watched the mid-day hustle of people and traffic, it was soothingly familiar, but also foreign. He felt cast adrift without an anchor, a home, or even a country. He told himself to snap out of it, stop being so annoyingly melodramatic.

The next morning Clark headed to LSE to try to find Professor Doctor. The school term had ended, but he hoped that the professor would be around.

During the long layover in Rome he had re-engaged with his situation with courses, credits and his future at school. He had found his notes for his Philosophy of International Law research paper stacked neatly on the desk in the flat. He wondered if he could stay and finish it, but he didn't think so. He really wanted to go home.

The professor was around but in a faculty meeting, so Clark went into the student union to wait for him to be available. As he glanced over his notes, it dawned on him that his experience in the prison and with the Turkish legal system gave him a perfect real-world foundation for his paper. He had had this theory about the conflicts between religious and secular laws, but now he had seen the consequences first hand, as evidenced by many of the men in the prison, and by the two attempts on his life. The problem was that he didn't think he had the energy, the stamina, or the desire to incorporate all of that into a research paper.

Deep into that dilemma, Clark didn't notice Arthur until he took a seat across the table from him.

"I'm sorry I was a bloody toe-rag mate. Do you still hate me?" Arthur got right to the point when Clark finally noticed him.

Clark didn't think so. He hadn't thought of him in a long time, except to worry about him surviving in Greece. That irony wasn't lost on him. He finally shook his head. "No, all's cool."

Arthur relaxed a little. "Is it true, the rumors about you and Nigel?"

Clark thought of deflecting the question but decided that it was better to just get it over with. "Yeah, had a bit of a ballsed-up mess. But we're back now. Everything's groovy." He tried to smile and hoped that would be the end of it.

Arthur could tell that Clark wasn't eager to expand, so he moved on. "Gwen was really upset when she heard. She'll be happy that you're back safe."

"How is she?" Clark asked, as an image of her with a big pregnant belly formed in his head.

Arthur hesitated long enough for Clark to begin to get worried. "She's good. She's still home, didn't come back after spring break with what was going on." He paused. "She was royally pissed at you for leaving."

"I'd like to go see her."

"I don't think that's a good idea. She made it pretty clear that she didn't want to see you."

"Well, maybe I was wrong to leave, but she pushed me away also." Clark paused to see if Arthur would get defensive of his sister, but he didn't react. "I really do need to talk to her about the…"

Arthur looked away and finally he said quietly, "She isn't pregnant anymore."

Clark didn't know how to react. He felt conflicting emotions - concern, loss, happiness, relief. "What happened? Did she…?" He couldn't come right out and say abortion.

All Arthur said was, "It's complicated."

After Arthur left, Clark realized that he hadn't asked about Cynna, and Arthur hadn't mentioned anything. He figured that it was better that way.

Seven days later, Clark was back on Pan Am flight one, this time bound for New York and then a connecting flight home.

Professor Doctor had given him an oral exam on the conflicts between Sharia and Turkish criminal law, which turned out to be a three-hour recap of Clark's time in Turkey. He then wrote a recommendation to Dartmouth College that Clark should be given credit for his year of study based on his work in class, his first-hand research and experiences, and his intellectual growth as evidenced by an outstanding final oral exam. He compared Clark's academic work very favorably to his peers in their second year of university. Clark accepted it as mostly bullshit, but it was beautifully written, and he hoped that it would ultimately be persuasive with Dartmouth's Government Department.

Maya had left her letter for him at her department office, and it glowingly described the stories that he had developed and mentioned his work with other students to help their stories. As his biggest accomplishment, however, she mentioned his third place prize in the Smithson contest, which didn't include any money but carried plenty of prestige.

Clark figured that he could survive one more year at school in the wilds of New Hampshire, but he knew that he couldn't spend two more years there. Everything depended on these two letters.

After many failed attempts, he had finally been happy with a letter to Bernadette that expressed his gratitude for their friendship, his happiness for her prize, and his hopes for her future. He could not bring himself to address the heart-wrenching desire he felt whenever he thought of their night together or the sadness, the sense of loss, that overwhelmed him whenever he allowed himself to consider any kind of what-if scenario. He always crashed up against the reality of who she was and would always be. He had given her a brief account of Turkey without mentioning getting shot.

Several days after he saw Arthur, Clark had received a short letter from Gwen. She expressed her happiness that he was back safe, but she was firm that she didn't want to see him. And her only mention of the pregnancy was a reference to her situation that had changed. She planned to finish her degree at the University of Cardiff and then read for the law so she could work to bring Wales into the twentieth century for women's rights and governmental accountability to the people. He had written her an equally vague note in response and then began to pack.

Clark had not made any attempt to contact Nigel. Nor Nigel him.

As the plane flew west over the Irish Sea, Clark realized that it was the end of another school year, and he was moving again - leaving people and relationships behind. He felt comfortable with that, but not completely. He wondered if he would ever find a normal relationship and was he mature enough to recognize it if he did? He hoped so.

Coming...

The Education of Clark Westfield is a trilogy about a young man coming of age, becoming a man, and striving for maturity in the late 1960s, early 1970s. *Lovely Rita* was the first book. *Curse of the Nice Guy* is the second. And Clark will finish his journey in the third book, *Clark's Choice*, which should be available in the summer, 2018.

Acknowledgements

This is a fictional work based on my imagination and my experiences as a young man in England and Turkey in 1966 to 1967. I met many wonderful people who gave me ideas for these fictional characters, but they are not these characters. This is a work of fiction. Names, characters, organizations, places, events, and incidents are either products of my imagination or are used fictitiously.

I would like to thank my family for all their support. First there's my mom, who encouraged all her kids to be true to themselves and was always there for us, no matter what. And, of course, I couldn't have done it without Amy "Perky", my amazing wife and best friend. And my three wonderful daughters: Michelle, Carolyn, and Claudia. I would also like to thank my beta readers, Debbie Rhodes, Lawrence French, and Kimberly Johnson, who were such a great help.

Thank you for reading *Curse of the Nice Guy* and supporting independent fiction. If you enjoyed it, please review it and tell your friends because word-of-mouth is critically important for all authors. And I'd love to hear from you at blairfilms@hotmail.com